DISBANDED

A SERPENTIA NOVEL

FRANCES PAULI

Disbanded

Production copyright © 2020 Goal Publications
Cover artwork copyright © 2020 Ilya Royz
Text Artwork copyright © 2020 Wesley Brown
Story © 2020 Frances Pauli

Distributed by Goal Publications
Norwich, Connecticut
http://www.goalpublications.com/

Print ISBN 978-1-949768-11-4

Published in the United States of America.
First Edition trade paperback March 2020.

FOR MY SCALY FRIENDS

Prologue

The darkness inside my egg split, a razor slash of pale white against eternal blackness. I peered at it from the warm sea that encompassed my entire world, small as it was. That glow was the first thing I'd ever seen, and the oddity of it enchanted me.

Come forth, for you are special.

A voice sang inside my head. It pushed in from all sides, not painfully, but with urgency and music to the words. The universe chanted for me to be born, and I coiled tighter against my shell walls and watched the light exist.

Perfect one. Child of gods. Be born.

My tongue stretched toward the gash, a slow probing, just a taste of what might be inside the light. And I thought of it as *inside* at first. My small, black universe was all I knew, and the slice breaking across it seemed tiny by comparison. It tasted of heat and something I would learn to recognize as dust.

Come out, beloved. Come to the light and breathe for us.

I flicked the tips of my forked tongue, twisting my head in an attempt to reach beyond the edges of my world. What was in there, and how could someone as huge as I, who filled up every crevice of my universe, fit into that narrow thread?

Hear us, child. You are the one to come. Chosen and perfected. The world needs you. The light needs you.

My tongue passed into the blaze and found more space beyond, room to flicker and gather scents to taste. I moved my head forward, bumping my nose against the soft barrier that was my eggshell. For all my days, that contact had been my only sense of touch. I'd twisted and turned, writhed and wiggled. But now, the first tap of my rostral scales to the egg and another tear blazed into being. Two lines of light, glowing, marring the perfect darkness...and beginning to irritate me.

Come out, dreamer. You are late.

My tongue returned to my mouth, carrying more dust and scents that I couldn't place or even imagine a source for. I retracted that probe and turned, instead, to press one eye to the gashes. The light ached against my lens, larger than the whole universe and speckled with shades of gray and grayer. Worse than the sight of a world bigger than my own was the realization that there was movement in it. Shapes passed my narrow viewpoint, casting shadows that twisted in an instinctively familiar fashion.

You are the one, the child that must be.

The voice sang a continuous chant, urging me to rise up and join those other bodies. To emerge and be what it claimed I was.

Special. Sacred. Come to us. Come.

I felt the words slide down my body as if I'd swallowed them. I felt the urging as a physical probe. Move, twist, slash. My nose bumped and bumped at my egg, birthing light even as it destroyed my universe. Even as it left my world in tatters. The light flowed in now. My shell split across the top, and my nose expelled a bubble of fluid that was all I'd ever known or understood.

Come out. Be who you must. Change the world. Be.

The chant moved me at last to try, first with only the tip of my nose and the gentle protrusion of a soft tongue. The world of light proved so vast that it stalled my advance. I was left to gasp at it, to blow my bubbles and suck in something cold and far more fulfilling. I *breathed,* and I listened to the song of my making.

A larger existence unfolded out there. I tasted it, drew it in, and believed what the chant said. I would *be* and *change* and *answer.* The warmth beyond my egg dried my nose, and suddenly being wet became unbearable. I shifted, daring to lift my head enough to peek.

It took me long breaths to understand the wonders outside the egg. A high ceiling covered the space, curved like a shell but never smooth. Patterns and pits scrawled over it in dark and light. Below it, all around me, were other eggs. They gleamed white, as did my own from the outside. Some were still full and fat, and others, like mine, had deflated, shrank in upon themselves as their fluids leaked away across the cavernous floor.

I tasted them, distantly. Similar and at the same time unfamiliar. I smelled so many new things that the scale between my eyes began to ache. Things that I would soon label as dirt and blood, musk and feces. Curious and full of awe, I flicked my tips in all directions and pressed my head higher, freer into the bright, dry world.

Yes. Well done, beloved.

I tumbled down the side of my now-empty egg, landing on hot sand. The rest of my scales dried quickly, hardening and tightening at the same time. I itched, for movement and growth and also to satiate the hollow settling into the middle of my length.

You must eat.

This command confused me. Eating was nothing, a worry I'd never experienced. My sustenance had always been constant and freely delivered. Still, the voice pushed at me to move. A will that was not fully my own drove me to hunt. I smelled the sand, the air, a nearby egg. My tongue explored and gathered. I found a dead thing inside a shell that looked bruised and wrinkled. The scales reeked, driving my nostrils away. I sucked in my tongue as if that might clamp out the invasion of the latest taste.

Death. An unfortunate soul so similar to myself that I cringed away from the egg and refused to move for long moments.

No. Eat.

I coiled tightly around myself, smaller and smaller until I might have vanished back into my egg again. When I looked for it, however, I saw only a row of unfamiliar oblongs. From the outside, I'd never know which one was mine. Something told me that was as it should be. There would be no fitting back into darkness now. It was too late; I knew how large the world could be.

Move, beloved. Eat or perish.

That pressed me to unravel. I tasted the rotten snake again, and felt my first stabbing of fear. To end that way, trapped in the tiny, closed-in egg, was suddenly the worst thing I could imagine. I slithered forward, not in any particular direction, hoping the voice would guide me to food. Instead it fell silent, quieted for the first time since it had begun.

My belly rubbed against the heated grit, and through it I felt the vibrations of my hatchmates. Those who had survived their emergence moved between the eggs, and their passing felt like low ripples. Between those sensations, the occasional tickle of something smaller and faster buzzed. This motion triggered a reaction that began in my empty belly and spread outward until it prickled at my scales. I focused on it, on the scattered, panicky rhythm, and let my tongue and my instincts guide me.

Though the most frenzied vibrations came from the center of our cavern, I moved around the edge, seeking a smaller eddy of motion. My caution led me around an egg so large that three of mine might have fit inside it. Though one side was punctured, the orb still held its swollen shape. Only a trickle of fluid drizzled from the crack in the leathery surface, and as I passed, a single eye peered at me from that shelter.

I paused, thinking at it in the language of the voices which had chanted for my birth.

Who are you? Why do you not emerge?

The eye stared out, round pupil shimmering and wet, but the snake did not answer.

We must eat, I thought.

He cannot hear you, the other voice answered. *You cannot help him.*

Why?

To eat is to live. You must eat. Some will not.

The voice chanted in the same low and gentle tones, but the message sank into my skull heavily. *Some will not.* I stared at that moist eyeball, at my unmoving brethren, and felt a chill despite the heat of the sand. My tongue flicked out and back. My worry moved me to speak aloud, something I had never known I could do.

"Come out of there." I nudged the huge egg with my coil and hissed my anxiety. "Come out and eat."

The hatchling withdrew from his gash. One flick the eye was there, and the next, it had vanished. The fluid drizzle thickened, leaking in a slow river down the egg's side.

You must hurry. There is little food left.

Fear clutched at me. Little food? But there were many of us, dozens of eggs both empty and full. What would happen to my reluctant hatchmate inside his mammoth egg? What would happen to me if the food was gone before I'd found it?

Move. Hurry, beloved.

I wanted to linger, to rail at the big snake to come to his senses. I wanted to shout for him to emerge and join me in the hunt for sustenance. My fear and the urgency of the voice pushed me away. Slithering as fast as I could manage, I rounded two more eggs as large as that one—one rotting from within, and the other empty, torn asunder with its fluids darkening the sands around it.

Beyond this, I found my first sibling, for that was how I regarded all who hatched around me. His size and shape would have claimed a far different parentage, but in that moment, we were all brothers. His length was easily thrice mine, and his girth so fat I couldn't imagine it crammed into *any* egg. Patterns of light and dark made splotches over his scales, and his fat tail thrashed against the sand in a frenzied movement I found utterly hypnotic.

I followed his length with my eyes and found an odd lump near his halfway point. His body narrowed after that, never reaching my threadlike

4

nature, but becoming relatively slender at the neck. An arrow-shaped head turned in my direction. I met its gaze and let my tongue slide out in what I intended as a friendly greeting.

The huge hatchling ignored me. His head turned away, great tongue flowing in and out. His body tensed, and for the first time I saw the source of the other movement, felt the erratic vibrations even as my eyes landed on the soft shapes. Twin bundles lay near the huge snake's head. They bore no scales, but were covered in a velvety down. Four protrusions sprouted from each body, and two slits pressed tight where the eyes should have been.

Each sad, sightless deformity twitched and wormed its way through the sand, and the big hatchling fixed his arrow-head upon the nearest and froze mid tongue-flick. I tensed along with him. My muscles prepared for the other snake's strike, and when his neck curved into an ess, I mimicked his posture. I held my breath, held my tongue, and fixed my attention on the scene.

When the strike came, I flinched, recoiling as the other hatchling hit its target with enough force to shake the ground. He twisted around the squirming bundle with a speed my eyes could not track. His massive jaws, stretched wide in his death grip, already ground together, walking their way over the unfortunate animal's nose.

My belly grumbled, contracting and urging me to act. Another meal waited on the sands, but its movements spawned as much pity as hunger. I hesitated, watching instead the progress of the first victim as it vanished into the big guy's jaws.

Eat, beloved.

The voice dragged my gaze back to the pitiful animal. Perhaps, to end its blind suffering would be a kindness.

Yes. Eat. Live.

I let my tongue loose, reached toward the vibrations, and tasted something that screamed of satiation. The fuzzy shape twitched, and my coils gathered nearer. I eased into proximity, wholly focused on the squirming thing now. My neck curved back. My tongue fluttered. I froze, tensing in an imitation of the other snake's successful attempt.

A low hiss rumbled nearby.

My hunger argued that I could snatch the meal first and answer the challenge after. I flicked and tightened, made my ess, and tasted my quarry from just the right distance.

Yes. The voice approved of my bloodlust.

I readied to strike. My jaws opened.

A huge coil thrashed into view, blocking my trajectory and sending me cringing, backwards. The other snake hissed again, and this time I knew the warning for what it was: greed.

I spun to face the bigger hatchling, whose jaws had already ended two of the little meals if the bumps along his length meant what I believed. He hissed and slithered, injecting his fat body between my quarry and myself.

"Mine." His voice rumbled against my scales, deep like a pit.

"You've already eaten." I sounded thin and stretched as an echo. "There's not enough for everyone."

No sooner than I'd said it, my invisible guide confirmed my suspicion. *Not all will eat.*

"I'm hungry." The big guy hissed again, positioning himself, coiling and coiling until my eyes refused to follow his moving pattern.

It was the food that mattered. It was eating that would keep me alive, and if I were as special as my guide insisted, I must live. The larger snake had consumed two meals already, and though his body could easily crush mine, I was the swifter of us. I feared his snapping jaws, but my confidence in the voice's promise insisted I must eat. I must live.

Additionally, the big snake's gluttony infuriated me. If he'd only restrained himself, another of our kin might have survived the day. Now he meant to steal a third sup, take a second life. Even if it hadn't been mine, I would have fought against it.

I slid to one side and the big head swung to follow. As it came around, I shifted direction, darting whip-like past the fat coils. He came around behind me but unwound as he did, revealing the prey we both wanted in the process. As soon as I had a clear space between my nose and that wiggler, I rose up into a striking pose.

Hiss.

Again I opened my jaws, and again the big hatchling maneuvered between me and my prey. He stretched his mouth wide, gaping at me and exposing a row of backward curving teeth. I feinted and he came with me, but by the time I'd raced back around again, he pushed his big body into the way.

Hurry. More come.

The silent commentary drove my nerves even higher. If I couldn't battle this one rival and succeed, what would happen to me when more hungry hatchlings arrived? Frantic and terrified, I dodged again, and this time my robust sibling struck at me. I dodged low, slithering underneath his narrow neck, and lunged forward, brushing past the treasure he guarded in my haste to avoid his jaws. When I spun again, the meal lay between us. We drew ourselves up, me barely reaching half his great height. Our tongues danced, and this time we both hissed a warning.

I had no hope against this brute in a face to face conflict. Nothing in my limited experience, nor in my guide's assurances, could change that. If we struck together, I would not eat. If I didn't eat, I knew I would not live. Between us, my only hope of survival wormed. Inside my skull a new thought whispered, daring, dangerous. But there was no time to argue.

I swayed in one direction, dividing my foe's attention between my motions and the animal we both meant to swallow. His eyes shone, his round pupils dark as my egg had been. How I longed for that peace now.

The big snake feinted toward the meal, and I matched his lunge, balancing myself in the very middle of my length. I knew there would be one chance for my plan to work. Only one. My stomach howled with hunger, and the vibrations echoing across our cavern suggested too many similar contests for me to find sustenance anywhere else.

This meal must be mine.

The next time the big guy hissed, I acted, throwing my tail-section directly at him as if in a strike. The arrow-head lunged for my defenseless tail tip, and I felt the scrape of teeth against my scales. My fore-length, however, already moved. I struck in earnest, mouth open and teeth landing squarely around the blind head of our quarry.

Pain lanced through my tail, but a glorious victory filled my mouth. I rolled around it, wrapping my length into a ball and letting the momentum carry me away, prize secured at my center, held fast between my needle teeth. If the big guy pursued, I never noticed. My instincts already forced the small thing down my gullet, one flex of a jaw after the other. I rolled to a stop at some point, landed beside someone else's egg, and there, in the shadow of either death or victory, I finished my meal.

Well done. The voice filled my mind, dripping with approval and affection both. It whispered to me, again and again. The secret of my birth, of my deepest desire now that my hunger was assuaged. *Live, beloved. Live. Grow. Change the world.*

DISBANDED

1

"Get up, Sookahr. The day will not wait for your drowsy pleasure."

"Go away." I tucked my head deeper underneath my coils and ignored Kwirk, despite the fact that he was absolutely correct.

My den echoed with the mouse's soft steps. He paced away from my nest and back, bringing a cool rush of air from the far side of the room and forcing me to press my body nearer to the heated wall where I slept.

"I've prepared your tools." Kwirk's voice, squeaky and high-pitched, indicated his exasperation. "You're trading-up today."

I lifted the front third of my body, swiveled my head, and fixed a hard stare on my soft mouse. "I'm awake."

"Good thing. Here." His paws worked at gathering up my pencils, my stylus, and compass and a roll of tracing paper. "Last time in this one, eh?"

Trading-up day. I nodded my head and looped my body out of the nest. The skymetal band that encircled my middle clanged when it met the den floor. It pinched my scales, and the remnants of my last shed, trapped beneath the metal, crinkled. Reaching with my mind, I pulled at a loose bit of skin. The band hummed softly, a vibration that worked its way through my entire body, amplifying my telekinetic ability. The trapped shed crimped, rattled, and slid free. It fell to the floor and a soft brown paw reached for it.

"You might have waited," Kwirk huffed as he bent over, snatched the shed skin, and then waddled to the refuse bin with it.

"It itched."

"The new band will itch for days."

"But it's my final one, Kwirk." I swayed from one side to the other, imagining my last banding with shivers of anticipation. "It's finally time to show them what I can do."

"I'm sure you'll do well, Sookahr. Your designs are quite *original.*"

His tone lowered my head a little. If Kwirk didn't believe in me, who could I expect to? The mouse had been my companion for as long as I could remember. His presence and his approval should have been a given.

"But we must hurry, sir." Little paws dancing, he stuffed my tools into a leather satchel and threw the strap over his fuzzy shoulder. "I'd hate for them to give your band to a *lesser serpent* simply because you'd dawdled the morning away."

He scampered to the door and waited without looking back. No doubt, the little rodent knew he'd said exactly the right thing to get me moving. He'd also likely woken me just early enough that my "dawdling" would get us where we needed to be precisely when we were expected. Kwirk was fully adept at manipulating me, an expert in "Sookahr" in every way.

"Just a quick wash."

My den was a humble abode, curved clay walls arching to a flat ceiling. The floor was packed but not paved, and one wall, where my nest hugged the edge of the room, hid the pipes that carried warm water from deep in the geothermal crevice up through the entirety of the Burrow. A shallow basin sat opposite the door where my attendant waited, and I slithered to it and submerged my head.

The cool water succeeded in terminating my urge to return to sleep. Kwirk had the right of it. I needed to hurry, and no matter how warm my bed had been, the allure of trading-up day moved me faster than any heat could. My last band would be applied today, my apprenticeship ended, and my future fixed like a stone before me.

"Did you get my drawings?" I shook my head, letting the droplets cascade down my neck and over my belly scutes. "The outpost design?"

"Right here."

I twisted to see the tube he held. My final project as a student architect had taken me since before the all-dark to complete. I'd worked on the concepts for most of my apprenticeship, and in order to be certain the design would impress my mentor, I'd ventured from the Burrow during the coldest time of the year in order to obtain an extra special all-dark offering for my den's altar.

My gaze drifted to that now, the narrow archway set in the corner of the

10

room, farthest from my nest and facing true north. The Sage peered back at me, his onyx eyes set in the mosaic mortar and surrounded by little bits of glass to represent his scales. I'd left the feather Kwirk and I had found in the niche before settling in for my all-dark rest. Now, the narrow shelf held only a thin layer of dust. I should have cleaned it before today, should have found something new to place before my god for trading-up day.

"You're going to do fine, Sookahr." Kwirk shifted gears, aiming straight for reassuring, a tactic that almost always got me moving. "The outpost is perfect. A fine design."

Before responding, however, I gave the Sage one final, penitent look. The god's body wound into a spiral, not unlike my own in nature except for the arching wings sprouting from his back near the point where a band would have rested. Each plume glistened. The mosaic pieces had been faceted to refract the dim light which filtered into the room through small shafts set in the ceiling. It might have been a humble altar, an artwork intended for the Burrow's less-than-elite, but I'd always imagined the tiles were real gems.

Their sparkle spoke to something inside me, a whisper that said I could be much more than just an apprentice architect.

"Can we take the spire?" I left the Sage to gaze out at an empty room, and joined my mouse at the exit.

"If we get moving," he said. "There shouldn't be too many serpents on the ramp this early."

Usually, we chose the faster route down a level to the classes and workrooms. The spire lay nearly at the center of the Burrow, and would add to our travel time. Kwirk knew how much I loved it, and he must have managed to wake me early enough that the detour could be allowed. I let him totter ahead, taking care not to trap his long tail beneath my coils. The passages on the housing levels had less room to travel, as if they'd packed so many dens into the level that there hadn't been room for more than a thin strip of hallway. More than once I'd been forced to duck into a random den to allow another serpent to pass, and this morning was no exception.

We'd made a dance of it over our seasons living in this quarter so that, even with the darting and stopping, the dodging and positioning, we traveled to the nearest cross-tunnel without issue—not even when a large constrictor and his rodent came barreling into us. Kwirk and the other mouse exchanged a brief series of whisker flicks, paw flutters, and squeaks, and then the duller serpent stretched forward. He lowered his stout head to the floor, rolled against one wall, and allowed me to simply glide over him. My mouse scampered ahead, doing his best not to let his claws snag on the constrictor's scales.

When we reached the main tunnel, the traffic was heavier, but the corridor twice as wide. The serpents of the Burrow organized themselves easily into two lanes, one moving in either direction, and our pace through the level doubled. We arrived at the spire, and Kwirk dashed out onto the ramp. I slowed, lengthening the gap between us and turning my head up to admire the central column.

Generations ago, the serpents who dug the Burrow had encountered a vein of rock running vertically through the earth. Initial efforts to remove it had proved too costly, both in time and lives, and the decision had been made to incorporate the obstacle into the Burrow's design. A wide ramp was dug in a spiral around the column, and some clever architect had rearranged the tunnels so that all primary branches came and went from the spire.

The flaw in the original design had been metamorphosed into the very heart of our every-growing city, and the story of the spire had become legend in architectural circles. Which happened to be the circles I moved in.

"Sookahr?" Kwirk's pointed nose bounced into view.

I tore my gaze away from the carvings and focused on his rough vest, the soft fur poking out around his collar. "Sorry."

"We have to keep moving. There's more of us about than I expected."

"Yes."

I eased onto the ramp, feeling the difference against my belly. The rough grit of the passage gave way to smoothly ground clay. It was warmer here as well, as several of the geothermal vents passed near enough to the spire to keep the column's proximity toasty. The heat gave me enough energy to match pace with my scampering mouse. But I longed to linger and admire the work we passed too quickly, as if it were not the most extraordinary achievement of our era.

Aspis artists had spent lifetimes working on the relief sculptures that covered the spire. Our history was recorded there, beginning near the surface and winding down, one stone scene at a time, to the deepest level of the Burrow. The architects and builders might have borrowed genius to design the structure, but the artists...

I believed they'd been divinely inspired.

"This way now. Come on, Sookahr. Shake that scarred tail of yours."

We exited the ramp only two levels lower than my den. Only a few others took the passages here, and most of those were fellow classmates, architects, or teachers. I flicked my tongue constantly as we went, tasting the familiar scents or waving a casual greeting to the few who passed us.

Most traveled in the same direction. Schoolrooms lined the tunnel walls, and for many, the day of study and work had already begun. Between the open archways, smooth walls broke only for the shafts that bounced light all through the Burrow. Another marvel of architecture. I set my spine straight and lifted my front third into the air as I went. Here, in the classrooms, the Sage governed our fates. Here, of all the disciplines learned, it was architecture that reigned supreme.

I felt destiny brushing against my scales.

"Morning, Sookahr." A slender, striped female slithered past us. Her mouse bounced ahead of her, laden with bags and the satchel that would hold her final project.

"Morning." I didn't remember the thin girl's name, but I knew she studied medicines and worked very near to the spire. Kwirk didn't care for her attendant much, and though he refused to tell me what their spat concerned, my sense of loyalty never allowed me to bear her presence for long.

We slithered past, and Kwirk's tail lashed before me, thrashing like a newly-banded hatchling.

"I hope they give me a thicker band," I mused, nodding a greeting to a couple of stout vipers on their way to the spire. "Less pinchy would be nice as well."

"I'm certain Laarahn has recommended you," Kwirk said. "He was very impressed with your progress."

"He seemed so." I stretched taller, flicking my tongue slowly out and in and imagined I smelled victory in the air.

"Of course, if you'd spent more time on the drawing and less wandering with that wretched *aspis*..." Kwirk trailed off, letting his judgmental tone fully deflate my ego.

"The drawings are good though?" I felt my head sinking despite knowing he was only working me again, taking any chance possible to drive a wedge between my friend, Viirlahn, and I. Kwirk did not approve of mixing castes, and as an *aspis*, Viirlahn lived far above my station.

"That doesn't mean they couldn't be better."

"I know, Kwirk." The weight of all the levels above us suddenly pressed down upon me. I dragged against the hall floor, head nearly touching the grit. "I should have worked harder."

"Of all the snakes in all the classrooms on this level, Sookahr, I believe you worked the hardest." Kwirk stopped, placing one paw on the top of my head. The rare physical contact sent a jolt through me. I wanted to cringe from it, and also to lean into my mouse and let him keep reassuring me.

"Really?"

"Yes. If anyone's drawings come even close to yours in originality or sheer brilliance, I'll eat my tail."

The heat of his paw burned against my scales, a trick of the rodents that I both envied and feared. Making their own heat, living free of the vents and the warm spots as if they carried their own geothermal reaction somewhere inside their tiny, furry bodies. To a serpent, that power represented a strange magic far beyond our own telekinetic skills.

I used *those* powers now, ruffling the fur on Kwirk's head with an invisible paw. Another rare contact, for I knew he also preferred not to be touched. The day's import, however, combined with his initiating the contact, excused our sentimental breach.

"Now come, Sookahr." Kwirk lifted his paw and shook off the moment. His whiskers twanged to attention and he nodded once. "Let's get you inside and busy impressing Laarahn with your talents."

He led the way through the arch and into the school of architecture. A short ramp led to the floor, which had been dug as a stepped bowl so that seven terraces encircled the central space where our teacher, Laarahn, relayed to us all the secrets of planning and design. Along the outer wall, banners fluttered, depicting the tools of our trade, maps of Serpentia, and the blueprints for various sections of the Burrow.

On the domed ceiling, the Sage himself gazed down at us. This mosaic made my own shrine look like a cartoon sketch. Each scale tile was easily as big as one of my eyes, and the wide, feathered wings on either side of the serpent god covered the room in a protective embrace. Looking up at that visage for the last five years, I sensed generations of architects gazing back at me.

Today, I felt only a nervous squirming, like worms in my belly.

"Take your place," Kwirk whispered.

My classmates already gathered on the first three tiers around our mentor. Laarahn coiled below them, his lowly, speckled scales making a dull pattern of circles. His head rested on his broad podium, and I couldn't have said if he slept or woke if my life had depended on it.

The students' mice gathered at the topmost tier, shadowed and clustered together, but ready to rush forward one at a time as needed. Kwirk joined them, carrying my precious designs with him, my bag of tools. The new band should have a compartment for these, and I prayed again that it would be larger than my juvenile skymetal girdle had been.

I slithered down the steps, enjoying the pattern of rough and smooth, warm clay and cool space against my belly. I'd arrived late enough not to be the first serpent in the ranks, but early enough not to draw attention by my entrance. I could blend in until my turn, and I settled on an empty space between a wide-banded male who I'd often exchanged humor with, and a new student with erratic lines across his scales that reminded me of lightning.

Neither looked in my direction as I coiled between them. They stared, like the rest of the class, at Laarahn, just in case he was actually awake.

I followed suit, keeping my head forward but letting my tongue slide leisurely in and out, tasting the smells in the room, the musk of the other students, the heated clay, the dust clinging to the banners. The tier underneath me sat above one of the water pipes, and I could feel the vibrations of the fluid moving past. My belly warmed and I drifted in and out of alertness, not quite sleeping but aware that many of the other students were.

"Class." Laarahn's voice rumbled from the podium and we all startled awake. "Welcome to your final project grading."

A few hisses erupted from a tier higher, serpents behind my row who had less chance of being caught in the disrespect. Not that I would have challenged Laarahn for all the world. He might bear a lowly, speckled pattern, but his skill could not be denied, even if his applications for promotion had.

"I know you're probably nervous," he continued, raising his head high, higher than his scale pattern would have allowed outside his classroom. "But today is the culmination of years of work. You only take the final step, the step that generations of our kin before you have taken. I have absolute faith that your fine efforts will be rewarded, and any half-hearted attempts will be likewise given exactly their due."

If he meant to reassure us, he'd have chosen different words. The room filled with the buzzing of tails. More hissing echoed from the higher tiers, and for my part, the nerves in my belly swelled until my tongue fluttered against my lips.

Laarahn smiled. With the speed that could only be achieved by a long bask on his hot spot, he uncoiled in one burst, stretching himself into a circle that nearly made its way completely around the inner tier. The students in the front row all leaned backwards, and I had to sway to one side to avoid the retreating head of the serpent in front of me.

"Are you awake now?" Our teacher swiveled his neck, scanning the tiers as if he could see our lethargy, or pick out the few who'd hissed and make an example of them. "Today you will be judged, class, and that means I will be as well. Those of you who fail will enjoy another season in this room. With. Me. Those of you who pass, well, I shall expect great things of you."

I leaned forward, brushing against the still-cringing snake in the first row, and let my tongue slide out to sample the air. To taste our teacher's speech. His words settled in my head, and a certainty spawned in my guts. Great things. This was where I rose above the others. My moment to be more than my simple pattern would dictate. A whisper of memory hissed inside my thoughts.

Go forth and change the world.

I shivered. If anyone in this room was meant to pass today's test, I believed it was me. As I always had, I believed in the promise of that voice. I had to do more than pass; I had to prove myself—to Laarahn, to the Burrow, and to the Sage himself.

It was my destiny.

DISBANDED

2

"Unroll your papers, please." Laarahn's voice gave nothing away. Any expectations related to my designs, he kept secret. His body rested beside the podium again, as flat as his voice—as if the hours of examinations had deflated him. Half the class had already displayed their finals and subsequently been led away for re-banding, pass or fail.

I'd tried to guess those outcomes as they went, but the monotony had, eventually, pressed me to sleep again. When Laarahn called my name, I'd been deep in dreams of future architectural glory.

"I've chosen an outpost," I said.

Kwirk's deft fingers unlaced the stopper on my portfolio tube, and as soon as the flap was free, I used my mind to latch hold of the contents. The roll of drawings rose from their prison, floating at my will toward the podium where I unfurled them with a subtle shift of focus.

"A simple but vital building," Laarahn said.

"The design of which has not changed in seven generations," I countered, unsure if his statement meant I'd chosen well or poorly. Each of us had selected an existing, standard Burrow structure to adapt, and I'd been wholeheartedly certain of my choice...until now. "Despite the fact that the outpost network is our primary line of defense against the avian hordes."

"We're not at war currently." Laarahn would do nothing to assuage my fears, not during an examination. "Continue."

"I've truncated the pyramid," I said. Kwirk used one finger to indicate the new shape on my design. "To allow for an additional hatch and increase the ability to spot an airborne invader."

"You have." Laarahn leaned over my work, his tongue tips barely visible between his lips. He had a wide head, courser than my own, that didn't suit him even with his much greater size. It was his pattern, perhaps, that pinned him in a teaching position, but many times I'd seen that dullness reflected in his thinking as well. It felt disloyal to think that now, preposterous. And yet a part of me wondered if he were even capable of appreciating the subtle changes I'd made. The soft lines and delicate elaborations.

"Your aesthetics are lovely as usual." The compliment surprised me, but I knew better than to show it and was grateful for my restraint when he continued. "But the vast majority of your changes are cosmetic, correct?"

"The old designs were made in a time of war, in a rush and out of only necessity. It seemed like now, during a truce, we could finally afford to add a little grace to the structures."

"We can afford it, yes." Laarahn nodded. "But should you not consider the primary function of a building before anything else? Is that not the first order of business, and decoration something to be added once function has been perfected?"

I stared at him. All my lovely lines seemed to writhe and tangle on the page. My heart slowed as if the water flowing beneath us had chilled. I think my head nodded, but I don't remember willing it. My brain scrambled for an answer, for some justification behind my choice to make the outpost prettier. A choice that had seemed perfectly reasonable short breaths ago.

"Even without the war to drive them," he continued, "we still endure attacks, face the occasional rogue bird. Just last week the agricultural district suffered losses."

"I was unaware—"

"Tell me, Sookahr." Laarahn continued to flick his tongue, to examine my lines even though, to my thinking, he'd already fully dismissed them. "If you had an opportunity to add another feature, a defensive one, do you think you could do it?"

"Of course he could," Kwirk squeaked, and both Laarahn and I swiveled in his direction.

"You will hold your tongue in this classroom, rodent." Laarahn punctuated the order with a rumbling hiss.

"I could," I interjected before my mouse could do more harm. I saw it in his eyes, the urge to answer back, and though his loyalty moved me, I feared the repercussions if he overstepped again. "I would love the opportunity to remedy the oversight."

"Oh, this is fine." Laarahn shifted gears, focusing on me as if Kwirk had vanished. "Your work is always on point, Sookahr. But I would very much like to see your more functional ideas. I'd like to discuss this further with you. Perhaps, after your banding?"

"T-Thank you, sir. I'd be happy to discuss it."

I tried to guess what that meant for my grading, but Laarahn had moved on. The word "fine" hung in the air between us, however. I imagined it as a black cloud ready to rain failure all over my future.

"Have your mouse roll these up and then report to the banding room."

"Yes, sir."

"And come by my office this evening. After your free time."

"I will." I watched Kwirk gather my papers and tried to digest what had just happened. My work was on point, and yet this was "fine". Laarahn was done with me far too quickly, and yet he'd asked for a private conference.

I might have passed with flying colors or failed miserably for all I knew.

"Come, Sookahr." Kwirk slid my work back into its case as Laarahn called for his next victim.

We made our retreat up the tiers and back out the door we'd entered through, and I couldn't decide from one second to the next what had just happened. I replayed the conversation in my mind, letting Kwirk lead us down the corridors, as if he held my leash. No matter how I twisted and turned the encounter, my designs, which I'd been so proud of earlier this morning, now felt heavy and flawed. My assurance in my destiny dragged down into doubt and the first shadow of depression.

Kwirk avoided the spire this time, taking a much shorter route to the deep levels where all spiritual matters took place. On the way down, we passed by no fewer than three floors of housing, each one caste echelon above the next. The serpents who worked the skymetal came primarily from viper stock, heavy bodied and fully envenomed. Individuals with rough scales and hooded eyes which protected them from the fumes and flame, their status allowed them a life only one short step below the nobility.

Or in the case of housing, one level above.

The deepest dens in the Burrow belonged to the *aspis*, slighter but often deadlier snakes who focused on art, politics, and the dreaming. I'd only ever set scale one level below the banding room's depth, where my dear friend and companion dwelled. That he paid even a fraction of his attention to me was an honor that even Kwirk's disapproval couldn't tarnish.

"Watch your path!" A voice like crunching gravel broke my train of thought. I startled just in time to dodge an iron crucible, only slightly smaller than my water basin, as it hovered past us. Behind it, a viper slithered. His disc-shaped head fixed on the moving vessel and his tongue extended fully in concentration. A massive rat trailed behind him.

"Our pardon," Kwirk squeaked.

I pressed against the wall and watched the big snake go by. Each of his scales keeled sharply, making a prickled armor over his thick length. His patterns were sharp and formed of concentric diamonds. Fancy enough to keep him to heavy work or teaching, but clean enough that, with his viper nature, he outstripped my standing far enough to press my head down.

My own scales were a uniform black aside from a hint of rings, barely a shade lighter, at regular intervals. If I'd been born to an envenomed caste, I might have been a senator, a poet, someone's boss. As a harmless snake, my aspirations were limited. I would not, however, be held to teaching or manual labor. I could rise a good deal higher than Laarahn for instance, but I would still have to earn each step along the way.

We continued once the metallurgist had safely passed, and this time I kept my head. Kwirk scampered down hallways that were as familiar as my own den, though I'd only entered them once a year to have my band resized. This year would be my last trip. My shed, only weeks prior, had terminated my growth cycle. I was as large as I would ever be, though I'd likely still slough somewhat regularly, and I'd never require another upgrade. My current band would pass to a younger serpent, and my new one would, finally, be fitted to my profession as well as my girth.

The banding room had double arches, one at each end. The chamber was a long, unimaginative rectangle with only rows of shelving to adorn it. A freestanding furnace dominated the center of the room, and one viper or another manned this at all hours on all days.

Today that guardian coiled around his brazier's heat. His rodent dwarfed my Kwirk. The pale rat had a tail nearly as large as mine, and it held a pair of steely tongs in its paws. The viper bore gray scales, a hint of patterned saddles, and rough spikes above his eyes as if he wore a crown of thorns.

"Sookahr the architect?"

I wound in a back-and-forth pathway toward the cauldron. "That's me."

"This is your final banding, serpent. Your examination has been passed. Your career begins once the bolt is tightened."

"Yes, sir." I spoke the required words, but my heart leapt into my throat. I'd passed the examination. Laarahn had sent a favorable recommendation.

"Are you ready to be *finished*?"

"I am." I slithered closer, straightening my body and holding my head and the tip of my scarred tail aloft.

"Do you, Sookahr, accept the duties of your office? Do you promise to work to your best ability in your field of choice, to strive always for the good of the Burrow and the serpents of all Serpentia?"

"I do."

The pale head lowered. Spiky eyes drilled into mine, and though we both bore slit pupils, the bander's were nearly twice the size of my own.

"Come forth, architect," he said. "Accept your banding and your future."

I shifted my motion, sliding to the side and bringing my midsection into range of the rat's tongs. He brandished the tool, blackened metal touched with the fiery reflection of the brazier's contents. The pincers clanged together once, twice, and Kwirk stepped against my flank, placing his paws on either side of my current band and guiding me into just the right position.

It hurt when the tongs bit through my ring's bolt. The circle halves pressed into my hide, pinching like they hadn't done even when I was shedding. I held still despite the agony. I held my breath and filled my head with memories. Other bandings, year after year of cutting and replacing. The acrid scent of my scales overheating as the hot tongs pried my band apart. The sound of the brazier's hiss.

Who shall you be, newest of hatchlings? What path will you take?

I huddled beside the burning basin, trembling in my scales, alone, filled only with the promise of a disembodied voice. Who would I be? The full-grown snakes circled me, flicked their tongues, and spread wide hoods at either sides of their faces. They spoke, not to me, but to one another, and to the gods I'd yet to understand.

"Who shall he be? He has a uniformity of scale, a darkness to him," one voice suggested.

"There is a pattern still." Another snuffed the idea.

"He has a good mind."

"But a small body."

"The Sage, then. But in what field?"

"Indeed. The Sage."

I tried to follow them, but my mind was fresh and my belly full. Instead, I let their words lull me into a stupor, let their discussion decide my fate forever.

"Medicine, business, tactics?" They chanted professions while I dreamed of greatness.

"His markings are even, as regular as bricks in a wall."

"Not a builder; he's too slight for that."

"Then there's only one path for him."

"The Sage has spoken."

They sang it together. "The Sage has spoken."

My band fell away, taking the last vestiges of my recent shed with it. I jerked as the metal clanged against the ground. My muscles flexed involuntarily, loosed from the constriction of a band that had grown too tight. My scales, free for the last time from the weight of skymetal, looked like the tiles in a mosaic as I examined them. I'd been given to the Sage in this very room, promised as an architect for all my days.

It was my oldest memory.

Except, as the images faded, I realized it *hadn't* been in this room. It couldn't have been. The ceiling here was far too low, the space too cramped for that many adult serpents to circle even the smallest of hatchlings. And thin as I was, I knew there were others even smaller than I.

If there were other banding rooms, I'd never seen one. Every subsequent growth spurt had been solved by a trip to this very chamber.

The rat carried my old band away, and I remembered that *this* banding was more pressing than any memory. Now I would see my permanent band, the one tool common to all citizens of the Burrow, all snakes who followed the gods of Serpentia. The precious skymetal girdle that would forever enhance my abilities, carry my tools, and encircle my scaly hide.

It would be as fully my companion as Kwirk was, and I felt the weight of that in my bones and in the pressing of the little mouse's paws against me.

"Your teacher has made his suggestions," the bander hissed. "And we have selected your band with care."

My tongue stuck to the roof of my mouth. All students heard the horror stories. Tales of snakes saddled with uncomfortable bands, of tiny compartments and flawed skymetal that forced the owner's powers to stutter and weaken. To live forever lessened by the tool that was supposed to serve you was the nightmare of every apprentice.

The pale rodent stalked to a shelf behind its master. I swallowed and focused on the heat of Kwirk's paws. My bander slithered into a tight knot beside his cauldron of fire. His pale scales gleamed on one side, turned to ebony on the other. The triangular head followed his attendant's motion, and his tongue slipped all the way out, forked tips fluttering through the air.

"No. One to the right."

The rat shifted down the shelf. He reached into the stacked metal rings.

"Let me...help." The viper froze, tongue sticking from his lips like an arrow. Even without a band, I could feel his focused power, his absolute concentration of will as he assisted with lifting my skymetal free.

The rat grunted, heaved, and then turned around with my permanent band in his ghostly arms. It should have weighed too much for him to carry, but the telekinetic assistance of his master allowed him to carry my treasure back to the brazier. I watched his progress, tongue flirting with my lips and heart racing.

The band was thick, far thicker than my last one, and wide as well. It would take more effort to shed with that around my middle. It would take time to get used to the heft of it. But as soon as my eyes latched hold of the ring, my heart clenched with joy. A beveled edge marked the storage compartment set in the band, long enough to hold my stylus and twice as deep as the one I'd just vacated. The skymetal had been polished to a high sheen, and I couldn't spot a single blemish in that surface.

Despite the perfection of the functional design, my approval settled first on the ornate, decorative etching. Guiltily, I admired the loveliness of the artist's work far above my appreciation of the engineer. My band was beautiful, and though Laarahn would have argued otherwise, I found that the most appealing part.

"Ready?" The viper loomed over me, spiky eyes reflecting his firelight.

"I am." In my seven years of life, I'd never spoken truer words.

The viper's will carried my band to the brazier. His rat guided the half-circles into position. Silvery tongs plunged the bolts into the fire until they glowed and made the air a constant rippling of heat. My permanent band hugged my sides as if it was forged specifically for them.

My new life, firm as the skymetal against my scales, opened up before me, a straight path toward a superior fate. Just like the gods at my birth had promised. But when the rat fit the bolt into my band, when the hammering of metal against metal rang through the room, a flash of terror gripped me. I saw, instead, a branching of lanes, innumerable forked tongues stretching like the tree limbs I'd seen on the surface. Many, many pathways in all directions, so diverse and so full of potential that my mind reeled.

The bolt slid into place with a dull thunk. The rat squeezed his tongs. The viper hissed, "Yes. Good." But as my path was riveted to my body, I felt only the cool weight of the metal and a sudden, sinking feeling, as if all the levels over our heads were dropping down upon us.

DISBANDED

3

"Well isn't that fancy?" Viirlahn curved his elegant neck and lowered his nose right up against my band. His tongue brushed against it, tasting my prize. "It suits you."

"Does it?" I twisted and tried to see all of my body at once.

"How does it feel?"

We'd met at the spire just moments after our rodents were released for their afternoon reprieve. Kwirk had a few hours of free time each day, and his absence provided an opportunity to socialize with Viirlahn free from comment. The morning of testing had finished, and now that the students were attendant-free, the spire ramp swarmed with serpents of every caste. We coiled together in a niche beside the ramp and watched three constrictor girls ascending.

"It feels all right." I rippled my fore-third in a shrug and turned back to the band. "A little itchy."

"Always is. I meant how does it *feel*?" He tilted his elongate head to one side and fixed cat's eyes on me. "How do *you* feel?"

"Mostly nervous." I shrugged again and shook my head. "A little disappointed, maybe."

"In that bauble?" Viirlahn pulled his head away. "You're nuts. Anyone on *my* level would be happy with that band."

"I know. It's really nice."

He looked at me like I'd grown a second head. Viirlahn's slender body stretched twice my length, covered in smooth scales that blended together in a lacquer finish. His large eyes stood out from his slim head, and everything about him oozed elegance. When he moved, even the highest of cobras looked clumsy. Not a single trace of pattern marred his slick finish but for twin dark lines below his eyes.

"You're never happy," he said. "That's a problem. The Circlet themselves could offer you commendation, and you'd find a reason for it to make you miserable."

"If the Circlet paid any attention to me at all, I'd likely die of embarrassment," I said, fully aware that the statement only proved his point. "It's not like I want to be nervous, Viir, but when they crimped my band on, I felt something."

"Felt what?" He twisted his neck and eyed the ramp traffic. "I mean, it's pretty normal to be nervous. When I got my final band I almost regurgitated."

"Did you ever wonder about doing something else?"

His head swung back around. "How do you mean?"

"Haven't you ever thought about doing something aside from weaving?"

"I do lots of things besides weaving." He wiggled his head from side to side and gave me an expression that put heat into my tail tip. "I *excel* at lots of things besides weaving, in fact."

"Ugh. Never mind." I knew better than to expect him to be serious, even for a moment, but the blasphemous idea had nagged at me all morning. And there was no way I could broach it with Kwirk. Aside from my mouse, Viirlahn pretty much counted as my only confidant.

"Oh, you make a sour face," he said. "Let's get into trouble?"

"Not today, Viir."

"You know you want to." He swayed, slender and lovely before me. Pale scales unbroken, slit eyes held as high above me as his station. I'd never expected to befriend an *aspis*, and still had trouble believing this one wanted to hang out with me. Even now that I knew what a pain in the tail he was. "Come on, Soo. Let's find some mischief."

"Sure."

It was easier to give him his way, to let Viir lead us into temptation and brood in silence. When he slid onto the ramp, I followed, dividing my attention between his delicate green tail and the heavy stone reliefs on our right as we climbed.

Viirlahn had found me during our first year as students. Mistaking my slit pupils for a venomous nature, he'd slithered right up to me and started talking so fast that it had taken me three days to correct his mistake.

When I finally confessed my lack of venom, I'd been certain the tentative friendship was over.

Viir surprised me. He'd shaken off my flaw with his customary joviality, and glued himself to my side throughout our year of basic studies. By the time our career training began, I'd almost begun to believe he actually enjoyed my company. Still, when he'd continued to seek me out after our days' study was done, I'd thanked the Sage for my luck. And I'd fully expected him to come to his senses at any moment.

That feeling I'd never quite shaken, though our camaraderie had grown and deepened over the years. Always, there was a sense that I was living above my worth, that at any moment I would lose Viir forever.

"Where are we going?" I hissed at his tail and earned a rude stare from a descending constrictor. Making sure to raise my head high above the fat-bodied passerby, I glared back and waited until he'd moved out of range to hiss again. "Viir?"

"It's so exciting!" Viir didn't look back, didn't slow his upward wiggle. "There was an attack last week."

"I know."

My friend halted so fast that I slithered across his tail before managing to stop as well. For a brief moment our scales twined together, mine feeling as rough as a viper's against Viir's super fine surface. I whipped my tail free and leaned against a sculpture depicting a scene from the first avian war. We'd nearly reached the surface, if the story of our people had gotten as far as that, and I'd been too lost in thought and pursuit of Viir to notice.

"How did you know?" He rolled toward me, twisting his cat eyes nearer and brushing against over a quarter of my body in the process. "Who told you?"

"Laarahn." I choked out the word, tightening every muscle and clamping my jaws tight on a tongue that wanted too badly to flicker. "During my exam."

Once, during the spring awakening, Viir and I had tangled in our excitement to reach the festival grounds. For only a tongue flick, our bodies had twisted together. While extracting ourselves, Viir's tongue had brushed against my own, tips to tips, and I'd experienced an involuntary shudder of pleasure that could not have gone unnoticed.

Since then, I'd been ever vigilant about the distance between our scales.

"I can't believe he told you." If my friend noticed my distress, he had the grace not to mark it visibly. Just as he'd had the tact never to mention what had happened. Still, I knew in my heart that he remembered.

"It was in the agricultural district."

Viirlahn tilted his head to one side. His eyes glazed over for a second, and the black tips of his tongue waved slowly between his lips. "I thought they wanted to keep it secret."

"Who?" I held as still as a fly in range of a chameleon.

"Who do you think?" Viir's trance broke. He rippled a shrug and turned away, slithering even faster now.

I waited, letting him increase his lead by half his length again. Then I followed, certain that he led me to the surface now, that making friends with someone far above your station was a bad idea, that Kwirk was right. My thoughts churned, half occupied with my fear over my reaction to Viir and half still obsessing over the revelation of my banding.

What if there were more than one path? What if I was meant for something other than drawing buildings? I skimmed up the spire ramp pondering my own nature, and nearly missed Viir exiting into an upward sloping side corridor. Only the flash of his scales saved me. They caught my attention as he scooted away, and I was able to divert from the ramp and follow.

The passage we took was new to me. I'd less of an adventurous spirit than he, and my Burrow explorations were usually limited to places I was supposed to be—the housing levels, the classrooms, supply rooms, and the great cavern where all students took their weekly meals. Viir had lured me out of that comfort zone on a dozen occasions, but this was the first time he'd shown any interest in agriculture.

The first thing *I* noticed was the smell.

My tongue flicked once, then retreated into my mouth and refused to emerge again.

"By the Dreamer, Soo, do you taste that?"

I nodded and tried to speak without opening my mouth. "Dsgstng."

"What?"

"It's gross!" When I spoke, a wash of the stench filled my mouth. I clamped my jaws again and shook my head at Viir. Trust him to find something horrible for us to do. As if my day couldn't have gotten any more disconcerting.

It was too late to turn back, however. Viirlahn skated ahead, closer and closer to the surface, and I followed, refusing to speak and doing my best not to breathe except when my lungs began to ache.

We passed a section of small rooms with arches covered by heavy curtains that made the tapestries Viir wove look like gossamer. Even the covering over *my* door seemed elevated by comparison, and that bore no decoration at all aside from a thin stripe around its edge.

After the farmer's quarters, the passage split. The left fork wound away, level and spotted with more doors. The right angled even more sharply than the previous hall, and Viirlahn slithered into that branch without hesitation. Whether I liked it or not, we were going to the surface.

My last trip to the above-ground had not instilled any urge to return there. Kwirk and I had ventured forth from a forest outpost during the frigid winter days before the all-dark. The chill air had slowed my body until I'd nearly ceased moving entirely. Only Kwirk's magical internal furnace had saved me.

As we climbed, I remembered that journey and imagined coiling back around and turning tail.

"They keep the beetle herds up here." Viir's enthusiasm had not dimmed despite the horrible stench. "One of the pastures was hit by sparrows, and all but five of the stock were killed."

"I thought they put nets over the herds." I leaned into the slope and used my tail to drive against the rough passage, closing the gap between us by half again.

"The corrals are netted, but the fat bumblers eat everything in sight. Have to be turned out a few hours every day and the pastures are too large to net. Spotters keep an eye on them, but my guess is, once they saw the birds coming, they abandoned the beetles to fend for themselves."

"Who wouldn't have?"

He made a noise in answer that I'd learned meant he was choosing to tune my pessimism out. We continued in silence, and I spent the time counting light shafts, noting that they punctuated the walls with less and less frequency as we neared the surface, and trying to gauge how much longer I had if I meant to bolt before it was too late.

Despite the lack of shafts, the passage grew steadily brighter. The rooms became less frequent, and a soft vibration filtered through the floor that felt like tiny prickles—or the moving of many insect feet. I risked a brief flick of my tongue, and found the touch of fresh growing things behind the reek of beetle dung. Oddly enough that had faded now, almost to a point that I could resume my regular, reflexive testing of the air.

By the time Viirlahn became nothing but a slender silhouette, I'd found my lungs again. We slithered forth, emerging from the Burrow via an unadorned crack in the earth. My eyes balked at the brilliance of direct, un-bounced sunlight. The brightness forced my nose down. I gazed at dry dirt studded with slight, patchy spikes of grass until the urge to flee had subsided.

When Kwirk and I made our excursion, the sky had been flat with winter overcast. But spring was upon us now, and as much as that meant the danger of freezing immobile had passed, it also meant brilliance, light that those of us who dwelt in the below-ground had little exposure to. I tasted the soil, the blades of grass, and when the aching in my lenses subsided, lifted my snout and scanned for my companion.

Viirlahn gazed back at me. His huge eyes were all iris. Only a thread remained of each slit pupil, but otherwise he looked as unfazed as ever.

The beetle herds grazed in the tall grasslands of our western border. Fences of woven twigs and deadfall ringed in the netted corrals near the Burrow's entrance. Beyond these, a vast sea of waving green rippled. If the pastures had fences, I couldn't see them from here, nor did I care to venture out into that expanse. It looked far too much like fur, like something that tickled the back of my mind and refused to form a clear memory.

High perches studded the fields, distant poles where the scouts coiled, hanging from cross beams and keeping their keen eyes, always, pointed toward the sky.

Much closer, fat constrictors guarded over the corrals. Most of them wore dull, overly patterned scales and would not expect either Viir or I to speak to them as we slithered along the fence line. Though they dwarfed us, we outranked them, and not one of the snakes in charge of the insects made so much as a flick to deter us.

Viir lifted his head as high as he could while still slithering. I did my best to mime his posture, realizing that, to the constrictors, I might yet again be mistaken for an *aspis*, a noble. The idea sent a rush of excitement through me and I nearly stumbled into Viir in my ridiculous and failed attempt to match his grace.

The herd beetles fascinated me. Their domed bodies gleamed like gems in the sunlight, supported by six flimsy legs that never seemed to all be still at once. They waddled in tight groups, rattling their carapaces and filling the air with a cacophony of clicking.

Viirlahn paused beside a corral containing six of the brutes and turned his gaze in my direction once again. "I can smell the roast already."

I cringed and gazed guiltily at the nearest stag. A curving horn sprouted from the center of its head. I imagined the job of killing and cooking the thing with a ball of horror swelling in my midsection. Roast beetle, in fact, was my favorite meal. Somehow the density of it left me more satiated than other fare. After a good roast, I could sleep like the dead, and my dreams were always more interesting.

"You there!" Viirlahn shouted for the nearest constrictor.

I curled my head lower and tried to merge with the fence. The beetle I'd been salivating at clicked and waddled farther away. Viir coiled into a full strike pose, looking like a cobra who'd gone off his feed too long. He waved his head back and forth while the constrictors tried to decide who had the bad luck to answer him.

"You." Viir flicked his tongue and stretched his jaws into a gape. The inside of his mouth was jet black, darker than my scales even, and it convinced the reluctant snakes that he meant business. The nearest one slithered closer.

"What?" His voice shook the fences.

"Show me where the attack happened," Viirlahn commanded as if he were a member of the Circlet.

"That pasture there." The beetle-tender turned his head toward the end of the corral, to a spot where the fence stopped and the grass sea began.

"They hit fast. Snapped up them clickers like they were worms and then flew away with 'em. All but the five that hunkered under the deadfall."

"And where's that, exactly?" Viir's dominant posture sagged as the story unfolded. He'd no doubt hoped to see disaster and ruin. Plucked easily from the open grasslands hardly left anything exciting to discover.

"Right out that way. The dark spot. You can see them spikes if you lean like this." The constrictor raised his body, topping Viir's height after lifting only a fraction of his length. It was inadvertent, I would have bet on it, but Viirlahn snapped and hissed at the offense.

"That's enough." He stretched high and gaped until the beetle-tender's belly kissed the ground again. "We'll find it on our own, thank you very much."

"Whatever you say."

Viir darted past the cowering behemoth and I raced to keep up with him. Certainly my ruse wouldn't hold without the higher serpent to back me up. I might outrank the giant constrictors, but that margin was much slighter than the difference between venomous and non. I didn't relish the idea of lingering long enough for the beetle-tenders to take their irritation with an uppity *aspis* out on my hide.

Viirlahn, however, had put distance between us. He moved through the grass as if it were, in fact, an ocean. His smooth-as-glass scales provided no resistance, and even laboring at my top speed, I continued to fall behind. He reached the protrusion of black deadwood long before I'd made it half the distance.

When I caught up with him, my breath gasped in and out, my mouth refused to fully close, and my tongue sagged like a wet piece of string. Viir coiled in a circle around a pile of fallen branches. They must have been cleared from the field and dumped there, for no natural force would have placed each stick in an upright fashion. As it was the wood formed a ring of spikes, and my friend waited no longer in twining his way between them.

"What are you doing?" I found my voice at last. The tips of my fork brought the sweet taste of grass into my mouth, and my body softened and relaxed. "Get out of there."

"Why?" Viir's head popped up from the black spikes as if the first quarter of his body had been severed and planted there among the dead things. "Why do you think they fled in here? It's not like there's a roof on it. No walls. Just a cluster of pointy sticks."

"Probably panicked and ran in all directions." I looked to the sky then, eyed the open plane that was the avian's domain, and imagined dark shadows falling around us. "We should go back."

"They won't return this soon."

"Now you're an expert on birds?" My fear twisted into irritation. He'd manipulated me into following him again, and this time he'd landed us right on the enemy's plate. "I'm going back to the below-ground, thank you. There's nothing here to see."

"But the beetles who ran here didn't get snatched." He ignored my rebellion and continued to mull over his question. His eyes glassed. He turned his head to the sky and then began twining again, moving absently back and forth between the branches. "Maybe the old aves don't like this kind of wood."

"Yes. I'm sure that's it." Agreeing with Viir usually saved time.

"Or maybe they couldn't see them among the twigs."

"Birds have amazing vision."

"They might just have had more than they could carry." Viir's scales made a soft noise as his coils brushed together, a soft echo of the rustling grasses.

"Most likely." My gaze drifted to the sky as well.

"We should ask exactly how many they took. And how many birds there were."

"Why?" I thrashed my tail and hissed.

Viir's head vanished into the grass and then popped up again beside me. I startled, shot backwards, and heard his laughter mocking me. When I looked back, he'd vanished again. The waving of the grasses suggested the trickster already raced back the way we'd come.

I started after, ready to squeeze the mirth right out of him. A breeze surged across the pasture, clattering the deadwood and dragging my gaze back to the beetles' life-saving shelter. The black sticks looked like the bones of some huge creature. Viir's questions hissed at me, despite my determination to ignore him. The wood made no sense as shelter. There were gaps in that defense large enough for even the constrictors to slither inside the tangled branches.

I shivered once, imagined hunkering between the spikes while a falcon dove from above. The wood creaked. The grasses swirled. I turned tail and chased after Viir as if an entire flock of airborne shadows pursued me.

4

"Your mouse can wait outside." Laarahn glared at Kwirk, apparently still irritated with my insolent rodent. My attendant's paw clung to the bell rope beside the door, and the look in his eyes alone counted as defiance.

I tried to get his attention, to will him to soften his expression as Laarahn slithered back through the office curtain, a thin fabric bearing the logo for the union of architects and engineers.

"I'll be right back." I chose to ignore Kwirk's grunt of disapproval and followed my former teacher into his office.

The room had a level floor but for an uprising where Laarahn's desk sat. That was round and tiered so that the architecture professor could lie across the lower level and use the topmost surface for his papers, drawings, and student files. He had mine open, I noted, and several of my early sketches laid out around my grade history.

I slid across the floor and coiled in front of the desk. A light shaft pointed directly down on the surface, illuminating whatever Laarahn worked on and leaving the squared corners of the room in shadow. There were many shelves there, I knew, full of books and blueprints that the professor allowed us to borrow on a case by case basis.

"You ready for real work?" Laarahn settled in on his desk shelf and eyed my file.

"I am, sir."

"That's good." He let his tongue slide out, whisk over my grades, and then retract. "I see an opportunity here, Sookahr. A real chance to see what you can do on your own. You've been my star pupil for years, but I'd like to see just how much brighter that star can shine."

"I'd like a chance to show you, sir."

All the nerves left over from my exam softened, twisting into a prickly, anxious feeling. This time it was not dread that nibbled on my confidence, but an eagerness to do my best, a certainty that my moment had come. And with it, a chance to fail as well as an opportunity to succeed.

"Can you keep a secret, Sookahr?" Laarahn's voice shifted. He hissed, and lifted his snout to eye me directly. "I shouldn't be sharing this."

"I can. I mean, I will, sir. Of course."

"Good. Good." Instead of elaborating, he shifted his weight, rolling and turning his head to face the wall behind his desk. A framed certificate hung there, woven paper painted with metallic letters. "I graduated at the head of my class too," he said.

"I wasn't aware of that." I lowered my head a touch in respect, and Laarahn's tongue fluttered approval.

"I had the gift I see in you. Sure. But I also had this pattern. These blotchy, dull speckles that pin me to this office as surely as if I were made of mud."

My scales itched, as if an invisible paw riffled them in the wrong direction. Surely there was some joy to be had from teaching, some honor in it. Did Laarahn mean to question his path, even as I'd begun to question mine? Not that I allowed myself to fully formulate those questions. No. I held only a silky, slippery feeling that things could be different, a curiosity about the *why* of our system.

Why did a patternless hatchling have more promise than a blotchy one? Why did someone who got top marks, someone like Laarahn, not deserve as much chance to elevate themselves as someone like me? Even more sharply I wondered at the assignment of my career. What had it been about me that told the dreamers I was an architect, and had they ever, in all our history, made the wrong decision?

"I-I'm sorry, sir."

"What?" Laarahn curved back, shook his pale head, and rippled all the way down his body. His tail buzzed against the clay floor, and I decided I'd taken his word the wrong way. He'd only been musing, and my weird funk had interpreted it as blasphemy. "No. No. It's just the way things are, right?"

"Right, sir."

"Thank the Sage." He turned back to the desk and poked just the tips of his tongue through his lips. "But there's this opportunity, you see. The

Circlet is interested in our work here, looking for a candidate to guide the building of new outposts."

"The Circlet?"

I'd seen a member of the Circlet once, years ago, while waiting for Viirlahn in our niche beside the spire. The image that cobra had made, surrounded by squirming assistants and followed by a long train of rodent attendants, had imprinted on me a sense of awe that bordered on fear. The gleaming hood, glossy scales, and sheer size of the snake had minimized the trace of pattern he bore. If each of the five rulers of our people had a similar stature, I doubted I would survive meeting them all together.

"Yes." Laarahn showed less distress, but his tongue moved in a quicker flutter than before, and I knew he was as excited as I. "This is not to be repeated, you understand, but we have heard rumors of late. Whispers of a new conflict brewing."

"Avians?" I buzzed my own tail and recoiled despite myself. Surely the truce would hold. Generations had passed since the last war, but both sides had suffered enough losses to keep that lesson dear. There were attacks still, of course. Solitary incidents where hungry aves found the Burrow's easily available food supply a little too tempting, but I'd always assumed those were rogue individuals. All birds did not dwell in the towered city of their leaders, no more than every snake in Serpentia lived in the Burrow. "You don't think the beetle attack was a prelude to war?"

"No." Laarahn shook his head. "Of course not. And it's nothing for you to worry about either. No. I want your attention fully fixed upon your design."

"Of course." I nodded, tucked my tongue away and then registered what he had said. "My design?"

"The outpost. Yes. If you can incorporate a few functional adaptations, I believe it might impress the Circlet. But they'll only be accepting submissions during their next convention, which doesn't give us much time to get your ideas refined and tested."

I heard Laarahn's words, but their meaning only skimmed over the surface of my attention. He meant to show my outpost to the Circlet, and as surely as I'd wanted recognition more than my next meal, the idea of actually receiving it left me feeling raw, exposed like a beetle roast. Armorless.

The lines would have to be cleaner. As much as I'd labored over their definition, my target had been passing Laarahn's test, not the highest governing body in Serpentia.

"Sookahr?"

"I'll have to redraw it." I turned toward the door, ready to begin fixing what seemed suddenly a clunky and unrefined design. "It has to be perfect."

"But also functional." Laarahn's tone drew me back around again. Set in a half twist, I tasted the air in the room, my own nerves and, oddly enough, his as well. Perhaps he didn't have as much faith in my work as he claimed. "You'll remember what we discussed. If the Circlet believes a war is coming, they will favor function, require... No. They'll demand it."

"I understand." His comments on my exam were clarified now. Laarahn wanted me to propose my outpost to the highest judges. And pretty lines would not impress a council determined to protect their subjects. "I will modify the design, now that I know—"

"But you know nothing," Laarahn said. "Outside of this room, you know absolutely nothing about the conflict, the submissions, even the Circlet's meeting. You must do this on your own time, I'm afraid, Sookahr. Your placement and ordinary work will continue as if this conversation never happened."

"Of course, sir."

"Don't sag so." His voice softened, lost the authoritative tone for one breath. "I'm not going to leave you to it alone. I've sent down a requisitions list. Supplies, things I've set aside for you from our department budget."

"Thank you, sir." My head snapped up. I could pull long hours, late nights, skip dreaming if it meant getting my work before the Circlet. If it might mean my design on the brand new outposts. "Thank you so much."

"You might not thank me in the end." Laarahn's eyes glazed over. He looked directly at me, but I'd have sworn he didn't see me at all. Eventually, when his long tongue had slid out and in three times, he shook off the trance and gave a short hiss. "Take the list to the supply level. They'll get you sorted out. Tomorrow morning you'll report to the work floor. Do your best, get the job done, but remember, this outpost could mean more than a simple promotion."

"I won't forget it, sir." How could I have? My dreams before the all-dark had been full of promise, whispers of a future where I might change the world. Today, Laarahn had dropped the key to that future before me. The Sage had accepted my offering and chosen my reward.

The Circlet.

I slithered from my teacher's office with my head fully in the above-ground. My brain filled with nebulous ideas, defenses I'd learned of in my studies, the weapons and armors of wars past. During times of conflict, each outpost would be staffed with soldiers, and I had an inkling to make them part of the plan, to think forward in my design as if we were already at war.

"Sookahr?" Kwirk's squeaks pulled me back down, fully, into the dimly lit tunnel. "Hello? What happened in there?"

"Everything." I'd never lied to Kwirk before, and my first instinct was to confide in him now. Surely, when Laarahn swore me to secrecy, that promise had not extended to my rodent, who was really but a function of myself. Yet I also hesitated to bring the mouse into our conspiracy. Laarahn had specifically kept him out of the room, and in hindsight I feared it was not simply a punishment for impunity. "Nothing. He's given me time to revise my outpost."

"But you've passed the exam already."

"Yes. I start work tomorrow." I slithered away from Laarahn's curtain, down the shaft that would lead us to a periphery ramp. "I'll redo the design after work."

"Why bother?" Kwirk scampered at my side. His whiskers were held tight to his little face, a sure sign of his distaste over the matter. "That dull twit has passed out of your life now. He can't give you orders, not on top of your ordinary work."

"I want to do it, Kwirk."

"Whatever for?"

"Personal satisfaction?"

My mouse made a noise I'd never heard him manage before.

"Did you just hiss?"

"You do what you like," he snapped. "You're the boss. What do I know about what's good for you? I've only been your attendant for seven years."

"Kwirk."

"He's taking advantage of you, you know? Hasn't a creative bone in his over-decorated body."

"Or maybe he just sees something promising in my design."

We reached the ramp, empty this late in the day. Most of my kind had either gone to the hall to dine or retreated to their dens for the evening. Their rodents would remain at their sides until they slept, so for a few hours the Burrow fell as close to silent as it ever did.

"Can you divide your attention and still impress your new supervisor? Or will working for Laarahn put your future at risk?"

I wound my way down the ramp, knowing exactly where my future lay: at the belly of the Circlet. In just a few weeks' time, I'd have my shot to rise above anything my new job could bring. My star would shine, just as the strange, silent whispers had always insisted.

You are special.

"I can do this, Kwirk."

"Of course. You can do whatever you want. Who am I to form an opinion? You know best. You always— Where are we going?"

"To the supply level."

Kwirk had let me pass him up and now stood at my tail, arms crossed over his vest. His furry face scrunched into a sour twist.

"Laarahn has given me a special requisition."

"Him again." My mouse huffed, pulling his whiskers close to his cheeks and flattening his ears.

37

I'd never seen Kwirk so irritated, nor had he expressed this distaste for Laarahn before. He'd always, for the last five years, held his position at the top of the classroom tiers, quietly brought me my tools as I needed them, and never once spoken directly to or about my instructor. I stared back up the ramp and tried to worry out where his odd behavior came from.

"Are you feeling well?"

"Oh it's on me now, is it?" His black eyes sharpened and the reflected light inside grew to an exaggerated precision. He uncrossed his arms and used both paws to tug at his own whiskers. Fidgeting. Something I'd only ever seen him do on rare occasions when he'd gone too long between meals.

"When did you eat last?"

"Yesterday evening!" He snarled the words, grabbed two fistfuls of whisker, and lashed his tail.

"Go back to your room and eat now," I ordered, dropping my voice into the nearly sub-vocal range that any rodent would have to obey. "No argument, Kwirk. Go now and eat."

He spun on one long foot, tail whipping, and skittered away at my command. I watched until the last of his tail was out of sight before turning back to my retrieval mission. Without Kwirk to carry my burden, I'd have to use my band. My new band. A shiver of excitement crept along my scales. I had a perfect excuse for a test run, and no rodent voice of reason to argue me out of it.

The supply level hallways were considerably wider than any other I'd found in the Burrow. Serpents carried their work materials back and forth through the sector, and side alleys had been dug to allow for easy passing should two oversized loads meet along the way. The supply room for architecture and building was as familiar to me as my own den, though I'd never found the way so vacant during regular classroom hours.

At the huge, stone-framed archway, I paused, tasted the air, and found the musky hint of a serpent's recent passing. So when I entered I was not surprised to find my path blocked by another snake. The constrictor's body wound back and forth inside the door, marked by deep splotches with pale centers. His great head lifted just to the top of the requisitions counter, and when it turned to mark my entrance, his round pupils grew large.

My throat tightened, nearly choking me on my own tongue. Despite my certainty that I'd never met this mammoth, fat-bodied lowlife, he instilled in me an unmistakable, irrational, and immediate fury. I swallowed a hiss, but couldn't mask the vibrating of my tail against the doorway. It buzzed, and the enormous beast cringed, lowering his head until it bumped the floor.

Never in my short years had I taken such an instant dislike to another serpent, but it was as if my body reacted of its own volition. I slithered into the room, lifted high as a cobra, and forced the big guy to curl himself tightly into a submissive knot.

We stared at one another, me from higher than I had any right to raise and him from belly level. I stretched my tongue out, rigid as a tree limb. My gut squirmed. Perhaps, as Kwirk had, I'd only gone too long between meals, except I wasn't due in the communal dining room for another three days.

The constrictor's body seemed too short for his enormous girth. His head made a long triangle, and I saw little aggression or intellect in his eyes. His completely submissive posture seemed overexaggerated even in the light of my posing. Was he mocking me? Did he find me equally infuriating?

"Here we go." From the dim rows of stacked materials, a clownish mouse appeared. It hunched forward as it walked, bent beneath the weight of a wooden pack strapped to its back. Long fur covered what I could see of its body, colored in black and white patches. "They had everything master Nuutahr requested."

The constrictor mumbled something so low that I didn't catch it. He turned his head toward the door, but didn't move a scale until I'd slid farther out of the way. Not interested in exploring my bizarre reaction, nor in actually engaging in a conflict that might get me into trouble or eaten by the monstrous idiot, I coiled myself into the front corner, still raised into a striking pose. Still trembling with anger.

I waited thus, as the bigger snake retreated, waited until his mouse and their goods and every last scale of my enemy had vanished through the archway. Then I relaxed. My belly settled. I turned to the rows of shelving at last, and landed face to face with the requisitions master.

"Sookahr?" She had a slender body, like mine, and no venom. But her scales were as pure and unmarred as glass. I had no business looking at her straight on.

"My pardon, Tohvaar." I lowered my head and uncoiled. "Laarahn has sent me to fetch some—"

"I have it all gathered." She lifted her chin and held her tongue extended for another breath. Round pupils glared at me from a face that was short, wide at the jaw, and covered in gently keeled scales. "Where is your mouse, student?"

"I've sent him to eat." I lowered further, heat coursing through my body. Tohvaar's form was pleasing, had always brought my nerves to the surface in the same way that too much proximity to Viir did. "Kwirk missed breakfast and lunch today."

"Then you were very right to make him eat." She softened, relaxing her length into a gentle curve that seemed to glow when backed by the dark rows of her domain. "Can you carry these, or should I loan you Mosh?"

"I'll manage, thank you. I've a new band."

"And a very nice one. I see." Her voice carried a note not unlike a rodent's squeaking, though coming from Tohvaar the sound grated a great deal less. "Most of this should fit nicely in that compartment. Only the paper roll is too large."

She rocked back over her own coils and her eyes gleamed. From the shadow of a shelf beside her, a small box lifted into the air, wobbling for only a moment before drifting toward my banded body. I rushed in to help, focusing my will on the new compartment and prying the silvery door open for her.

Her mouse, Mosh, waddled from the back of the room, grabbed a second box, and carried it to my side while his master continued to levitate the goods one at a time. I was left to marvel at the zinging of my new band, a vibration much higher and faster than the hum of the old one. Keeping my focus on holding the compartment open, I let the heat radiating from the operation flow out through my scales until the power felt as swift as the currents running underneath my nest.

My own personal thermal tide.

Too soon, Tohvaar's voice ended my concentration. "That's the last of it."

I settled the hatch back into place and released my telekinetic intent. The ring hummed a second longer, then silenced and returned to normal temperature.

"Here are the papers. Linen, very high grade. What are you working on so soon after your examination?"

My tongue tried to slide all the way down my throat. Laarahn's orders repeated in my head. *Outside this room, you know nothing.* Tohvaar's pretty face swayed above mine and I cringed lower.

"It's special, a special project."

"Must be very special with this paper."

I nodded my head, afraid to say another word. She levitated the paper roll between us and I reached out with my mind, enjoying the flare of heat from my band again. Special paper. Special new band. Gently, I took the roll from her mental grip and carried it from the room. My band zinged, my heart raced, and I passed the levels on the way to my den with my head high and the fancy paper brandished before me like a weapon.

5

The open sky turned black with shadows. I felt them coming in my bones, long before I heard their ragged, scraping cries. Attack from above. The flapping of a thousand wings. The air churned, cascading around me in chilly downdrafts. The grass, swaying like the coat of a fat snake's rat, turned into a quilt of pale blades and dark, circling blotches.

Flee, Sookahr.

The voice in my head screamed for me to act, and yet my belly scutes had glued to the earth. I shivered, looked up, and caught the first glint of talons descending.

Flee! Live, beloved.

But there was nowhere to go. I twisted my head left and right, turned in a coiling circle until my scales brushed loudly together and my head grew dizzy. Grass and more grass. Open sky, and a flurry of dropping shadows. Death falling, pain and destruction.

Something caught my eye, but I spun too quickly and lost it in the rippling pasture. I turned back just as the screeching of an ave sounded directly above my head. My body flew forward, slipping through the grass without friction. Another cry drove me faster, and once again I caught the glimpse of dark shapes. A stipple of spiky wood piled in the middle of the field.

Yes. Flee.

The deadfall loomed ahead, stretched somehow, much taller than it had been when Viir had played among it. Each black spike aimed toward the sky, sharp as a tooth and solid as stone. I dove between them, twining back and forth as if just the touch of the wooden spikes would keep me safe.

Something screamed over my head. I flattened myself, pressing the grass to the earth below my belly and rolling, twisting my neck to see my attacker. Ice fell over the deadfall. A blanket of heavy air slammed into me, pinning my body in place and putting every muscle to chill sleep. I lay frozen among the spikes.

A round silhouette blotted out the sky. I watched helpless as the bird spread its wings wide, reaching for me with curved claws, talons as long as my head. It fell straight for me, growing larger and larger as it came. The air trembled with the monster's screams.

The deadfall would be my prison now, an open tomb for only my bones and teeth to rest in.

The bird reached the spikes and threw its wings back, veering to the side and fluttering there as if a wind had knocked it off course. It steadied, cried again, and scrabbled at the wood with its feet. The spikes held. My attacker mantled its broad limbs and curved its neck, reaching with its beak now between the sticks.

Closer and closer, I heard the clacking of its bony maw. The great wings beat wash after wash of cold air like hammer blows upon me. I lay twisted in the grass, and the ave opened its beak and lunged.

And came up short.

It tried again, claws scraping at the wooden spikes, neck twisting its head sideways. The space between the spires was too narrow to admit that head. The wood, which I might slip easily through, held the devil avian at bay.

Live, beloved. Live.

Heat flared in my midsection. My band fired to life and I focused on the enemy above. The zinging of my new ring echoed over the pasture as if amplified. A single, droning note. I bent my will, my attention to the bird, latched onto the massive body, and heaved.

Special.

Change the world.

You are the one who must be.

My foe fell away, taking his shadow and his breeze with him. I moved again, freed by the touch of the sun, lifting from the grass, lifting while another shadow dropped in to take the first bird's place. This time I froze too close to the tips of the spikes. The talons came on, shining knives reaching for my eyes. My band sputtered and went cold, and somewhere near my head, I heard the sharp, distinct cracking of wood.

"No!" I squirmed in my nest, thrashing coils over the side, up the hot wall and onto the cool floor. The dream images faded abruptly, but the voice echoed on.

Special.

I flopped out of my basin and curled into a ball. My band clanged once and then zinged as I drew on its power, letting heat spread from the skymetal and burn away the last traces of terror. I breathed, settling my tongue between my lips and eventually relaxing.

The den was empty and warm. The floor vibrated less than my hot wall, but I could still feel it, the faint flow of the pipes beyond the clay. I unrolled slowly, keeping my head tucked in beside my band until the very last moment. Then I stretched, gaped my jaws, and hissed out at nothing.

Black spikes against wan grass.

I replayed the attack again, this time awake and distant enough to see through the dream-terror. What did it mean? I coiled into a loop, resting my head beside my band. My sides still heaved, pushing my nose up and down. The beetles had run to the deadfall. A wall of spikes, easily breeched by a snake, but sufficient to keep a fat-headed bird at bay. Spikes.

My den lay in darkness. The shafts wouldn't catch the sun for a few hours yet. Kwirk had long since returned to the rodent quarters. He'd be back before I usually awoke, but I had a few hours left of solitude, and the Sage knew I would not be sleeping again tonight.

Tomorrow my life's work would begin. I'd be assigned a station and supplies, a project to fumble about with. A chance, perhaps, to earn my mark. Years to make it, struggling to twist mundane structures into a semblance of art. If the gods meant for me to focus on that upward slog, they would never have handed me Laarahn's secret opportunity.

The dream, then, was a gift from the Sage. A message I'd be a fool not to heed. I shook myself, nuzzled my new band and, alone in the dark, tasted the skymetal. My tongue buzzed against the warm ring and an electric jolt raced up to hit the roof of my mouth.

The taste of power.

I yawned, stretched out my jaws, and reached for my sketching paper with my mind. The fine linen could wait until my ideas were finalized. For now, I focused on my student supplies, leaning against the wall beside my worktable. A sheet of dull paper danced down onto the surface and a pencil stub, straight-edge, and eraser floated to join it.

I slithered across the room, perched over the empty page, and went to work interpreting my dream.

By the time Kwirk arrived, I'd worn through my stub and half another pencil. The floor around my workspace was littered with eraser dust, which also frosted my scales where I looped around the desk. I'd almost fallen asleep twice, but the paper bore a rough design, a whisper of something my instincts said just might be brilliant.

"You're already up." Kwirk's whiskers drooped. "Am I late?"

"I had a dream." I barely looked up from the page at his entrance. My efforts gripped my full attention, and it required the utmost concentration to keep a pencil moving this long. My band had long since lost its zing, only humming faintly as I forced the stick of lead across the paper. Too much longer and the lines would suffer. "Almost done."

"You've another hour till we report to your new workspace." Kwirk scurried to his niche beside the washbasin and retrieved a broom and dustpan. "My tidying won't disturb you?"

"Go ahead."

I stared at my page while the broom whisked against the floor. Kwirk's domestic tasks usually occurred while I was still asleep, and despite my reassurance, the sound of his fussing made too much of a distraction. My pencil faltered, dropping uselessly onto the drawing.

I sighed and let it lie. Rearing back and up for a better perspective, I eyed the outpost I'd sketched, turning my head sideways and then upside down.

"That's ghastly." Kwirk's voice shattered my self-congratulations. "It looks deadly."

"As it should." I gave a soft hiss and used the last of my strength to roll the design quickly, not bothering to remove my tools in my haste to get it out of the rodent critic's sight. "It's meant to be a defense."

He rubbed his paws over his nose and made a grunting sound that was anything but complimentary. "The other one was pretty."

"But this one will work."

"You'll be too tired to have a good show today. Spending all night using that fancy new toy. How are you supposed to make a strong impression on your first day of work if you've exhausted yourself on this?"

"It'll be fine." In truth, I hadn't considered the repercussions. I'd been so caught by the dream. Now that Kwirk's pragmatism pointed out my error, I felt a new sense of dread. My fine band felt nearly depleted, and I had a full day's work ahead. A day that would constitute my first impression upon the world of architecture.

"Take a rest," he offered, tucking his broom back into his nook and replacing it with a stout dust rag. "Have a wash first or I'll need to sweep all over again."

I slunk to the basin and lifted my coils over the rim, careful not to spill the eraser residue in the process. The water flowed from a spout set in the wall and out again from a drain at the far end of the sloping bath. Though it carried the same heat as the runoff racing through my walls, the depth never quite managed to allow me full submersion. I rolled and twisted until my scales gleamed, thinking of Viir's multi-chambered den complete with a pool deep enough for swimming.

My fangs might never carry venom, but with a commission from the Circlet, I could easily earn better quarters. Perhaps not as fine as Viir's, but as I bathed the crumple-scarred scales near the tip of my tail, I deposited all my hopes on that goal. First day of work or not, the outpost and Laarahn's competition were my priority now. If I failed, if I missed this chance somehow... I couldn't allow myself to think of it.

Every day since my hatching I had heard the voices tell me I was made for more than this dirty room with its shallow pool. Every day I'd worked and excelled and stretched myself to prove the truth of it. There was no room to falter now. My outpost had to win the Circlet's favor. My design had to win.

With that certainty to guide me, there would be only victory. I clung to the thought, slipped from the bath, and let Kwirk worry about the mundane details.

Viir waited in our niche. I slithered off the ramp with the day's work dragging at my body, praying he wouldn't notice.

"Hard day?" His tongue fluttered between us. "You look like my last meal right before the dung beetles carried it off."

"Thanks a lot." I pulled my tail out of the walkway seconds before a passing mouse could trample it. "They gave me a redesign for maintenance closets."

"Ouch." Viir jerked back and hissed. "How did that even happen?"

"Kwirk would tell you I spent the whole night dawdling over a figment of my imagination." I threw myself into the niche and sulked lower.

"He does have a way with words, your little mouse. But what would *you* tell me?" Viir, not one to tolerate my moods for long, slid out into the ramp traffic, forcing me to follow if I wanted to tell him my side of the story.

"I had a dream about that deadfall in the beetle pasture. It gave me an idea for—"

Viir's long head twisted, aiming his huge eyes in my direction even while he continued to slither up the ramp. "For what?"

"Look where you're going," I chided and succeeded in getting him turned around, but I knew better than to hope he'd drop the subject. I needed an answer quick, before he got any more suspicious. "It's a side project. Just something I'm working on."

"You work too much." Viir paused long enough to watch a skinny mamba girl slither past. "Maybe Mr. Crankymouse is right."

"Never thought I'd hear you side with Kwirk. But this time, I think he might have been. I could barely lift my pencil today, and of course they held a placement assessment."

"Which is why you got closets." Viir's voice held far too much amusement. "That'll teach you."

He had a point, but I didn't care to admit it. He'd also chosen a safe place to exit the ramp—a well-traveled corridor that led to recreational areas and went absolutely nowhere near the surface. I followed obediently, paying far less attention to the passing serpents than to my own thoughts.

I'd been too tired to make a good show at work. On the first day. The idea of that would have been nightmarish if Laarahn's surprise challenge hadn't dangled so temptingly overhead. If the unthinkable happened and my designs were not enough to impress the Circlet, I could apply myself more forcefully at work. I'd be there long enough, trapped there in fact, if the other test went sour.

Forever should be plenty of time to make up for a poor first impression.

"Maybe you should see Mohjiir?"

"Who?" I pulled to a stop, just short of tangling with my *aspis* friend again.

"My friend, Mohjiir." Viir's eyes looked deeply into mine. "He's working on his dreamer training, and you could use guidance. I can hook you up."

"I don't know, Viir. I haven't been to the dreamers in years. The venom makes me sick to my stomach."

"It makes everyone sick." He laughed, causing his scales to ripple and catch the light. "But better a proper dreaming with a trained guide than letting your fantasies play tricks on you."

I refused to make an answer to that. My dream, the dream that showed me a clear solution to Laarahn's functional riddle, had not been a fantasy. Nor would I believe that any dreamer guide would have steered it in a better direction. They might, however, have made the scene a little less terrifying.

Viirlahn chose an archway on our left. The room beyond was a gaming hall, and a scene where we often came to relax and practice our mental skills. This close after work hours, and during the designated free time for our attendants, the room writhed with bodies. A crowd of serpents twisted around the game tables, slithered back and forth between the checkout counters and their games, or lounged on the many shelves lining the walls in order to watch the action.

The rumble of dropping stones bounced against the high ceiling, as did the cheers and hisses of players as they celebrated or mourned their luck. I flicked my tongue, letting it guide me toward our regular group of players, but Viir thrust his body across my path before I'd gone half my length.

"Not tonight," he whispered. "I want to play at a different table."

"Why?"

Viir ignored my questions and headed into the fray. I hurried after, casting a last nervous look toward our usual crowd, mostly non-venomous snakes like myself, but a few of whom I enjoyed spending time with. A few I would have been happy to spend *more* time with.

Instead, Viirlahn led us to a back corner and a table of stout, fat-bodies serpents with splotches in dull shades and a familiar, unpleasant aroma clinging to them. These were the beetle wranglers, the agricultural workers that might not be the same individuals we'd spoken to on the surface but definitely slithered along the same path.

I swallowed a protest when the large heads turned toward us, and kept my tongue glued to the roof of my mouth.

"What are *aspis* wanting in our little corner?" One of the constrictors lifted his head, rising above his cronies and their game. His pupils made slits not unlike my own, and there were jet-black lines trailing from his eyes away down his neck. A rough scar crossed his snout just above the nostrils. "Don't you have your own games to play?"

"Tables are open to all." Viir shrugged and lifted his head just high enough to top the bigger serpents.

The long surface already had enough coiled bodies around it. The game cups were in use by two females, one with black rings on a muddy background and the other solid drab aside from a few pale specks. Their friends had been cheering them on until Viir interrupted them. Now, all eyes were on us, but I watched the stones still rising from the table. One of the girls, whoever had chosen the white stones, was able to watch us *and* continue her moves. Rather than face the conflict between Viir and the rest of the table, I tried to determine which of the players was, in fact, still playing.

"You want to play?" The constrictor made his question a challenge, and I knew exactly how Viir would react to a challenge. We were staying, whether they liked it or not.

"Unless you're opposed to losing to an *aspis*," he boasted and lifted his pointy nose to the ceiling.

"So long as *he* doesn't mind losing to one of us." The whole crowd chuckled, vibrating the cups and causing the covert player to miss her target. The levitating stone dropped to the table, and her opponent finally noticed.

"That's a foul." The dark-spotted girl threw her tongue out and hissed. "You never called a time out."

"But we were all looking, Neetahl."

They continued to spar, but Viir had slithered to the other end of the table where the challenging constrictor busily set up a new game. I threaded my way around the many tails until I found a gap through which I could see the action. Two clay cups were set in the center of the table, and a pile of stones—half white and half black—were currently being scattered around them by the spectators' minds.

Once the game began, any interference from the crowd was strictly forbidden. Each player chose a color, and the race to get all your stones into their cup before your opponent was on. Not a complicated game on the surface, but fantastic practice for building telekinetic skills. The real challenge came in speed, precision, and not letting yourself be distracted by the crowd, which *was* allowed to make as much noise as possible in an attempt to swing the results.

I usually beat Viir, despite his status, and I didn't put much stock in his winning when the entire table would be supporting his opponent. I could only assume he meant to lose, and when his first rock stuttered clumsily and missed its cup, that idea became certainty.

"Sloppy, *aspis*." The constrictor plunked a black stone dead-center into his cup and lifted another. "Hope you have a lot to lose."

"Give me time." Viir's tongue fluttered between his lips. "You'll see, beetle-wrangler."

He tossed me a look then, found me in the crowd while his constrictor counterpart scored another stone and the snakes around the table hissed and shouted. The look in his eyes sharpened, telling me he had a purpose here far different from winning a match of stones.

He'd come to mingle with the agricultural set, which meant he wanted something from them. I could guess what it was. Today was no casual afternoon of gaming; Viir was still investigating the avian attack. He wanted to know what happened on the surface, whether it was his business or not.

His third attempt actually landed a stone in his cup, but the constrictor was busily filling his. The girls' match had ended and every serpent in the corner watched Viir now. If they knew he threw the game, no one mentioned it, and by the time the second round had been laid out, the constrictors' ribbing had turned jovial, even friendly.

Viir blended in with a new crowd as easily as he slithered through long grass, naturally, leaving me behind. I pulled back and sulked while he chatted, listening only for the inevitable questions. It didn't take long.

"I heard you had some feathered trouble last week."

Bingo. My friend might have been as smooth as glass, but I could see right through him. He might have thought my dream was nothing, but it turned out I wasn't the only one obsessed with the deadfall. For whatever reason, the birds' attack had captured Viir's mind as well, and now we'd both be dragged under it, hiding between black needles while the sky swarmed with shadows and with death.

6

Two days later, Laarahn visited my new office. I worked in the middle of a grid of tables, curled around my designated surface and surrounded by other architects who'd done better than I on their day one assessment. Despite the fact that they hadn't half my talent between them. Or possibly, that was just the maintenance closets talking.

Regardless of my confidence, I'd drawn the short lot and it had neither endeared me to my new coworkers nor spawned in me any interest in interacting with them. I arrived early each day, worked past our designated cutoff, and once Kwirk had stowed my things away again, I left the room without giving it another thought until the next shift began.

Our supervisor was Daamohn, a thick, saddled serpent with round pupils and enough length to wind his way two thirds around the edges of the room. He was six times my size and, thankfully, dismissed me completely right out of the gate. I might have been doodling cartoons at my center table for all the boss took notice.

So when my old teacher appeared in our doorway and asked for me by name, most of the serpents in the room looked about, confused and unaware exactly who I was. Kwirk grabbed his whiskers and tucked his tail around his fuzzy body. He leaned toward my drawing and whispered.

"What's he doing here?"

"I'll see." I dropped my pencil and left my mouse to guard the desk. Hissed whispers followed me between the tables, and by the time I reached Laarahn, most of my coworkers had stopped their drawing to watch me instead.

Daamohn circled the room in time to meet me at the exit. As my direct supervisor, he outranked me despite his saddles, not that my tiny body could rise above his even if I'd tried. So it surprised me when he lifted into a dominant posture until I saw Laarahn dip lower in respect.

"Architect." My former teacher fluttered submissively. "I wonder if you could spare Sookahr for a few moments."

"Who? Oh." Daamohn stabbed his tongue through the air. "I doubt he'll be missed if you need him for something."

Heat boiled behind my eyes. Kwirk would have had something to say about my boss's ambivalence to me, and I thanked the Sage that I'd left the little rodent at my desk.

"Are you caught up on your work?" Daamohn asked.

"Yes, sir."

"Then go ahead and cut out early."

We waited for him to return to his circling. When his tail had passed us, Laarahn hissed softly. He lowered his head and though his tail still lingered in the hall outside, I could feel it thrashing.

"Arrogant twit," he mumbled. "How has it been? Missing me yet?"

I hesitated to admit my lackluster impression upon the world of architecture. "It's going well."

"Do you have a drawing for me?"

"Yes. Well, mostly in the sketch phase at this point, but I've got the idea down." I'd restarted the design four times, but settled on a final arrangement and managed to pin down the overall idea of my outpost that morning.

"I need to see it."

"It's really just in the beginning stages—"

"Do you have it with you?" Laarahn twisted and tried to peer around me, as if the outpost sketch would be on my table here. "Does your mouse have it?"

"Kwirk? No, sir. I've kept it in my room and haven't really explained things to him. Or to anyone."

"Good. Good. Let's have a look then."

"What? Now?" I squirmed closer to the door, turned my head, and caught Daamohn halfway around the room again. His circuit would lead him back here soon. From my desk, Kwirk's tiny face scowled at me. Or more likely, at Laarahn. "I'll just get my—"

"Better if he stays here, isn't it?" Laarahn already pulled back, retreating fully into the hallway. "If he doesn't know already, it's better to keep as few as possible in the loop."

"Of course, sir." I looked back once to catch Kwirk's eye, trying to convey what I could in a glance. *Everything is okay. Stay here. Don't rush after us, don't give me that look.* None of which would work. I had, perhaps, a few moments lead before my mouse would have stashed my tools in the designated cubby hole and bolted after us. "They're in my den, though. Should I bring them to your office?"

"No need. Halfway there now. We may as well go on up."

Laarahn had never seen me outside his office or the classroom, and I balked a little at the idea of dragging the teacher to my tiny den. In particular because only part of him would fit inside it. The urgency in his voice and the way his eyes continued to dart toward my new master convinced me quickly enough. "I'll lead the way."

He withdrew, allowing me to slip from the room. Once outside, I turned toward the nearest ramp, not the spire way but one much faster and less likely to see traffic at this hour. Laarahn followed behind, and I caught him looking back once, checking side hallways we passed as if he didn't want to be seen. Not that I could blame him. The oddity of a teacher visiting with his student outside class might have earned us a few questions, and he'd made it very clear that this project was between the two of us alone.

Which, of course, gave me a shiver of delight. Of all his students, it was me he trusted with this. It was my work he wanted to put forth, my design. If he approved of it.

"I'm just down this way." I suffered a moment of fear. What if the design was all wrong? I'd been so excited by my dream, so driven to act on it. But the new outpost bore little resemblance to the one I'd put up for my final exam. I could easily be working in the wrong direction, could easily push Laarahn to select a different confidant.

"A bit tight up here." He had to lower his head considerably to travel down my corridor. No serpent would enjoy that restriction, but as my master, it had to be particularly off-putting.

"Higher ceilings in the den," I offered. "We're almost there."

By the time we'd reached my curtain, I'd convinced myself he'd toss me off the project just for the inconvenience. I should have insisted on bringing the drawings to him, but now it was too late. My former teacher squeezed into the hallway, and I had no choice but to offer at least a part of him to come inside. I slithered in, making as tight a coil as I could manage beside my work desk.

Laarahn's face appeared in my doorway. His tongue made a slow circuit, out and in. While he eased inside, I used my band and my focus to retrieve and unroll my most recent sketch of the outpost, the one I'd designed as a response to the dream and my visit to the beetle pastures. As the paper unfurled, I remembered Kwirk's reaction, how much he hated the design.

My scales chilled despite the warmth emanating from my nest and hot wall.

"This is it." Laarahn's oblong head hovered over my paper. His tone held a sharp note, one I'd never heard him use before, and could not interpret.

"It's only an initial sketch."

"Spikes." His nose dipped. The tips of his fork flirted with my design. "Formidable. Visually intimidating, but easy enough to maneuver around."

"For us," I said. "An avian is going to have trouble getting close—"

"Which gives us time to fight back." Laarahn nodded. He stared at the paper until my scales itched.

I couldn't keep my tongue from fluttering. Did he approve or not? Had I sacrificed too much of the aesthetic for my deadfall imitation?

"This is it." He said it again, hissing the words now. "You've done it."

"D-Do you like it? I can clean up the lines a lot and I'm not completely certain about the placement of the spikes. Maybe a different pattern."

"How soon can you have it ready to build?"

"To build?" I nearly swallowed my tongue, jerked back from the desk and rapped my coils against the wall, knocking over another roll of paper. "I thought—"

"The Circlet meets in little over two weeks, Sookahr. Two weeks to present a *proven* design. Do you know what that means?"

"I wish I did, sir."

"It means we have to hurry. If I can get you a team of builders, fast, we might be able to make it happen."

"You want me to build this? But...where?" It was the least of the questions romping through my brain at that moment, but for some reason, "where" was the first one I latched onto. The easiest one. Far less significant than why, how, and also, what.

"An abandoned outpost. We lost two scouts there last month, and had to send out an additional team. Reports suggest an attack, but for all we really know they might have just wandered off into the jungle."

Jungle. Laarahn meant to send me to one of our furthest outposts, to the very edge of Serpentia where the avians still pressed our border, treaty or not. He meant to send *me*, however, trusted *me* to get this thing done, to get the Circlet's attention, and that thought overruled any rising terror.

"With a team of builders, supplies, and an already standing outpost to modify, we should be able to get it done in time."

I spoke the words, even as my mind recoiled from them. I'd never done anything but design buildings. I'd certainly never worked with builders, but as an aspiring closet-designer, the odds of that ever happening were slimmer than my tail tip. This was my chance, and though my anxiety might not want to recognize that, my ego leapt in to seize the day.

"I can do it."

"Good." Laarahn withdrew from my den, one scale row at a time. His eyes fixed on the paper while he retreated, never once looking up at me. "I'll get working. Be ready to go quickly, as soon as the team and supplies are arranged. And, Sookahr?"

"Yes, sir?"

"Tell no one."

"Of course not, sir. But—"

"I'll arrange leave for you. Best not to tell even your mouse until you're on the way. They talk together, you know. After hours."

"I'll keep Kwirk in the dark, sir." I tried to imagine how that would go over, but didn't care for the idea enough to explore it far.

"Good. Be ready. Soon as I can." Laarahn vanished through my den curtain, inadvertently ringing the bell. I stared at the fabric, rippling, as if only a breeze had moved it.

My heart raced. The paper on the desk began to re-curl, and I reached for it with my mind, helping it along, stowing it tightly away in its corner. Kwirk would flip out, but by then we'd be on our way to the jungle border.

My tail twitched, rattling my supplies and knocking over the design I'd just straightened. Jungle territory meant birds, feral insects, and the City of Tongues. At least the four-legs living there had never warred with Serpentia. But the aves. A recent attack even.

A chance to impress the Circlet.

All my trepidation died in the face of that simple thought. I was born to do this, and no danger between me and my future could be large enough to make me falter. If only I could get one cranky, overly loyal mouse to agree.

"Mohjiir needs two more dreamers for his final exam." Viirlahn slithered beside me, head bent close to mine in conspiracy. "I told him we'd volunteer."

"I suppose that's fine." My afternoon had passed quickly. I'd managed to avoid Kwirk's unspoken questions, though it had required some uncomfortable contortions to pretend I didn't see his expectant expression. Now the rodents were off on their own. Possibly gossiping about us, if Laarahn had the right of it. "Sure."

"You don't mind?" Viir had obviously expected to have to convince me.

"No. Are we going there now?"

He'd directed our progress so far. My mind continued to chew on the immediate future, switching rapidly between shock, terror, and excitement until I had the mother of all belly aches. Maybe a guided dreaming could help with that, and maybe the venom would make me vomit. It wasn't like I didn't feel nauseated already.

"Yeah." Viir tilted his head to the side. "You okay?"

"Sorry. Weird day at work." I shrugged and he let it slide.

Viirlahn must have been as distracted as I, and I was grateful for it. The dreaming as well, I'd decided, was a good idea. If death and horror waited for me on the jungle's edge, at least a dream could warn me ahead of time. I found myself looking forward to it, leaning into my slither and so distracted by my inner turmoil that I didn't even bother to dodge when Viir's lithe body brushed against mine.

I'd be leaving soon, and what was I to do about Viir? For months now, I'd been forcibly ignoring what had happened, but there was no denying my interest in him, at least from an abstract, intellectual perspective. I found Viirlahn every bit as lovely as the female in requisitions, but our friendship made that attraction incredibly complicated. Too much of a puzzle to unravel when my whole work life was in flux.

It was as if my *aspis* friend and I coiled on the apex of a cliff, and neither of us had any intention of being the first to slither over that edge. Or possibly, Viir didn't return my interest. He'd made no effort to keep apart, however, not even in the aftermath of my *faux pas*. It meant something, and if I hadn't been in knots about the dreaming and the Circlet, I might have felt strong enough just then to broach the subject.

Instead we took the ramps, side by side and brushing our scales together more than I'd allowed since my initial reaction to him.

Mohjiir might have been a student, but he was still an *aspis*. Viir led us down ramps I'd never touched before. We traveled below his own den, an expansive dugout that fully suited Viir's elegance. He led me into the *aspis* student levels, into wide halls lined with soft hangings instead of cool clay.

"Where do they get all of these?" I flicked my tongue over the fabrics as we passed.

"Student work, mostly," Viir answered. "One of these days I'll show you mine. If I can drag you back down here once whatever you're brooding over is resolved."

"I'm not brooding."

"Sure you're not." He lifted his head and gave a tongue flutter that suggested I was full of dung. "Jiir's gonna meet us in the classroom. Just ahead a little."

"Is that okay?" If he'd led me into another slightly-outside-the-rules adventure, I was going to kill him. Today, that was the last thing I needed.

"Of course it's okay. I told you this is for his exam. He has to guide us through a dreaming to get his final grade. Relax a little, big guy, and you'll live up to those eyes yet."

"Not funny." Somewhere along the way my venomous friend had equated rule-breaking with being an *aspis*. Despite being currently annoyed with him, I hoped he never learned the opposite. One of these days his adventures were going to knock him down a peg or two, and I only believed he deserved that when I was really irritated with him.

"Here we go." He slipped through an open archway and began introducing me before his tail had left me room to follow. "Hey, Jiir. This is the friend I told you about. Soo, this is Mohjiir. Oh. Here he comes."

I poked my nose into the room. Viirlahn coiled off to the right of the doorway, tail tucked now and front third lifted high into the air. Not quite as high as the serpent facing him. The room was dimly lit, as if the sun had already begun to set, though I knew it was still bright just a few levels above us. The shafts here must have been dug at a different angle. That or some device had been installed to diffuse the bounced light.

Either way it gave the room an eerie, shadowed atmosphere. Long couches rose from the floor at regular intervals in two rows along the room's sides. The paved space between them had been etched all over with deep grooves that made an esoteric pattern. The walls were draped in sheer cloth, and the designs woven into those panels showed only faintly against the gauzy background. No mere student had directed the weaving of these, and they gave the entire room a feeling of floating, as if my scales were not directly in contact with the floor.

"Soo, this is Jiir." Viirlahn's voice reached me, sounding soft and far away.

"I think he's dreaming already," the other serpent spoke, and his words pulled me from the symbols and the curtains as if they'd been an order. I lowered my head far below the level of respect I'd offer Viir, and looked up at the cobra.

"Hello."

Mohjiir swayed back and forth. His blunt head rose at my groveling, and the fleshy hood to either side of his face spread twin ridges that ran down a quarter of his body in a gentle, striped tapering. His tongue hung free, long and only twitching at the very tips of his fork. If he tasted me at all, it was a more courteous inspection than I warranted.

He stretched even longer than Viir and with a stouter girth than either of us possessed. His scales were not so smooth as my *aspis* friend's, but there was not a speck of pattern on him save for the hood stripes and, I guessed, a signature marking on the back of his head.

"Not much for words, is he?" Mohjiir hissed and rocked from side to side, miming the slight riffling of the many curtains. "Oh well, strong and silent. Definitely your t— What?"

"Soo's here to help you out, Jiir. You wanted dreamers, so here we are." Viir rocked back, not lifting but definitely posturing.

"Right." The cobra nodded and his hood fell close to his neck again. "So which one of you would like to go first?"

"He would," Viir answered before I could open my mouth. "I got the rest of the day free, but if his mouse catches us down here, he'll make Soo pay

55

for it for weeks."

"Kwirk's not that bad," I defended my attendant, though I knew Viir had the right of it. Kwirk wouldn't say a word, but there would be all the little signs of his fury. The looks, the passive-aggressive cleaning, the mumbled comments just outside my range of hearing.

"If Noch acted like that, I'd replace him," Viirlahn said. "Don't you want to go first?"

"Yes." I did need to get done and back to the den, but not because I feared Kwirk's wrath. Nor did I resent it half as much as Viirlahn suspected; my mouse had always fussed over me, and I was used to it. Kwirk's diligence to my welfare made me feel safe and loved. If Viir couldn't understand that, it was only because his own rodent showed a lackluster, automated obedience that held little personal interest.

"Okay, Viir will need to wait outside." Mohjiir swayed and flicked his tongue at Viir. "Dream work is strictly private. Can't have you butting in with comments that might rattle our friend here."

"Fine," Viir snapped. He'd obviously intended on watching. "But I'm not going to wait in the hallway. What time should I be back?"

"Sookahr." Jiir ignored him and focused on me. "Climb up on that second couch there, where I have my tools lain out. I'll get rid of this slacker and be right with you. Just try to get comfortable and relax."

"Sure." I slithered toward the couch he indicated, trying hard not to hear his conversation with Viir. The truth was, I needed this dreaming, like it or not. I hadn't been to the venom couches on our level for two full cycles of the seasons, and my head was a mess.

Between my aspirations to prove myself, my constant studies, the secret and sudden onset of an attraction to my best friend, and now my lackluster performance in a brand new job, my stomach had twisted into a constant knot. Was I thinking clearly? Maybe taking Laarahn's project was the last thing I needed. Maybe I should be focusing on impressing my current boss with a series of fabulous, creatively inspired maintenance closets.

I eased my body up onto the couch and curled around and around. The clay was warm and dry, convex at just the right angle to make a soft cup for my coils. The sound of voices faded into the background, behind the soft rustling of the sheer drape beside my bed. I listened to that instead, letting the heat and the whisper of silk lull me into a quick stupor. Too long, indeed.

I drifted the instant I allowed myself that luxury, and my head filled with images, with dreams that meant everything and yet had nothing at all to do with venom.

7

The black needles of the deadfall rose around me, though this time they didn't sprout from a beetle pasture. Instead, a facade of smooth brick waited at my back, rent in the middle by an open doorway. Above that slim maw, the outpost pyramid reached its point toward the twin suns. Those blazed down, nearly touching, round edges butted up against one another like two tails almost twining together.

"Sookahr!" A familiar voice called my name, not from the tunnel at my back, nor the wall of foliage that was a jungle before me. Viir's words fell from directly above, from the sky, and I strained my neck around and back in an effort to find him. "Soo!"

A shadow blotted out the suns—wide wings opened, eclipsing the light and glowing with a fiery halo. I fell to the ground, flattening and pressing my face against cool grass.

"Sookahr!" Overhead, the bird called to me with Viir's voice. "Look up, Sookahr. The danger is behind you."

My tail thrashed in the outpost doorway. My body twined between the spikes. I tilted my head just enough to see, just enough to catch the bird body falling toward my defenses.

"Danger," Viir's voice sang from the bird's beak. The claws reached for me, and the round head twisted side to side, examining me with a pair of slit-pupil eyes that should never have been set in a feathered head. "Danger, Soo. Watch your back."

No sooner than I heard the words that I felt something latch onto my tail. A cold grip, squeezing my scales until they ached. It tugged me backwards, toward the outpost entrance, and despite the safety of the Burrow, I thrashed and struggled against it. That grip meant me no good. The Viir-bird had warned me, and yet I'd fallen easily into its trap.

I thrashed and strained, but the thing holding my tail would not give. It dragged me, one scale row at a time, deeper and deeper into the tunnel. If it scored my entire length, I knew that was the end of me.

"Fight, Soo," Viirlahn chanted overhead. "Don't give up."

But no matter how his words stirred me, no matter how hard I struggled, my body continued to be devoured by the Burrow's entrance. The outpost, my outpost, consumed me, back and back until the bird shrank into a dot overhead, and the tall spikes grew like naked trees toward the sky.

"Sookahr. Sookahr. Soo." The voice that had been Viir's deepened, twisted into another I almost recognized. "Don't start without me, Sookahr. Easy."

I jerked awake and found the cobra, Mohjiir, coiled beside my couch. His tongue waved near my face, and beside his head, a cup floated.

"Sorry," I muttered and shifted my coils.

"Viir wasn't lying, was he? You're way wound up. One sip should do it though. Just as much as you think you can handle. The cup floated closer to me, and I saw the flash of Jiir's band hugging his scales, humming in a low, ground-rumbling tone.

"Is it yours?" My nerves caused my voice to crack. "The venom, I mean. Do you use your own?"

"We learn to extract and distill in a different classroom," he said. "But the final brew is never from a single snake. Could this contain some of me? Likely, but we never know for certain."

"Oh." I breathed in deeply, aware that my fear showed and that Jiir would probably tell Viirlahn as soon as we were finished. "So, what if something happens that's...embarrassing?"

"Don't worry, Sookahr. I might be Viir's friend, but this is my final exam. I'm taking it very seriously, and dreamer confidentiality is non-negotiable."

"He'll try to make you talk."

"Of course he will." The cobra chuckled. "It's part of his charm."

I had to agree but couldn't quite laugh. Instead, I found myself wondering exactly what sort of relationship Jiir and Viirlahn had. A jolt of jealousy caught in my throat, but before I could process it, the bowl of venom bobbed impatiently.

"Start with just a taste, hmm?"

I liked this cobra despite myself. He had a gentle manner and fit perfectly into what Viir referred to as my inaccurate hero-worship of the *aspis*. I slipped my tongue out and danced the tips of my fork over the surface of Jiir's cocktail. Bitterness. A burn against my tongue that spread into fuzzy numbness. I tensed, waiting for my stomach to process the first taste of poison.

When it didn't complain, I lapped again, this time plunging my nose into the bowl and sucking up the tiniest of mouthfuls.

"There you go," Jiir crooned. "That should do it for now. You're an easy dreamer, I imagine. Probably why the ordinary dose makes you sick."

"You think ssssss?" My tongue numbed all the way down my throat. I saw Mohjiir above me, blurry, as if he moved through water. Back and forth. Back and forth.

"Good. Just let go and relax." His voice droned, beating like a heart above my head. I felt my own pulse match that rhythm, felt the heat of the drug racing through my veins. "Now. Where shall we begin, Sookahr. What is it that you desire? Where are we going?"

The beetle pasture spread out in my mind's eye, stretched from horizon to horizon so that the distant corrals were only dots against a blue sky. A fat beetle waddled past me, carapace gleaming, rocking as it went from side to side. I twisted around, scanning the long grass until I found the spiky, black branches of the deadfall.

"There you are," Mohjiir's voice continued, despite the fact that the cobra failed to appear in the scene. His guidance echoed from all sides. "What do you seek?"

I focused on the deadfall. The grass rippled and I slithered through it, swimming in the dream as Viir did in real life, without effort. The branches rattled, clacking together like a bird beak. I looked skyward, but spotted only puffy clouds and blue emptiness.

"Show me," Jiir droned. "What does it mean, Sookahr?"

I stared at the branches, out of place among the soft grass. Contrasting, not where they belonged. A voice that was my own whispered. *Like me*. Not where I belonged? I'd assumed my obsession with the pile of sticks had to do with the outpost and my designs. Now, it felt far more personal. As if *I* somehow were those black and twisted spikes. Prickly and impossible to approach.

"Show us what it means," Jiir urged. "Show me."

"I don't know." I spoke in my mind, but the words reverberated through the pasture. The beetle clicked and ambled away to join its herd. The spikes rattled. A familiar snake popped up from the center of the branches. Viir's body lifted higher, bringing his huge eyes well over the top of the deadfall. He peered down at me, swaying like Mohjiir had. I shivered. "I don't understand."

"Show me," Mohjiir urged.

I watched Viir. Surely my body's reaction to him hadn't been so significant that my dream would focus on that? I had so much else to worry about, so many other things to sort out first. I had the outpost, Laarahn, my design, my new job, and...Kwirk.

A huge shadow loomed behind Viir. It fell across the deadwood and over my scales, bringing a chill that soaked deep into my bones and turned my muscles to stone. A monstrous face, larger than the entire deadfall, hovered behind Viir's. Rodent teeth gleamed. Two arms the size of tree trunks spread out, claws flashing. They moved in slow motion, slashing down toward my adventurous friend.

No! I screamed the warning, but this time, no sound came out. Viir continued to watch me, swaying, unaware of the beast about to tear him to pieces. A beast that looked exactly like Kwirk, if my attendant were twice the size of my entire den.

I darted forward, tail threshing the grass. My scales caught on the blades, as if they'd suddenly turned backwards. The grass held me, and all I could do was twist and watch, and scream without a voice as the claws fell upon my friend.

"Breathe, Sookahr. Let it free," Mohjiir's voice cooed, oblivious to the horror. "Let yourself free."

The shadow blotted out Viir and the deadfall. The grass darkened, and the giant Kwirk came down around me like a heavy blanket, crushing me, squeezing the air from my lungs.

"Breathe."

I sucked in a breath, coughed, and tried again. My stomach tightened. The long room of couches and drapes replaced the beetle fields. Still blurry, still a dance of light and shadow. I clamped down the urge to vomit and followed Jiir's orders. *Breathe.*

Slowly, I returned to the room. Mohjiir hovered at my side, hood extended fully and slit pupils dilated until they were nearly round. The venom's effect. My own would look just as strange. The new guide had taken venom at my side, and he'd been with me in the pasture. Had *he* understood the vision?

"I.." I moved to lift myself, but a wave of dizziness pushed me back into the couch. "That was...different."

"How's your stomach?"

"Not going to vomit." I said it more to convince myself than anything, but discovered the nausea already subsided. The room settled into its ordinary sway and rustle, and I felt better, more relaxed than I had in days. "Thank you."

"Take your time moving again. No need to rush." Jiir's band thrummed and the bowl of venom lifted into the air, floating toward the next couch in line, to a spot where, as soon as I'd recovered, Viir would lie for his own dreaming.

What would he see?

That thought put a squirm into my muscles, warm from the couch and the drug. I lifted and spilled slowly from my dreaming bed with a shiver of anxiety replacing the sick feeling in my belly. Would Jiir keep his confidentiality promise? Would I feature in any of Viirlahn's dreams?

"Was there anything you wanted to discuss?" Mohjiir eased between the two couches, lowered his hood, and looked at me with interest and compassion. He would make a fabulous dream guide. I had no doubt he'd ace his examination, and in fact, I would happily seek him out again should I need another dreaming.

"I think," I began, paused, and swallowed my insecurity. "I think I'm more bothered by Kwirk's disapproval of my friendship with Viir than I thought."

"A fine interpretation, based on what we just saw." Jiir's tongue fluttered a friendly agreement. "Additionally, the giant Kwirk might represent your worries in general. They feel overwhelming, perhaps, and Viirlahn could stand for safety or possibly comfort?"

"Possibly." I didn't think Viir fit that role, but I didn't care to tell Mohjiir exactly how I felt about our mutual friend. "I've definitely been feeling overwhelmed."

"You've just begun your adult work, right?"

"Yes."

"Then I'd say that's a pretty natural reaction. We're all feeling the pressure, the uncertainty that comes with change."

"Like there's no solid ground beneath me." It slipped out. I hadn't meant to confess so much, but when Jiir nodded and waved back and forth, I felt a knot of tension slipping free, releasing me from its grip. "Thank you again."

"You feeling better?"

"Yes." I'd never expected that, but the dreaming had released a lot of my fears. It had also set a resolve in my bones, a steely defiance to see the thing through. To follow the path *I* wanted, with Laarahn, toward what I believed I deserved. "I'm not sure why, but I feel a great deal better."

"We experience our greatest emotions in the dreaming: fear, joy, lust. It doesn't matter that it's just a dream, the release is real. Once you've faced it, these demons have far less power over you."

"Thank the Sage," I said.

"Thank the Dreamer." Jiir fluttered his tongue playfully. His patron, of course, had a more direct hand in the dreaming, but it felt disloyal to address another god out loud.

"Yes. And you too."

Mohjiir tilted his *aspis* head at me, stared with dark, drug-laced eyes, and then nodded. "You did well, Soo. I sincerely hope it helps."

"I should go so you and Viir can continue."

"Anything else you want to talk about?"

"No. Thank you." I slithered around him, around the couches and through the center of the room where the carved symbols tickled my belly as I passed. The last thing I wanted was to talk to him about Viir, but I had the oddest sensation that he knew, that he saw through me somehow. Maybe, he'd have answers for that too. Eventually. "But perhaps if I need a dreaming in the future..."

"Any time."

Grateful for that offer in more ways than I'd expected, I slithered from the room. Meeting Viir in this state was the last thing I wanted, and I couldn't be sure when to expect my friend's return. So I hurried to the nearest ramp and raced up it, intent on my own den and filled with a renewed sense of my purpose. My worries I could face down, now that I'd survived them in the dreaming. My focus could shift entirely to my work, and my outpost needed a final polish if Laarahn meant to send me off to build it.

By the time I reached my den, I'd summoned a renewed enthusiasm. I could feel the hand of fate at my back, driving me forward toward my rewards. My band zinged as I unrolled the freshest outpost sketch, and I reached for the fancy linen paper with my thoughts.

"Wasting your time." Kwirk's squeaky voice chastised me from the den curtain.

"You're back early." I ignored the jab and gently laid the expensive paper over the sketch. "Didn't you enjoy your free hours?"

"I did." He huffed and scampered up to the desk. "I always do. But I don't enjoy watching you throw away your future on an old serpent's whim."

"What do you mean?" I reached for a new pencil and my sharpener. It wouldn't do to mar this surface with sloppy nubs.

"This is Laarahn's doing. Don't bother arguing. I smell his meddling all over you."

"It's a side project, and one I want to work on." I ground the pencil to a fine point. "What does it hurt if I spend *my* free time doing something I love?"

"It's landed you at the bottom of your work crew." Kwirk peered over my drawing, popping up onto his toes to see the entire desktop. "And it's wearing you down."

"That's my decision, Kwirk. My problem."

"And it's my job to see that you're taken care of." He rubbed his whiskers with both paws and sighed pointedly at me. "A job I've been seeing to since you first crawled into this room, freshly banded and with that big, empty head full of your own importance."

"Is it a crime to believe in yourself?"

"No." He shrugged and turned away, waddled toward his niche for his afternoon chores. "Not a crime, and whether you think so or not, I believe in you too. I always have. Which is why it's so frustrating to watch you waste your time and your talents on a no good *aspis* delinquent or doing busywork for that washed up old teacher of yours."

"I can't decide if you hate Laarahn or Viir more, Kwirk."

"At the moment?" He tightened his whiskers and showed me a scowl I hadn't seen since I was a youth.

"Yes?"

"Both of them."

I released my focus slowly, setting the pencil down near the edge of the paper in case it made an inadvertent mark. Kwirk, despite his current mood, deserved more than dismissal from me. Even if I disagreed with his worries, they were for my benefit, as was everything he did.

And there might be a way I could relieve his concerns. Laarahn had specified that I tell no one about our plans, but he'd also been surprised when I'd kept my mouse out of the loop. Kwirk's loyalty had always been beyond question, and I felt suddenly as if I owed him a great deal.

"Listen, Kwirk," I began, slithering away from my desk and softening my tone. "I know you're only worried about me, and that you have my best interests at heart. But there's more to this project than just doing Laarahn's bidding. This is for me, and I want to do it. More than I've wanted anything else."

"He's using you." Kwirk's tail swiped a path through the dust on the den floor. "I don't like it."

"I know you don't. But I promise, there's more to this than I can say."

"Secrets!" He threw up his paws and pressed his round ears flat to his head. "Of course. Secrets you can't even tell me."

"Not exactly." I looked into his dark eyes and sighed. It was probably fine to tell him about the trip. At least enough so that he could prepare for it. It wasn't like Kwirk would tell anyone, not if I asked him not to. "We may need to leave the den for awhile, Kwirk. Likely soon, and for at least a week. Less than two."

If the Circlet was convening in two weeks, we'd have to be finished and back before they arrived. I'd have to have my design in place, tested, and ready for inspection if Laarahn and I convinced them to take it under serious consideration.

"Where are we going?" Kwirk's eyes squinted, but the darkness in them remained full and round. He'd eaten a good meal, and his mood was far less volatile than on an empty stomach.

"I can't say exactly. Not yet. And I'd appreciate it if you kept the whole thing between us."

"I'm no gossip, sir. Never." He sniffed, offended and ready to argue again.

"I know, Kwirk. I know. But this is important enough I have to say it."

He crossed his paws over the front of his vest and tilted his head sharply to one side.

"It's important. But you deserve to know, to have time to prepare in case we have to leave quickly."

Kwirk gave me a nod, curt and backed by a look that told me he still held his own opinions. In fact, I'd probably just convinced him I was up to something nefarious, something even more stupid than he'd suspected. It would do little good to continue discussing, yet as I turned back to my work and began to re-draw my outpost, I felt that look boring into my scales.

My tail twitched. I focused, letting the pencil glide over the linen and admiring the lines it made. Beautiful lines. A strong design, but still original. Still mine. That mattered more than Kwirk's approval.

I'd done right by him, defied Laarahn's orders not to tell a soul. It had been the right thing to do. And even if Kwirk disliked the plan, he'd do the right thing, do right by me in return. Everything would probably be fine.

Just fine.

The pencil lead scratched softly against the white linen—stark contrast I'd never been able to get on student paper. My outpost grew slowly from my strokes. My skymetal band zinged and heated, and I knew in my heart that this was the right path. This outpost, the deadfall, and the dreaming. It all directed me forward, toward the jungle. Toward my chance and my date with the Circlet.

So when a shadow fell across my paper, a trick of something passing over the light shafts, I did my best to ignore it. I did my best not to imagine an enormous bird, a giant mouse, or claws that fell and fell until there was nowhere at all to run.

8

My maintenance closet did not impress Daamohn. He wrote my decorations off as frivolous, criticized the adjustable shelving unit as too complicated, and requested I begin again from a fresh slate.

Kwirk stood silently beside my station while the boss shredded my ego, and when Daamohn at last slithered away, said nothing at all. The worst reaction my mouse could muster. For a breath, I considered that he might be right. Work was not going well and there was no guarantee, possibly no chance at all, that my design would catch the eye of the Circlet.

Perhaps Laarahn had too much faith in me. He'd not enough experience on his own to be the truest judge of my talents. I sulked over my desk, whipped a new sheet of paper from the roll mounted below the surface, and stabbed at it with a pencil until I'd poked a hole clean through.

Kwirk's whiskers drooped. His tail curled around his feet. The other architects scratched away at their brilliant designs and I considered, for the first time in years, the possibility that I might be a failure after all.

Go forth and change the world.

My dream echo surfaced, as it often did in times of doubt, but today it brought little reassurance. It was a mad whisper, an elusive promise with no proof to it. I stabbed at my paper again. Kwirk flinched.

"Perhaps a new piece," he offered.

My band hummed. I focused my frustration on the parchment and thoroughly enjoyed crumpling it into a ball.

"Better?" My mouse asked.

"Yes," I snapped at him, regretting it right away. "Sorry."

"You've time," he said. "Time to apply yourself and sort this job out."

I tried to smile for his sake. Time. Two weeks until the Circlet convened, and I was stuck here, designing a space I had no interest in. The next piece of paper I laid smooth across my desk. Instead of stabbing it, I drew a simple outline of the proportions allowed for maintenance space.

"Sookahr!" Daamohn shouted from the far side of the room.

I jerked my head up and found him glaring at me. His tongue prodded the air in a stiff, curt gesture, and he'd wound his substantial body into a tall pile so as to better tower over us.

"What now?" I mumbled to Kwirk and let loose my hold on the pencil. It thudded to the paper, marking a long scribble across my unwanted closet.

"Hurry," Kwirk whispered and scrambled over my coils toward the boss.

I followed, head low and feeling the weight of my fellow architects' stares. They pressed me down further, as if all their combined delight in my reprimand were a heavy blanket over my scales. I slunk to the boss and lifted only enough to meet his steely gaze.

"It appears someone has gone over my head," he said.

"I don't understand."

"Zip it, Sookahr. You're being pulled on administrative leave for some field assignment I was never consulted about. A field assignment. I can think of a dozen better choices in this room, but perhaps they require a highly ornamental toilet in the *aspis* quarters."

Laughter circled the class. The shame of it burned beneath my scales. I lifted my head, just the same. This was it. Laarahn had set me free of this place, at least for the time being, and if I had my way of things, I'd never be required to return. I imagined myself, personal architect to the Circlet, and lifted a few scales higher.

"I don't know what they're playing at with this," Daamohn continued, "but don't think for a moment that it won't have repercussions. If I could stop it, I'd have you pulled back to your desk and put you on sewer design for the next ten seasons. You understand me?"

"Yes, sir."

"Then get out of *my* room." His tail buzzed—enough of a warning to make Kwirk squeak aloud. His meaning rang clear as fresh water. When I returned, if I returned, Daamohn would make my life here torture. "You're to report immediately to requisitions."

"Yes, sir."

Kwirk beat me to the door. I chased after my mouse, trailing the scorn of my teacher and the mockery of my peers. It stung, to be certain, but I focused ahead. That was my future, my only goal, and if everything went according to plan, I'd never have to look back.

So long as everything went according to plan, I told myself. As if anything in my short life ever had.

We hustled down to requisitions and paused there, at the bottom of a deserted ramp. I caught my breath while Kwirk trembled beside me. Once my pulse had returned to normal, I tasted the air and found a hint of Laarahn's passing. He'd already come this way already, and I had no intention of keeping him waiting.

"Come on, Kwirk." I slithered down the huge hallway with my mouse scampering to keep up.

We passed no one on the way, and I had a chance to peer inside the doorways, curtain-less and all opening on huge rooms full of shelves and supplies. The majority of goods made by or traded for in the Burrow ended up in one of these rooms, ready to be used by our workers and crews, and available upon requisition for any serpent citizen. Some of the specialties, I understood, also exported their wares, and those were stored on a different level. Viir's weaving might one day grace some lizard's den in the City of Tongues, or dangle over a doorway in Swampfog.

As an architect, my work belonged to the Burrow. The farthest my designs might reach would be the edges of Serpentia, and of the Burrow itself.

"Where are we going?" Kwirk squeaked. "I know you're up to something. You and Laarahn."

"You'll see. It's going to be fine, Kwirk."

Better than fine, if I could seize my opportunity. If Laarahn had found me a qualified team of builders to set my concept firmly into reality. I tasted the air again, found my teacher and another scent, one I recognized only as a faint memory of association.

We reached Building and Architecture, and this time the door was not blocked. Inside the room, however, there was little space to squeeze into. Laarahn coiled, tighter than his usual, directly in front of the counter. He spoke with Tohvaar while a second serpent draped his fat body around the rest of the space. The sight of that stout, splotchy bastard sent a flare of indignant fury through me. What was he doing here, again, when I needed to be about my business?

"Sookahr." Laarahn turned as I poked my head inside. His rat sat on the end of his tail. It held a list in both paws and had been reading off the equipment to Tohvaar. "Oh good. We're all here."

"All, sir?" I tossed a glare at the big constrictor. Whoever he was, I didn't like him, and despite having no rational reason for that, I both guessed and dreaded what my teacher was about to tell me.

"Right. This is Lohmeer. Your builder."

I glared at the object of my irrational dislike. He tilted his huge, arrow-shaped head and his tongue slid out and back. Black tips between splotchy lips. I shivered, felt a start of terror, and barely resisted the urge to curl into a striking pose.

"It's an honor to meet you." He dipped his head, but his eyes tracked me. I wasn't imagining the wariness there. Of course, I was also acting like an ass. "Laarahn says you're the best student he's seen in years."

"Does he?" I straightened my ess and lowered my head, keeping it higher than his and doing my best not to make direct eye contact. "I doubt that's true."

"Lohmeer will run the build crew," Laarahn said. If he noticed my reaction to the big builder, he didn't comment on it. "We've got two other constrictors for the heavy lifting, and one metallurgist to form your spikes."

"G-Good." This was really happening. I shivered again, and this time it had nothing to do with Lohmeer. The constrictor's mouse was barely visible; the spotted female had been sandwiched between her massive serpent and the far corner. I could smell her, but only made out the very tips of her ears behind the splotchy girth of Lohmeer. "How many rodents?"

"Just your personal aides." Laarahn had turned back to the counter, and Tohvaar peered over it to examine the rat's list. "We were told there were no free rodents to spare, but I got you two carts and draft beetles to pull them."

Wow. That had to have taken some doing, and I suspected not for the first time that Laarahn had an endorsement from some snake higher up than either of us. To get my leave alone would have required strings to be pulled. Which was likely why Daamohn had been so irritated.

My stomach clenched. I'd never directed the actual building of anything. Suddenly this felt like madness, like something far over my head. I'd drown in it, fail so spectacularly that returning to Daamohn's ire would be the least of my worries.

"You have the drawings?" Laarahn continued. "And your personal needs packed?"

"I-I can be ready quickly."

"Be ready now," Laarahn hissed and turned to his rat. He checked the list, nodding for Tohvaar and then turning back to us. "You'll set out at dusk. that should get you to the outpost by dawn the day after tomorrow. Lohmeer has the route and will meet you at the mouth of the eastern outposts tunnel."

"I'll be there."

"Is there anything you need to add to this list?"

The rat climbed over Laarahn, paper sheet rattling. He thrust it forward so that I could inspect it, and I read through the supplies they'd requisitioned. The draft carts and beetles were at the top, already crossed off. Below these he'd listed brick and metal rod, lumber, fasteners and nails, and then tools. We'd obtained a welder and sander, polish and sealer. After the job's needs, Laarahn had listed our sundries, food for my crew and their rodents, bedding, and storage boxes with fuel for heat should we be required to spend time on the surface in inclement weather.

Not likely, but also not out of the question at this time of year.

I read the list twice, trying to imagine any contingency, anything else we might require. As I scanned it, I felt the sudden proximity of another body. The giant builder, Lohmeer, had shifted position. Now he leaned his head forward to peer at the list. His nose hovered near mine, and I had to force myself not to flinch away.

"Food," he said. "Is that enough? What if we're longer than expected?"

"He's estimated for that," I hissed. "There are only five of us."

"Some of us are bigger than others."

I eyed his jaws and something flashed through my mind, a lightning quick image of the huge serpent with his mouth stuffed full of...something. My pulse revved again and I leaned back, putting space between our scales.

"We can add more dried grubs," Laarahn said. "Adult beetles won't last long without pasture."

"Add them," I said. "Dried is fine."

I pulled farther back, letting the constrictor continue to read the rat's list. The air in the room felt thicker now, tasted of Lohmeer more than anything. I wanted out, and fast, or I was going to regurgitate despite having an empty belly.

"It looks fine. Just fine as it is."

"Good." Laarahn twisted to face me again, tongue fluttering in slow motion. His pupils dilated slightly. "Then we'd better get it all packed onto carts and ready for you."

"Do you need me?" I imagined staying, working with Lohmeer to load the carts and prep for our journey. My tail shuddered, thankfully still out in the hallway. It would be torture enough traveling with the big snake, working with him for more than a week.

"No." Laarahn let me off the hook. "You need to gather your things and make ready."

"Then I'd better go." My mouse already scooted through the doorway. I felt his little claws against my tail scales as he climbed past me into the hall. "Until tonight."

Without looking directly at Lohmeer, I withdrew from the room. The rat carried his list back to the counter, and Laarahn fixed his attention on his task. But the constrictor's gaze followed me out. I could feel it, as heavy as his splotchy body, even after I'd cleared the doorway.

"What's the matter with you?" Kwirk whispered, sounding like a serpent in his attempt to keep his high voice low. "You practically struck at him."

"I know. I'm not sure."

"And where are we going? Two weeks in the eastern outposts?"

"Come away first." I started back toward the ramp we'd come down, then changed my mind and took the first branch leading toward the spire. I needed to see it, to watch those deep carvings pass as we rose. Anything to soothe away the unsettled feeling spreading through my insides. "I'll explain in my den."

We went alone until we neared the spire. From there the hallways filled with other duos, snakes and rodents off early from their jobs or classes, all traveling back and forth between dens and common rooms. Kwirk dodged between the crowd, popping up and down while I was forced to move with the flow of other snake bodies. I watched his brown head bouncing here and there, but only caught up with him when we'd reached our level.

The spire carvings failed to improve my mood, though I was glad to see them once before leaving. It took twice the time it should have to reach my curtain, primarily because two serpents who both had taken engineering classes had decided to compare notes in the middle of the tunnel. By the time I'd squeezed past them and made it to the den, Kwirk had already pulled out my tools and my rolls of paper.

"Known about this for days," he mumbled. "Might have told his old mouse."

"Kwirk. I did tell you."

"Cryptic hinting." He sniffed and his whiskers twanged. "No details. Keeping the rodent in the dark as usual."

"I'll only need that last drawing and a few blank sheets in case I have to make adjustments."

He sighed and unrolled my outpost design, glared at it and then added four sheets of plain paper before rolling it up again.

"And we're going to be building that," I said. "Remodeling an outpost that's suffered damage."

"Damage? Why? You mean to wander into the east, where the blasted birds are still attacking?"

"It's for a good reason, Kwirk."

He huffed and tied a strap around the papers. "I'll have to pack as well."

"You can go now, if you like." I watched him fuss with his paws, sorting my pencils and sharpeners, my straight-edge, and the erasers I would need. "That can all fit in my new band, but if you have enough to carry, you can sling the paper roll over my head."

"What reason?" His head snapped up, dark eyes fixed on me. "If we're to traipse about the eastern border, don't you suppose I deserve to know why? What are you risking everything for?"

"The Circlet." I sighed, watching him stiffen and stretch his eyes wide. It was almost time to leave. Almost no time at all for the news to spread, and I trusted Kwirk. "The Circlet is convening in two weeks to hear presentations for defensive improvement. Laarahn thinks my design might have a chance. You know what that means, right?"

"It means you'd be set for the rest of your life." Kwirk nodded. His paws clung together. "It means I'm an old fool. *If* your design is chosen."

"I have to try." I sagged, letting my head drift toward the floor. If Kwirk didn't believe in me...

"Of course you do." He crept nearer and pulled at his whiskers. "And that prickly outpost of yours is bound to catch their attention."

"Thank you, Kwirk."

We stayed quiet a moment, my mouse fidgeting with his whiskers and my tongue fluttering happily through the air between us. Whatever came next, I could handle it with Kwirk on board. And I think he knew that too. I could have enjoyed the moment a great deal longer, but our deadline and my anxiety pressed at me.

"You should go and pack," I told him.

"And you should go and eat." He straightened, threading his tail across the floor. "You visited the defecation closets yesterday. Best to leave on a full stomach."

"I will." Laarahn said the trip would take tonight and all of tomorrow, and since emptying my body I'd felt the first dull aching for my next meal. "I'll go and meet you at the passage?"

"The eastern tunnels." A trace of his usual scorn entered his voice, but he shook it off quickly—no doubt for my benefit. My little rodent likely knew fear of the far-off tunnels and the jungles beyond. Our northern neighbors, the four-footed, kept their primitive traditions in place, and at least on festival occasions were known to dine on what smaller mammals they could catch.

"It will be safe," I said. "Five serpents and an outpost with guards. The treaties with the City of Tongues are much older and more respected than the one with Avian Tower.

"Let us hope." Kwirk scampered to the door. "The tunnels at dusk."

"I'll see you there."

I waited for him to scamper through the curtain. Once alone, I slithered to my basin and crawled into the warm water, letting the liquid soothe my scales. The dreaming had nearly eased all my nervousness away, but the entrance of Lohmeer into my traveling party, into my life, had set a new tension in my muscles. A fight or flight instinct that I couldn't explain.

I ached with it.

The water allowed me to relax and think for a moment. My reaction to the big constrictor was completely without reason, and yet, I'd seen something too. Something that felt a lot more solid than a daydream. Those huge jaws working away at a meal, something both wonderful and disgusting. Trying to invoke the memory now proved useless. It had vanished as quickly as it came, and all I was left with was the uneasy certainty that Lohmeer was not my friend. And that I would be trapped with him for nearly two weeks.

Worse, I needed to eat. Kwirk had been correct on that count. My belly rumbled at the thought, but my mind balked at the idea of slithering down to the dining hall for a few beetles. I was hungry, but every time I considered eating, I saw Lohmeer's fat body. *With bulges along the middle.*

I shook myself from nose to tail tip. It was an irrational reaction to a stranger. No sense at all to it, yet I knew I wouldn't be eating before we left. Waiting the two days until we'd arrived safely at our destination would not be fatal. Serpents could go much longer when necessary between meals.

He was probably down there eating right now.

I rolled over in my bath and felt my resolve solidify even as my muscles, finally, relaxed. It would be easy enough to wait. We had a journey ahead, a task at hand, and though it might not be beetle roast, we had two carts full of provisions.

I could eat my fill once we got where we were going.

Tonight, I had more pressing needs, like settling my mind. It wouldn't serve the outpost's completion if I continued to react violently to my lead builder. I needed to rest and meditate upon my future. I needed to prepare, and I had very few moments of opportunity left to do so.

I slithered from the basin, stretched my jaw, and moved closer to my corner shrine. The Sage peered out at me, wide wings like falls of water at his sides. His eyes flashed, and for a moment I saw Viir's face. Viir's head on a bird body, warning me of danger.

Viirlahn.

Regardless of my nerves or any desire to meditate, I realized there was something I needed far more. With a final glance around the apartment and a check to see my band compartment was sufficiently packed, I raced back out into the hallways to find my friend.

And to say goodbye.

9

"Two weeks?" Viir's pupils tightened into threads. "And you can't tell me where you're going? Do you realize how crazy that sounds?"

"Yes, actually." I raised my head until I could look into his bulging eyes. "I just can't. And I didn't want to go without saying goodbye because...I didn't want you to worry about me."

"What about work?" Viirlahn rippled, sending a wave through his glossy scales. He'd stretched out on one of the shelves above the game room floor, and I'd coiled onto the neighboring ledge. Below us, the cavern rattled with dropping stones and friendly shouting. "They're just cutting you loose for two weeks?"

"Daamohn wasn't happy about it." I turned my head down, staring at the top of our new beetle herder friends' table. Viir had been playing with them when I arrived, and though he'd chastised me for being tardy, had left the game willingly enough. I wasn't sure if he still lost on purpose, but he'd definitely managed to pay the constrictors more homage than he'd initially intended.

"I can imagine. You're going to have a rough go when you come back."

"Sure."

"Okay, who are you and what have you done with Sookahr?"

I jerked back to attention. "What? I'm fine, Viir."

"My friend, Soo, would be freaking out about this right now." He tilted his head and stared. Stared until I caved, I usual.

"I might not be going back to work there at all."

Viir hissed, a long note of appreciation and awe. "You're up to something big. Something sneaky. And I didn't think you had it in you."

"Thanks a lot." I looked out across the room. Beneath the sounds of gaming, the low thrum of several dozen skymetal bands played a background note, a deep vibration that worked its way up through the clay to the shelves we lounged on.

"Are you coming back at all?" He spoke softly, almost in a whisper, and there was a touch of fear in the words.

"Of course I am." I turned to face him, finding strength in the way his eyes shimmered. "And there's something else, something I want to talk to you about when I return."

"Something important." Viir made no question of it. He kept his gaze fiercely fixed upon me. "Right?"

"Yes." For a breath, the weight of our unspoken conversation settled over us. Viir's eyes remained locked on mine, and his long tongue drifted out and down, fluttering softly. My scales tingled. I stared back as long as I could, but Viirlahn had a lot more confidence than I could muster, even on the eve of my ultimate triumph. I looked away, letting my gaze travel over his shining body, the thin elegance of the skymetal band around his girth, the dainty trailing away of his tail as it fell over the edge of the shelf.

"How is Kwirk taking all this?" He kept his voice low.

"About how you'd expect." I rippled a shrug and watched the game below. "He's hurt that I didn't tell him everything, worried about me, angry with everyone involved."

"That's Kwirk all right."

"I should be going." My throat tightened as soon as I said it. Viirlahn and I had spent our afternoons together without fail for years. Two weeks without seeing my friend felt suddenly impossible. "You... I..."

"Give them hell out there," he said. Casual, as confident and Viir-like as ever. Still, the intensity in his eyes didn't falter. "Whatever you're doing, do it like you always do: perfectly."

I laughed despite the sinking in my belly. "And you'll continue to lose spectacularly to our new friends down there."

"You know it." A flash of shadow crossed his expression. It was gone in a tongue flick, but there was no denying it. Viirlahn was as up to something as I was. We'd have more than one thing to discuss when I returned. "You know me."

"Yes, I do." I stared back at him, couldn't resist a long flutter of my tips, a final taste of my best friend, my...possibly something more. Unless I was imagining everything. "I'll see you soon."

I dipped over the edge of the shelf, lowering myself slowly to the gaming floor. As my head reached the ground, I felt a gentle brush against my tail—Viir, saying a more tactile goodbye. His voice floated down, falling softly in the wake of that touch. But the words sent a jolt of something darker through me.

"Watch your back."

He echoed my dream warning, called out the same eerie chant as the bird-Viir had. *Watch your back. Danger. Danger behind you.* I heard it again and felt the cool grip against my tail as if it were real, as if it dragged me backwards. My head filled with the thrill of Viir's flirtation, and the terror that his final warning spawned. I slithered out of the room, and though my tail still tingled, the rest of my scales suffered a creeping itch.

A warning, just like in the dream. And though Mohjiir had soothed away my initial nervousness, I began my journey for real with a fully renewed horror in my gut.

The eastern passage had few light shafts, and those had long since faded to a dull, powerless glow. It made the walls of the tunnel into dark curves spotted with wan circles, and whatever geothermals heated this space were deep and barely enough to keep my scales from shivering.

It didn't help that the hallways were massive here, easily large enough for the beetle-drawn carts to go two by two. They waited in single-file however, and the rest of my new team was already coiled beside them when Kwirk and I arrived. I carried the front-most fourth of my length aloft, driving my body forward with just my tail, and trying my best to look larger than the massive constrictors filling the tunnel. My mouse stuck to my side, one paw hovering near my skymetal band. I flicked my tongue sharply and all heads swiveled in our direction.

The constrictors dropped immediately. Three big heads lowered to the sandy tunnel floor. Lohmeer hovered, I noted, just enough higher than the other two—a black mammoth with pure white saddles and a muddy, splotched female who was even duller than my lead builder. The last member of our party, however, kept his eyes level with mine, even lifted his body a few scale rows to match me pose for pose.

He would be my metallurgist, and though on paper I was the leader of this project, his smooth, un-patterned black scales would not allow him to give me any leverage in posture. I held my focus on him, slowly dipping my tongue through the air and tasting his defiance, as well as his musk.

"Lohmeer," I began. My eyes remained on the other snake. I needed to establish my place at the top of the pecking order quickly or this entire endeavor would be one struggle after another. "You may introduce us all."

Kwirk's hand settled for a brief moment against my scales. I chose to interpret the gesture as a pat of approval, and didn't dare shift my gaze to look and confirm this.

"That's Tuhmaak," Lohmeer's voice rumbled, vibrating the floor and adding to the irritation in my gut. "He'll be working your fancy points for us, and helping with the welds."

"Very good." I nodded to the blemish-free snake in as condescending a manner as I could. Then I looked away quickly, dismissing him and immunizing myself against any further attempt to out-pose me. "And these two must be our other builders."

"Yeah." Lohmeer's voice turned on a note, raising in volume and pitch and sounding friendlier than I'd ever heard him. "This is Mehreet, and that's Paalahv."

"Hello." I nodded to the two constrictors and then lowered my body into a normal traveling stance. Without glancing back toward the metallurgist. "We have quite a journey ahead. So as long as everything is ready, we should start immediately."

I slithered toward the nearest cart and Mehreet and Paalahv curled out of my way. At the fore of the wooden craft, a huge stag beetle stood in its traces. The carapace gleamed, even in the dark, and a humongous horn crowned its hard head, sprouting between two shining compound eyes. Six jagged, segmented legs grew from the thorax. The beast's slender feet left odd scratch marks in the sand. I eyed the two wheels, inspecting the spokes as if I could see weakness in them. As if I knew anything at all about carts and draft animals.

"Everything is here?" I fluttered my tongue and gazed at the boxes and grain bags piled inside the bed.

"Laarahn delivered the cargo and we loaded it ourselves," Lohmeer answered. He'd turned jovial, and I suspected that this, hauling loads and traveling through wide tunnels, was far more in his field of comfort than in mine. "This one is supplies and the fore wagon has your building materials."

"Good." I turned from the beetle and made my way to the second cart.

Lohmeer followed close at my tail. "The bricks were too heavy for a small cart, so we had to borrow one from the expansion construction team."

This vehicle had four wheels and two fat beetles harnessed to it. They were smaller than the stag beetle, squatter and hornless, but their legs were easily twice the girth of their solitary counterpart.

"Will it hold?" I tried the wheel-inspection trick again.

"It should, sir."

I jerked upright. No serpent had ever referred to me with an honorific before. I wasn't sure how to take it, in particular from the first serpent I'd ever developed an instant dislike for. If there was danger on this trip, I'd been certain it would come from him. That was, until I'd met Tuhmaak the Perfectly Scaled. As if he heard my thought, the other black snake lifted his head even higher.

A soft presence at my flank reminded me that Kwirk was with me, one certain ally at my side. The bi-colored mouse that shadowed Lohmeer held herself in a permanent hunch. If she ever straightened she'd likely be larger than Kwirk, and both Mehreet and Paalahv brought stout brown rats along. Tuhmaak's rodent looked sickly thin, bore a coat of satin black, and huddled near its master's tail.

We were not a heroic-looking group, nor did I suspect any of my team to be experts in their fields. Laarahn had chosen us from newly graduated students, and this project would likely be a test for each of us. I needed to seize control firmly, and then I needed to keep it.

"I will go with the first cart," I said. "With Mehreet and Paalahv. You and Tuhmaak will escort the rear vehicle."

Lohmeer nodded slowly, as if moving that huge head took all his concentration. His tongue poked out, but stopped halfway, clamped between his lips. His eyes slid down, and I could have sworn he stared at my tail.

"Is that all right with you?" I shouldn't have asked. I'd given an order, and taking opinions would undermine its validity. Still, my question snapped the big constrictor back to attention. His eyes darted to mine and he nodded, faster this time.

"Of course, sir."

"Do you have directions?"

"A map of the tunnels, sir. Yes."

"Then keep your cart close behind this one. I'll need to consult it when we reach a branch." It would have made more sense to keep him with me, but despite the fact that he'd kowtowed appropriately, I couldn't stomach the idea of his presence. "I believe the arterial here goes quite a ways east before we'll encounter any side passages."

"Probably won't see any until tomorrow," he agreed.

His tone of voice still vibrated the floor, but I found it less grating. Either he'd lowered it or I'd begun to adjust. Either way, he'd been perfectly respectful, and my ambiguous anger flagged in the face of his non-threatening presence. Everything about Lohmeer was submissive, and after my few initial sparks, it just felt silly to continue raging at him. It didn't mean I had to like him, however.

"Laarahn said there was a second team of guards sent to the outpost after the avian attack." I lowered my head to a comfortable stance, still above him but without straining. "Are they aware we're coming?"

77

"They failed to report in," he said it in a matter-of-fact, unconcerned tone, as if two teams going silent at a remote outpost were no reason for alarm. "But the message was only due a day ago. It's likely just late. Laarahn sent a runner ahead to announce us yesterday. The messengers will probably pass one another."

"Right. Good." If Laarahn had sent a mouse ahead, I would trust everything to work out before we arrived. I didn't care to show up and have to explain our presence myself, nor to deal with prickly vipers who resented us being there in the first place. Hopefully the supplies we carried would be a welcome enough addition to the outpost stores to smooth any lifted scales. "Then tell the others our gliding order and I'll speak to you at the first branching."

"Yes, sir."

I watched him slither over to the others, his big body moving like a plump caterpillar's. My tail twitched, and the scars that crimped the scales along the very tip of my body throbbed. I curled them beneath another coil and tried to see just the arched walls and the shining backs of the beetle duo beside me. Instead, my mind filled with a sense of two places, the one I waited in overlain with a much larger cavern, a place that I was certain did not exist inside the Burrow. It stretched too far, lifted too high, and my head filled with the chanting of unspoken voices.

Go forth.

Telepathy. A rumored talent restricted to the *aspis* alone. Something so rare it wasn't even talked about. I heard it in my mind, in the voice I'd always just labeled *the echo*. The voice of my oldest dreams, the ones I couldn't even be sure I hadn't imagined.

Eat.

Now I saw *him* there, the big constrictor. Lohmeer. His body bulged and his mouth opened, wide and threatening. He hissed, and the floor rumbled below me. My body trembled. My tail throbbed.

"Sookahr?" A builder, Paalahv, stared up at me. Her partner coiled behind her, and their two rats stood beside my beetle cart. The constrictor's head dipped to the sand, but her tone suggested she'd called me more than once. "Sorry, sir. Lohmeer said you'd be needing us in front?"

"Yes." I shook away my vision and glanced back to the other cart. Lohmeer and Tuhmaak, a pair I'd instinctively put as far from myself as possible. Was it a mistake, though, to let them conspire along the way? Perhaps separating them would be worth enduring one or the other's presence.

Danger behind you!

Viir's dream warning sang over the faded memory, a whisper that was unlikely to be anything more than fancy. I'd never met Lohmeer before that day in acquisitions. Telepathy, even if possible, was beyond the likes of me.

At least if the danger was behind me, I knew exactly where to find it. I could be wary, watchful of the duo following us, and still keep them where they were. I'd just have to go with care and keep my eyes open.

"Let's move out!" I shouted, and the beetles clicked and heaved against their traces. Wood creaked. Mehreet hissed and leaned into the rear wheel. His band, a heavy but unadorned ring, buzzed like a hornet until the cart rocked forward and began to roll.

We were on our way with only the dim tunnels ahead of us for many long hours. My thoughts needed to be there, focused on the journey and the job we had to finish. Time would quickly run out if I spent it mulling on the fantasies of my hatching. Two weeks barely gave us enough room to accomplish our task *without* distractions. Without irrational anger and contention, without a pair of serpents at my back that I didn't trust for one flick of the tongue.

How could I keep sight of them when I didn't dare look back? Only the next passage mattered, the next tunnel and the one after that. How could I build the outpost I'd envisioned when my team was already half set against me? Except, despite my fear of him, Lohmeer had obeyed so far without question. Aside from the dream warning, everything had gone far smoother than could be expected.

And no matter what lay ahead, or behind me. I'd have no choice but to face it down, deal with it, and keep going. The outpost would be finished, or I'd be back in a room full of architects at Daamohn's mercy. My body shivered at that thought, at the idea of failure. Onward was the only option. I wanted it, this opportunity, more than I'd wanted anything before.

No matter what, I couldn't turn back now, not until the deed was done and my future was as set as the heavy skymetal band around my middle.

DISBANDED

10

We traveled all through the night. Once the light shafts went completely dark, Mehreet took point, using the heat-sensing pits above his top lip to guide us. The beetles' clicking grew more steady in the absence of light, until I suspected they steered by some sound-reliant system of their own. For my part, I slithered directly beside the domed carapaces, eyes forward except when I twisted around and tried to spy on the vehicle behind us.

Lohmeer's labored breathing gave him away. He hung beside the box full of supplies, and Tuhmaak took my position, guiding the big stag beetle and, every time I checked, looking straight ahead. I could just make out the shine of his scales in the dark. His body blended into the tunnel walls and floor so that he seemed only a pair of huge eyes floating in a field of darkness. Always looking right back at me.

It took all that I had to keep checking on them.

The light returned so slowly that I couldn't have picked out the moment it began. I noticed, eventually, the dull shifting against the tunnel walls as we passed each shaft. Within moments, I could pick out the faint circles ahead, the first sign in hours that there was anything in front of us besides blackness. With the return of the sunlight, my nerves settled, and I felt for the first time the tension that had been seeping into my bones, the aches in my muscles where I'd been clenched and taut for too many hours.

"Thank you, Mehreet, for your guidance." I nodded as the big guy fell back, returning, now that the way was easily seen, to his post at the rear of our cart.

"No problem," he rumbled.

The vibrations his voice made did not spawn the same creeping sensation I got from Lohmeer, though they spoke in the same range. I glanced back, twisted my neck, and found Tuhmaak gazing at me. His tongue fluttered lazily. Behind him, Lohmeer sagged against their cart, resting his large head on the side as he went.

We'd been moving all night, and I gathered Laarahn's calculations had allowed for at least a moment's resting here and there.

"Halt!" I stopped, but the beetles trundled another four steps before obeying. When the carts had rattled to a stop, I let my tongue free, tasting the air in front of us and behind. "A brief rest only, or we're liable to sleep."

"There's so little heat here," Tuhmaak said. "We're liable to stop entirely if we don't pass some pipes soon."

I looked past him. Lohmeer's big head tilted in our direction. His body still looked deflated, and his mouse stood, patting his flank in reassurance. In my group, both constrictors showed the strain of our all night trek. I shook my head. "We stop here, just for a few minutes. Catch your breath now, and as soon as we near a pipe we'll take a longer rest."

"You're the boss," Tuhmaak added, increasing his height and letting his tone make his feelings perfectly clear. *He* could keep going. The rest of us didn't matter in the least.

Mehreet and Paalahv, however, seemed as grateful as Lohmeer, and like him or not, I didn't intend to kill my team before we'd even had a chance to reach our outpost and begin. I turned my back to Tuhmaak and pretended to check on our beetles.

"That was a good call." Kwirk rested his paws on the wagon and whispered. His whiskers danced when he kept his voice down, and it gave his face a comical expression. One far too cute to point out, but that I enjoyed immensely. "The big guys were struggling."

"I should have noticed sooner." I sagged a little under the truth of that. My lighter body could go a lot farther, had an easier time of it, and I'd been as oblivious as Tuhmaak to the constrictors' condition. "We'll need to plan some stops along the way."

"Perhaps you should talk to that Lohmeer, see what route Laarahn has given him."

It was a good idea, an idea I should have already thought of. The obvious idea. I'd been so averse to interacting with Lohmeer that I'd let it cloud my judgment. He wasn't along on this trip to be my buddy, he was here to work. And I needed to set my personal bias aside and let him.

"I'll go talk to him now."

I used the beetles again, pretending to inspect the draft animals while my two constrictors sprawled out on the sands. The floor held a trace of heat, and I hoped that would recharge them enough to make the nearest warm area. Of course, it would help to know exactly where we could expect to find that.

As I moved toward their cart, Tuhmaak slithered around behind it. I hadn't wanted his attention anyway, but the slight still prickled my scales. Lohmeer lay much like his kin, spread wide and low with his head resting on the ground. When I approached he lifted it enough to look at me, but not a fraction more.

"You have a map?" I asked. "From Laarahn?"

"In my band." His voice came slowly, as if each word cost more effort than the last. I heard his skymetal humming, and the hatch to his carrying compartment rattled.

"I'll do it, if you don't mind?"

"Go ahead." He sagged back to the floor, and I suffered a fresh surge of guilt when his head thudded against the ground.

I reached out, set my own band zinging, and pried his band open with my will. The tools inside clanked together as I mentally sifted for the paper I sought. It had been packed in the bottom, and took precise control to wriggle free, but once I'd removed it, it fluttered obediently into range.

"Kwirk?" I began unfolding it, but my band heated uncomfortably, and the paper trembled in the air. Slim-bodied or not, our trek had taken a toll on me as well.

My mouse skittered to my side and snatched the map from the air, unfolding it the rest of the way and then spreading his paws wide so that I could gaze upon it.

A diagram of the eastern tunnels had been drawn in neat scale over the paper. The outpost we sought was lined out in red, and a dotted line traced the route we currently followed. The initial trek east continued without a break or a branch for over half the distance, and we were to take a northern angled passage shortly after that. Along the line, at regular intervals, were small blue dots.

"Lohmeer?"

"Hmm?" His head shifted again, raising even less this time.

"What are these blue dots? Are they hot spots?" According to my calculations, we'd already have passed at least two.

"Break points," he hissed. "To keep the beetles at top performance."

"But we've missed two already." If I had to venture a guess, I'd say Laarahn had meant to keep more than just the beetles in prime shape. Lohmeer obviously could have used the rest. "Why haven't you said anything?"

The constrictor's huge head tilted. His body cringed as if it meant to sink through the tunnel floor. His eyes darted toward the back of the wagon, toward the shadow where Tuhmaak coiled against the wall.

I lowered my head and my voice. "He gave you a hard time?"

Lohmeer's tongue slid out, fluttering once. "I should have told you, sir. I'm sorry."

My irritation with him shifted, found a better mark in the serpent who'd actually done something to warrant it. Tuhmaak had likely mocked him for wanting to rest, that or he'd directly ordered my lead builder to keep information from me. But in truth, the fault was mine. I'd failed to examine our route before departing, and I'd kept Lohmeer in the back when he most certainly should have taken point. In short, I'd let my personal feelings get in the way of my job, and we hadn't even been gone a full day yet.

"I want you with the fore cart," I said. "With me. We've missed two breaks, so we can stretch this one a bit, but we do need heat at some point. Do you think your builders can make it to the next dot before we stop to sleep?"

"We can do it."

He perked visibly and his head came up. Too quickly. My body cringed away from him and my tail buzzed softly. I tried to cover the reaction as quickly as possible.

"Which of your constrictors would you recommend I post back here? With..." I trailed off, letting him think on who I meant and why I needed his advice. It took longer than I hoped. He tilted that arrow-shaped noggin again and let his tongue flap this way and that. Finally, he nodded.

"Paalahv. I don't think he'd pick on a female."

That answer told me I'd guessed correctly. Tuhmaak was going to be a real problem, but for now, I agreed with Lohmeer's solution. In the long run, I'd likely have to deal with the other snake more directly, and from our interactions so far, I didn't look forward to that confrontation.

"Rest a bit more," I said. "When you're ready to move out, come with us."

I slithered back to the lead wagon where my other two constrictors sprawled. Mehreet's heat-pits made him vital to our point group, and I agreed with Lohmeer's suggestion that Paalahv would fare better with Tuhmaak, not only because of her gender. She'd more mass than either of the other two builders, and I couldn't imagine any serpent intentionally sparring with her.

Then again, Tuhmaak didn't seem to care who he hissed at.

"I'm going to switch our traveling order," I began.

Both big heads tilted, but failed to lift from the sandy floor.

"Lohmeer will join us up front, and I'd like Paalahv to take the rear with Tuhmaak."

Her tongue fluttered at the mention of her name, and I saw the large muscles tensing to move again.

84

"Wait until you're rested." I cringed inwardly, imagining Laarahn's reaction when he discovered I'd run our builders into the ground in my haste. "Please. We'll have more breaks going forward."

The mice had all scrambled underneath our cart to nap, and I let them sleep, only suffering a brief flicker of jealousy at the sight of Kwirk's curled up little body. The beetles clicked as I approached them, stamping their spiky feet as if anxious to be off again. They showed no sign of fatigue, unlike the rest of us. My belly burned softly from the rough floor, and I could have slept for hours if I'd let myself.

Even so, I knew I was in far better shape than my stout companions. The light filtered in now, brightening the passage, and I allowed myself a moment's rest, a tight coil, and a settling of my chin against the cart box. Sleep, however, I refused to entertain. I needed to get us moving again, and if I meant to deprive my team of slumber, there was no way I could indulge in it myself.

I watched instead—the shadows of the beetles' movement, the rise and fall of Mehreet's body as he breathed, and the soft drift of dust motes through a slant of light, bounced from far over our heads and growing stronger by the moment. I tasted the air, sighed, and prayed our journey had seen my last stupid mistake. My last failure. I tried to imagine my outpost finished, our triumphant return, and my glorious moment before the Circlet.

Instead, my tired mind conjured only an image of black spikes and the persistent warning of my dearest friend. *Danger. Danger behind you, Sookahr.*

We traveled without further ordeal, stopping where Laarahn had indicated in spots that didn't always intersect with the heating pipes, but did often enough to keep our muscles limber and obedient. Our northern passage loomed after the third pause, and Lohmeer and I consulted the map together before we confirmed the route and changed direction.

The extra rests did wonders for my constrictors and the mice and rats, who perked up enough to scamper ahead. Kwirk led them and dutifully returned every few passages to check in with me and confirm the route. I allowed their play, certain that a life beside our slower bodies did little to expend their natural energies. In short, the extra running about was good for them, and I noted a shine in my attendant's eyes that I hadn't seen before.

For the first time since joining my life to Kwirk's, I tried to imagine what his moments without me were like. Did he have mouse friends that he ran off to during his free hours? Did he have a game room? A buddy who excelled at getting him into trouble? Somehow, I'd never considered his existence outside of serving as my paws.

Watching the rodents run through the tunnels ahead of me, I felt an odd envy of that internal mechanism which allowed them freedom from hot pipes and running warmth, but also a shiver of fear. Though I relied on Kwirk for so much, it was apparent, here in the dim underground, that he had little need for me.

Only his loyalty and our traditions bound my friend to my side.

A shadow of worry dimmed my heart. I loved my mouse as truly as I'd ever loved anything. A serpent's parentage was never known, their hatchmates dispersed upon banding to their own fates, but the rodent attendant was a constant companion, both family and friend. I might be able to imagine Kwirk on his own, but my life without him would be inconceivable.

The beetles clicked beside me, their feet making soft thumps against the sand. Kwirk rocketed back from the tunnel ahead and perched on his heels in front of me. Both his paws pulled at his whiskers and his round eyes gleamed in the bounced sunlight, which had grown considerably brighter.

"I think we're nearing our destination," he squeaked.

We'd cut some time off the trip by skipping the first two of Laarahn's way points, but I didn't expect to see the outpost for some time yet. Our naps had felt as if they dragged, and I'd actually feared we'd fallen behind schedule. Still, I trusted Kwirk's judgment, and I knew he'd been examining our map as thoroughly as I had.

"What have you seen?"

"Supports." His paws waved through the air, miming uprights and crossing lines above. "A ways yet, but there are wooden supports in the tunnel ahead."

"Good news." I resisted the urge to ruffle the fur on his head. My sudden rush of affection would likely only terrify him, or convince him I'd lost my mind. "They shore up the tunnel as it nears the surface because the ground here is so sandy. We shouldn't be long out now. Maybe close enough to skip the last rest stop."

My anxiousness to arrive surged back to the surface, bringing all sorts of new concerns and drowning out my over-attachment to my rodent. We'd have to talk to the guards on duty, possibly find out what they knew about the last attack.

Though we'd expected our messengers to cross, we'd seen no one at all along the way. If the guards knew nothing of our coming, it would cause difficulties. Once we arrived at the outpost, we'd need to settle in, find room for our group in their barracks, and that could only strain the relationship further. Additionally, I brought the news that we were redesigning around them and that I, a freshly graduated architect, was now in charge.

I eyed the carts sideways and prayed the additional supplies would be enough to win a tentative peace. At least long enough for me to finish my work.

"Are we stopping?" Lohmeer scooted up near my flank and eyed Kwirk through his big, dull eyes. His round pupils gave him a naturally vapid expression. "It hasn't been that long, has it?"

"Kwirk and the others have noted wooden structures ahead." I watched him deflate. He might have welcomed another nap, but my anxiety won out now. We were close enough to push the fat-bodied snakes just a little. "We're going to drive through and arrive early. Give us time to talk to the guards and sort everything out before dark."

"Oh." He dipped lower, but this time I read less of submission and more disappointment in his stance. Still, he nodded amiably. "That makes sense."

"I'd like time to smooth any ruffled scales," I elaborated. Not that I owed him an explanation. I was in charge. I was the one who'd have to deal with things if the outpost soldiers decided not to cooperate. "To make all our lives more easy. So we can get the work done and get home as fast as possible."

"You think they won't want us here?" He lifted his nose and his tongue drifted out, slowly, to what I hoped was its full length. Any longer and I could have tied the thing in knots. "You're worried."

"Not in the least." I hissed and pulled myself higher.

"Well," he ignored my lie and persisted, "there are more of us."

"I'm not talking about fighting," I snapped. "Nor will I allow it. There are plenty of ways two annoyed vipers could make our job a lot more difficult than it needs to be."

"We'll have your back," he said.

I gaped at him. A head that size couldn't possibly house so little brain. It was as if he processed my words at a slower rate, and his mouth hadn't caught up with the conversation. Still, a part of me appreciated his reassurance. There *were* more of us, if it came to a confrontation, and it was good to know at least my constrictors would side with me. I glanced back toward the rear cart.

Danger behind you.

Tuhmaak's slit eyes stared back at me. A creeping chill worked its way up my spine. I saw bird-Viir's black claws reaching, reaching for me.

"I'm glad to have your support." I said it off-handed and wasn't sure yet if I even believed it. Lohmeer triggered something angry in me, yes, but along the way I'd decided whatever that was, it was on me. The big constrictor hadn't an aggressive bone in his long skeleton. I'd no sane reason for my dislike of *him*.

Tuhmaak was another story. If the danger was at my back, I knew whose

87

name to pin to it. If the guards ahead should give us trouble, I had no doubt whose side my metallurgist would take. Everything about him questioned me, and he couldn't pass up a chance to prove his superiority any more than I could shed my skin without Kwirk's assistance.

I was trapped between the unknown ahead and the enemy on my own team. If the dream message could be trusted, it was the snake in our midst that I should worry about. And I didn't like the idea of him making friends. I turned back to Lohmeer, who looked like he was still trying to parse my last sentence.

"Switch Mehreet and Paalahv for the last stretch."

The constrictor nodded and looped back to enact my orders. I was left with Kwirk, still fidgeting with his whiskers. Still waiting for my approval.

"Thank you, Kwirk." I let my guard down, using my band to reach for him and ruffled his fur ever so gently. "You can go ahead again if you like, but be wary. I want you all back with the group when we reach the outpost."

"Yes, sir." He spun and scampered off, obedient, unquestioning.

I let out a sigh and signaled for the beginning of our last stretch. "Move out!"

But as my voice echoed through the passage, as the wood creaked and the beetles clicked, all I could think of was Tuhmaak. We moved again, creeping forward, and I felt the pressure of his slit-eyed gaze drilling into the back of my head.

As if I were completely transparent.

11

The tunnel sloped upwards soon after the wooden supports began. The beetles leaned into their traces and I ordered the rodents to stay put, to remain with the group behind me. I slithered ahead of the first cart, taking point and continuing up the ramp toward the surface with my head higher than my rank allowed.

Just to be safe.

The floor, which had been sandy for the majority of our trip, smoothed into hard-packed clay which quickly gave way to a series of huge, fitted bricks. The ridges between these bumped against my scutes. The walls became studded with wooden supports and, right before we reached the first storage room, shifted to a smaller brick structure. Light shafts broke more regularly, and the corridor narrowed so that, even if we hadn't already been traveling single-file, we would have been forced to here.

Kwirk discovered the first stockroom, dancing inside and then dragging his tail as he crept back out. His ears drooped, and his paws clung to the hem of his vest.

"What is it?" I'd known him too long not to understand that posture. A chill lump lodged in my throat. "What?"

"There's nothing in there but some broken boxes," he said.

"Well..." My heartbeat quickened. If the guards were low on supplies, they'd be happier to see us. But Kwirk's attitude suggested something more dire. "There are two more storage areas. Perhaps our reception will be warmer than I feared."

The admission slipped out, that Lohmeer had been correct and I was, in fact, afraid of our impending encounter. I covered it as quickly as I could by ordering a sharper pace forward and moving out before the beetles had even begun to strain at their harness.

The second storeroom was equally bare. It lay on the opposite side of the aisle, and according to the plans on our map, was the last room we'd encounter before the leveling of ground where the barracks and a final stock space waited. There, I fully expected to find our hosts. If supplies had run low, it would have been prudent to bring whatever remained to that final storeroom as well.

I argued the logic of that in my own mind, and did my best to believe that nothing out of the ordinary was occurring. But as the light grew brighter, my mood dimmed. The empty rooms lay behind us, and they grew in my thoughts until they loomed as largely as my other fears. Confrontation, Tuhmaak, failure, even the fear of facing the Circlet all hissed at my back as we infiltrated the far-too-silent outpost.

The barracks did little to assuage my concerns. I went in first this time, signaling for Kwirk to restrain himself. If I'd hoped to find a friendly face inside, that died with my initial peek. Where the stockrooms had been empty, this room overflowed. But it was not with the evidence of life and duty. The wooden sleeping shelves had been torn from the walls, smashed into dark sticks and scattered over the floor. Torn sacking and broken furniture littered about until there was no room left to move inside.

I pulled back out, turned to my team, and saw my horror reflected in their reaction. I knew, without looking, that we'd find nothing in the final storeroom. The outpost had fallen, and if there were any serpents left to guard it, I'd be more surprised than if Tuhmaak were to suddenly bow before me.

"I believe there's been another attack," I said. "Stay together. Lohmeer?"

"Yes, sir?" He slithered to my side.

"Keep close." I cringed inwardly, but managed to hide my distaste. The bulk he provided gave me the courage to continue, and after checking to confirm that the last stores had indeed been ransacked, I needed courage more than ever.

"Leave the carts here. Can your rats keep the beetles quiet?"

Mehreet answered. "Dawl and Peet can manage them."

"And what if we're attacked from the rear?" Tuhmaak snapped, lifting himself from the ground and zipping forward faster than the heavy-bodied serpents could manage. "What if we just leave our food here and someone takes it?"

"We came from that direction," I snapped back. "But if you wish to stay with the carts that's fine with me. You can begin unloading the supplies into this room."

"Unloading?" He curled back into striking pose, and I heard a low hiss from Lohmeer in response. "You can't possibly expect to stay here."

"We have a job to do," I said. Turning back hadn't occurred to me. Now that he'd mentioned it, I liked it even less than the idea of facing whatever ransacked the barracks. "But before I make any decision, I need to see the whole situation. I'm not about to panic and turn tail before I know what's actually going on."

Tuhmaak hissed, but he lowered his head and softened his ess. I hadn't figured he'd embrace being accused of cowardice, and I was right. When we continued away from the carts, the surly snake came with, following Paalahv and making no further objection.

There was little outpost left to explore, and yet I still held out hope we might find a single survivor here, a wounded guard, or possibly a note or hint of what exactly had happened. Before the exit to the surface, two bolt-holes stood on either side of the passage. I knew from the plans where they led, and ordered Lohmeer to stay with the others while Kwirk and I explored the first.

Inside the narrow doorway, a single ramp made a corkscrew path to the lookout post. Kwirk skittered up ahead of me, and when I poked my nose into the square room, my mouse already gazed out of the slits set around three of the sloping walls. We were inside the pyramid top of the outpost, and from here should be able to see 180 degrees of the surface terrain.

"Anything?" I moved to a different wall than he'd chosen, trusting his assessment.

"A lot of trees," he answered.

I hissed and pressed my nose down, gliding to the wall for my first peek of the jungle outside. Before I even looked, I could taste the difference, the odd moisture in the air, the thick, sweet smell of more growing things than I'd ever imagined could be packed into a single location.

The jungle had been painted in a gradient of shades, bright to dark, speckled and splotched and striped. Whatever trunks supported the cloud-reaching trees were obscured by layer after layer of fronds, overlapping and only offering sparse peeks of vine-encrusted undergrowth. The base of our outpost nestled in the sandy soil, but it held a dark hue here, rich through with organic matter. An area around the building had been cleared, wide enough to park three of our carts end to end inside it.

At the very edge, a short fence had been woven of fallen limbs. It circled the clearing as far as I could see from this vantage, but I moved from wall to wall, gazing out just to be certain there was no breech in that barrier, and no viper guard coiled anywhere inside it. I'd just decided to check the opposing lookout tower, had begun to turn away from my slit, when a movement in the foliage dragged my gaze back.

"Kwirk?" I called my mouse, whose eyes were often sharper than my own. "Come and look here."

The fronds overlapped, but behind them, about even with our position, I'd seen something shifting. I knew I had, but now the leaves held still, and my mouse's tiny voice squeaked at my side.

"What am I looking for?"

I peered out, staring into the spot where I'd have sworn something moved. My tongue stretched through the open slit, tasting, fluttering through surface air that brought too many new tastes to decipher. There had to be something out there, and yet the longer I stared, the more still the jungle was. Eventually I had no choice but to look away.

"Come, Kwirk. Let's see the other side."

We descended and found Lohmeer peering up the corkscrew ramp. He retreated quickly, but I could understand his curiosity, the need for answers in light of our discoveries so far. When I slithered into the hall, all four other snakes had pressed close together. Even Tuhmaak looked eagerly in my direction.

"I'm going to check the other side," I said. "But feel free to go up and take a peek."

I crossed in front of them and paused in the opposing doorway. Not one scale had moved, and all eyes still tracked me as if I would somehow have the answer. Logical, considering I was meant to be their leader, but off-putting when I had nothing at all useful to share.

"Two at a time at most. It's not a very large space." I ducked into the next bolt-hole, where Kwirk already danced up the ramp. Twisting back, I added, "And keep your eyes on the trees. Let me know if you see anything."

They gaped at me, and I turned away first, headed up the ramp after my rodent and didn't hear them moving at all until I'd nearly made the top. I poked my head into the lookout room and Kwirk skittered past my tongue.

"You need to see this." He popped onto the tip of his toes and waved one paw toward the viewing slits.

The rooms were open and, though the sun was up, chillier than the tunnels below had been. I slithered to Kwirk's side, already planning rotating shifts, night times with two of us stationed in these rooms and the rest hunkering near the warm wall in the barracks. During the daytime we'd have to be about our work, but I might be able to assign a few of the rodents to watchtower duty.

I joined Kwirk, certain that I could defend the outpost. My redesign would now involve widening the slits, for one thing. The addition of the spikes would make the openings far more defensible, and the visibility left

92

a lot to be desired now that I'd actually gazed out from them.

For one thing, they offered a terrible view of the sky. The jungle grew too tall around the outpost, and I'd had more of a view of trees and ground than the air above, which was exactly where I'd expect an avian attack to come from. The original architect must never have seen the jungle where his design would be installed.

My eyes went automatically there, up as far as I could twist to see. The fronds and vines blocked all but a thin strip of the heavens. And I was so focused on solving that problem that it took Kwirk's paw on my neck to show me the error of my ways.

"What do you think happened?"

I let my gaze drop, following Kwirk's stare down past the jungle to the ground, the clearing, and the fence. The brush barrier stood between the sand and the jungle, just as it had on the other side, but here a gap had been torn in that defense. Trampled branches littered the yard, and the soil was churned into heaps and valleys in a swath leading from the outpost to the broken fence and away, I assumed, into the black undergrowth of the jungle.

"Great Sage," I hissed. 'They were attacked from the ground."

"From that wretched wall of leaves," Kwirk said.

I stared into the undergrowth. Vines and fronds, prints on the ground, and the breaching of a fence that was too low, too flimsy to keep even the smallest ave outside. The serpents here had been attacked, possibly twice. They'd vanished as well. But who were the attackers if not birds?

"The truce with the four-legged," I mused. "They'll never believe it back in the Burrow."

"Why would the lizards start a war?" Kwirk scowled at the jungle as if the trees themselves had done the damage. "They'd have no hope of winning. They're far too primitive, and our weapons have already proven that."

"Maybe something changed." I curled away from the view, dreading relaying what I saw to the team. Dreading the decisions that had to come next. We were alone here with a task to do, but someone should definitely pass this information along. If the four-legged had moved against us, maybe their weapons had improved. Maybe...

I looked around the room again. A cold gust skimmed in through the slits, slowing my thinking. Making me want to pause and rest. To nap.

"We should go down." Kwirk's hand landed, warm and alive against my scales. "Sookahr?"

"There should be weapons here." My thoughts clarified, sharpening to a point. "There would have been weapons here, darts, arrows."

"They took everything."

"Yes."

All the supplies, the weapons, and possibly the guards themselves. I shivered again, and this time the air had nothing to do with it. Whoever had attacked the outpost had done so easily and quickly, twice. They'd defeated two teams of viper guards, trained soldiers, and they'd taken their weapons. Which meant, of course, that they still had those weapons. That they were armed now with the sum total of the outpost's defense.

We were on our own, alone, and we'd packed nothing but building supplies and food. It should have been all I worried about, should have been enough to make us turn tail and flee for home. But as I slithered down the corkscrew ramp, my mind wrestled with two things. First, the dream had insisted my enemy was behind me, *inside* the Burrow. And second, the thought which nagged most persistently in the face of the damaged fence: if it hadn't been aves who attacked us here, would my spikes still work?

All my efforts turned around the beauty of my design, a design I'd drawn with avians in mind. If the enemy did not fall from the sky, my remodel and my future would be worthless.

I raised myself, bumping into the low ceiling and hissing at the impact. All the facts here had stacked against me. All signs pointed to failure, and yet I wasn't ready to concede. Not even in the face of that shredded fence. We had more serpents, more eyes to watch the jungle. We had a little time, and if we worked quickly, might finish the job and retreat before whatever enemy stalked the outpost knew we'd even come.

But I would not make the same mistake the guards here, two teams of guards, had made. Our first order of business would be to send word of this disaster home.

"We must tell the others," I said. "And begin as soon as possible."

Kwirk gaped at me. I caught the look out of the corner of my eye, but swept over it with a twist and flutter of my tongue. Down the spiral ramp I went, head up and thoughts churning. *Tell the others, and send word. Get to work and be done as fast as possible.*

I built a plan around these ideas, set my will to the task and refused to let myself consider the obvious answer: run away. Soon enough, the others would suggest it. I needed to be ready to counter with solid strategy. I needed to be ready, because I was far too close to getting everything I wanted to give up now. Not with avians dropping from the sky, and not in the face of a jungle full of enemies.

12

"They've already taken everything." I coiled beside the large stag beetle, as if his horn might lend me strength. "It's very unlikely they'll return a third time."

"And we have no weapons if they do. No defenses at all." Not surprisingly, it was Tuhmaak who argued for an immediate retreat. "We're ants in a bowl if we stay here."

"We'll repair the fence and make weapons," I said. "You are a metallurgist, are you not?"

He jerked back, trying to lift himself above me. I matched him scale for scale. This time, I couldn't afford to let him play his tricks. Not when the other three watched us as closely as a game of stones.

"There is enough rod to spare a few for spears and darts," I said. "You'll get on that first, while we unload and clean up the barracks. I'll send one of the rodents back to report on the situation here. Replacement soldiers will only take a few days to arrive, or less, and I'm certain they'll bring weapons."

"Whose mouse will go?" Lohmeer broke in, low and submissive, but for once, a welcome interruption.

"I was thinking of yours? If you can spare her." I made it a question, though I'd already decided on the bi-colored female. The rats would be too valuable during the building, Tuhmaak would only fight harder if I deprived him of his little mouse, and though I'd considered sending Kwirk, no one else here knew my designs as well as I did. We needed him, in particular if we had to divide our time between the remodel and defense. "I could send Kwirk, but he knows the plans for the build too well to spare."

"Rapt will do it," Lohmeer said. "She's fast, and brave enough to go alone."

"Thank you." I turned from Tuhmaak the same way I'd brushed over Kwirk's objections, rolling forward as if pulled by an irresistible tide. "The remaining rodents will work on the barracks. Mehreet and Paalahv can unpack the wagons here, and Lohmeer and I will rebuild the fence. If we begin right away, we should have this place back to functional before Tuhmaak finishes those darts."

I put a dare in that, and I saw it register in the rebellious metallurgist's eyes. He'd be done before we were, no matter how fast we worked. Perfect.

"I'll send Rapt now?" Lohmeer looked up at me, already nodding.

"Give her some grain and water first. She's had a long trek already. If she needs rest, let her have that too."

"I will!" Lohmeer shouted, and lifted his head from the ground long enough to nod fiercely at me.

Tuhmaak hissed, but I ignored him. The other two constrictors exchanged a look between them—though kept their eyes from landing directly on me—and ordered their rats to begin work on the barracks. I turned to Kwirk and caught the look I'd been avoiding since we first saw the destroyed fence. My mouse most certainly didn't approve of staying. He'd have too much sense to argue it in front of Tuhmaak and the others, but I knew I was in for one hell of a chastising eventually.

"Go and help with the barracks, Kwirk. Make sure there is enough space cleared for both snakes and rodents to sleep. We'll likely be taking shifts manning the towers during the night, but I want at least two shelves near the heat and enough floor clear for you guys to make a nest."

"Yes, sir." He snapped to attention and spun on one heel. His tail whipped against my side, stinging, not likely on accident.

Once the rodents had entered the trashed barracks, I headed down the hallway, trusting that the others would have little choice but to do the tasks I'd given them—not because I believed in my own authority, but because I had no idea what I'd do if they refused. The final slope to the exit ended in a heavy door. It should have shown signs of damage, should have hung, as broken as the rest of the outpost, on its hinges.

I examined it from both sides, opening it with the help of my band, and slithering into the sunlit yard. I found no damage. Not even a scratch in the wood. How had the enemy gotten through that panel? I gauged the thickness against my body and came up short. Had the door been open

96

during both attacks? If so, we'd have a simple answer: keep the wretched thing shut at all times.

With that in mind, I closed it behind me. With the zinging of skymetal and a push from my thoughts, the door slammed. It echoed with a thud that I hadn't meant, but hoped would serve my purposes with the serpents still inside. I felt as much fear as they did, surely. My body seized at the sound of that portal closing. I glared at the surrounding foliage and pictured savage lizards armed with our darts and spears.

But I would not flee from this. I couldn't.

Go forth, beloved.

The echo whispered to me of courage. I glared at the fronds once more, lifting this time until three quarters of my length strained for height. My tail buzzed the sand and I hissed, low and long, before relaxing the pose. The fence stared back at me. The fronds rustled in the fingers of a soft wind. I sighed and slithered around the side of our pyramid, finding the first tossed twigs only a tail's width from the sloping bricks.

My band hummed into action. I began by sweeping the detritus back toward the gap in the fence. Loose fronds rolled across the sand, followed by dancing twigs and stout branches. A cloud of dust rose from the movement, smoking around my scales as I slithered from one side of the mess to the other.

I paused once the debris had been piled near the edge of our clearing and let my band rest. The breeze continued, stirring the dust and shifting the jungle all around. The air echoed with the ring of metal, Tuhmaak busy at his own task. If I'd judged him right we'd be well armed soon, and I could begin posting guard rotations. I stared into the layered jungle, through vines that interlaced so many times they appeared like a solid wall around our clearing.

The damaged fence gave the truth away. Anywhere in that mask of growth, an enemy could be watching. Even as I thought it, the scales along my spine prickled. I felt the weight of unwanted attention, a creeping sensation at my flanks.

The outpost door banged open. The thud echoed out, reaching the jungle edge and stirring a rattle of activity. Tiny insects scuttled through the detritus littering the floor, and above that, something dark moved behind the leaves. I twisted, craning to see the movement I knew I hadn't imagined this time. A huge black thing traveling through the fronds, high up, level with our spying slits.

"Sookahr?" Lohmeer's rough voice vibrated its way across the yard. His heavy movements reached my belly scutes, telling me he crept in my direction.

I stared into the jungle, flicked my tongue, and held my breath. Something waited in the fronds, and it had been watching me.

Lohmeer joined me, sliding to a stop nearer than I would have liked and angling his head to follow my gaze. He said nothing, only waited in a lower replica of my pose. As if he had a clue what I was doing. His breath huffed in and out, the only sound now that the disturbance had passed and the jungle fallen silent again.

"Do you see anything?" I asked him.

"A lot of leaves," he said.

"There's something out there." Perhaps I shouldn't have confided in him, but in the shadow of those humongous trees, I'd never felt so alone. "I think it's watching us."

"What?" He dropped his nose and looked three times between me and the dark leaves before hissing, "What is it?"

"I'm not sure. But I think we should finish this and get back inside as quickly as possible."

I leaned into my band, felt the flare of the metal, and tried to focus on moving sticks, on interlacing twiggy supports for the flat, frond-laden branches—most of which had been broken and were too short or too weak to support even their own weight. Lohmeer attempted to help, but his clunky efforts worked more like a bulldozer than anything. In the end, we only managed to pile the detritus into a somewhat orderly heap along the perimeter.

It was enough for me.

"That's good," I said. "Let's get behind that door again."

He slithered for the pyramid's entrance, and I forced myself to hold back, to go last and to steal another covert examination of the foliage beyond our ragged repair job. It looked almost as bad as the gap had, but then, a perfect fence hadn't stopped whatever attacked the outpost. Mending it now was more about our feeling of security, of doing everything, the only thing, in our power to feel safe here.

I had no illusions about the low fence holding anything out. Not birds, for certain, and not the four-footed either. Something about that dark shape in the trees, the texture and the slow movement, had convinced me our spy was reptilian. Perhaps our treaty with the City of Tongues was so old that it had worn thin.

Nothing moved now. The insects had settled back to their business, and the wind contented itself with brushing softly at the dust in the yard. I followed Lohmeer, keeping one eye on the jungle. I watched for our watcher, but all that looked back at me now was darkness and vines.

Still, my heart raced. My band hummed softly, ready. I drew in a slow breath and didn't let it out until we'd both slithered inside and the heavy door thudded closed once more.

"What do you know about the four-legged?" I'd led Lohmeer back to the wagons, where Mehreet and Paalahv had already unloaded all of the sundries and half of our building materials. "Have any of you encountered one?"

Three long, triangular heads fixed on me. My constrictors stared as if I'd just asked them if they'd grown wings and flown.

"That's a no?" My tail twitched irritably. "Very well. I think we should finish here and then regroup to discuss—"

"Your weapons are ready." Tuhmaak's voice flowed down the hallway, reaching me seconds before his head popped out from the right-side bolt hole. "Two spears and six darts, and I only used one of your precious rods."

He slithered fully into the passage. I could see how much he'd hurried in the sagging of his body. His band had been forged with a narrow width, but was deep enough to contain his tools. Now its surface dulled. Tuhmaak's sides heaved and I could see the line of his spine every time he exhaled. His head, usually held in a way specifically to challenge me, drooped now, and there was a fatigue in his normally sharp eyes.

"You need to rest." I waited for the argument, but he only nodded. "And eat. Kwirk? Is there enough room in there for Tuhmaak to nap?"

My mouse popped out of the barracks. Dust coated his brown fur, making him look like a ghost. He blinked three times to dislodge it from his lashes, shook himself, and still had visible bits of fluff stuck in his whiskers.

"We've cleared a path through the mess and repaired one shelf, sir."

"Perfect. And well done." I turned back to Tuhmaak. "Well done both of you. Lohmeer and I can finish unloading. Mehreet and Paalahv can take the first watch."

"Yes, sir." The constrictors echoed one another, then slithered toward the forward bolt holes.

Tuhmaak leaned into the wall as they passed, most likely for support as much as getting out of their way. He needed rest, had worked himself too hard in his effort to show me what he could do. Stupid, perhaps, but exactly the sort of thing I would've done.

"Lohmeer, can you bring one of those grubs we added last-minute?"

When he ducked inside the stockroom, I turned back to the beetles. The single stag stood in his traces, clicked and stamped when I slithered nearer. The cart had indeed been emptied, and its draft animal would need tending. Though we'd brought a small amount of bark silage, the plan had been to stake the animals out, to let them graze the jungle's edge while we worked. I pictured the high-domed back gleaming beside the dark leaves, below a black shape that moved just out of sight.

"We're going to have to come up with a new plan for you guys." I tried clicking to him, but my tongue had not been designed for sharp sounds. "Perhaps we should have let Rapt take a cart back."

Lohmeer emerged from the storeroom. A wrinkled grub nearly as big as my head hovered beside him, and his fat band rumbled with the effort of teleporting it.

"Give it to Tuhmaak." I cringed inwardly, watching the meal float beside that splotchy body, imagining huge lumps in Lohmeer's already substantial girth.

"There are only three more in the box." Lohmeer sent the dried grub wafting in Tuhmaak's direction, keeping his eyes fixed on it and speaking with enough effort to make his words choppy. "There should have been eight."

"Three?" I flinched as Tuhmaak struck the grub. He latched onto it in mid-air and rolled around it only once before beginning to work his jaws. "Tohvaar must have grabbed a partial crate by mistake. Thank goodness there were extra."

Lohmeer nodded, but his head sagged toward the floor, nose down.

"I'm glad you thought to request more," I added. "Very sharp thinking."

I'm not sure why I felt the need to placate him, but when his head snapped up again, I felt satisfied. I didn't have to like my team, it turned out, but I definitely needed to keep them happy enough to work. Healthy enough to get the job done, and contented enough to follow my orders. Right now the most pressing of those was Tuhmaak, who looked about to pass out even with his meal lodged halfway down his throat.

"As soon as you're done, get some sleep. If you need to kick the rodents out, they can tend to the beetles while you rest. Lohmeer, help me with the rest of this."

We turned our attention to the bricks, to the remaining cart and its contents. The first shift had lain our sundries on the storeroom shelves and begun a tidy pile of brick inside the doorway to the left. Lohmeer and I finished that stack and built a twin on the other side. We placed the long metal rod in a pile to the side of the room, and stacked the small amount of lumber we'd need against the opposite wall.

Together we worked well and quickly, emptying the cart before the sunlight began to dim. The rodents scampered out of the barracks, and I set them to feeding our insects and unhitching them. I ordered the beasts stabled in the rear stockroom, and Lohmeer and I put our bands and minds together and tipped the smaller cart on its side to block the doorway and keep the beetles in.

They'd have to survive on silage for the night, and I assigned Tuhmaak's rodent to foraging fresh greens and wood for them in the morning. Once that was finished, we pushed the second cart across the passage as a rear defense, which drew a few questioning looks. I ignored these, and felt a great deal better for the wall at our back. My dream voice still insisted the enemy was behind me, and I had no plans to take chances here.

Not with the jungle outside. Not with my future on the line.

As the passage darkened, I relaxed for the first time since arriving. My muscles ached. My band barely responded when I prodded it with a thought. It hummed, but so low that only my scales could feel it. The night was coming on fast, and Mehreet and Paalahv would need to be relieved. Lohmeer had to be as tired as I, but at least for a few more hours, we'd have no rest coming.

I caught him tossing nervous glances into the storeroom, and had to fight to still my tail. He and I could take the next watch, could wait a little longer for our turn on the warm shelves. I sent Kwirk to gather the rodents for sleeping, and gave the fat constrictor the bad news.

"You and I will watch while the others sleep."

If I'd expected an argument, I'd picked the wrong serpent. Lohmeer only nodded, lowered his head submissively, and dragged his heavy body toward the front of the outpost and his next duty. Perhaps I should have woken Tuhmaak, let the constrictors all sleep while we ordinary snakes kept an eye on the jungle.

But Lohmeer made no complaint, and I couldn't shake the feeling that he deserved a little more work, a little more punishment for whatever crime my gut insisted he'd committed. Perhaps I deserved it too. As I slithered to my station, into the bolt-hole and up the corkscrew ramp, I couldn't shake that sensation. The idea that I was punishing us both.

That Lohmeer and I should suffer just a little more.

And when I emerged into the tower room, when the dark slit surrounded me, open to the jungle beyond, I felt certain that of the two of us, I would resent that punishment the most.

I found Tuhmaak's spear, neatly pointed and looking like deadly comfort. Three short darts lay beside it. The craftsmanship was excellent, as Laarahn had promised. Dark weapons on a dull floor. Black spikes like the deadfall twigs. Protection. Safety.

But as I gazed out at the layers of jungle beyond our tiny yard, safe was the last thing I felt.

DISBANDED

13

I woke suddenly, cold and aching. A chill breeze flirted with my scales, and my eyes registered only shades of darkness. The solitary warm spot against my side told me Kwirk had found me sleeping at my post. His whisper brushed against the side of my head.

"Sookahr?"

"Oh no." I jerked upwards, banging my head against the ceiling and sending a flash of stars through my head.

"It's okay," Kwirk squeaked. "No one else is awake."

"The jungle." I peered through the slit in the wall, pressed my face to the cold night and reached with my tongue.

Fronds rattled, but the breeze could explain that movement. The air tasted of crisp earth and dense growth. Nothing more. No warmth or musk or hint of mammal, bird, or insect. I saw only shades of darkness, and the only vibrations that reached me were the soft tread of my rodent's paws and, somewhere below, the deep rumble of someone snoring.

"How long did I sleep?" I cringed. The outpost hadn't fallen while I'd napped, but sleeping was not watching, and we'd needed to be alert. My lack of control had put everyone on my team in danger. "Is Lohmeer—"

"Also sleeping. I only woke moments ago, but everything seems quiet and secure."

"No." I hissed and thrashed my tail. "I could have killed us all on the first night."

"But you didn't." He walked the line of practicality, but it didn't ease the shame burning beneath my scales. "And now that the others have had enough rest, you need to sleep in earnest."

"No." I checked the jungle one last time, expecting to find a horde of four-legged rushing our walls. "I've had enough rest. Wake Lohmeer. Send him to bed. I'll meet you in the barracks."

I slithered down the ramp without waiting for his answer. The hallway lay as dark as the night outside, and I found my way to the barracks with my tongue. I needed heat, at least for long enough to warm away the chill that had made me sluggish. But I wouldn't sleep again tonight. At least, not until I'd gotten the day's labor sorted and begun.

The snoring, it turned out, came from Tuhmaak. I'd envisioned one of the larger serpents when I felt that rumble, but there was no mistaking the source when I entered the room. Two shelves had been reassembled, and Tuhmaak took the one farthest from the doorway. Both Mehreet and Paalahv coiled on the other, twined together tightly enough to make me suspect more than lack of space at work. Their curves folded around one another, and my tail tightened, prickled.

I slithered to Tuhmaak and nudged him with a thought only. My band hummed and the other snake shifted, hissed, and lifted his obnoxious head.

"It's nearly sun-up," I said. "I'm going to put the others on the guard towers so you can work on the spikes. They'll take the longest of our tasks, and most of the renovation requires them."

"Where?" He flicked his tongue and a tremble traveled from his head all the way to his tail tip. "Should I work in the yard?"

"I'll send the rats out with you."

If he wanted to argue, it didn't show again, nor could I blame him for hesitating to venture into the open yard. Not when all I could think about was a dark shape moving behind the leaves. The forging of my spikes, however, would require space we didn't have inside the outpost. I meant to keep Tuhmaak safe, but I meant to get our job done too.

"I'll need the rod out there," he said. "And the rodents, yes. And—"

"Mehreet and Paalahv in the towers, and myself and Kwirk helping you." I nodded and turned back toward the door. "I'll wake them; it's not quite light out if you need to use the closet or—"

"I only ate yesterday." Tuhmaak slithered toward the pile of sleeping rodents. "I'm fine, but *you* look like shit."

I spun around to glare at him, but he hadn't raised his head, and his expression held more concern than confrontation. Perhaps Kwirk was right and I should rest, but I couldn't see time for it in my current plan for the day. "I'm tired, but I can go a little bit longer before a nap."

We woke the rest of our team, and the two constrictors stretched their big jaws, unwound their bodies, and obediently reported to the watch rooms. The rodents shook themselves, groomed their fluffed fur with their paws and then, at my direction, skittered over to the storeroom to eat before getting started.

Tuhmaak and I went to work moving the rod. Our bands chiming together, we selected two long metal staves and began the weighty job of maneuvering them to the front door. Kwirk stayed with the rodents, so I had to set my rod down to open our fortress to the coming day. The air still bit at my scales, but the sky had begun to lighten around its edges. The jungle scents thickened as the first rays of sun hit the farthest corners of the foliage, and a glow spawned around the tips of the high trees.

We carried our rod into the sunlight, and I let Tuhmaak decide where to lay them before setting mine down beside his. I waited, too, for him to reenter the pyramid before following, and I watched the jungle, certain it watched me back. When we returned to the storeroom, the rodents had all gathered around the shelves. They'd huddled together, and their round eyes had gone dim. They all looked to Kwirk, who held his whiskers in both paws and shuffled his feet.

"What's wrong?" I knew a frustrated Kwirk when I saw one. His tail drooped, and his ears made flat disks against his skull. "What's happening?"

"I'll take another out." Tuhmaak lifted a rod, forcing me to duck to one side as it passed.

When he'd headed out the door with his cargo, I turned back to Kwirk. "Well?"

The rats curled their tails around their bodies. Tuhmaak's mouse glanced to the door behind me, as if his master were still lurking there.

"What's going on?" I hissed and buzzed my tail. Kwirk ignored it, but the others flinched. "Kwirk?"

"The food supply is compromised," he finally spat. "All our grain is wet, starting to mold."

"How?" I leaned my head forward, raised and looked over their little bodies at the sacks they'd pulled from the shelves. "All of them?"

"Yes." Kwirk's voice had taken on a low monotone. His ears stuck to his head as if glued flat. "We've nothing to eat, and..."

"What? What else is wrong?"

"Your supplies are low as well. The sacks marked 'beetle' are full of bark mulch."

"What about the mulch bags?" I grasped at a thin straw. Maybe the sacks had been switched. Maybe our food and the draft animals' had been mismarked.

"Also mulch," Kwirk said. He turned glassy eyes toward me, as if I would have a magical solution to us all going hungry out here. "You have only three dried grubs in a crate."

"The extra Lohmeer ordered."

"Yes."

That meant three of us could eat. Tuhmaak already had, which left the three constrictors and myself. Of that group, I had the least to offer physically. Who went hungry was easy to answer: me. The rodents were a much larger issue. Their bodies required sustenance daily, burned their fuel much faster than ours. They couldn't wait a week or more to eat. Most likely, they couldn't wait a day.

"We'll need to forage," I said. "Do you think you'll be able to eat any of the local plants?"

They huddled again, whispering while I poked my nose through the rest of our sundries. All draft food and nothing usable for my team. How had it happened? I'd seen Tohvaar's mouse fill the order. Laarahn had checked off each item from his list, and he and Lohmeer had packed the carts.

Lohmeer.

Suppressing a shudder, I calculated the possibility that the dopey constrictor had sabotaged us. Was it possible? It could just as easily have been an error on the shelves—a mislabeled box or a load that was packed incorrectly. There were too many variables, and I'd been completely out of the packing process. I couldn't say for sure, nor could I summon my initial dislike of Lohmeer now, in the face of what might be a critical failure.

Something had changed along the way. I couldn't imagine the huge constrictor doing anything intentionally to harm us. Inadvertently, like a sloppy mistake or possibly a greedy, late-night gobble, I could still believe. I needed to talk to him, but I needed to calm the rodents, and find a way to feed them first.

"What do you think? There has to be something out there. Seeds, fruit?"

"Dawl thinks he might know something." Kwirk pointed to the smaller of our two rats. "His grandfather worked near the jungle."

"Good." I felt a little flaring of hope, but Kwirk's posture remained deflated. "What? What is it now?"

"He's not... That is, none of us are very keen on going out there alone."

"No. Of course not. I'll accompany Dawl. The rest of you will need to help Tuhmaak. If he doesn't get those spikes made, we can't begin our work at all. And if Dawl and I don't find anything you can eat... I hate to even think it, but that might be the end of our efforts. At the very least, we'd have to send you rodents back with a cart."

I didn't know if they could make it that long without eating. It seemed like such a short time to go without food, but then, my body didn't have the rodent's magic. I couldn't create my own heat, and I had no idea how much that power cost them in longevity. Either way, my project depended on finding them food, and I didn't intend to fail at that.

"Come, Dawl."

I shifted toward the exit, could feel the vibration of Tuhmaak's return already down the long hallway. If we had to venture into the jungle, so be it. While I was there, perhaps, I could find something edible for myself as well. I caught Kwirk's eye as I left the room, caught a full dose of concern on his face now. I hadn't eaten before leaving, and I had no intentions of taking one of the remaining grubs in our store. I hadn't slept more than a few moments in the watch room, and it didn't look like I'd be resting anytime soon.

"We won't be long," I threw back at my loyal attendant, half to soothe his worry and half for my own mind. "Everything will be fine."

The rat, Dawl, followed me, hanging a few steps behind my tail. A peek into the barracks confirmed that Lohmeer had found a shelf to warm and rest upon. We passed Tuhmaak on the way out, and when he questioned me with a look, I only lifted my head higher.

"I'm taking Dawl into the jungle," I said. "You'll have my Kwirk and the others to get the spikes done. As soon as they're finished, you can rest again."

If he had anything to say, I didn't hesitate long enough to give him the opportunity. My body ached. My bones still carried the chill of a night in the watch room. If I let myself think about it, my belly felt hollow and out of sorts. But none of these discomforts meant a thing in the face of our current task. The rodents needed to eat, and for that to happen, I had to enter the jungle.

Just the thought of it set a shiver against my scales, a cool creeping that I prayed was only my fears at work. Let there be nothing in those fronds to challenge us. Let there be warmth there, enough to keep me moving, to keep me going until the task was finished. Until we were saved.

Because salvation was what I really sought now. The outpost had offered us only one disaster after another, and I felt its walls pressing in on me, resisting. I felt failure looming. The dark jungle lay ahead of me, yes, but as I slithered from the pyramid, I heard my dream insisting yet again that the enemy, the real danger, was at my back.

"There's good fruit up there." Dawl lifted his pointy nose and gazed up the broad tree trunk. "The yellow cluster."

I peered through the fronds and curled closer to the trunk, brushing against the rat's tail and trying to make out what it was he meant by "yellow".

We'd only gone a few of my lengths into the jungle, and I could still hear the ring of metal as Tuhmaak worked. I doubted Dawl would embrace the idea of straying much deeper than that. Not any more than I would. So we circled our pyramid, just inside the foliage, and now it seemed he'd found something edible.

Except I couldn't make it out.

"Darker or lighter than the leaves?"

"Much lighter." The round globes.

That I understood. I peered through the fronds, looking for a shift in texture. Grainy bark covered the trunk, which grew on fat folds near the base and shifted to a smooth and slender profile overhead. Vines wrapped this, and the reaching branches drooped under the weight of their glossy fronds. As I followed the trunk up, my eyes picked out the shapes Dawl had settled on—a group of four round balls each the size of the rat's paws.

"I think I can pry them loose." I focused, and my band zinged. "Step back in case they—"

A crack echoed overhead, followed by a crashing of fronds. Dawl leapt backwards just in time as the three fruits I wasn't mentally gripping fell to the jungle floor. The last I wafted down gently and set beside the others, two of which had cracked open to reveal a soft pulpiness inside.

"We can eat these," he said. His nose twitched and I noticed he held his whiskers tight to the sides of his head. His paws rubbed beneath his chin, and he bent forward and began fashioning a bundle with the fruit inside and a haphazard weaving of fronds around them.

"Good. Maybe there are more." I slithered to the next trunk and craned my neck back. The bark was crisscrossed with vines that bore tiny, pale flowers. Despite looking like the same tree, the fronds had more lobes and no round fruit clung to the trunk. Still, I believed our luck had turned. If one tree held edible fruit, more would as well. I only had to find them, and the most pressing of my problems would be handled.

I tried a third, looking for the telltale bark and scanning up and up until I landed on the undeniable pattern of black scales. Something dark as pitch moved over our heads.

"Dawl!" I threw a coil toward the rat, shielding him. "Hold still."

My eyes remained on the strip of glossy black, but my mind scrambled to identify the owner of those scales. The most primitive of the four-legged still ate rodents, and even the rare non-Burrow-dwelling serpent might consider my furry friend to be too hearty a meal to resist. I tasted the air, hissed, and heard a deeper echo from directly behind me.

Snake.

I lifted my body high into the air, spinning around and leaning clumsily to one side as I tried to simultaneously posture and protect my companion. Rocking back upright, I fixed my focus on the slender neck and disc-shaped head currently descending from the fronds above.

Viper.

I tensed from nose to tail tip, curving into an ess that would prove the end of me if I was forced to use it. My jaws were no match for a viper's keeled scales, and my teeth had nothing to deliver except for a barely painful pricking. The viper's attention fixed on me. His black tongue stretched out and fluttered. Slit eyes regarded me. I thought I saw a flash of insanity behind them. An unpredictable light.

"What have we here?" He hissed and lowered his head until I could almost look him dead in those eyes.

Another loop of his narrow body dropped down from the canopy, and I tried to judge his length from just those two glimpses. His body was skinny. I could see bones, the ridge of spine where fat and muscle should have masked it. A hungry viper, and one not prejudiced against eating either Dawl or myself.

I shifted slowly, angling to put myself between the stranger and my rat. The viper turned with me.

"Take the fruit back to the outpost, Dawl." I waved my body back and forth, forcing the stranger's eyes to follow me. When the rat grabbed his bundle and ran, I dodged, placing myself between him and danger.

The viper's mouth yawned, exposing a pair of fangs the width of my tail.

"We don't want any trouble," I said.

"You'll still get it." His voice stretched out, as if he spoke through a haze spawning either from his own thoughts or the venom coursing through his body. "We didn't want any either. We didn't want to die."

"I'm on official business for Serpentia." I eased my coils tighter. "This outpost—"

"Our outpost," he hissed. "Our job. And all of us gone."

His words, at last, registered over the racing of my heart. "Wait. Your outpost? You're from the Burrow?"

"Guards," he hissed. "Doing our duty in this wretched wilderness. Serving and protecting until..."

He wavered, head dancing back and forth. This time, I felt less threatened. Not enough to relax my posture, but enough to consider I might not already be dead. "You were stationed here with the others. What happened?"

"*They* happened." His head danced, back and forth, up and down. The U-shaped coil swung back and forth. "They killed the rest of us. Killed them all and took everything we had."

"You got away." I meant no accusation there, only a prayer of hope that perhaps this enemy was in fact survivable. "Who attacked you?"

"I... I ran away." The viper froze, stilled as if he'd never moved, as if he

109

were in fact a vine dangling from the canopy. "Not. Not without damage."

A fluttering of fronds prepared me for his next move. I spun, stupidly, away from the viper's head. Behind me, his long tail dangled, all shredded scales and swollen, purpling flesh. Something had torn into him, and infection raged in the wounds.

"By the Sage." I reeled from the stench, but that motion brought me nearer to the viper's head. "You. You need help. We can. We might. If you'll come inside with us, perhaps."

"Inside?" His hiss turned into a laugh, and then a dry, hacking cough.

The echo of it shook the fronds, but I heard another sound behind it—brush rustling, the scrape of scales as my team responded to whatever Dawl had told them.

"Yes," I tried. "We might be able to tend those wounds. We have carts. Someone could take you back to—"

"No!" The spiky head twisted from side to side. "I'll never place scales in the Burrow again, friend, and neither should you. The enemy is already inside your walls."

"Inside?" My throat tightened. I heard the dream again.

The danger is behind you.

The rustling became a crashing now. My constrictors hurrying to my aid, but it was the viper who had the answers I wanted. And he already retreated, pulling himself up and back into the cover of the fronds.

"Wait!" I shouted after him. "Please. What's your name? We can help—"

"You can call me Ghost." His voice drifted down even as his body vanished, taking the scent of his impending death with it. He faded, as if he'd never existed, but his last words landed like a venomous strike. "And no one can help us now."

14

"The guards were killed." I coiled inside the outpost yard, close to the door and with my entire team around me. "All but that one, and I doubt he's long for this world. The infection..."

I couldn't describe the smell, nor could I get it out of my nostrils.

"But who killed them?" Tuhmaak coiled beside his mouse, upright and indignant again. "And what's to stop them from doing the same thing to us?"

They looked at me. All of them. Four serpents, the rats, and mice. Even Kwirk stared, waiting for my answer. What would we do? The sane part of my brain suggested we leave, slither back to the Burrow and abandon the outpost and our project. The insane part, the part that believed in anonymous echoes and the voices of my dreams, surged right over the top of my sensible reason.

"We'll send Tuhmaak back, as soon as he's finished the spikes." I shifted all my attention to the other snake, not ready to face the constrictors' reactions to my leaving them here in danger. "How much longer do you need?"

"I can finish tonight," he said. "With the rats' help and no interruptions."

"Good. Dawl's fruit will last them for today, and I'm confident we can find more now that I know what to look for." I turned to Lohmeer. "You three can make sure it goes smoothly for him. Whatever he needs done. Then we can work on the build while he goes for help."

"Yes, sir." Lohmeer lowered politely, obediently. "We'll make sure he has what he needs."

If the other constrictors shared his enthusiasm, they didn't show it. Both maintained a traveling height, and their arrow heads turned to face one another. It was Tuhmaak, however, who asked the question I'd expected all along.

"And what will *you* be doing?"

"Kwirk and I will man the watchtowers," I answered, ignoring the worried look from my mouse, the way his paws fretted with the hem of his vest. "Until we see you off. Then I'll be working with the others on the build."

"And not sleeping." Kwirk muttered it. I couldn't be sure if anyone else had heard him or not.

No one commented further, and I didn't give them the chance to think of any more complaints. I scanned the desert one last time and then spun toward the door, trusting that Kwirk followed, that he'd obey my orders even if the rest of the team, if the rest of the world, revolted against me.

I left the door open. The constrictors would close it once they'd brought all the tools they needed out to the yard. Tuhmaak could give them orders for awhile, and I would drag my sorry scales back up to the slit to watch. This time, without sleeping. I doubted I *could* fall asleep now, with my nerves zinging as deeply as my band, my nostrils full of the viper's sickness, and my head full of his story.

Something had killed two sets of guards—viper guards, that had far more in the way of defense than we did. Even with our new weapons. I should have asked more questions of Ghost, should have tried harder to get him to come in for aid.

The enemy is inside the walls.

Who could sleep with that echoing in their thoughts? I wouldn't rest now, or even after my shift ended. Not when the jungle outside had grown less terrifying that the tunnel at my back.

We reached the bolt-hole rooms, Kwirk and I, and paused in the wide hallway to regard one another. His whiskers had gone tight. Ears drooping, his fuzzy paws worked together, and his eyes...

"You need to eat." I stared into those black orbs and found shards where there should be only soft reflections. "There should be enough fruit."

"I did eat," he said. "Mushy, sweet stuff, but filling enough."

"Oh." I peered closer, trying to see the gentle soul inside the dilated pupils. Perhaps it was only me on edge, only my fears reflecting back from Kwirk's fearful gaze. "That's good."

"And you will be sleeping when?" His tail jerked around and curled between his feet. "And eating what?"

"I'll be fine." The familiar chastising soothed me. This was the game we played, my mouse looking out for my welfare. "It's my project. My name on the line and my stupid ambition that got them into this mess."

"And your stubbornness that's keeping them here."

I nodded, relaxed, and let him win this one. "That too."

"It will all work out, Sookahr." Kwirk reached with one paw, as if he meant to pat me on the side. He froze halfway through the gesture, letting his arm hover there, outstretched but not moving any closer. "You're going to be fine."

"We all are," I said. "We have to be."

"Shall I take this side?" He swung his paw around and pointed at the left-hand ramp. "Watch the jungle and wait for your next orders?"

"Yes. Please, Kwirk."

I waited until he'd climbed his ramp and vanished into the watch room. Then I slithered into the opposite room, made my ascent, and stretched my body out around the perimeter beneath the slit. The spear and bolts still lay in a tidy line against the wall. The sun glared down on the yard now, warming even my sheltered scales. The jungle brightened, shifted in a soft breeze and rustled softly.

Somewhere out there, Ghost still watched us. I had no doubt about that now, but it also lent me no terror. The dark thing in the branches might be wounded, dangerous, but it was ours. I feared what was out there a lot less than my own imaginings of what might be in here. Of who I should be afraid of to begin with.

And as I watched, I understood Ghost's decision. He might have fled, but in his way, the wounded viper still guarded this outpost. He still did his duty, and I believed he would continue at his post, steadfast until the fevers finally took him.

So while I stared out at the fronds, hoping to catch a peek of black scales behind the leaves, my thoughts worked, furious and frantic, to unravel the puzzle. The broken fence, the trashed barracks, and a door that should have been shut tight. It was possible Ghost had destroyed the fence while fleeing, but the trail of debris led inward, from the jungle to our door.

Was it also possible that someone opened that willingly? That the danger outside was invited in? If so, I felt we had less to worry about. Despite my initial concern about Lohmeer, I'd found him ready to obey my orders to a point that rivaled Kwirk. Tuhmaak had an attitude, definitely resented my authority, but I could no more picture him turning on us than I could imagine sprouting wings.

The team was frightened, possibly frustrated, but there was no serpent among us that I didn't trust, at least to be sane and safe. There was none

I would believe capable of treason. With that thought foremost in my mind, I let the kinks in my muscles unravel. And though I'd no intention of sleeping anytime soon, I let a fog settle over me. I watched, certainly. I heard the sounds of the others working, and I smelled the metal and the earth.

But I also let my body rest, my mind numb, and a stupor that was not quite sleep wash over my scales, soothing, relaxing. Promising I had nothing at all to worry about.

When Kwirk roused me, the sky was still light. I heard his steps ascending and lifted my body well before his brown head poked into view.

"I believe they may have finished," he squeaked. "Tuhmaak has gone to the shelf to rest and the yard is... Well, you can see it from my side."

I followed him down the ramp and back up the other side. Despite the warmth of the day, my body was sluggish, fatigue counteracting the balm of the sun. The watch room where Kwirk had been posted smelled of rodent and dust. He moved directly to the front-facing wall and peered out, tail curling behind him like a miniature snake.

"Are they still out there?" I slithered to join him slowly and with tiny pains crimping at each curve of my body. "They're done much sooner than I'd expected."

"Look." Kwirk's ears lifted, round and fully upright for the first time since we'd arrived here. He waved a paw for me, and I tried to follow it with my eyes.

Below us, the yard had grown prickles. My spikes stood now, stabbed into the sandy earth for safe-keeping perhaps, or possibly as a joke. Either way that black stipple chilled me. I saw the needles of the dead fall, and I heard my friend calling to me in warning.

Behind you.

All of it, the beetle yard, the dream of Viir, and the spikes below us blended into an eerie tableau. It was as if those black branches had snared me, and now I was helpless to escape their influence.

"They're ready for you now," Kwirk said. "For your poky pyramid."

"I thought you hated my design." I stared at the rod sticking out of the ground. Tuhmaak had chiseled down one end of each into a deadly-fine point.

"I do," Kwirk answered, "but the sooner you're done with it, the sooner we can head for home."

"Well." I scanned the yard, but aside from my spikes, the open ground was empty. "At least we can agree on that much."

With a final glance at the foliage, and a disappointed heart when I found no sign of Ghost, I turned back to the ramp. Kwirk wanted to run as much as the rest of them. It should have been enough to shake me back to reason. What if I was wrong about Ghost? What if he'd gone mad, killed the others, and then slunk off into the trees?

I shivered and considered revising my plan, giving up and turning our tails straight for home. The rough grit of the bolt-hole floor scratched at my belly. I coiled inside the room, waiting for Kwirk to descend so I could tell him I'd gotten it all wrong. So I could give in and abandon my outpost redesign, my Circlet convention, and my future. So I could go back to a room full of better architects and accept my fate.

"He is not." Lohmeer's voice rumbled from the hallway outside. He'd growled the statement, and dust rained from the bricks over my head. "He knows what he's doing."

"Getting us all killed?" It was not Tuhmaak who spoke with him, but Paalahv, and right after her, Mehreet.

"We should leave, and you know it."

"Sookahr will keep us safe," Lohmeer insisted. "He'll get us home. I know he will."

"He's sacrificing us for his own designs," Mehreet argued. "He's an ordinary snake. What do they care about us?"

"When we were coming here, he did. When we were exhausted, he went against that other one and let us rest."

"And now you're his disciple," Paalahv hissed. "Your hero, Sookahr. But his ego and our combined wits are not going to keep us alive against something that killed at least four vipers."

I tucked closer to the wall as they passed. My facial scales burned with embarrassment, and I had to pin my tail beneath another coil to avoid buzzing. Lohmeer defended me, for no good reason aside from allowing him the appropriate amount of naps. The amount that Laarahn had ordered to begin with. I recalled my initial reactions to the constrictor and my flush heated further. Shame shivered through my long body.

Also, I was definitely going to get them killed at this rate. My ego, Paalahv had said, and she'd been right on the mark. It was time to revise my thinking, and yet, I wasn't quite ready to abandon my outpost. Tuhmaak's spikes were done. I could send him back for help, send him to safety, and pray we survived the four days it took him to return with reinforcements. Or I could send them all. A four-day delay might destroy my chances of finishing in time, but it was still a chance. If I remained here and kept working alone, I might still be able to finish on time.

"Sookahr?" Kwirk stood on the bottom of the corkscrew ramp.

"Just a moment, Kwirk." I waited for the constrictors to work their

115

way further down the hall. The outer door opened and shut again, and I counted breaths until Tuhmaak passed us. Once his mouse had skittered by, I moved, slithering in behind them and following to the barracks where the constrictors had settled in on their shelves again.

"A minute, before you sleep please." I spoke, and Tuhmaak spun to face me. The others lifted their slow heads and regarded me with expressions I could fully read now. "Is your work done, Tuhmaak?"

"Yes. Everything I can do with the rod we had."

"Good." I lifted my head a touch, slowly, and not enough to inspire a response. "The four of you sleep now. When you're rested, you'll take the remaining rodents and the larger cart and return to the Burrow. Use the same schedule on the return, and take what you can to feed the rats along the way."

"What?" Tuhmaak lowered his head and flicked his tongue in my face.

I ignored it. "Get to Laarahn as soon as you're back. Make sure he knows what happened here. Then the constrictors can reload the cart with food and return as soon as possible. Four days on the outside, if you move fast."

I finished, pulling my coils around myself and my tongue in tight between my lips.

"You're staying behind?" Tuhmaak asked. "Alone?"

"I'll have Kwirk with me."

"And me." Lohmeer's heavy body flopped off the shelf, shaking the floor enough to rain more dust down on the group. "I'm not leaving."

"It might not be safe here," I argued, despite the rush of relief at his offer. "I can't guarantee that."

"We'll get more done if I stay." Lohmeer pushed his way forward, forcing Tuhmaak to scoot toward the rodent nest. "And they'll move faster."

"Lohmeer." I swallowed nothing and flicked my tongue softly. "You don't have to stay. I can get some of the prep work going, and maybe it will be enough to finish on time."

"I'm not going," he said.

"Then you two can watch while we sleep," Tuhmaak said. He didn't raise himself, but his tone of voice was challenge enough. "The sooner we get going, the sooner we can send food and reinforcements."

"Eat before you leave," I said. If I had another stint in the watchtower to look forward to, I definitely didn't have the strength to argue with him here. "You'll need the food for the exertion."

"Fine," the other snake answered for them all, took the reins and the lead easily, at least for that part of our team.

I had a feeling Lohmeer was all mine. He was the only one of us down a rodent, however, and I felt a sudden urge to care for him. He'd volunteered to stay behind, and we'd need all the paws we could.

"Pick one of the rats to leave behind as well. Lohmeer will need paws if he's staying to work."

I could see Paalahv wanted to argue, but she said nothing to my face. Even so, I was betting it would be Mehreet's rodent who remained behind. Leaving them to decide it, I retreated from the barracks. The beetles would need to be fed before leaving as well, but I trusted Tuhmaak to think of that, and I left the responsibility for their care to him. Then I retraced my path back to the watch room, parting ways with Kwirk in the hallway and noting, once again, the sharpness behind his eyes.

The fruit might sustain him, but it was clearly not enough to replace the burrow-made grain. We'd have to forage farther afield. I set my mind to that, to a plan to feed my mouse, to keep us going for the next few days. Just enough to keep the project alive. Lohmeer and I could begin the build much more effectively than I could alone. His volunteering might have saved my remodel. Might just have saved me.

As I gazed out at the jungle, watching the sun sink behind the fronds, sink and cast the world into shadows, I hoped only that I could return the favor. If Ghost was out there watching us, I hoped he still lived. And I hoped most of all that I could save them—Lohmeer, Kwirk, even Ghost. I watched the dark stripes stretching over the yard, the lengthening of my spikes as their shadows grew, and I prayed. To the Sage, and the echo, and my dreams as well.

Let me keep them all alive. Let me keep them, just for a few days, safe and breathing.

A breeze lifted the fronds outside, dancing across my scales in an invisible caress. Cold, aching, and tired. I leaned my chin against the slit in the wall and listened for an answer, for a hope, for anything at all to cling to.

DISBANDED

15

"They've all gone." Lohmeer's head popped into the watch room long before the sun had re-emerged. "They took one cart and left."

"Good." I lifted my nose from the break in the wall and turned to face him. "You could still catch up. I wouldn't hold it against you."

"I would," he said. "This way we'll have half the work done by the time they get back."

I sucked in a breath, tasting the night and the bricks and my own stupidity. "First thing we need to do is gather more food for the rodents. They won't do us any good if we can't keep them moving."

"Speaking of that." Lohmeer pressed further into the room, spilling from the ramp hatch and easily taking up over half the space left. The walls seemed to move in around me, and the constrictor just kept coming.

"What's wrong?" I eased toward the far corner, coiling over myself in an effort to clear more floor space. To not touch him.

"You look half dead already. And I don't think you've slept at all."

"I'm fine." I tried to shrug, began a ripple from my neck down, but the room around me started to spin. Lohmeer became a splotchy blur. Constrictor everywhere. I stopped mid-gesture, and bit down on my tongue. "Maybe a little nap on the hot spot wouldn't be a bad idea."

"As long as you need," he said. "I'll watch here, and the rat has gone up with your mouse already."

I slithered toward the opening his tail had just barely cleared. "But you have to wake me when the sun's up. We have too much to do."

"And we need to do it right the first time."

"What's that supposed to mean?" I didn't even have the energy for an indignant tone, just a flat question I already knew the answer to.

"It means you should rest, and I'll take the rodents out to find food."

"*Then* wake me up."

"Deal."

I eased down the ramp, feeling the weight of my flesh hanging from my bones. The lower room had less breeze, and clung to a whisper of heat that the night air had sucked from the watch room. It was that warmth alone that gave me the strength to drag myself down the hallway and into the barracks. No sounds filtered this far into the outpost, and no bodies lay on the hot shelves. The rodents and Lohmeer had the towers, and despite my determination, there was nothing for me to do now except sleep.

It didn't take long. The nearest shelf was also the lowest, and no sooner than I'd pulled my body onto it that the rush of hot water through the walls enveloped me, turning my body liquid and unresponsive. My vision fogged, I drifted, and despite my hopes otherwise, failed to dream at all.

When I awoke, my body felt like my own again. The heat filled me and I lingered, reveling in it, as if I were back in my den getting ready for school. I even heard Kwirk's voice muttering, soft squeaks that I couldn't make out over the rushing inside the wall.

Lifting my head, I scanned for my mouse. The other shelves were empty, and the light in the room suggested Lohmeer had let me slumber long past dawn. I stretched my jaws, swiveled, and found Kwirk hunched in the center of the rodent nest. His paws worked at his whiskers and his nose dipped forward, low and tight to his body. His voice came in a sing-song muttering, as if he sang or chanted under his breath.

"Good morning," I said.

He jerked, snapping his nose up and dropping both paws to his sides.

"I think that constrictor let me oversleep. The day is wasting out there."

"What?" Kwirk turned to face me, and the bounced light reflected off his eyes. Knife-sharp reflections in hard black marbles.

"They were supposed to find food. When was the last time you ate?"

"Fruit," he said. "I ate the fruit last night."

"Well, let's see if they have anything else today. Come on." I slid from the shelf, gliding easily now, as if my body were brand new.

I left the room, assuming he would follow, and slithered for the front door. If Lohmeer was out foraging with the rat, that left the watch rooms empty. I listened at the door before opening it, fluttered my tongue, and then leaned into my band and felt the additional heat flaring.

How long had it been since my skymetal had responded so willingly? Perhaps I *had* driven myself too far, gone too long without resting. The door flew wide at my slightest touch, and a wash of golden light spilled into the outpost.

"Ready, Kwirk?" I turned my head, as much to give my eyes time to adjust as to check on my mouse. When I looked, however, Kwirk was not at my tail. "Kwirk?"

The hallway behind me echoed my voice. Dust sparkled in the sunlight. As I watched it descend, Kwirk poked his head out of the barracks door, far back in the dimmer section where the light barely reached.

"Are you okay?" I curled around and began slithering in his direction.

"Fine." He snapped the word, flipping his long tail out and back and then trotting toward me.

I waited, praying that the team outside had found some grain, something with enough substance to return Kwirk to an ordinary level of crankiness. If Viir could see him now, I thought, he'd never complain about my attendant again. As soon as he'd reached my tail, I turned back and, tongue fluttering, slid easily into the yard.

The long spikes made a metallic forest to my left. The repaired fence curved away to the right. Lohmeer and his rodent had left tracks leading out from the door, and it looked like they'd taken my orders to heart; they'd gone straight out into the jungle. I'd planned to begin removing bricks from the pyramid's apex today, installing the spikes from the top down, but Kwirk's mood thrust feeding him to the top of my priorities.

I headed for the fronds and called for him to follow where ordinarily I would have assumed his presence at my side. "This way, Kwirk. There has to be something out—"

The brush directly ahead rattled. Fronds parted and vines thrashed. I pulled back, lifted into strike pose, and leaned on my band enough to activate it, to be ready for anything.

Lohmeer burst from the jungle. He trailed vines from his body on both sides, and traveled with his head higher than I usually saw it. The big rat who belonged to Mehreet stumbled along at his tail, arms full of a frond-wrapped bundle that would have eased my mind considerably more if the two of them hadn't looked terrified. I fluttered my tongue and tasted fear on the air.

"What is it?" I rushed forward, but Lohmeer shook his big head.

"Inside!"

He barreled onward and I flipped myself around and followed near his side, searching for Kwirk as I went and finding the mouse just outside the doors. Lohmeer dove through the opening, followed by the rat, and Kwirk only stared outward, as if the jungle held him, transfixed.

"Go, Kwirk. Get in, now!" I waited, but threw a coil wide and used it to herd him into the outpost. When he'd finally jerked away from the view and scampered inside, I followed, grasping the door as I passed it and pulling it closed just as I snapped my tail out of the way. The panel thumped into place. Dust rained in the hallway.

Lohmeer panted against the wall. His fat tail buzzed.

"What happened?" I turned to him. "What was that about?"

"We heard something," he said. "Something moving in the jungle."

"Ghost?"

"On the ground. More than one." He lowered his head, but fixed his nose on the door. "Can we bar that?"

"Absolutely." I reached for the heavy bar and lifted it with my band's assistance. The metal warmed, and the wooden rail settled into its cups across the door. "No one's coming in here."

Except we needed to be out there, in the yard, working.

"Good." Lohmeer huffed and his body expanded. In the center of his length, the scales stretched apart in a lumpy knot, as if he'd just eaten. I'd ordered the others to finish off the grubs, but if he'd sniped one of them, I'd deal with him later. I had bigger things to worry about at the moment.

"What food did you find?"

"More fruit." Lohmeer flicked his tail, and the rat deposited his bundle on the floor and began unrolling it. "And a few flowers that Peet thinks are edible."

"Make sure they eat them, then." I flashed a peek at Kwirk, whose front teeth were showing. His ears flattened to the sides and he stared at his paws, didn't look up to meet my gaze. "You and I should go over the plans for the day, maybe in a watch room so we can—"

"See what comes out of the jungle?" He tilted his head to one side and sucked in his tongue.

"Yeah. Kwirk, take the food and Peet up to the right, and Lohmeer and I will take the left.

I waited, listened for the "yes, sir" that had to be coming. Peet rolled his bounty back into the leaves, and I tried to get a look at his eyes. If there was something in the fruit, we might be better off tossing it out. But starving the rodents wasn't the answer either, and a little belligerence was a small price to pay for Kwirk's health and well-being. I decided to endure his behavior and watch him carefully.

When the rodents had scampered into their bolt-hole, I broached the subject with Lohmeer. "Have you noticed anything weird about Peet?"

"He's hungry." The big constrictor shrugged his forward third and lowered his head guiltily. The lump in his middle, he tried to push behind a fatter coil. "Just a little cranky."

"Good. You don't think the fruit is toxic?"

His head jerked up and his tongue slid out, stretching as if to taste any poison lingering in the air. "Could it be?"

"I think we should keep an eye on them going forward," I said. "But first we need to sort out what you heard and whether or not we're going to get any work done today."

I hated saying it aloud. Everything depended on getting something done. I'd come all this way to do it, and now, the waiting around and wasting time was eating at my nerves. How could I report to the Circlet with a proven design if I couldn't even get the thing built?

Lohmeer waited for me, and I led the way into the other bolt-hole. We both pressed our noses to the slit in the wall, and we both let our tongues gather what information they could. Outside, the fronds seemed still as one of Viir's tapestries. The wind had died and the sun blossomed, turning the world bright and making all the textures into a pattern of contrast and shade.

I tried to hear what they had heard, but only quiet answered. Only leaves and dirt and hot sun flirted with my tongue. If it were just me, I would dare the yard. If it were only my neck I risked, I would begin building immediately, as fast as I could manage. But then, what would I manage on my own?

I looked at Lohmeer, at glossy scales that had stopped huffing, but still heaved more than would indicate relaxed breathing. He was scared. Peet and Kwirk might be compromised. It made way too much sense to wait, to let the day stretch while my chances at success burned away like the morning mist.

"Let's give it a little while," I said. "Just to let the rodents eat. We'll see if anything else happens."

Lohmeer nodded, but his attention didn't shift from his vigil, from the wall of jungle out there.

"I'll go get the design." I sighed. We might not be leaving the outpost anytime soon, but we could still get something accomplished. If Lohmeer and I could develop a plan of attack, we'd move faster once we did begin. If we began. If all the world hadn't conspired together to stop me.

The day passed without another sound from the jungle. I sent Lohmeer to nap before dusk so that he could take the first nighttime watch. While he slept, I reviewed our plan for the morning. Kwirk and I would begin the initial removal of bricks, and Lohmeer and his borrowed rat could patrol the yard's edge and listen. Then, when it was time to install our first spikes, we could switch duties.

It would work, so long as no more trouble found us. So long as the noises in the fronds were only Ghost watching. Wind and worry, and nothing more.

So far, we'd solved each disaster as it occurred. The rodents could find food now, and though my belly was empty, the others had all fed. I could survive, certainly, long enough to return to the Burrow. Word of our troubles already slithered its way toward Laarahn. Relief would be sent. The project could go forward and, I hoped, a new group of guards could stand at our watch room posts while *we* worked.

With those thoughts foremost in my mind, I watched the darkness come.

Shadows elongated the individual leaves, made serpent-kin of the vines and turned the smooth yard into a dance of flat, black snakes. The breeze swelled, stirring the images and drawing a background symphony of rustling foliage and creaking trunks. It carried less chill than the night before, and still I shivered at its touch. What had Lohmeer heard out there? Were we not alone here, on the edge of our dominion?

"Ghost?" At first I whispered it.

The fronds crinkled, in a motion that could easily have been blamed on the wind, yet I retained a certainty that the former guard still watched us, still waited just outside my vision.

"Are you still out there?"

The response came slowly, beginning as a hiss barely distinguishable from the moving foliage. It grew until I could make out the words, faint and lacking in any semblance of vitality.

"What's left of me," he said, "is still here."

Relief shuddered beneath my scales. My long muscles relaxed, let loose a day's—a week's worth of tension. Knowing we were not alone here, that our Ghost kept watch, gave me enough solace to brave the next question.

"Is there something out there with you?"

The wind whistled. I pressed the side of my head against the viewing slit and listened, felt for an answer.

"Many warm bodies." A branch cracked as he shifted his weight. To my right, and very near the border between yard and jungle. "Low to the ground."

My blood iced. Our walls were strong, our door stout and barred, but as I stared into the dark leaves, I imagined teeth and claws. I remembered our stolen weapons, and I withdrew my head from the slit. Warm bodies. I tried to recall if the inhabitants of the City of Tongues made their own heat like our rodents did. I tried to remember anything at all I'd learned about them, but my thoughts had frozen.

The dream might have warned of danger behind me, but looking out at that dark wall, I couldn't believe it. Nothing inside our outpost could be scarier than that jungle. Using my tongue, I tasted, reaching out for a hint about our danger, our invisible enemy. Only the same scents answered: leaves and dirt, serpents and mice.

The Ghost hissed softly, or perhaps his breathing had now turned to wheezing. The sound, this time, brought little comfort.

"Should we flee?" I asked, half certain that I'd never build my spiky outpost here, that I'd never return to the Burrow alive, let alone victorious.

A dry laugh echoed from the trees. It crackled like the branches, stretching out and then breaking on a fit of coughing. There was an impending death in that sound, as if the last traces of air were rushing from the feverish serpent's body.

"What?" A fit of terror seized me and I yelled through the slit, shouting now, though I guessed the enemy could hear me. "Should we go?"

"It's too late, little serpent," Ghost rasped. "Too late to go, and you have nowhere safe to flee to."

I held my breath, stretched my tongue toward the vines, and leaned out again, hoping to catch a final word, a soft comfort as the big guard slithered through the fronds. Surely we could still go home, still pack ourselves and our rodents and flee this place. The doors would not be opened this time. Not a one of us would...

I thought of Lohmeer then, of my first overwhelming reaction to him. How enraged I'd felt at the sight of his lumbering body, his huge, arrow-shaped head. Could it be that I'd known he'd spell my doom somehow? That the fat constrictor might open the door and let our mysterious foe inside?

If the enemy was actually inside the outpost, I had to believe it was Lohmeer. Yet he'd been the most loyal, defended me and supported me when the others would have refused my authority outright. I pulled back into the watch room and pondered the night ahead. We could go now, travel through tunnels both dim and cool. Or we could wait out the darkness, make that decision in the light of dawn, with a night's sleep behind us.

But even as I thought it, I knew I wouldn't sleep. How could I, when Lohmeer was the only defense I had against the jungle? I heard the canopy crashing, heard Ghost's movement, and wondered how much longer he would last. If I was lucky, it would be at least till dawn.

And when the dry, wheezing laughter echoed again from the fronds, I told myself it didn't sound anything at all like death.

DISBANDED

16

I slept, despite my intentions. The worry alone had exhausted my reserves, and my body was running on so little that the moment I lay up on that warm shelf in the barracks, I drifted away.

In the dream, I awoke alone. The outpost lay as chilly as my winter adventure with Kwirk had been. My bones felt like knives as I moved, and my muscles dragged at me to stop, to lie down and let the cold put me to sleep forever. The hallways were black and tasted of rot. I tightened my lip and kept my tongue still, for fear of smelling more of it. Nothing moved that I could sense in either direction, but a soft vibration of sound tickled my belly.

It hummed beneath me, and I followed it through the frigid passage. The vibrations increased as I neared the doorway, and a gust of wind knocked me backwards over my own tail. Wind. My heart hammered. The door was open. Our walls had been breached, and yet I saw no sign of enemy or danger.

With my tongue fully extended, I crept forward, one scale row at a time, sensing, listening, tasting for anything that might give away the threat. Instead, only fresh air and distant jungle reached me. The blackness broke on an oval of light: the outpost entrance, thrown wide open.

I stalked toward it, certain there was only death beyond that portal. When I reached it, I stared out into the yard. The spikes had been moved. Nothing stuck from the sandy dirt, yet I could see shadows of long needles. Curiosity took me and I eased out of my shelter, twisting as I went to look behind me.

The pyramid loomed above, backed by a full, bright moon. My spikes adorned the structure like a crown, poking in all directions just as I'd intended them. But we hadn't done the work. There'd been no time and too much worry over the—

Danger! The echo whispered inside my head only seconds before another voice joined it.

"Danger!" Viir's voice, echoing all around me. "Danger, Kwirk!"

"Where? What is it?" I spun my coils, looking to the jungle, the yard, the passage behind me.

"Up here." Viir's words fell on me, and I craned my neck back.

A shadow fell across the pyramid. It had a snakey silhouette, but also the unmistakable outline of jagged wings. *Viir.* My bird-friend descended, and I retreated to make room for him. This time, there was nothing terrifying about him. His body remained long and elegant. His head rested on a slender neck, and the only avian features about him were the two waterfall wings at his sides. He looked like a god. Like the Sage himself, and I lowered my head to the sand without hesitation.

"Don't do that." For a moment he was all Viir again, all mischief and casual nature.

I lifted my head and came face to snout with him. Huge, slit eyes regarded me up close, and his spread wings blotted out both the moon and the outpost.

"Viir. I'm so lost out here," I whispered. "What do I do?"

"Well..." He tilted his head and a sliver of moonlight made a halo around him. "For starters, you should wake up."

I felt the rushing of water first, the pipe inside the wall where I'd rested my head. Warmth spread through me and I returned to the moment, slowly, easing in as the sensation of ice was replaced by heat. Something moved beside me, the softest flutter. I heard a mumbled voice, familiar and yet alien in the darkness.

"Kwirk?"

It was definitely his voice, and yet, when I twisted my head, I saw a stranger. He tasted like Kwirk, sounded like him, but the mouse standing beside my shelf had a stiff spine, rough and unkempt fur, and a gleaming metal dart held in both his paws. As I watched, the weapon lifted higher.

"Kwirk!" I rolled toward the wall as the dart fell.

My mouse growled, a sound I'd never heard him make. He bared his teeth, and I felt the bite of metal in my flank, the slow burn of a new scrape. The pain cleared my head, bringing home the very real danger of the dart in Kwirk's grip. My head spun to face the little rodent, and I hissed, opening my mouth and showing him my insubstantial, but still very sharp, fangs.

"What are you doing?" I pulled into a striking ess, though I had no intention of biting him.

"Killing the devil."

His words came low and with more edges than his voice had ever shown. In the dim light from the nearest shaft, I caught the flashing of his round eyes, the hard reflection and a wild look, an expression that screamed to me of insane things. Rage, violence, impossible avarice.

"Why?" My own question sounded meek, like a squeak in the face of that dart lifting again, lifting with every intent of impaling me.

"Freedom!" He screamed the word, tensed his body from tail-tip to whiskers. His eyes gleamed, and I knew he meant to kill me. Whatever had possessed my friend, he would do it if I didn't stop him.

My mind reeled, but my body tensed. Survival instincts took over, and I shoved down the questions and readied myself for whatever madness came next. Kwirk's teeth flashed, flat razors. His paws lifted the dart, but his arms were trembling.

When he leapt at me, I lunged to one side. His weapon slammed against the hot shelf and I threw a coil toward him, lashing out with my lower body while my head danced out of range. The impact, scales against fur, slammed the rodent into the heat wall. He let out a soft breath and then crumpled to the shelf. The dart clanked against the floor, and Kwirk lay still as stone in the place where I'd been dreaming.

"Kwirk?" I whispered it, chilled again by the sight of that immobile body, by the very idea of what had just happened.

When he didn't move, I lowered my nose, leaned over him, and let my tongue collect his familiar flavors. My companion, confidant, lifelong attendant lay in a heap, face down and— I let out a relieved hiss. Still breathing. The barracks were warm, but I suffered another shiver. The fruit had been poison after all. I should never have let him eat it.

My guilt drew me closer to the small body. I had no idea how long it would take to wear off, if it would wear off, or what I'd do if it didn't. My throat seemed to shrink, and I felt a sudden, desperate need for air. The rat had also eaten the fruit. Lohmeer stood watch now, but what if the other rodent had been struck with madness as well?

I moved then, out of fear only, toward the hallway. At the barracks door, cold air met my scales. It was only then that I remembered the dream, the open door, and the warning from my friend-turned-Sage. The chill told me what I'd feared the most: our door was open. Whatever had happened here before, we hadn't prevented it at all. Which meant I had more than Kwirk or Peet to worry about.

The skymetal around my middle hummed. I reached back, toward the shelf and my unconscious mouse, and latched hold of the weapon Kwirk had turned on me. The dart lifted into the air, hovered, and spun until it pointed toward the doorway. I eased it forward, focusing my intent on keeping it aloft, and my other senses on listening, feeling for what might be happening outside the room.

At first there was only the soft shifting of the breeze, more confirmation that our outpost lay exposed. Kwirk or the rat, under the influence of the jungle fruits, had opened the doors. But why, and who or what might have seized upon that opportunity to invade our defenses? Soft sounds from beyond the doorway gave me little answer. If I strained, I could hear movement deeper inside our tunnel, toward the storerooms. Something larger than a mouse shuffled there, no doubt rifling through our supplies.

I considered confronting it, whatever it was, but then I remembered Lohmeer. Had the rat slain him? If not, then I wasn't alone, and facing an unknown enemy with another serpent seemed a lot more possible than doing so alone. I eased my head into the hallway, tasting only snake and rodent on the breeze. Maybe there *was* no other enemy. Maybe the guards' mice had eaten the fruits too, slain their partners, and then ransacked the outpost and run off.

First I needed to find Lohmeer—or what was left of him.

Keeping my body tight to one wall, I slithered from the barracks and forward, toward the twin bolt-holes and their vantage. The scent of jungle thickened, and I could make out the darker square of doorway where the wood panel should have blocked our entrance. Lohmeer had relieved me, and so I began on the side where I'd watched earlier, slipping into the room and testing the ramp with my dart at the ready. His scent lingered here, but as I climbed it grew staler, and I guessed before I'd reached the top that the watch room would be empty.

Still, I poured from the ramp and coiled inside. No taste of blood either. No sign that my fellow serpent had been slaughtered in his sleep here. I'd let out a soft breath and determined to check the other side when a harsh, raspy voice reached me.

"Is it secured?" The words were gruff and sharp.

"As far as I can tell. They didn't bring much of use. More weapons and some scrap," a second stranger reported to the first.

I eased myself against the forward wall and dared to lift my head, careful to keep to the shadows where moonlight did not reach. It illuminated half the yard, and in the center of the glowing sand, two rats stood. They wore coarse clothing, not unlike Kwirk's vest, but with matching garments to cover their stout legs. A harder material covered their chests and shoulders, almost like a turtle's shell. The taller of the two carried a sword in one hand, its tip currently resting against the sand beside his long tail.

I'd seen hundreds of rats and mice in my short life, but none had carried themselves like this one. He posed as an *aspis* might, and I had no trouble labeling him both enemy and leader. The rodent reporting to him had dense, satiny fur in a shade similar to the shadows around the yard. Though they dressed alike, this one's weapon was slung across his back, leaving his paws free to carry a familiar roll of paper.

"The fat one had this with him."

My heart seized as the rat unrolled my outpost plans. As they examined my life's work, I took stock of the yard. Paw prints crossed back and forth through the sand. Our spikes had been uprooted and lain in a tidy pile, and beside those, several of the crates from our supply room had been stacked.

They hadn't mentioned the remaining beetles or our cart, and I held hope that the invaders hadn't ventured that far into our boundaries, that they'd busied themselves with the stockroom and gone no further. They'd obviously found Lohmeer, for who else could "the fat one" refer to? My heart tightened, for the loss of Lohmeer, and because I was now alone.

"We've got less than a week until the attack." The leader's words drew my attention from my own dilemma, snatching me back from the edge of panic only to hammer home a new danger. "We'll hold the tunnel here until it's time to move on the Burrow."

I nearly swallowed my tongue. Attacking the Burrow? These rats had lost their minds. Perhaps the jungle fruits were a staple of the rodent diet here, and that consumption had given them delusions.

"And if they send more serpents?"

The other rat only laughed in answer.

I held my breath. The wind danced through the fronds, shaking them into a fierce dance. From the shadows around the yard, more rodents sprang, as if they'd only been waiting for the breeze to announce them. Huge spotted rats, tiny gray mice, even a skittish shrew wandered in from the jungle. I counted as fast as I could, but the little bodies moved too much. I lost track after ten.

However many there were, they all held weapons. Swords and knives, curved wooden bows, and long spears. They all wore the rough clothing, and not one of them looked as if he'd seen a day inside the Burrow. If this was the rats' army, we had little to fear. Yet something nagged at me. Something about the leader's confidence suggested he had far more than the resources he'd stolen from us. There was a larger danger afoot.

I had to get back. That thought chased my fear down long enough for me to think. I had to warn the Burrow, tell them what was happening here on the edge of our world. If Lohmeer had perished, it was up to me to warn the others, to stop Laarahn from sending more of us to our deaths here. To send in soldiers ready for the unthinkable defense: a battle against rodents. Any attendants we sent with them would be potential liabilities.

Like Kwirk.

Sliding down the wall, I eased toward the ramp opening. I'd left my mouse behind in the barracks, but I couldn't abandon him to the hands of these ruffian rats. He might have been under the influence of the fruit, but I had to believe that would wear off eventually. Knowing he'd attacked me, wounded me... I wasn't sure what he'd do when he came to his senses.

The ramp slid away below me. The bolt-hole was empty still, but I'd heard something near the stockroom. How many more rodents infested our space? Could I slip past them, and if so, would I be able to keep Kwirk unconscious long enough to steal him away from this madness?

I brought the dart along, hovering at my side and right at rat height. The hallway air stung my scales as the night stole in through our open doorway. I hugged the wall again, led with my fully extended tongue, and slithered as quickly as possible deeper into the outpost. Just before I reached the barracks, movement ahead brought me to a standstill. I tried to blend into the crevice where wall and floor met, to look like a shadow, though my size made that impossible.

A crate of goods emerged from the stockroom. It rocked softly as it came, but hovered above the tunnel floor and floated forward, directly toward where I lay. Behind it, a familiar splotchy body slithered. Lohmeer's arrow head poked out to one side as he tracked his path toward the doors.

"Hi, Sookahr." He fluttered his tongue and continued to ease the crate forward as if I weren't there.

"What are you doing?" I pulled myself into a proper position and blocked his path.

"I'm carrying the supplies outside."

"Put it down." My body trembled with rage. I felt the urge to strike at him, and that crate was in the way. No sooner than I'd ordered it, however, the big snake settled the box against the floor. I stared at him, and he looked back at me with pupils that had gone fully round and fuzzy at the edges. "Lohmeer?"

"Hey!" a squeaky voice shouted behind him, from inside the stock room. "Keep that crate moving."

"Okay." Lohmeer nodded fiercely and his band buzzed. The crate lifted from the dust.

"Stop!" I hissed and showed him my fangs. "Put it down."

"Yes, sir." He settled the box again and stared at me. Blank expression, total obedience, and eyes that looked like a mouse's should.

"You're helping them?" I'd adjusted to the fact that he wasn't dead, but the idea that he'd gone to the rats sat wrong in my thoughts. "Why?"

"What?" He waved from side to side slightly, still held himself low and submissive. "No, sir. Helping who?"

"Yo, fatty! I said to keep that thing..." A rat appeared behind Lohmeer. It stepped out of the stock room, paws on its hips. A sword hung from a thick belt around its waist, and its spotty fur bristled at the sight of me. Whatever order it had meant to give died at the sight of my scales. The pointy face twisted into a grimace and the rat shouted a new directive. "Kill him!"

Lohmeer lifted into the air. His tongue went rigid and his neck curved back into a striking ess.

"Stop!" I ducked to the side, expecting to feel his teeth embedding in my flesh. Instead, Lohmeer had frozen in place.

"Get him," the rat ordered.

"Don't listen to him," I countered.

Lohmeer made a noise in his throat, half hiss and half groan. The rat shook himself, reached one paw for his sword hilt, and changed tactics. He shouted again, but this time, his words were not meant for any serpent. "I need help up here!"

From farther down the hallway, from the dark recess where our beetles waited, I heard the pattering of feet. Too many feet, and if each of the summoned rodents held a similar weapon, I didn't care to stay long enough to count them. The one behind Lohmeer raised his weapon and showed me his razor front teeth. Lohmeer wavered, side to side, and at any minute I feared he might decide to follow the rat's command instead of mine.

I leaned into my band, felt the shock of heat against my cold scales, and fired my dart directly at the rat's middle. The metal impacted his heavy outer garment and threw the little body backwards. If it pierced the vest, I couldn't say, nor did I intend to wait around to see.

"Lohmeer, follow me." I coiled around and headed back toward the front of the outpost. "Whatever happens, don't listen to anyone but me."

I had no time to verify if he'd heard me, that he obeyed at all. The rats from the rear already shouted, their cries flowing past us and likely meeting their allies outside the gate. Any second, the pounding of furry feet would echo from both directions. I raced to the right bolt-hole and ducked inside, pressing myself to the wall as Lohmeer's huge body flowed in behind me.

"Get out of the doorway. Here. Out of sight."

He moved automatically, as if I directly ordered his nervous system.

"Quiet." I held my breath as the floor began to thunder beneath my belly scutes. Trampling rodent paws rattled through the hall outside. They flowed past us, racing for their compatriots who, in turn, raced forward. We had maybe a second to act, and I had no idea how many still remained outside, where I would go, or what I could do once free of them. The only thing I was certain of was that I needed away from this place, free of the madness that had gripped Kwirk, that held Lohmeer now. An insanity I couldn't blame on bad fruit any longer. My only goal was to live, in that moment, to get away and to find somewhere safe to think.

"Follow me, Lohmeer." I eased to the doorway. "Follow me as fast as you can, and don't you listen to anyone else."

His "yes, sir" chased me out. I felt him behind me, and that weight lent me courage. We went unmolested through the short stretch between bolt-hole and front door. The air sharpened, and I suffered a flash of hesitation. Out there we would be at risk, exposed to the elements and without our hot shelf and warm pipes. In here, however, we would be dead.

That thought drove me past my terror. I listened to the soft voices of rats outside, let my tongue flutter once, and then exploded into the open with a final order for Lohmeer. "Only to me!"

The lead rat still stood with his sword in the dirt. His eyes grew as we emerged, and those round orbs filled my vision. His shock, I would never forget, nor the speed at which he recovered his senses and began to shout direction to his remaining men.

"Draw arms. Come together, on my mark!"

Perhaps he expected a battle, but I had no intentions of attacking, not when we were two against twenty, and not when I couldn't trust Lohmeer to remain on my side. I barreled past him, sliding like a breeze against the sand. Two mice ended up in my path, and I hissed and struck as I went, scattering them to the flanks. The jungle waited ahead, and inside it, a third of our kind. A trained soldier, even.

I focused on my path, directly toward the fronds, and flew like the Sage on wings forged of my own fears. Lohmeer shouted once, as I neared the jungle. His call drew my head around, though it did not slow my slither. I saw the rats behind him, swinging their weapons, drawing bows. My large companion still came on, but there was a spear lodged in his fat tail, and his eyes blurred and wavered toward confusion.

"Flee, Lohmeer!" I screamed it and fastened my vision upon our pile of spikes. My band howled to life, blazing fire against my scales. I meant to lift them all, to fire the enormous arrows through the crowd of rodents. But my focus and my power failed. Instead, I succeeded in tumbling the shafts, rattling the metal, and scattering the spires haphazardly in the direction of the foe.

Enough to scare them, only. Still, they ducked their fuzzy heads, and Lohmeer's attention focused again on me. He drove toward me, bleeding and out of his wits, and I had nothing left to do but pray he'd make it.

I turned around again and plunged, head-first, into the dark jungle.

17

We continued long after the foliage devoured us. A blind fury gripped me, and despite the labored sounds of Lohmeer's breath at my tail, I pushed my body onward through vines and fronds that slapped at my sides like many flat paws. When a trunk appeared in my path, I'd curve around it. When the vines wove too tightly together, I veered, slithering like a drunken hatchling in a direction that could only be labeled random.

By the time my lungs gave out, I could no longer hear the sound of pursuit. The squeaky shouts had faded to nothing, and no more tramping paws crunched the fallen twigs. Only the panting of my stout companion interrupted the soft whisper of the breeze through the jungle.

Lohmeer, miraculously, had kept with me. He stalled when I stopped, panting and sagging as if his body melted from his bones. The spear in his tail had broken off, so that only a jagged bit of wood stood over the embedded metal tip. My own scrape burned from repeated thrashings by the foliage. We needed to rest, to tend our injuries, and to find water to clean them. Otherwise, we'd end up as feverish and full of rot as Ghost.

Secretly I hoped the guard still lived, that he'd watched our attack and marked our escape. That he'd lower himself from the canopy at any moment and join our cause. But the jungle remained dark and unfriendly. The vines shielded us, but they also masked anything that might sneak upon us.

"Are you okay?" I turned my desperation on Lohmeer. "What the hell happened back there?"

"I don't. I'm hurt," he said. Then he shifted his body and, wincing, shoved his tail further into view. The broken stub of spear waved at me.

"You were helping them," I pushed on. "Taking orders from a rat."

"He..." The big constrictor's eyes went fuzzy. He tilted his head as if trying to remember, as if he'd been dreaming. *In the dreaming.*

"Never mind." I shook off a shiver and coiled around my own wound. "We need to find water and shelter, to get away from here as fast as possible, and find a way to warn the Burrow."

"Yes."

"See if you can smell anything that way." I jabbed my tail in one direction and turned my head in the other, stretching with my tongue and praying for the scent of water or rock. Anything but jungle and rat.

While I tasted, I listened with my whole body. The only vibration I sensed was the soft movement of the wind through the fronds. I felt its touch against my scales and I focused, not realizing my band had come to my assistance until the branches in front of my nose parted. They curved aside, though I hadn't willed it. My mind had been on finding...Ghost.

"This way." I slithered into the gap, only half trusting Lohmeer to follow me. His odd obedience to the rats made him suspect, possibly traitorous, and yet I couldn't bear to leave him. To face this maze of dark foliage alone. I fixed my thoughts on the old guard instead, and let the skymetal guide me.

As far as I could tell, we moved away from the outpost, slightly north and east. Laarahn's map hadn't indicated anything outside the Burrow, but there had been a branch, a day back that led to another outpost. It would be a good goal, if we survived the jungle, another way into the Burrow, and a chance to get the warning out before the rodents made their move.

If we could get there first.

I had no idea how long that journey might be through the above-ground, nor did I relish spending the rest of the night exposed to whatever lived here. Rats, for one, insane rodents with weapons that hadn't been forged inside the Burrow.

"What's that smell?" Lohmeer's voice came. I'd slowed and he'd been following closely; he'd nearly lapped me by the time I tasted what he meant.

Rot in the air.

"I think it's Ghost." I slowed now, and the band failed and went cold. The effort of using it again so soon turned my muscles to rubber. I sagged, the pain of my scrape seeming to swell, as if it fought for my attention again. I flicked my tongue with some effort, and scanned the fronds above. "Ghost?"

"Over here." Lohmeer crashed through the brush too loudly.

I cringed and hissed for him to be quiet, but the big constrictor continued to wiggle his splotchy body through the vines. I followed, scenting as I did and begrudgingly agreeing with his choice of direction. The stench thickened quickly, and I caught a shimmer of black scales beyond Lohmeer's gigantic head.

We both stopped together. From the canopy, Ghost's tail dangled, turning from one side to the other as the breezes played with it. The wounds puckered and writhed with parasites. The smell filled my nostrils and clung to my tongue, though I refused to draw it into my mouth again. Nothing about that casual movement suggested life, and yet I clung to my last hope one breath longer.

"Ghost?"

It was Lohmeer's band that hummed to life. His unseen will that nudged the guard's body ever so slightly. I saw only the briefest jerk and then, with a crashing of vines and branches, the long carcass of our Ghost fell from above. Twisting on the way down, the body landed in a heap, flat, viper head staring out from a tangle of broken coils. Beneath the eye-ridges, Ghost stared, lifeless, at our intrusion.

"Warrior's tongue," Lohmeer cursed, and then turned his head to the side and made a retching sound in his long throat.

I wouldn't have guessed my chunky companion followed the Warrior, but his epithet was appropriate considering Ghost most definitely did. Despite the stink and my stomach's insistence that it should follow Lohmeer's lead and evacuate itself, I slithered past the splotchy body of my former builder and rounded on the dead viper's head.

"He died with honor." I wasn't sure who I spoke to, the jungle, the Warrior, or Lohmeer. It didn't matter. Someone had to say something, and judging from the sounds, it would have to be me. "Stuck to his duty to the last, stayed by the outpost when he might have gone for water or..."

My mind filled in the word "help". Disrespectful, that thought, and yet as I swayed above the dead viper, I wondered why he hadn't left. Why not seek another Burrow entrance? Why not warn the Circlet that there were wild rodents out to destroy us?

In the end, I choked out less than I'd intended. "Go in peace, Ghost."

When I turned away from the corpse, I found Lohmeer watching. His eyes still had a dullness to them, but the pupils had begun to retract back to their normal shape. Beside him lay his last meal, steaming, and looking nothing at all like a half-digested beetle.

"Is that grain?" I didn't exactly want to examine his regurgitation, but there was an unmistakable texture. "What have you eaten?"

His big head lowered, nose down in shame.

"Lohmeer, is that the tainted grain?"

"I was hungry," he mumbled. "They weren't going to eat it."

"It was moldy!" My thoughts scrambled. Perhaps the grain was the

137

culprit. Maybe it wasn't the fruit at all, and Lohmeer's obedience to the rats could be explained by his last meal. But the mice had gone off their grain. Gone off it and turned on us with eyes sharp as daggers. "I wonder if the Burrow's whole supply of grain has been contaminated."

"Is it poison?" He looked at his vomit as if it might bite him now. "Am I going to die?"

"No. For one, you've just evacuated the majority of it. Unless you've been dining on rodent rations for longer than that?"

He shook his big, dumb head.

"For another, our mice have been eating it and no one has dropped dead yet."

"But they didn't eat it," he said. "They ate the fruit."

I eased away from Ghost, and from the stench of both death and vomit now. "Come away and listen to me. The rodents reacted to the fruit or...to not eating for so long."

I remembered Kwirk's eyes, sharp and defiant when he'd skipped breakfast. I remembered that same look, amplified a thousand times, as he drove the dart down toward my scales. The pieces of a puzzle were all there, in Kwirk's rebellion and Lohmeer's docility, but I couldn't quite make them fit together. Nor did I care to at the moment.

"What a stupid thing to do, eating grain. It's probably going to rot in your fat gut." I turned my nose up and tried to catch sight of the moon, to reorient myself toward a direction that was as near to "east" as I could guess. "You probably *have* poisoned yourself."

"It didn't feel like poison." Lohmeer sulked along beside me, head at my halfway point and barely lifted above my band's height. "It felt like the dreaming."

"Which is induced with venom." I hissed and lifted higher, hurrying my pace though I had no idea where I was going. "Venom distilled into a *poison*, Lohmeer. I certainly hope you survive this."

Taunting him eased the squirming feeling in my belly, but I suffered a pang of guilt when I looked back and saw the way his head hung. Dejected. Taking my foul mood to heart, just like I would have had Viir lashed out at me. I turned away and tried to focus on finding us a path in a world where everything was a tangle of growth.

Moonlight filtered down to us, but the canopy was a shield against the majority of it. I slithered from shaft to shaft, using the gaps above as waypoints and leading us in some direction that I was fairly certain wouldn't take us directly back to the enemy. Lohmeer followed in silence, still obedient, eyes still dull, though they shifted by the moment. When they'd returned to normal, would he still ally himself with me? If not, I'd face this dark patchwork and anything else it hid alone.

I shivered, though the breeze here held both warmth and moisture.

"There's another entrance to the Burrow just east of here." I tried my best to sound sure of that. "I heard the rat say he meant to attack in a week's time. We need to—"

"They're after the Circlet," Lohmeer interjected. "Going to take out the leaders and free the slaves."

"What?" I stopped, and one of his coils ran over my tail. I spun my head around and swayed above him. "What did you say?"

"I heard the rat say it." Lohmeer fixed his eyes on the ground. "When I was moving their stuff."

"Our stuff. You were moving our stuff so that they could steal it."

"They told me to move it and..." His eyes glassed over. The tips of his tongue flitted between his wide lips. "They said to."

"There are no slaves in the Burrow." I snapped it, biting my tongue in the process and hiding my wince of pain by spinning back around again. "The stupid rats were all mad."

"Yeah. They were really angry."

I cringed and pushed my way through a wall of fat vines. A round clearing waited on the other side, not large enough for both of us to coil inside it, but crowned by a substantial gap in the canopy. Light pooled on the matted ground, and the full of one moon gazed peacefully down on us.

"I need to sleep." My fears argued that we hadn't put enough distance between us and the rodents, but my muscles trembled, from adrenaline or fatigue, I wasn't sure. I'd be no use at all come light if I pushed on any further. "*I* haven't eaten in days."

My head was too fuzzy to count them, in fact, and that didn't bode well for my decision-making either. Too much had happened to us too quickly, and I couldn't process it, let alone select our best course of action in this state. For all I knew I'd led us in a circle, and the enemy waited just beyond the next tree.

"We shouldn't stay on the ground." I eyed the nearest trunk skeptically. "How well do you climb?"

I had little experience attempting it myself, but as I stared up the folds of bark leading toward the canopy, I imagined I could find a path to that lowest branch. I had a much harder time picturing Lohmeer's enormous body ever leaving the ground, however.

"Fairly well," he said.

I never discovered if his confidence was feigned or not. Though I could imagine no situation where he might have practiced or even attempted the skill, the splotchy constrictor slithered past me and began to ascend the trunk with uncharacteristic grace. His muscles bunched and clung, hugging the tree as if it were a beetle steak, and he lifted himself far more easily and quickly than I would have believed had I not seen it.

All that was left for me to do was follow, and I approached the bark

139

cautiously, tongue fluttering. My body was too slight to use Lohmeer's technique, and so I fit my length into a vertical fold and pressed outward with one coil after the other, each time wedging my body a little bit higher.

It was slow going, much slower than I'd hoped. By the time I reached the first branches, my sides ached. Lohmeer already lay in the crook, wrapped over and around himself with his head resting on one fat coil. The moonlight made his lighter splotches glow softly, and for the first time since our meeting, I found him lovely. His smooth scales and round body shone against the night, stretched tight.

Like a squirming thing against hot sands.

I gripped the bark with my belly, clenching against a sudden vertigo. Images swam through my memory—Lohmeer and I locked in battle over something. A soft hiss escaped me, and the constrictor cringed. I hadn't aimed it at him, and yet, who could blame him for being terrified of me?

Something small and furry.

Kwirk's voice screamed in my head. *For freedom.* The random rat's gossip echoed in Lohmeer's voice. *Free the slaves.* I clung to the tree and remembered rolling across warm sand with my first meal, stolen from Lohmeer's ravenous jaws. My first success, but it had been no beetle I'd eaten.

Yes. Good.

Even the echo betrayed me now. My whole life yawned between that moment and this, a series of events focused on one goal: recognition. I'd lost that chance when the outpost fell, and yet, I'd found something else. Something massive and secret and fully horrible.

Lohmeer settled back into his nap, sides rising and falling under the moonlight. I craned my neck up, stared into the pale face of that disk, and began to climb again. Though I'd meant to stop, to sleep as near to where Lohmeer had curled as possible, it was as if the moon drew me upwards. I chased her into the canopy where the trunk broke and divided into a web of lanes. Many forks and branches, many pathways like tongues flickering.

I settled there, alone, in the pale light. Settled and yet knew sleep would be hard-won. Too many questions fought for my attention now, too many nagged and turned to darkness. A little higher and I'd be able to see, perhaps, our outpost and its invaders, a pathway back to the Burrow. I left that discovery for morning.

My coils draped over and under the branching boughs, and I rested my head on a frond, staring at the shine of light on leaves. Staring, like Ghost had done, at too many truths to swallow all at once. Each one settled through me like a chilly meal, like a mouthful of poison grain that refused to be digested.

18

I woke to my stomach's clenching. My hunger pushed at me to be moving, and a pervasive heat lent my muscles the energy needed to lift myself. The sun burned through the thin leaf layer, dappling my scales and making my shelter as hot as my shelf back home. The wound in my side barely complained now, and I examined it fully for any trace of infection.

In the morning's light, my scrape seemed superficial, irrelevant when compared to the puncture Lohmeer endured. His would be the one to cause worry, if we didn't return soon. I yawned, stretching my jaws wide and pretending I had a juicy, fat beetle to wrap them round. Then I looked to the final leg of my climb, the last few branches before the canopy broke and I could survey our situation in its entirety.

Lohmeer would need tending. I owed him that much, to see him safely to water, to see his wounds healed and his injuries righted. In my long hours of rumination before sleep had finally taken me, I'd worked that out. It had been my pride that dragged us to the outpost, my vanity that kept us here long after the signs pointed to danger. I'd repaid his loyalty with harsher words than warranted, even in light of his actions.

I now believed those actions had been fully under the influence of whatever tainted our rodents' rations. Whether or not that taint was an accident of our trip, or a design of our society, I still refused to decide.

Instead, I climbed the rest of the way, pushed my narrow head through the leaves, and examined the world spread like a map before me.

The morning sunlight blazed, reflecting against the leaves. My head spun for a moment as my vision adjusted. My tongue tasted the heat of slowly cooking foliage. When my vision cleared, a distant stripe, pale and smooth, showed me where the jungle ended. Farther than I'd expected. We'd fled deep into the trees and now—just to my left, I could barely make out the sharp edges of our pyramid. Good and bad. We'd left the enemy far behind, yet we'd have a trek ahead of us if I meant to find the second entrance to the Burrow.

A trek south first, and then east, lest we miss it entirely.

I turned away, resting my eyes and preparing to duck back into the shelter of the leaves. Something shiny caught my attention. To the right, closer than the path I sought directly south, a ribbon of water flashed. The light bounced against its surface, making diamond scales, a mosaic like the one in my shrine. The scales of gods.

My wound no longer burned, but Lohmeer still bore a spear tip in his tail—unless he'd plucked it free in the night, an act which may have renewed the bleeding. I gazed down at the river, gauged its scope and direction. If we angled our way east and south, we'd hit it soon enough. From there we could aim directly for the border between dense jungle and open forest. The odds of missing the other entrance seemed slim, as we'd only skip a narrow section of our border.

Water had to be my first priority, even with the rat's threat echoing inside my head. A week's time. A week left until the Circlet convened. I'd worked that out in the long hours too. The odds of that timing being coincidence seemed a slimmer thing than the distant river.

We had no time to dawdle.

I poked my nose through the fronds and found one branch, and then another. As I descended, they thickened, came together, and decreased in number, the many paths narrowing into a single road. Only one choice. I passed the crevice where I'd finally found sleep and continued, sliding between the bark ridges with more ease now that my body had rested. My belly still yawned and complained, but at least I had my strength back. My determination too had refilled somewhere under the night's moon.

Lohmeer still draped over the same crotch of branches. His head lifted as I reached him, and the tips of his tongue emerged. He'd wrapped his tail up over his back so that the wound was aloft, an instinct to keep filth and infection at bay. The spear stub still sprouted from the puncture, and blood had dried into a seal around it.

"There's a river," I said. "Just to the east."

"What?" His tongue drifted out and back. His eyes fixed on me, and today, the pupils made perfect circles inside.

"You need to tend that wound. Get the spear out." I watched him, certain that his memory of the previous day had become as fuzzy as any dreaming.

He turned his head toward his tail and explored the wound with his tongue. His heavy sides flexed, in and out as he breathed. Had he slept the night through and woken with no idea of his injury? I guessed as much, but I didn't plan on filling him in either. Not at the moment.

"Does it hurt much? We'll need to start off as soon as possible."

"It's sore, but..." He flexed his tail, slid it off the rest of his body and tested his range of motion. If there was too much pain in that, he kept it to himself. "I can climb down now."

I wondered if he remembered climbing *up*, if Lohmeer had woken in a tree with no idea how he'd landed there. He said very little, but his head kept shifting from one side to the other, looking, working out where we were and what we were doing.

Though I felt for him, we didn't have time to linger and discuss. I led the way down the tree and waited only until his first quarter touched the matted vines before starting off, at an angle, to intercept the river. Lohmeer followed in silence, either ashamed of himself or still processing. I couldn't be certain but I enjoyed the quiet just the same, listening to the soft crinkling of growth under my scales, and tasting the jungle smells which I'd come to read as more nuanced than my original judgment.

Now, along with growing things and dirt, I picked out distinctly sweet-scented flowering plants, bitter roots, pungent loam and, once, a fresh pile of droppings left by some mammal I didn't care to meet. The air filled with sounds as well, as if our night sleeping in the trees had convinced the locals we belonged here. As if the jungle had been holding its breath, waiting for us to leave. We'd persisted, and now the chattering of insects droned around us. Overhead, wings buzzed past, sending me to my belly in terror until I worked out that they were not, in fact, the wings of avians.

I checked on Lohmeer every so often. He moved with me, not lagging, and yet his tail section moved stiffly as he went, as if bending it properly were too much to bear. I scented for any sign of rot, more than once, and checked my own scrape for good measure, though it had long since stopped bothering me.

From the ground, it was harder to be certain of my direction. I did my best to point us toward the southeast and to hold that course, but massive tree trunks and dense walls of vine required that we veer one way or the other. I'd expected to smell water before the sun had reached its zenith, but midday came and passed, and still the air carried only jungle to my senses.

The soft leaves beneath me became blades as their repeated scraping wore on. The fronds and vines that had been gentle paws at my flank slapped and dragged at me as I fought to keep moving between them. Well after midday, when I still could find no sign of water, we encountered a particularly large tangle of growth. The vines threaded together as if woven, and the patch stretched in both directions so that circling around it became a massive undertaking.

I stared into the web and flicked my tongue irritably.

"It's a long way in both directions." Lohmeer stopped half a length behind me. His breath rasped in and out, and I refused to look back and discover another problem. I doubted he'd benefit from a long detour out of our way, a long wait until we reached the river. Digging our way through the tangle might take more effort, but it would get him to water all the sooner.

I hoped.

"We'll go through," I said. In case he meant to argue, I moved forward immediately, using my band to shove at the vines until a reasonable path appeared. "I'll clear as we go."

My skymetal hummed and heated. I fixed my mind on the wall of growth, shoving and twisting, cracking and tearing a swath wide enough for Lohmeer's substantial girth to pass. The vines curled and sprang at me, as if the foliage fought back against my onslaught. We moved ahead, entering a dark tunnel of fronds until the sun was only a pale glow caught in snatches.

The heat of my band flowed through my scales. I leaned into it, tore a chunk of vine from the wall in front of me and felt the grasp on its fellows around my middle. I pulled forward, and the vines yanked me back. I jerked free, and a rush of cold answered. I heard Lohmeer's gasp before I realized what had happened. I froze, staring ahead and feeling with my mind only.

Scales, cool air, nothing.

"Your band," Lohmeer rumbled. "Sookahr."

"I know!" I yelled it, heard the tremble in my words and cringed. Slowly, I turned my head around, following my own scales and finding nothing to break than slick length except a paler patch where a band had rested at all times since first being made a citizen of the Burrow. My whole life. The skymetal device rested in the weeds now, held by vines and looking like a relic from a lost culture.

"You've lost weight," my companion continued as if my life had not just ended. "It just slipped right off."

"I've missed a meal." I stared at the band, not believing it was there, free of me. "It hasn't been that long."

"But you've been working hard."

I ignored him and slithered into a knot beside my misplaced ring. Without it I was no one, half a serpent, and unwelcome inside the Burrow. Oddly enough, as I examined it, I felt less of terror and more a slippery excited feeling. I was no one, but also, *anyone*.

You are special.

The metal glinted back at me, silent now, as if it had never sung around my scales. The breath of elation passed quickly and panic swept into its place. I hissed softly.

"Put it back on," Lohmeer suggested. "No one will know."

I nodded, but my body refused to act.

"Once you eat something, it will be fine."

Timidly, I uncoiled my tail, probing nearer to the band as if it might strike and bite. The vines held the loop upright, had simply slid it off my slightly deflated girth. Slipping it back on should be a simple thing. With my heart in my throat, I threaded my tail through the thing, easing the band up until I could pull it free of the vines' grip. Then I lifted my tail, angled it so that the heavy skymetal fell back into place.

I knew instantly that it would not stay there. The ring spun loose around my scales, and no amount of wiggling on my part could wedge it higher up.

"Maybe you can keep your tail in the air?" Lohmeer suggested.

"Not while we work through this. I need the band to move the vines."

"I'll clear for awhile." He crashed forward, brushing against my tail and the ring, and forcing me into the vines at the side of the path I'd made.

"Wait." I set the band down and let it slide off my tail again. "I think I can get it into position this way."

I doubled back on myself, testing the band with my tongue as if it might have changed its scent somehow, become foreign in its short time off my body. When it tasted as familiar as ever, as safe, I nosed my way into the ring. It fit over my head easily, sliding rapidly down my long neck to clang against the ground. My body expanded from my lungs to my middle, and I wiggled into the band, certain that it would tighten at any moment. That it would tighten *enough*.

A scale row before it reached its former resting place, the band stopped. I held my breath, and the skymetal held its position. Not exactly where it had started, but close enough to give me hope. Lohmeer must have considered it a success as well, for he nodded fiercely and then turned back to the brush.

"Is this the right way?"

"Yes." I let him break the vines, let out my breath, and felt the ring slipping. I sucked in again, holding my sides as wide as they would go. It didn't fit. If I didn't eat soon, it would fall off again. "I'm right behind you."

I waited for the constrictor to cut us a path, letting the panic swirl inside my belly. What would happen if I returned home with a loose band? I'd never heard of such a thing occurring, and wasn't certain that the viper and his cauldron would even allow me another visit. There had to be a way to resize the band, to bolt it back into place once my midsection re-inflated.

In the meantime, I would have to focus on holding it in place.

One good meal ought to do it, and as Lohmeer had suggested, I could keep my tail high, move carefully and possibly hunt up something to eat before we reached our goal. Hunting in the wild. Killing my own food. These were things only spoken of in theory. Every meal I'd eaten came to my plate already processed. Ever since...

The image came again. Lohmeer and I on the sands. Something fat and wriggling between us.

Almost everything.

If it meant my band, I decided I could hunt. If I were lucky, and right about his appetite, I wagered I could convince Lohmeer to help me. If we searched up a grub or two, and I managed to squeeze back into my band, everything would be fine. We just had to get home before the rodents made their move. We had to get Lohmeer's wound tended, get to the river, and—

A ground-trembling crash echoed from the spot where Lohmeer had been working at our path. I peered ahead, but saw no sign of the plump constrictor. The thicket we'd been traversing opened up before me, and the jungle brightened ahead. I stretched my tongue and tasted, for just a moment, the sweet hint of water.

"Lohmeer?" I eased forward. The ground fell away beneath the vines, making a steep slope with a swath torn through it where my fellow serpent had tumbled down. "Lohmeer? Are you okay?"

"Watch out," he rumbled from somewhere below. The tangled growth masked him, but when he moved, I marked the rattling of fronds. "There's a drop-off."

"I can smell the river," I called down, eying the ragged path he'd made and planning my descent.

"You can feel it down here."

That declaration proved enough for me to dare the slope. I went in a zigzag, from one side of Lohmeer's destruction to the other, back and forth over the vines, and only slipping a few times as the thicker foliage grabbed at my scales. The smell of water thickened as I descended the slope, and I heard Lohmeer crashing off again before I'd made level going. Still, his path was obvious. Not only for the tearing of the jungle, either. I could smell blood now, and I found the first spattering of it in the constrictor's broad trail.

His fall had torn the wound open—that or plunged the spear deeper. If he hurried to the river now, who could blame him? I slithered in his wake, as fast as I could manage with the vines dragging at my sides. When the jungle gripped me, I tore myself away. When the blood trail became a stream, I threshed my tail and raced forward between the fronds.

The ground vibrated with the water's movement. The air filled with iron and moisture both. I chased Lohmeer until the jungle thinned and parted, and only when I reached the soft sloping of the river's edge did I notice the cool absence around my girth.

My band, gone again. Lost in the tangle somewhere behind us while I worried about my companion. The matted vines broke and turned to sandy soil. The river rushed between two soft banks, curving here and full of riffles but not so huge or so wide to make any sort of barrier. Lohmeer sprawled on the sand, one tenth his length from the rushing water. His sides heaved, and his damaged tail lay limp in a puddle of fresh blood. I saw no sign of the spear, and prayed it too had been lost along the way.

"Into the water," I ordered. "Clean that before..."

Images of Ghost's tail, angry and purple, filled my head. I longed to turn around, to search the path I'd just floundered along and find my missing skymetal. Lohmeer's dilemma pressed more urgently, but the idea of waiting shivered against all my instincts to retrieve my band. To be a whole serpent again.

"Come on," I urged him, slithering closer and raising my voice to make it an order. "Get into the river."

Already, I scanned the fronds for suitable wrapping materials. Once we'd cleaned Lohmeer's tail, we'd need to bind it. Without my band or my mouse's dexterous paws, that became one more difficulty before us. I only prayed Lohmeer could manage it, once he'd cleaned his puncture, that his band would serve him where mine could not.

The sooner he'd been tended, the sooner I could begin my searching.

I nudged his flank with my nose and he groaned. His big head lifted, and his tongue gave a pathetic flutter.

"It's just a scale farther," I urged. "Come on."

He raised himself enough to slither, and I leaned into his side, pressing him forward with a coil. We crept across cool sand, and mist filled the air, landing on my scales and my tongue with welcome relief. I leaned forward, certain Lohmeer could slip easily into the water now and desperate for a long drink. My tongue flicked across the cool surface, but froze there when the foliage on the opposite bank erupted with a low hiss.

"Get back!" a feminine voice shouted.

I jerked my head up at the challenge in her tone. Lohmeer moaned softly, but my gaze had fixed forward. I swayed as the new snake poured forth from the brush. I held my ground, held my pose, as a pale keeled body flowed down the sand to the water. I held it until she reared back, flattened her head into a hood, and hissed again.

Then, my head came down on its own. My belly pressed into the sand, and my thoughts circled around a single word.

Aspis.

DISBANDED

19

The *aspis* drew herself into a striking posture. Her hood flattened at the side of a face with a square, slightly upturned nose. Two dark lines marked the underside of her eyes, reminding me of Viir and driving me instinctively lower.

"Back away from my river," she said. "I don't want you here."

"My friend is injured." I kept my head down, but only coiled my body into a knot. I'd no intentions of leaving the river, but no status at all against an *aspis*, even if I'd had a band around me. "We need to clean his wound."

"Do it somewhere else." She slid forward, easing to the water's edge and pressing her advantage with another hiss. Despite her pale scales, her belly scutes were jet black, the reflection in the water making her two snakes, dark and light, an image of *aspis* perfection. Except neither this girl nor her reflection wore a band of any kind. "Go on. Get out of here."

"He's bleeding," I tried again, tried because no serpent I knew could be so callous as to let another die over something so insignificant as territory. I tried, because I had no other option, and because Lohmeer was too weak even to argue his own case. "If we leave here, he won't make it."

I hoped he was too weak to hear me too. My fear for his life warred with my loyalty to the *aspis*. One did not challenge a higher serpent; the peace and glory of the Burrow depended on this. Yet Lohmeer's life spilled, red and dark upon the sands, and this particular *aspis* showed no sign of the grace or understanding that Viirlahn or any of his fellows would.

I began to suspect she was a rogue serpent, an outsider, and a villain too. Her presence here, band-less, suggested as much, and the idea that an *aspis* too disloyal to join our society would then bar one of our members from life, burned in my belly. My scales warmed with my fury. Still, I cowered before that too-familiar stance.

"Find another place," she said. "What's it to me? For all I know, you mean to steal my land, defile my body, and leave me for dead."

"What?" I lifted my head, just enough to gape at her.

She'd pressed forward, waited now in the middle of the river and, when I looked at her, opened her jaws and showed me the black inside of her mouth.

"Why would we do that?"

"How do I know? You could be outlaws, murderers. He could be faking."

"He's bleeding all over *your* sand."

"Take him somewhere else to bleed."

I pulled my neck into an ess and hissed, softly, but loud enough to get the strange *aspis'* attention. She swayed at me and I raised my head, one scale row at a time. Lohmeer's labored breathing became a metronome that both the girl and I swayed in time with. My fury turned hot as an ember, squirming inside me, driving me up to meet her aggression. My vision narrowed. The river turned into a blur of dark and light.

I hissed again and made my words spit with it. "Let. Him. Wash."

"No!" Her tail buzzed against the water, splashing the opposite bank and me as well. She puffed out her hood, but when I jerked forward she pulled back sharply, laying her head and neck back over her body. "Go away."

"No." Shame boiled beside my anger. I'd never defied anyone at all, let alone an *aspis*. I imagined Laarahn's reaction, the disappointment and embarrassment I'd become, band-less and manner-less after only one day in the jungle. At the same time, however, I saw Ghost's limp body and I heard Lohmeer's rough breaths. "No!"

I slithered into the river. The water hit my scales like ice, first sharp and then quickly numbing. If Lohmeer died here today, then so would I. Either from the bite of the girl or the shame of attacking a superior. It could get me banished, ostracized, and left to live like this, like she did, forever.

"I'm warning you." She eased back, reached the far sand and curled around herself. "Don't come any closer."

"*You* go away," I shouted and readied to strike.

"I'll bite you." She swayed, but her voice faltered. I saw something fearful in her movements, something I remembered only halfway. "I will."

She was bluffing. Even as I thought it, she opened her mouth wide, hissed, and showed me not a trace of fang. Her teeth were stubby and, while likely sharp, unlikely to hold any more venom than my own. Not only was she rude and unfeeling, she'd lied about her own nature.

Enraged, I struck toward her, not to bite, but to break her act at dominance. My open mouth breezed past the side of her hood, and I pulled back and essed again.

The girl deflated. Her hood vanished, her body went limp, and she flopped onto the far bank and lay, belly up on the sand.

Lohmeer's voice called from behind me. "You've killed her."

"I didn't." I hadn't even touched her and yet, as I looked at her now, she certainly appeared dead. Her tongue hung from her open mouth, like a drowned worm beside her head. Her black belly flattened, as if her body had lost all its shape. Had it not been for the subtlest of movements, I would have agreed with my companion. "She's breathing."

"Is she?" The curiosity, if not his open wound, drove Lohmeer into the water. His splashing startled the "dead" girl, and she fluttered her tongue.

"She's faking," I said.

The tongue moved again. Lohmeer reached us, and I noted with satisfaction that his tail end remained in the current, turning the water bright pink, but also cleaning any foreign material from his puncture.

"She's no *aspis*." I hissed and felt the relief like a bathe in its own right. My body sagged, and the heat that had coursed through me turned to chill again. I shivered, and looked up to where the sun broke through the canopy. "Why is it so cold?"

"She's just an ordinary snake." Lohmeer agreed with me, nodding his big head. "But she's pretty."

That worked magic on our phony *aspis*. She flicked her tongue again, flipped her entire body over in a single movement, and lifted her head to regard us evenly. This time she remained on my level, though I wasn't certain she should rate even that much.

"Who are you?" She poked her upturned nose in Lohmeer's direction as if I weren't directly in front of her. "You're banded. From the below-ground. What are you doing way out here?"

I hissed again. My hot rage had turned into cold fury. This idiot, this rogue, had fought to keep us from saving Lohmeer's life, and now she conversed with him as if they'd met in the gaming hall during their leisure hour. Lohmeer coiled onto the bank, trailing a thin drizzle of bloody water, and stretched his tongue out happily.

"Don't go near her," I warned. My body shivered, a wave of ice from tail tip to nose. "She's dangerous, Lohmeer. She tried to kill you."

"I did not." She lifted a third of her body and eased away from me. "And I was talking to him, not *you*."

The hiss began deep in my belly. It burst forth, backed by my indignation, my fury and shame and whatever this new shivery feeling was. I had no band. Did she think I was an outcast too? A non-snake living in the wild who wouldn't know good manners if they struck her in the face?

"I'm Lohmeer." My stout companion beamed at her, lifting his head higher too until we all posed at the same height, and my embarrassed rage spilled free. I pulled back and mock struck, once at her and once at him. Band or no, I outranked Lohmeer and he knew it. The girl was below us both simply by her rogue nature. I hissed, swayed, and struck the empty air between us in warning.

"What's his problem?" The girl coiled away, flattening her phony hood and looking, again, to Lohmeer for answers.

"He lost his band." Lohmeer said.

I swiveled between them. My head spun, and the jungle blurred into a streak behind two serpents that were both strangers if I really thought about it. All I knew about the constrictor was that he was a glutton and less than brilliant. The blunt-nosed girl was trouble, and now Lohmeer eased closer to her. Leaving me alone, outside, furious.

Ice beneath my scales made my skin crawl. I shivered nonstop now, as if convulsing. My band might have been lost, but I was still Sookahr, still more than either of them.

You are special.

I thrust my anger into a fist and reached out, slamming it down against the sand. The bank exploded. Particles flew up from the invisible impact, showering us all in a wash of grit. I reeled backwards, feeling for a band that wasn't there. How? Even with the skymetal, I'd never...

"Sookahr?" Lohmeer's voice called to me, but it sounded days away now. Much closer was the rushing of water, the tinkling of grains of sand landing back to earth. The roaring of my own thoughts.

I stared, realizing my mouth hung open. My tongue, when I attempted to use it, fluttered in a spasmodic jerking. The jungle seemed everywhere now, over my head and against my back. Sand made a vertical stripe to one side. I'd fallen, or lain down, and now the water rushed just over my head. Inside my body, ice flowed. I shivered and shivered, unable to stop, unable to make a sound.

"What's wrong with him?" Lohmeer's voice trembled with fear.

"There." The stupid girl joined him. How perfect. They'd make a wretched pair. "It's a fever."

"How?"

"He's let his wound close over. Who knows what's left inside it. You bled freely, wisely. Yours is deeper, but it's stayed clean."

"What do we do?"

Just like that, my companion allied himself with the stranger. I couldn't blame him for it; Lohmeer was the sort that needed a leader. It was the wretched rogue who earned my fury. She'd step in, of course, take his naivety and use it to forge him into her own tool. They'd leave me to die here on the bank, and if she was right about my wound, I had to believe I deserved that too.

I'd been focused on keeping Lohmeer alive. I'd underestimated my own scratch. Or maybe I hadn't wanted to believe it. I'd been unable to believe that Kwirk would strike a mortal blow against me. How I missed his soft paws now. His grouchy voice would chide me for being such a fool, and he'd squeak and remind me that only a neonate would fail to protect himself from such a simple injury.

Then he'd make it go away. With a touch of gentle paws, my mouse would save me. Kwirk would save me, tend me, take me home again. The jungle dimmed, as if a cloud had blotted out the sun. The water hushed in reverence, stilled and silenced, and I lay still and let the fog consume me.

I lay in a ring of black spires. My body curved and twisted between them, as if tying the spikes into a complicated knot, as if holding them to the pale earth. I lifted my head, but the needles reached higher, stretching to the point they seemed to meet above my head. Below, above, and around me, everything else was flat and gray, a void containing only myself and my deadly-sharp creations.

"And me."

I spun to face him. My tongue stretched, and my throat tightened. "Kwirk?"

"Who were you expecting?" His sarcasm had a familiar ring to it, but his eyes still glinted like knives, and I checked his paws quickly for any sign of a weapon. They folded together in front of his vest, empty. But I couldn't quite feel safe.

"I-I thought you'd left me."

"How can I?" In that, there was something darker than sarcasm. I remembered Lohmeer's overheard threat. *Free the slaves.*

"Your eyes are weird again."

"Perhaps you don't know what a mouse's eyes really look like."

I stared into the sharp reflections. I'd seen shades of it before, hints of that edginess whenever Kwirk would skip a meal. Whenever he'd go too long without his grain. Laarahn's voice mocked me, singing in my memory. *Get that mouse some food.*

"It wasn't something you ate, was it? It was something you *stopped*

eating."

"You always were clever." His tone made that less than a compliment.

"Are you a slave? All this time, with me?"

"What do you think?" He didn't twitch a whisker, but his long tail swiped once against the non-ground behind him. The black spires hummed, like skymetal, a single note, droning higher and higher.

"I didn't know."

"Does that make you innocent?"

I stared into those sharp eyes, into a face I'd known my whole life, loved my whole life. I had no answer for him, nor did my alleged ignorance soothe the twisting sensation in my middle. I had no words, but someone else spoke for me.

"It doesn't make him guilty."

I turned again, and this time, my heart leapt. Viir hovered, wings spread to the sides, just beyond my prison of spikes. His scales gleamed, as if a light glowed inside him, and his feathers sparkled like gemstones.

"Viir!" I would have rushed to him then, but the mouse snarled behind me.

"All devils must die."

I spun back, expecting a dart to pierce me. Only Kwirk's eyes stabbed at my scales, however, spilling over with hatred. With justifiable rage.

"It's not your decision." Viir's voice remained calm as a stone. "If you'd succeeded in killing him, you'd have committed murder. Would *you* not be just as guilty then?"

"*I* haven't killed anyone," I argued, but the instant I said it, a memory flooded back. Rolling over hot sand with something squirming in my jaws. "I... I don't think."

Both of them held their tongues then, held still and waited for me to connect the dots. If all rodents in the Burrow were slaves, kept docile by consumption of food laced with poison, then didn't that make us all guilty? From Lohmeer's reaction to it, I could only assume the drug was made from venom similar to the dreaming drink. Didn't that mean someone in the Burrow knew about this? Maybe many someones?

One week.

"There are many paths before you, my friend," Viir said. "It is almost time to choose one."

"What can he do?" Kwirk snarled, still familiar, still my lifelong companion despite his lack of consent. Would I ever be able to think of him as anything else?

"They're going to attack the Circlet," I said. "Aren't they?"

It was too tidy otherwise, too neatly similar. Laarahn had given me a deadline, and that time ran out exactly when the rodents planned their assault. All the pieces fell together, and my outpost was only a step, a false destination on the path to a greater goal.

"I have to stop them."

Kwirk growled. I looked from him to Viir, who'd spread his wings wider and begun to lift into the air. He didn't flap his great, feathery appendages, only waved his tail slightly as if swimming through nothing. His lovely head tilted. Big eyes fixed on me as he rose.

"It's time to choose, Sookahr."

"It's time to do the right thing," Kwirk echoed.

"Wait!" I looked between them, back and forth, over and over. Viir continued to drift upward, and Kwirk faded as if he were made of fog. Both of them left me, one breath at a time, and a new panic squirmed in my stomach. Time to choose?

But was I to do it all alone?

Go forth and change the world.

"No!" I slithered toward my mouse, trembling, shaking as if I meant to dislodge my own scales. "Don't leave me, Kwirk. I need you. I..."

His body solidified again. Tiny paws folded together underneath his chin. Long whiskers tightened against his pointy face. His furry head leaned to one side, and both ears pivoted to catch my words.

"My band is gone." I shivered, fighting back the urge to cry out, to wail and throw myself at his tiny feet. "It's gone. I need your paws. I need—"

He began to laugh. The sound started low, as if it rose through him, before bursting forth. Each guffaw came louder and louder, and as they grew, Kwirk's body faded.

"Do you?" His voice became an echo, a far-off whisper. It mocked me, shamed me, but also dared me. There was something of the old Kwirk in his final words. Something of advice and warning both. "Do you need me, Sookahr? Do you really?"

I swallowed further protest and stared in silence. The black spikes ringed me in, and Kwirk, Viir, everything I loved, faded away into the empty void.

DISBANDED

20

"There was metal in it. Look." An unfamiliar, but somehow annoying voice, spoke nearby. "A sliver of something metal."

I felt a quick pain, so fast I had no time to react. Not that I was certain I could move at all. My whole body felt numb and out of control. Every few breaths, a seizure of shivering took me.

"Will he be okay?" That question, I recognized. Lohmeer had remained with me, which meant I knew the other voice as well. I'd only blotted her from my memory.

"I think so," she answered. "It's out now, clean and dressed. He'll have to rest though."

"Thank you," Lohmeer groveled, expressing his premature gratitude. I hadn't survived yet, nor did I trust my future if the rogue girl was involved.

"I suppose he can stay here."

I opened my mouth to argue, but the movement set off another round of shivering. I assumed they meant to leave me on the river bank. When the spasm ended, however, I sensed the difference. Somehow, I'd been moved. That or I imagined the warm earth beneath me, the firm wall at my back. Not quite as hot as my geothermal shelf, but comfortable, sheltered.

How long had I dreamed?

Their voices faded in and out, or perhaps I drifted into sleep and back. This time I didn't dream, only wandered back and forth between dark unconsciousness and a groggy awareness of shapes and sounds. The third time I came to myself again, my shivering had subsided. My scales felt warm, and I heard the conversation clearly though it had moved, perhaps, farther away.

"What did you do?" Lohmeer's voice rumbled softly.

"What could I?" The girl sounded as sharp and irritating as ever. "I had no choice, did I? Had to find shelter and learn how to eat on my own. *What* to eat on my own."

"I think I'd have died."

"I nearly did once or twice. Before I found this place, I lived under a rock." She laughed, but even that sound had little mirth to it. "I was much smaller then, of course. It was after I found my first meal, followed a bug into its niche and ate it. Then I just settled in and lived right there."

"They didn't even give you a band."

"Didn't need one, did I?"

"But how did you know what to do? Who told you what you're supposed to be?"

"No one. I do what I want, Lohmeer. And most of the time, all you can do out here is survive."

"Without a band."

"It's not so bad, really."

I twisted my head at that, and caught my first glimpse of the room I lay in. The walls and ceiling were cut from grainy soil, and only the floor had been packed properly. Still, the corner I slept in had a smooth concavity, a sleeping basin almost as comfortable as a Burrow shelf. Not nearly as warm, but hardly chilly.

An open doorway marked the far wall, and light spilled from that oval. It cast the contents of my room into deep shadow, a pile of something soft to my right, two huge baskets beside the doorway to the left. It was a serpent's den if I'd ever seen one. The fact that it lacked a shrine and a wall with pipes inside it told me exactly who it belonged to.

Lohmeer's new friend had taken us home.

"What about you?" the girl spoke, and a shadow crossed the lighted portal. "You're happy with your band and your job? What was it again?"

"I'm a builder," he answered with a wistful note in his voice. "But..."

Suddenly, the conversation gripped me tightly. I sensed it. My sturdy companion was about to confess something I knew was coming, something I'd suspected since my final banding. Something I'd seen again and again in the many branching of forked paths.

"I always wanted to cook," he said. "I remember thinking that's what they'd pick for me."

"And they didn't."

"No."

Something rustled, and I heard a scraping of scales as one of them shifted position. I held my breath, shaking from something that wasn't fever anymore.

Finally, the girl asked, "Are you any good at cooking?"

"How would I know?" Lohmeer answered directly, simply, as he always did. "I'm a builder."

If he didn't see the issue with that, if he didn't hear the truth I feared, the girl most definitely did.

"That's stupid," she said. "You just do whatever they tell you to?"

"It's my destiny," he said.

"But they're the ones that told you that."

"Yes."

"And you just believed them?"

Her tone filled me with shame. I'd believed them too. Of course I had, but unlike Lohmeer, I'd never even considered an alternative. I, despite my certainty that I was destined for greatness, hadn't even had the imagination to question.

Did I want to be an architect? Even now I couldn't say. I was certainly good at it, but that could easily be attributed to my training, to applying myself and driving always to be the best I could.

Would I have been equally effective as something else? A weaver like Viir, an engineer, or an artist, or one of the rough-natured beetle tenders? None of them seemed likely or desirable, and yet, I couldn't quite swallow that I was destined for architecture either. Not now. Not when those who'd labeled me such were likely a party to slavery and murder.

"Let's find out for sure." The girl sounded different now, less grating and more playful. "I have some dried beetle and spices here. Cook me something, Lohmeer, and we'll see if you're any good at it."

"Can I really?"

Lohmeer's predictable awe diffused some of my jealousy. He had the strength of a builder, the body for it. Who was to say it wasn't his destiny? Who was *she* to say it? Still, his unmistakable joy at the prospect of cooking weighed against his dull nature. I couldn't begin to guess the answer.

As they began to move about the room outside, I considered dragging myself to join them. I should have, perhaps, stopped what they were doing. Called the blasphemy for what it was. Eventually, Lohmeer would return to the Burrow, to a life cemented into the path of a builder. Would it be kinder or crueler to send him back knowing he preferred to cook?

I should have stopped it, and though I decided as much, I didn't have the strength to move, to drag myself out of the warmth just to crush Lohmeer's excitement. I couldn't do it, and possibly, I thought the rogue girl might be right. I lay in the dimmer room, surrounded by shadows, and thought that she might be right about everything.

And if the strange serpent was right, I had to believe the opposite was true as well. The Burrow was wrong. About the mice and about our paths, and... I tried to think of everything I'd believed simply because it was how things were. Our bands? The ranking of our many types? The benefits of the below-ground and the dangers of above? Everything I'd known was suspect now, but then, maybe it had been for days. Maybe it all fell to shit when my rodent stabbed me.

Maybe everything went back to Kwirk.

A shiver took me then, the cold returned, and I couldn't have said if it was fever or grief. I only knew that I mourned there, alone in the dark. I mourned the loss of more than my faith in society. I grieved for my mouse, for his life as a slave at my side. For the affection that had been false, forced, unwarranted. For my skymetal band and my outpost that would never be built. For my future.

I mourned everything I'd lost, and everything I feared I was about to.

"We have to get back to the Burrow." I held a fourth of my body aloft, the most I'd managed since I'd woken in the girl's room. My muscles trembled at the effort, but I considered it a win. Enough. "They're going to attack the Circlet. I have to warn them."

"You're too weak to go anywhere."

"Teerahl is right." Lohmeer poked his head through the bedroom doorway. He'd made himself at home in Teerahl's den, and both of them had united in an effort to keep me from getting on with my life. "You can barely slither."

"We only have a few days."

"At least five," Lohmeer bobbed his nose up and down, and something out of sight behind him crashed to the floor. "Whoops."

"Concentrate, big guy." Teerahl, our pale, *aspis*-impersonating host, had made it her personal mission to teach Lohmeer to cook. So far, he'd produced a passable beetle stew, and some cakes made from herbs and grub flour that I had to admit were one of the more pleasant things I'd ever eaten.

Which only made her interference more frustrating. What would Lohmeer do, now that he'd discovered how to cook, when he was required to slip back into life as a builder?

"Sip your broth." Teerahl had also taken on the job of nursemaid to me, something I didn't need nor had I asked for. "It'll get your strength back faster, and then you can dash off to warn your overlords of their impending doom."

"They're not my overlords." I leaned toward the bowl she'd rested on the floor beside my bed. Steam wafted from the liquid, carrying a smell that stirred my hunger despite my desire to remain petulant. "I can't even be sure the Circlet knows about the...problem with the rodent's food."

I couldn't bring myself to say slavery, though Teerahl had happily warmed to that term. She'd taken the news of my epiphanies with a glee that only drove my annoyance with her deeper. Lohmeer, for his part, had expressed an initial shock, followed by a stoic acceptance of things that was very true to his nature. It also annoyed me, however.

While I lay incapacitated, the desire to rail at something, to shout and throw things, had only grown more intense. In contrast, both of my companions remained unmistakably, maddeningly calm. They showed absolutely no outward sign that the massive imprisonment and unwilling use of multiple species surprised them in the least. In fact, they both seemed perfectly content to fiddle about the den, making food and chatting about nothing of significance whatsoever.

Through the two days of my recovery so far, I'd learned that Teerahl lived alone in a den she'd discovered as a hatchling. Its previous owner had either moved on or perished. She was a few seasons older than Lohmeer and I, who I now knew had hatched on the same day. I kept that secret to myself, as well as the memory of our first meeting, the ensuing battle, and the meal that followed.

Just thinking about it made my stomach tighten, and Teerahl insisted I still had to eat more before I could leave. She also insisted I rest. And so I remained in the warm basin while she was free to influence Lohmeer without my interference.

Suspicion filled my head as I tapped the broth with my tongue. It was hot, but not enough to burn—sweet, but also rich and heavy. I pressed my nose to the bowl and sucked in a warm mouthful. Teerahl had taken to Lohmeer immediately, and it hadn't take much to work out that the girl was lonely. She'd told us her entire life story at least three times already.

I pieced her history together as I drank, drawing more conclusions, matching the tale of Teerahl with my own, freshly uncovered memories.

"I didn't want to leave my egg at first. It was so warm and the light hurt my eyes. Maybe I stayed too long, but that doesn't excuse what they did. I mean, I was just a baby."

The broth went down too quickly, burned a little in my throat. I reminded myself that she'd been born before us, that she couldn't possibly have been in one of the eggs I'd passed by. I remembered, too, calling and calling for the others to come out, begging them to hurry.

Not all will eat.

I remembered that voice too, knew now where my echo had originated.

"When I did hatch, there was nothing but empty eggs around me. Everywhere I went, the others had already gone on. The sands were warm, but no one remained to greet me. There was nothing. And I was so hungry."

"That's better," she chirped at me now, voice filled with her own success. "You'll be yourself in no time if you drink that up. Ready to take on the world, right? Rush back and save your over—er, your big ol' city."

If I'd had time to get over my crumpled pride, I might have been able to like her. As it was, her story only added to my consternation, to the disaster area that had once been my certain, infallible world view.

"I finally found the exit. They'd left the door open for me, though all the others were shut tight. I assume that's where they took the snakes like you, the ones who got bands and food and a life. I got shown the outside. Just a big ol' "off you go and be on your way, thank you".

"How far is it to the Burrow from here?" I tried to focus on the task at hand: the Circlet and the rodents' plans. Even if my leaders knew about the slavery, I wasn't ready to let them fall just yet. I wanted answers first. I wanted to know why and how and who. Mostly, I wanted it all to be a lie. I wanted to believe our great civilization had grown from more honorable means, that it deserved to thrive.

And turning a hatchling out to fend for herself was kinder somehow than what I'd originally feared. They'd given her a chance, hadn't they? And she'd managed to make the most of it.

"I only heard one thing, just as I was leaving: a voice from somewhere I couldn't see. I remember how scared I was, how cold the outside seemed, and how big. But just as I passed through the door, it whispered to me."

"What did the voice say?" Lohmeer had hung on her story, fixing his gaze on Teerahl as if she were made of truth and freedom.

"It just said, 'good luck'."

I swallowed another mouthful of soup and waited for the outcast to answer me. I needed to go, to get free of this place and the stories. I needed to get Lohmeer away. When Teerahl failed to answer me, I pressed her. "How many days to get there?"

"Not many." She sighed and her body deflated. The ability to puff herself up had lent a great deal to her *aspis* routine, but outside of her threat dance, it just seemed silly. "There's a road your people travel, to and from the place where I was born. It's less than a day from here, and I'm not sure how far south after that. I've never gone that way."

"You've gone the other way? Back to..."

"Sometimes they drop things on the road." She puffed again, pulled herself back and up, and in my current condition I could do nothing to out-pose her. "I found those baskets by the way, and a few other things. I learned how to do stuff by watching them. What to make and how to use it."

162

"I..." In the end, I couldn't imagine it. Teerahl's den had all the comforts of home. Almost. She'd made a life here that was more than satisfactory, if lonely. I tried to believe I could have done as well on my own, but every time I thought of it, my shivers flared up again. "I hope you know that Lohmeer is coming with me."

I hadn't meant to challenge her, only to warn her of the impending separation. A flash of unmistakable fury flickered through her eyes and tongue. She hid it quickly, and rippled in a shrug that was suddenly very Viir-like.

"He can do what he wants."

"Yes, he can."

"And you can leave as soon as you're well enough. Now finish your broth."

"Thank you."

We stared at one another, both of our tongues still and mute. There could be no denying her intentions where Lohmeer was concerned, but in truth, I'd feel bad for her when we left. Maybe there'd be a way to integrate her back into the Burrow. Certainly she'd shown enough strength, enough skill at survival to prove her worth. I almost suggested it then, even opened my mouth before I thought better.

What if they refused her? I no longer trusted the justice of my society, and I was in no place to offer anything. In particular what I wasn't certain I could deliver. I vowed to ask, though. Set my mind to finding a way for Teerahl to come home. Maybe there were others like her too, serpents who'd proven that life without the Burrow was possible.

And even as I thought that, I feared the answer would be no. How many within the Burrow would welcome a change so great? That required so much effort? How many would willingly free the rodents they'd come to rely so heavily upon, even in light of the truth?

I wanted to believe they all would. I wanted to.

"You get some rest." Teerahl eased backwards through the doorway, back to Lohmeer and her treachery.

Lohmeer can choose for himself.

"I know he can," I snapped, and her head jerked as if I'd struck at her.

"What?" She fluttered her tongue.

"I know Lohmeer can choose for himself." I immediately regretted saying it. Teerahl essed and hissed at me, and I scrambled to retrace the conversation. She'd said... Or had she? The words had come clearly in her voice, and yet I'd heard them as I heard the echo. Inside my own head. "In case you were trying to help him decide."

I added it quickly, awkwardly, but it seemed to satisfy her. She puffed again, turned her already upturned nose toward the ceiling, and retreated from my presence.

The sound of Lohmeer clanking filtered through in her absence, and I swear I heard an echo of her previous, unspoken statement.

Lohmeer can choose.

Which should have been impossible. My band was lost, tangled in the viney slope somewhere beyond the river. I had no idea how to get back to it, and no time to waste on the effort either. The Circlet waited. The truth waited. Despite my best instincts, I waited too.

But if my body wasn't ready to race for the Burrow just yet, it didn't mean I had to be idle. My skymetal was lost, as good as gone forever. I should never have been able to smash an invisible fist against the riverbank. I shouldn't have been able to do much more than scratch an itch.

I needed to recover, yes. But while I did, I had some closer truths to work out. To work out on my own, like Teerahl had done.

With a deep breath, I lifted my nose from the broth and focused my intent on the basket beside the doorway. Nothing hummed. No warmth spread through my middle where the skymetal had been. Still, the woven grass crinkled. The basket wobbled where it stood. A little push, a simple thought, and the vessel tumbled onto its side. The flat top fell off, and a cascade of seeds and nuts spilled across the bedroom floor.

"Sookahr?" Teerahl's voice called aloud, an echo whispering behind it.

What now?

"I'm fine," I said. With nothing at all, I willed the contents back into the basket. With a soft thought, I pressed the lid into place and righted the thing, settling it back exactly into the round, dust-free mark it had left on the floor. My tongue extended, flicked, and tasted the miracle. The band was gone. The skymetal was lost.

But I was not.

I coiled back into a knot inside my basin, resting my head against my scales. I breathed, tasted, and thought harder than I'd ever had to. The skymetal amplified the snake. The band boosted the will.

And the mouse served with all his heart, willingly.

In the darkness of Teerahl's room, I rested, though I felt less fatigued than I should have, less strained. My body filled with the warmth of the broth, strengthened and relaxed, and my brain busied itself with counting all the lies.

21

"I'll go with you as far as the road." Teerahl swayed beside her wooden cart. It bore two wheels and had a rod sticking out with a loop on one end which fit over her head, allowing her to guide it along at her side. Lohmeer insisted that she'd built the thing herself.

Two days ago I might have doubted that.

"Thank you." I coiled just outside the entrance to her den while Lohmeer continued to bumble about inside. I feared he delayed our departure on purpose, just as I knew in my heart that he wanted to stay. My mood had soured long before the girl announced that I was ready enough to travel.

Her friendship with Lohmeer had bloomed while I recuperated, and as soon as I slithered from my convalescence, I'd felt like the odd snake out. The invader, pissing all over their good times. Lohmeer's reluctance to show any sign of urgency grated against my scales, even though I couldn't blame him in the least.

I still wanted him at my side.

"We'll barely have time as it is," I spoke to no one, merely spat the thoughts out of my head in the hopes that they'd stop tormenting me. "The attack could happen any second."

My calculations put me at least two days ahead of the rats' forces, but only if he hadn't changed his mind. Only if I had gauged his target correctly.

"Lohmeer, are you ready?" I cast a nervous glance at Teerahl, but she fiddled with her neck-loop and didn't turn in my direction.

I'd seen her use her will to move things more than once, though never anything that confirmed my suspicions about the skymetal. Her telekinesis seemed a frail and unreliable thing, just the sort of level you'd expect from a serpent without a band to amplify her. Mine, on the other hand, had grown undeniably stronger. I could move heavier objects, more things at one time, and suffered next to no fatigue after all but the most monumental efforts.

As if to confirm this, I reached for the largest stone lining Teerahl's pathway and shoved it out of position. The stone moved easily at my mind's touch, but instead of satisfaction, I suffered an uneasy trepidation. Why had my powers grown without the band, and more pressingly, what would happen when the Burrow discovered as much?

"Lohmeer?"

"I'm ready." His big head poked out of the den entrance, a crack between two protrusions of rock that would have been difficult to spot if its owner hadn't paved a little pathway to her door. Lohmeer peered out at this, and though he repeated his assurance, "I'm ready to go," I heard the echoing thought despite myself.

If I have to.

The loss of my band had opened that to me as well. I could hear, as clearly as if spoken, the more forceful of my fellows' thoughts. For the life of me, I couldn't figure out how to turn it off.

"It's not far." Teerahl had fit herself into the loop, and now she heaved against it. The wooden cart creaked and began to roll forward, roughly, as if its wheels were slightly off of round. "I take the cart in case I find anything."

"Can I help?" The rest of Lohmeer burst free of the den as soon as Teerahl began to move. He brushed past me, knocked over half her tidy rocks, and slithered to catch up with the cart. "Maybe I could push."

I glared at his tail. Then, with but a flick of my awareness, I righted the stones, shoving everything back into position, and feeling a sense of pride despite myself. No serpent I'd known could manipulate so many items in unison. Had Viir seen, he'd already be dragging me to the game room.

Perhaps.

My belly squirmed, as it did lately whenever I thought of my *aspis* friend. Did Viir know about the mice? I tried and tried to guess his reaction to the news, but each time I considered it, the sick sensation returned. Would my band-less strength please or horrify Viirlahn? I couldn't know for certain until I saw him again.

"I thought you were in a hurry?" Teerahl's taunting dragged me back to present.

"Coming." I slithered after them.

166

The day had begun in a chill shadow, but the sun already burned away the last traces of clouds. Warmth built in the stones and earth, and the fringes of the jungle stood in dark contrast to the bright forest where Teerahl had found her home. I stared back once, at that wall of fronds. My skymetal waited out there, and I'd thought more than once about suggesting we hunt for it.

Time pressed at me, but here the danger of the rats seemed far away, and my band so very close. I riffled a clump of nearby grass with my thoughts and turned my back to the jungle. A traitorous thought whispered that I didn't need it, that the band had been a chain, holding me back.

My body shivered. Even to think it felt like rebellion. But amplified powers or no, I'd still be a non-person inside the Burrow. I still had to fight my way back in, to convince whoever would listen that I was in earnest, that the danger I warned of was real and pressing.

I had to get to Laarahn.

Lohmeer traveled behind Teerahl's cart, head higher than I'd ever seen him carry it. His tail moved before me, back and forth. It had healed nicely. I forced my gaze up, to the pale sky, the bright clouds, and the flutter of leaves from the trees around us.

In contrast to the jungle we'd left, the forest here barely reached the height of that lowest branch where Lohmeer had slept. The growth was sparse, with wide swatches of wiry grass between the trees. The bark on those was flaky, peeling away in random patches like a snake having a difficult shed.

The cart bounced along a faded track which I could only assume Teerahl herself had worn, dragging the thing back and forth to the road for her stolen treasures. Not that I could blame her for gathering what she could of Burrow life. Her meager comforts, and the way she guarded them, only made me feel worse about her situation. About the situation of any hatchling too slow to win the prize of Burrow life.

A safe, pampered life.

My thoughts whispered blasphemy about the cost of that, hissing to me in Kwirk's voice. I silenced my doubts by focusing on the leaves, by subtly shifting one branch after another as I passed below them. Easy. As simple as wiggling my own tail.

"Do you think they'll let you in again?" Teerahl's chipper voice broke my concentration, causing one of my targets to lash back sharply. I heard the whipping of it above my head and glared at her.

"I think I can ask for Laarahn easily enough," I said, pressing more confidence than I felt into the statement. The guards at any exit would be vipers, stout serpents with scales like Ghost's, with hooded eyes and viper dispositions.

Maybe they'll turn us away.

I ignored Lohmeer's thought and focused on Teerahl. "It was Laarahn who sent us to the outpost. I'm certain he'll be relieved to hear *we've* returned."

The news of our dilemma would have long since reached my mentor. If they'd sent the help I requested, then those serpents would meet the same fate that we did. Rats in the outpost, mice stealing our supplies. I prayed to the Sage that they'd survive the ordeal. Maybe they'd defeat the rodents before they could execute their plan. Word of the attacks may even now be on the way to the Circlet through other channels.

Maybe they didn't need me at all.

"It's just over that next rise." Teerahl pulled her wagon to a halt and wriggled free of the loop. "I don't take the cart all the way to the road."

"You think they'd try to take it from you?" Lohmeer asked, voice dripping with sympathy and adoration both. He'd taken the girl's side the instant she'd told us her story, possibly the instant he'd laid eyes on her. "That's not fair."

"I dunno." She shrug-shivered and fluttered her tongue. "But it's better if they don't see it."

"Wouldn't want them to know you're taking their stuff." I felt compelled to add it, to remind Lohmeer that she scavenged the wood and wheels from a crashed Burrow vehicle, that she sniped whatever goods fell from Burrow carts as they passed.

"Only what they leave behind." Lohmeer defended her, but he had the sense to lower his head, to look sheepish about it.

My scales were all in a prickle just the same. I knew it had little to do with him, or even with Teerahl, but they made an easy target to lash out at. It should have shamed me, but deep in my belly, a dread had been building all morning. It turned my thoughts dark, stirring my old fear of failure into a whirlwind of doubts.

What if they *didn't* let me in? If Laarahn could not be summoned, who would listen to my tale? He'd kept the whole thing so secret. What if he hadn't told anyone about the outpost? He might have sent a select few to bring us supplies and assistance, but what if they died at the rats' paws?

Frantic, I turned to Lohmeer, certain that ordering him into a faster pace might relieve some of my tension. When I saw the way he drooped, however, I couldn't bring myself to crush him further. His head hung from his neck as if it had been broken, nose dragging, just skimming the tips of the grass as he went. He sagged as if his reluctance were a physical thing, a paw dragging him backwards even as he continued to move.

Guilt swamped my other misgivings. I felt myself sagging too, slithering with a sluggish gait toward the roadway Teerahl had promised. Two days at best to sound the alarm, if my message hadn't already been delivered.

We topped the hummock of grass and gazed down upon our

destination. The roadway had been packed into a rough pavement by Burrow engineers, but wheel ruts made squiggles over the surface, marking where the carts traveled. Many pathways again, but this time, all running in the same direction: either to or from the Burrow. At least three carts could have passed in the width of the road, and the sides had been bermed up to keep the beetles from wandering toward any off-road distractions.

Toward the south it curved and snaked between the scattered trees, but to the north, the jungle fell away quickly and the road followed its edge only until it broke on an expansive grassland which stretched as far as my eyes could see.

"It's very close to your den," Lohmeer said sadly.

"She didn't go far from the Burrow at all." I sniffed and stretched my tongue out as far as it would reach.

"Would you?" Teerahl asked.

Her voice held a challenge, but I heard wistfulness too, a deep sadness that lingered behind all of her attitude. I thought again of asking her to return with us, but my fear for my own reception argued that it would be far harder to bring two un-banded serpents through the gates. I would ask on her behalf, once the danger had passed, but I didn't hold any high hopes for the answer.

My faith in my people had died.

I held very little hopes at all for that matter, and standing beside the roadway, the truth of that could no longer be shoved aside. Lohmeer would never abandon me, never ask to remain behind; the constrictor's loyalty would never allow him to. I knew what he wanted just the same. I couldn't un-know that any more than I could stop hearing his dejected thoughts.

Which was probably why I'd imagined returning alone all along.

"I think you should stay with Teerahl," I said. I didn't look up from the road, didn't need to see their reaction to know I'd showered relief upon them. "You'll be happier there, and she won't have to be alone."

"What about you?" Lohmeer's concern failed to mask his excitement.

"I'll be fine." I sniffed again, raised my head higher into the air and lied my tail off. "Laarahn will let me in. We'll get word to the Circlet, and everything will be fine."

"Are you sure?" So much hope in those three words, and so much fear of my answer that I had only one to give.

"Yes." I turned my gaze south, toward home and everything I'd ever wanted. Everything I'd ever believed in. Everything I doubted now. "You stay here. I think that's for the best."

"Yes, sir!"

And just like that, I was on my own. Lohmeer had been waiting for an order, and he took it merrily. Teerahl fell uncharacteristically silent, and the road continued to exist below us. I fluttered my tongue in both directions,

found only faded traces of serpents, beetles, and wood. There was no one coming, no reason to wait any longer.

"I should be going." I nodded and failed to move.

"You could stay with us," Lohmeer offered, brave now that his own future was right where he wanted it.

I looked to Teerahl, expecting to see the opposite sentiment. Instead, she only offered me a sage nod, one with a little too much pity attached.

"No, I've got to get word back. Should have left days ago." I slithered to the lip of the slope, grass that rippled down toward the berm and the road beyond. "Goodbye Lohmeer, Teerahl. Thank you both for all the help."

I hurried then, sliding down the bank with their return goodbyes vibrating against the side of my head. I didn't look back, not until I'd reached the bottom, climbed over the berm, and made my way into the very center of the road. The ruts were hard lumps against my belly, but the sun had warmed them. I fixed my direction south, stretched into a long traveling pose, and then glanced quickly toward the rise again.

Only Lohmeer remained, and even as I looked, he turned away to follow his new destiny, and the rogue girl, away from his life as a builder. I couldn't blame him for leaving. In a world where my own mouse could betray me, where bands fell away and lies hissed from every corner, I hoped that Lohmeer found happiness cooking in Teerahl's den.

For me, there was only the road ahead, the task to be done, and the faint whisper of an old echo.

Go forth.

With a deep breath and a soft hiss, I obeyed. The washboard passed below me—warm, cool, warm, cool. The sunlight made my path a glowing plain that forced my eyes to rise a little toward the leaves and the branches above it. Teerahl hadn't known how far the Burrow entrance lay in this direction, but according to Laarahn's map, I'd passed the second outpost in arriving at her den. This road carried goods to and from a major exit, and it hadn't been of concern to my project and so hadn't been notated in the diagram.

I only prayed it entered the below-ground soon.

Despite the tending of Teerahl and the solid meal now digesting in my gut, I tired quickly, sooner than I should have. My wound, when I examined it, looked healthy and cool, but my body hadn't fully recovered. I wanted rest and refused to allow it. By the time the sun had marked its zenith, I dragged my scales over the wagon tracks.

In the distance, I thought I saw a lifting of the earth between the trees. It could have been the entrance I sought, or it could have been another hummock, a slight rise like the one I'd left behind me. Either way I pressed forward, certain that I was closing in on my goal. When the sound of cart wheels reached me, my heart leapt. I rallied my willpower and slithered faster.

Between the trees, a wagon appeared. Huge horned beetles pulled at the traces and the box had been piled with sacks and crates. Two rodents curled on top of the cargo, asleep or huddled together for other reasons. On either side of the vehicle, a serpent traveled. From this distance I couldn't make out their type or pattern, but the glinting of scales filled me with both a surge of hope and a tremble of fear.

The space where my band should have rested felt too cold, exposed and pale in the sunlight. I lifted my head, increased the fury of my slithering, but held that empty segment to one side as much as possible. As the cart neared, I watched its guardians solidify. Both of them were ordinary snakes like myself, thin of body and devoid of venom. The smaller of the two had saddles, dark against a pale background, and his companion bore three wide stripes down his entire length.

When we'd closed our gap enough that I could hear the clicking of the beetles, I coiled to the side of the road and, tucking my empty midsection behind a loop of tail, waited for them to reach me.

"Good afternoon, traveler," the striped one called out.

"Afternoon," I answered. Pulling myself into a pose to match the height they carried themselves, I fluttered my tongue in a peaceful wave and hugged my coils tighter. "Could you tell me how much farther it is to the Burrow?"

"Oh it's not much more than a..." He began to answer, but his spotted partner hissed and lifted two thirds of his skinny body into the air. I saw the flash of skymetal around his middle, and knew at once that he'd noted that lack on my part.

"Who are you?" the little one demanded. "What business do you have on this road?"

"I am Sookahr the architect," I said. "And I—"

"Band-less." The striped fellow caught up with us, interrupted me with a spat insult and a low hiss. "Get off our road, outcast."

"I'm not—"

"Go on," the little guy shouted over me. "He told you to leave the road. This is Burrow property, not the wilds."

I wanted to argue with them, to plead my case and my cause, but I'd have to do it all over again once I reached the Burrow entrance, and these two could not allow me access nor advance me toward my goal either. My indignation, however, lifted me higher.

"Don't you dare," stripes warned.

"Thinks he's an *aspis*," his partner eased closer to me, lifting despite his shorter body in an attempt to out posture me. "Keep it up and we'll show you what these bands are for."

Two bands hummed atop the cart. In the center of the road, a handful of pebbles lifted into the air. They meant to fling them at me, to strike me down if I dared continue occupy a road I had every right to travel.

I could have taken them both, perhaps. I could have flipped their cart and spilled their cargo to the ruts even without a band. Maybe *because* I lacked one. The stones and the little one's posing tempted me. One small nudge and he'd be pressed to the dirt. But there was something about him, something that reminded me of myself, and the shame of that pulled me back down, turned me away, and sent me slithering over the berm and off "their" road.

For some reason, I thought of Tuhmaak. Had I seemed to him like these idiots? Had I bullied him because of something as ridiculous as how he held his head? Perhaps. I'd been so focused on my outpost, on proving myself and increasing my status. It had meant everything to the Sookahr who'd left the Burrow, but what did it mean to the one who returned?

What did anything mean?

I slipped down the far side of the berm and followed it, as low as I could hold myself, slithering like a worm at the side of the road, but not allowed to tread upon it. What would all the status of the *aspis* mean without their rodent slaves to carry them? If their bands fell off, would even the Circlet be reduced to dragging their bellies in the dust?

I flicked my tongue, tasting rock and dirt and desperation. If my band were restored, could I go back, be that same Sookahr again? Once inside the Burrow, how could I possibly go on as I had before, as if my eyes were still closed? That egg had cracked, split open, and allowed the light inside. I feared, even if I passed the guards and made it inside, that I could never be a citizen of the below-ground again.

22

I stopped moving without meaning to. Long before the sun had reached the horizon, my scales stilled. I lay, stretched to my full length, in the shadow of the berm. I breathed, and from time to time I flicked my tongue, but I had no intention of doing anything else. Maybe I meant to die there and keep all my secrets from infesting the Burrow. Then I heard the echo singing.

You are special. You are strong.

My head lifted slowly, as if my chin had grown roots.

Rest, beloved. Sleep and dream.

I knew that voice so fully that it might have been my own thoughts. This time, however, it came from outside my memory, pressing against the side of my head as if it had spoken aloud.

You are special.

I raised myself until I could peer over the top of the berm. A cart like I had never seen before worked its way over the ruts, bouncing, one bump at a time. It was heading north and pulled by a single, flat-backed beetle with long antenna and round spots across its carapace. The box was low and wide, and supports at its corners held up a woven canopy which blocked any view of its cargo. No serpent slithered beside the beetle, but a white rat perched on the seat up front, and a stout viper brought up the rear. His scales made a thick armor along his spine, and the ridges over his eyes had been pierced and studded with heavy rings. The base of his tail ended in a series of translucent rattles.

My tongue fluttered, just above the mounded soil, but I didn't dare reveal myself any further.

Dream and grow. Be strong.

How many times had that voice sung to me? I knew it so deeply that it eased my fear of the guard. My head raised too far, and the viper spotted me.

"Halt." He stopped, but the cart continued to roll past. "Sahveen! Stop the wagon."

You are special.

All my life I'd believed that, that I was destined for greatness. All because *this* voice had told me as much. I stared at the covered bed now, and my whole length trembled.

"Who are you?" The guard moved his body in between the cart and the roadside. "Why are you lurking beside the road?"

"I am Sookahr, the architect. I've lost my band while stationed at an outpost near here."

"Lost your band?" His head raised. I saw suspicion in his eyes, and I heard a confrontation in the humming of his skymetal, a stout ring easily as wide as the one I'd lost.

"We ran out of supplies," I said. "I lost too much weight and it slipped free."

"Where?" He snapped the question. Behind him, the wagon's cover rippled.

"In the jungle." I swallowed a surging of fear and stared past him to that curtain. "Who is in there?"

"None of your business, band-less."

"But I know that voice. I heard her—"

"What voice?" The viper curled his neck into an ess and lifted. His flat head turned left and right, examining the berm to either side of me. "Are you alone out there?"

"But I heard her singing. I remember it."

"You need to move along." He eased toward me, still scanning, as if I'd hidden a band of rogues behind the berm and meant to leap upon his wagon. "Go on. Leave us be."

Sookahr.

"Yes, it's me!"

"I said move along."

"He is alone," a new voice spoke, soft as a breeze and coming from inside the wagon. "Let him come."

"He is band-less, an outcast." The viper made no move to allow me passage. "It's not safe."

Come closer.

I climbed the berm despite the rattling of the viper's tail. It would be suicide to press him further, but the voice was on my side. Whether he could hear it or not. My position, perched on top of the mound, lifted me too high, and I lowered my head to the ground in deference. Not retreating, but holding my ground as politely as possible.

"I said—" He essed and readied his deadly strike, but stopped short when a pale nose poked out of the curtain.

"Let him come, Naaraht. I wish to speak with *Sookahr the architect.*" A slender head, larger than mine and shaped similarly to Lohmeer's, emerged from the wagon. Every scale on it shone pure white, but the eyes were as black as the all-dark. "Stand down. We can camp here for the night."

"There's plenty of light left," the viper argued.

"I said we shall camp here."

He won't hurt you.

Despite the silent assurance, I waited until her guard relented. He flashed me a final glare, rattled his tail menacingly, and then turned back to the road, keeping his eyes on me until the last second. Once he had, I skidded down the berm and back onto the roadway.

The viper slithered to the far side of the cart, and I eased my way, one rut at a time, to the rear of the wagon. The white snake watched me come, but didn't emerge any further. Only her head and the first few scale rows of her neck were visible, and though her eyes fixed on me, her thoughts seemed aimed elsewhere.

Rest, beloved. Sleep.

"That's you, isn't it? Your voice?"

"It is." Her tongue slid out and down, fluttered softly and took in my scent. "And you can hear me. I wonder, Sookahr, how that is?"

"When I lost my band," I said, easing closer and coiling into a low knot, "I could hear my friend too, when he thought something really loud."

"How interesting." She withdrew her tongue and tilted her head to the side. "Come closer so I can look at you."

"I remember your voice." I uncoiled and slithered nearer, until our noses faced one another and her eyes looked down at me like twin black pools. "I've heard it in my head my whole life."

"Sookahr, Sookahr. Oh yes. I remember few of my children, you know. There are so many. Still, you feel very familiar. And also very lost."

"Your children?" My throat dried around the words.

"Well, not entirely mine. Look, see what I mean." She turned her head to the side and used her nose to nudge open the curtain.

I leaned forward, slithered a hair closer, and peered into the wagon. At first all I could make out were the folds of her body, silvery pale and piled up in great increasing loops. She was built like Lohmeer as well, and yet, without a trace of his clumsiness.

"I am Sahveen," she whispered. "And these have been entrusted to me. I will deliver them safely to the nursery caverns, and there I will watch over them until they hatch. Though they did not come from my body, I am egg-mother to each one."

"And to me?" I held my breath. Between two of her coils I could make out the shapes, curving surfaces, pale and rough, just a shade darker than their guardian. The wagon bed was full of eggs, and Sahveen hugged them to her as if they were the world's treasure.

"Yes."

"And the singing, 'you are special, you are the one'?"

"This is the birthing chant, the words of each egg-mother as she urges her children to emerge. Just as I will keep them warm and safe, so I must coax each hatchling toward its destiny."

"So you tell them *all* that?" I curved away, rewrapping my coils tighter and shaking my head at her. "I remembered it. All this time. You said I was special and... It's just another lie. You— I'm not any different? Not special, not destined for greatness?"

"Sookahr," Sahveen's voice purred.

I wanted to shout at her, to feel angry, but the revelation only settled on top of the rest of my horrors, comfortable there and unsurprising after all. "No. I understand."

"Sookahr, listen to me." She thrust her head forward until our noses bumped together. "Pay attention now, to your egg-mother."

"But—"

A low hiss silenced my protest.

"You've remembered the song your whole life, is that right?"

"Yes." Heat flooded below my scales. I lowered my nose to the ruts and let my muscles sag.

"Who else do you know that recalls their birth? Who else has heard the chant after their banding? And who, do you think, among all the Burrow's, citizens, could hear me sing it now?"

"I-I don't know of anyone."

"Nor do I." Something in her voice lifted my chin. I stared into her large eyes and felt myself falling forward, reaching for something inside them.

You are special, Sookahr. Of course you are.

Doubt hissed in the back of my mind, reminded me she told all her "children" the same lie. Still, those eyes held me, bored into me as if expecting me to argue. Or to do something. I leaned into that feeling instead. There'd been too much disappointment in the last few days for another loss to join them. I needed something, anything to keep me going, or I feared I would return to my rut beside the road and lay down forever.

Was it a test? Sahveen stared and I listened with my entire body, listened for a clue or an answer. The echo had been with me forever. Here was its source. What could I possibly give her in return that might impress myself upon her? That might prove she was right. I *was* special. The echo...

The echo.

I held my breath, pressed my tongue tight between my lips, and *thought* at her.

Is everything a lie?

Well done, beloved. Now do you see?

I do not. My heart raced. I felt a warm tingle of something pleasant, a sensation that stood in stark contrast to the desperation that had filled me. I could do it. My thoughts could echo too.

"How many do you know who can speak with their minds, Sookahr?" She returned to speaking aloud, and I heard the guard's scales rustle. He'd settled in near the beetle, but I knew he listened, that he didn't trust me any more for Sahveen's interest in me.

I lowered my voice to a whisper. "No one."

You see?

Sahveen stirred inside the curtain. I felt more than saw her body shiver.

"Are you well?" A dash of concern flitted over my newfound pride. If Sahveen was the only serpent in the world who knew I was special, my recent luck would have her dying of some mysterious illness soon.

"Very well. See for yourself." The curtains parted further, and as I looked on, the white coils trembled again. "I must keep them warm, Sookahr, for they have been entrusted to me. It isn't a long journey to the nursery, but surely too long for such fragile cargo."

"Do all egg-mothers sing to their hatchlings?"

"The chanting is one of our oldest traditions." There was so much pride in her voice then that my face heated. A little shiver traveled down my spine, a microcosm compared to her mighty efforts to keep the eggs warm and safe. Until they hatched.

"I remember," I began. "Hatching and...and my first meal."

Sahveen hissed softly, a friendly shushing sound, but her head turned toward the side of the wagon where the guard rested. I sensed she feared his rat would hear us, that the secret of our initial meal was exactly what I'd feared it to be.

"I never see them after that, you know." She shivered again and stared past me, toward the lowering sun. "You're the first of my children whom I've met again, after setting them free in the world. I would like very much to speak with you, to answer your questions."

"I have quite a few."

Sahveen laughed, a sound like a whisper in its own right. "Very well.

Camp with us, Sookahr. Stay with me tonight. I mustn't linger for long, but what answers I have will be yours."

"Thank you." I lowered my head.

The wagon creaked as my egg-mother settled herself more comfortably around her cargo. The eggs she guarded had not come from her body, but she tended them as if they had, crooning silently and shivering her scales to heat them. I coiled myself into a knot below her, against the edge of her wagon where the last rays of the sun still tapped the ruts. A heaviness settled around us both, and though I had a million things to ask her, we fell into a reverent sort of silence until full dark fell.

Even then, it was Sahveen who spoke first.

"You are fatigued, Sookahr. I sense your journey wears at you."

"It has been very long." My own voice sounded far away. I lifted my head, realized I'd been slipping away, and shook off the first fog of sleep. "And less than pleasant."

"You must tell me." She'd tucked her chin up on the wagon's gate, but the curtain fell around her head, so that only her nose and eyes were still visible. "I would know your story, little Sookahr. Tell me what has brought you back to me tonight."

"Where should I start?" I raised my head enough to prevent sleep from sneaking up on me. Sahveen's eyes reflected the stars, and despite my desire for answers, I couldn't resist her offer. Couldn't refuse a chance to tell her my story. "There's so much."

"Let's start with what brought you here. Where did your adventure begin, Sookahr, and what sent you forth from the Burrow to find me?"

"It was Laarahn that... No. That's not true. It was you, really. Your words that convinced me I could do it. Laarahn might have offered me the chance to go, but I *believed* I could change the world because of you."

"Can't you?" she asked. "Can't anyone change the world, Sookahr?"

"Maybe." I shook my head. She'd confessed that she told all her children the same thing, but still she believed it was true. I wanted to join her in that, but it left me feeling more confused than confident. "But Laarahn wanted me to design a new defense, an outpost to show the Circlet."

"For the convention tomorrow." She sighed. "So much fuss."

"Tomorrow?" I jerked up, suddenly fully awake. "No. I have to be there. I have to warn them."

I uncoiled, shaking, certain I was already too late. I'd been so sure that I had a few more days, so convinced that destiny had brought me to Sahveen, that it would allow me a breath to spend in her company.

"Sookahr." She poked the rest of her head from the wagon and hissed until I ceased my thrashing. "I had hoped to hear your story tonight. But instead you must *show* me. Hurry, little one, come closer."

"The Circlet is in danger," I said. "I have to go."

"If you travel well this night, you still might make the Burrow by dawn. You have time, though perhaps not as much as you'd hoped. If there is a threat coming, I must know of it as well. The eggs, Sookahr. The nursery could be in danger too. Now come."

The last was an order, and I moved to answer it without fully meaning to. My head swayed closer to the white snout. She glowed in the wan light, looking like a dream, and her voice came in an even meter, chanting inside my head.

Open your mind to me. Open. Give me your thoughts, your heart, your memories.

I felt a pressure behind my eyes, as if a great noise vibrated there. And yet, there was no sound, only the soft breathing of Sahveen and the gentle rattle of her scales as she continued to shiver around her clutch. My vision began to cloud, as if I drifted to sleep and her thoughts sang to me.

Open your mind. Show me.

I tensed for just a breath, an instinctive defense against so intimate an invasion. Then I let go. My muscles turned to water, my bones melted, and all my thoughts were lain open as Sahveen slithered inside my mind. I watched my journey unfold as if I were a spectator. I saw Laarahn again, evaluating my final project. I saw my banding and cringed as the bolt was hammered into place.

One by one the events of the last few days played out inside my mind's eye, and as they did, I felt Sahveen's presence, her observation, like a tiny prickle overlain atop my memory. She witnessed the night Kwirk tried to kill me. She watched as we discovered Ghost's body, and she knew my misery as the infection set in, as my fevered mind unraveled the new truths that had been bared to me along the way.

Teerahl and Lohmeer said goodbye again, and I felt Sahveen's touch inside my head as a whisper of sympathy. When I met the hostile wagon on the road, when I limped over the berm in shame, her presence soothed away my grief.

When it ended, Sahveen hissed softly and I felt her slip away from me. So many trials.

"The rat leader means to attack the Burrow." I fixated on the one thing that I could possibly act upon. "I have to—"

Hurry.

"You must hurry, Sookahr. Yes. You must warn the Circlet before they convene at midday. I fear their arrogance has left them vulnerable, and if these wild rodents are not stopped, we'll all face the same danger. But remember, your strength will not hold out forever. Even those who would change the world must rest."

"But..." I struggled to focus, head still swimming in the montage of my own thoughts. "Are our rodents really slaves? What about the..."

I trailed off, casting a nervous glance toward the side of the cart where Naaraht lay, certainly alert, likely eavesdropping. Did his rat listen as well?

"I regret that I won't have time to explain, that I cannot offer you the answers I promised." Sahveen lifted her head until her curtain bunched near the top of its support. "Know this much. Some of the things you fear are true, but some are...not exactly as you imagine them."

I thought of that first meal, then. Of stolen mouse babies and hatchlings that refused to eat them. Of turning out the weak, or rather, those perceived as less than worthy. I couldn't paint Teerahl as a weakling for a second, even if I wasn't her biggest fan. All the things I wanted Sahveen to explain to me danced past in that moment, but I latched onto the one that affected me the most, the curiosity she'd only just ignited.

"You said no one remembers their birth after the banding." My tongue slipped out and down, as if testing the air for lies. "Why not? Why can't we all remember our hatching?"

"Can you not guess that as well?" She fluttered her tongue and I heard the soft humming of a band, a sound that sent a pang of longing through me, even now. "Let me give you a hint. I suspect you have some resistance to the dreaming drug?"

"Actually, I've been told I'm very easy to set dreaming." I remembered Mohjiir's assessment, and the fact that I'd dreamed without the drug before we'd even started.

"Interesting," Sahveen hissed. "I wonder what it means."

Her fascination with me eased the blow a little, or perhaps I'd only already suspected it. They drugged us before they banded us, wiped our memories clean, and then locked us into a path of their choosing. How could I ever go back to that? Would I ever willingly slither inside the banding room again?

"One more thing, Sookahr, and then you must go." Sahveen's band sang now, a high-pitched hum that suited her perfectly. Whatever she worked at clattered inside the cart. "It would not be wise to show them, show anyone what you can do without your band. What you're capable of. Nor will they let you through the door without something like... Let me see."

The curtain rippled as a small object bumped into it. Sahveen's band hummed. Her nose nudged the cloth aside, and a miniature skymetal ring floated free of the wagon.

"It's only a neonate band," she said, "but it should get you inside the Burrow."

I eyed the tiny thing and then, as she guided it toward my tail, reached out with a thought and snatched it in the other direction. I had no desire to lose another band, and this ring would hardly reach my first narrow stripe. I guided it instead to my nose and slipped it over my head. It wedged there, just behind my eyes, hugging my lower jaw and not quite hindering my breath.

"Amazing." Sahveen stared at me. "You've given *me* a few questions to ask, Sookahr, and yet, our time has run out. You must come to the nursery cavern the moment you are able. Promise me that. I feel there is more to your story than what you seek today. You have more to show me, and I would get the chance to see it."

"I will try to come." I lowered my head in respect and thanks both. The tiny band stuck with me, not as tight as a bolted one, but in no danger of slipping either.

Come and find me.

"Now you must fly," she hissed and pulled her head back inside the wagon. "I fear you have a long night, a long journey ahead of you."

"Thank you, Sahveen." I stretched my coils for traveling and turned toward the south. The last glimpse I caught of my egg-mother were the tips of her forked tongue, the last bit of her to retreat behind her curtain again. The guard's tail rattled softly, but if it was a warning or a farewell, I couldn't have said.

I set my path firmly toward the Burrow, and began my race for home.

DISBANDED

23

The night passed without event. I slithered freely down the road, accosted only by the creeping chill which dared to drag at my flanks. I longed for a warm shelf then, either the basin at Teerahl's or my own den in the Burrow. My muscles felt heavier with each rut I skimmed over, and my mind slowed until I feared I'd lose my forward momentum entirely and sleep right where I slithered.

Eventually, the trees shifted from black skeletons to softer forms and more complex textures. Fluttering leaves and bark that flaked less here, that bore deep trenches and began to look a great deal more familiar. Before the all-dark, Kwirk and I had wandered amid such trees, and though the thought of my mouse brought a twinge of fear and shame mixed, I felt a renewed energy, an elation that feigned warmth enough for me to continue my slithering.

Or perhaps it was only that the sun had finally reached me.

Whatever the reason, I hurried once more. Before I'd passed three trees, I heard the rumble of a wagon's wheels. The ground before me lifted into a hill, but the road had been cut through this. As I approached the channel, a cart pulled into view at the other end.

My stomach tightened. Though I bore the neonate ring upon my brow,

I was no more banded than I'd been the day before. I held my head lower than I desired but kept moving forward. If the cart's owner meant to throw me from the road, they'd have to allow me to reach beyond the hill to do so, and that would only carry me closer to my goal.

This time, as I passed the beetle and her serpent guides, no one shouted at me. The nearest snake cast a curious glance, and the mice whispered. Wretched, squeaky accusations that chased me past faster than their masters' curiosity had. I continued with my heart racing and without molestation, though the next bend in the road brought a trio of stout constrictors on their way out into the world. Again I earned only the assortment of glances, a low whisper and nothing more.

Sahveen had done me a great service in lending me the band, and I lifted my head higher. The hills continued to rise beyond the first, but the road lowered so that I knew I neared an entrance to the below-ground long before the telltale pyramid poked over the next rise. At first sight, I cringed and checked the sky, looking around lest an army of rats were prepared to spring from behind the trees.

The next cut brought me to the base of the stone triangle, and there the ground opened. A pair of doors each twice as wide as the outpost's stood open, and two enormous black vipers guarded the entrance. They reminded me instantly of Ghost, save for the lack of eye ridges and the elongated rattles at the stub of their tails.

I slithered for the entrance as if I might pass unnoticed, as if the tiny ring would buy me free passage into the Burrow. My head lifted to just below the vipers' level, and I kept my eyes forward and the tips of my tongue just visible as I neared them.

"Halt." They both said it, but in such perfectly orchestrated timing that the word sounded amplified, as if it came from one mouth, but with twice the force.

I froze in my track. My head lowered without my willing it to. My plan had been to bluff my way in, to feign confidence and so convince them that I had every right to enter here.

"What sort of band is that?"

I couldn't have said which serpent said it, but the timber of his voice thumped against my belly.

"A neonate ring." The truth spilled from my lips, as if the tone of the guard's voice had summoned it. "Given to me by the egg-mother Sahveen."

They fell silent, as if the white snake's name had summoned stillness. A distant cart wheel creaked. Scales behind me brushed softly against the road.

"What business do you have here?" One of them spat the question.

I stared into the Burrow's maw and cleared my throat. "I have an urgent message for instructor Laarahn."

"Concerning?"

The sharp rattle of a tail prodded me to answer, yet my mind whirled. How much of my tale would serve me here, and what truth might get me tossed from this door forever? I remembered Sahveen's caution, but also the urgency of my warning. These two guards had no rats at their sides, but only a few more lengths inside there would be rodents everywhere.

"Concerning his presentation today at the convention of the—"

"Stop!" His shout was punctuated by the rattling of two enormous tails. One guard leaned his massive head down, and the other looked from side to side as if checking to see if we'd been overheard. "You're here for *that*?"

"Yes."

"The nannies sent you?"

I balked at his term for my egg-mother, but had already dug myself into this trench. Backing up now would only weaken my position. "I was sent by the egg-mothers, yes."

"Very well." He snapped back to his original position so fast that his partner buzzed at him. They exchanged a look I couldn't begin to decipher, and then a slow tongue flutter released me from my terror. "Go quickly. Find this instructor and keep your mouth shut about it."

"Yes. Yes, sir." I raced away, expecting them to call me back at any moment. If the convention of the Circlet was so secret that they assumed anyone who knew about it had a place here, how were the rats so well informed? I took the first ramp down once inside the gaping entrance. The hallway immediately narrowed, and I felt a flush of safety, a sense of being secure for the first time since entering the jungle. Still, I had no time to enjoy it, and threw myself down ramp after ramp, counting levels as I went.

Of course, no one kept secrets from their rodents. I realized how many times I'd confided in Kwirk, how I'd viewed him as an extension of myself. If just one of our mice were a spy, the enemy would know too much. Could easily know everything about us.

I'd never explored this end of the Burrow, and found myself unfamiliar with most of the levels I passed. Had I gone too deep and missed my target? How many tiers of housing sat above the instruction rooms in this section? I picked one at random, slithering past a group of students who all stared at me as if I were a ghost. The band on my head would draw attention anywhere I went, and if I continued to thrash around in a panic, I was liable to waste more time than I had.

I pivoted in the middle of my slither and turned back to find the group still gaping at me.

"What's the fastest way to the Spire?" I threw the question at them, and a few of the smaller snakes flinched. One girl, a constrictor of similar build to Lohmeer but with tidy saddles instead of blotches, raised her head enough to make eye contact.

"Take the next left and keep going past the libraries," she said. "You can't miss it."

"Thank you."

"Are you from the above-ground?" Her friend, a slender mid-shade snake with a single white stripe along her spine grew brave, leaning forward to peer up at my ring.

I lifted just a little higher. The walls were so dark around us, even with the bounced light glowing from its shafts. There was warmth flowing beneath the floor. Safe and comfortable. I eyed each snake in their little crowd, noting the wide eyes, and also the heavy skymetal bands bolted around their midsections.

"Are you?" The first girl repeated her friend's question, and there was a note of awe in her voice.

"Yes." I nodded and lifted myself high above them. "Thank you."

I turned on my tail and shot off in the direction she'd indicated. Their whispers followed me, filled me with a new sensation, a pride that had nothing to do with my type or my work either. Rooms passed in a blur at either side of the tunnel. The light shafts became bright dots traveling in the opposite direction. I went left when the next passage arrived, slithered faster as the rooms became larger. My tongue caught the scent of paper, of oil candles and dust. My belly drank in the heat of the geothermals, and my head spun.

Get to Laarahn. It was all I could manage to focus on. Once I'd delivered my warning, then I could ponder my future here, if I had one, and how I'd ever return to my desk in the center of a room full of serpents destined to be architects.

I barreled forward, and knew I neared the Spire before the next turn revealed it to me. The vibration of many serpents traveling up and down brought an unexpected jolt of happiness. The scent of many musks mingling filled my nostrils and sent a heady wave of dizziness through my body. I flew around the final turn, and with a revived heart, merged into the downward travelers.

I'd more levels to travel than my original estimate, but they passed quickly. When I spied our familiar niche, I half expected to see Viir waiting there. That the corner was empty dimmed my spirits only slightly. I would see my friend soon, and the idea of it, of Viir's large eyes and pointy face, warmed me in a way the geothermals never had.

Later. So many thoughts to arrange at a later time. So many revelations to tie together.

I burst from the fray on the student level, taking the hallways almost automatically now that I'd entered familiar territory. My fatigue wafted away as I went, as if my new exertion washed off the last traces of my previous ordeal. I heard, just before I reached Laarahn's door, the whispered echo of

Sahveen's warning.

Even those who would change the world require rest.

But there was not time for it now. I sensed the impending event like a tangible thing in the air around me. At Laarahn's curtain, I paused only long enough to brush my nose against the bell rope. If he wasn't in... My heart stuttered in the breath it took for him to answer.

"Come in."

I burst through and came nose to nose with Laarahn's rodent. A shiver took me, shaking the neonate ring enough that it threatened to slip for the first time since donning it. The mouse squeaked and I jerked backwards, lifting into a defensive ess and hissing a warning.

"You'll have to be quick, I'm a—" Laarahn's sentence died with a gasp. He coiled behind his desk, working at something, but when he saw me his pencil dropped to the surface with a thud. His mouth hung open around his unspoken words, and a single thought blared so loudly that I felt it in my tail.

Alive!

Laarahn made a choking sound. His mouse staggered back from me. Apparently I'd been declared dead, lost, and now returned from the grave. Their shock was palpable, unmistakable. It twanged through the room and echoed when my mentor finally found his voice.

"Sookahr."

"We don't have time to explain," I said. "The Circlet is in danger. Our rodents have risen up against us. They've joined the wild rats and plan to attack during the convention."

"What?" He uncoiled, spilling from his desk ledge and slithering toward me. "But how?"

"The rodent food in our supplies was damaged. Two days on native foraging, and Kwirk attacked me."

"So it *is* the food." He nodded, let his tongue flutter, and shooed me farther into the room with a flick of his tail. "And the wild rats?"

"Killed the guards, tried to kill us. Lohmeer and I had to hide in the jungle.

Alive.

He slid toward the door, and I moved deeper into the room to allow him access.

"Can you warn them? The Circlet? I think that's where they mean to..." As we shifted position, I caught sight of the papers on Laarahn's desk. I fully expected him to race away, to hurry to our leaders with my warning and yet, here was something I hadn't suspected at all. "This is my design."

"Is it?"

I closed in on the papers, leaned over them, and felt another shiver skitter beneath my scales. My architecture final lay atop Laarahn's desk, my original, too-decorative design. Except of course, this wasn't mine. It was, however, an exact copy, traced in every detail, but marked with a very different signature.

"You're going to turn in my design."

And yet he'd told me it was all wrong. He'd asked me to design a thing of spikes and shadow, and then sent me away to... Sent me away. Into danger. Laarahn had gotten me out of the way. I heard his band zing but spun too late, jerking around just in time to see the blow coming.

The dark square of a heavy box filled my vision, blotting out the room, the rat, and my traitorous mentor for a single breath before Laarahn smashed it against my head.

24

I came to in total darkness. My head throbbed, swelling around the neonate band until it pinched my scales painfully. I trembled from fatigue, my muscles jointly declaring that they'd had enough. It felt like effort just to lift my head, just to press my tongue between my lips.

Once I'd managed it, I tasted foul air—dampness, feces, and a metallic odor that was only faintly familiar. It wasn't until I heard the beetles clicking that I knew where Laarahn had dumped me. My stomach squeezed against the realization and I retracted my tongue quickly.

The excrement closets were scattered throughout the levels. Laarahn might have carried me here with his band's assistance. How he'd done it without being seen I couldn't guess, but I knew he meant to end me. Either to let me starve in the bottom of this well, or to return and finish me himself after he'd used my design to win the Circlet's favor.

The walls would be too high to climb. I resisted touching them; I'd seen enough from the top side to know that surface would be wholly unpleasant. The beetles who collected the waste had access tunnels down here, but they were a small species. One quick probing of my tail proved that route was closed to me. I had no escape, and no hope of surviving unless someone happened to open the door from above.

Laarahn would have thought of that. He'd have blocked the door or posted the room as out of order. I tested the beetle tunnel again, but my tail could hardly fit inside it.

My breath came too fast, sucking in foul air and making me gag. I had little strength, had spent it in my final flight for the Burrow. It was all I could do to hold my head above the filth and yet, somehow, I had to escape. I had to. At this very moment the rats might be attacking. My panic surged forward, jumbling my thoughts. Laarahn could warn them, but at what cost to himself?

I knew, even as my thoughts scattered, that he wouldn't risk it. He meant to use my work as his own, to earn the place that I deserved. It all fit together now. Our lack of proper supplies, the danger at the outpost. He'd sent me there with every intention that I'd never return. He'd been willing to sacrifice every member of my team just to be rid of me.

I laughed, a dry, shallow sound that echoed up the shaft overhead. If the rats got him, I'd owe them my thanks. If the rats got the Circlet...

Maybe that wouldn't be a tragedy either. But if the Burrow were overrun with armed rodents, if our attendants joined in and rose up against us? I imagined the students who had guided me here, my fellow classmates, Viirlahn. I couldn't let that happen. I couldn't bear to lose Viir too. To never get a chance to tell him whatever it was I needed to say.

Something important. To tell Viirlahn.

Viir.

Viir!

I thought of my friend with all the desperate force I could summon. A flash of pain lanced through my temples. The neonate ring hummed, and I felt the skymetal like a cold finger snuffing out my voice. Muffling me. Holding me down. With a breath that brought more discomfort than relief, I leaned my head against the filthy wall and dragged the skymetal forward, over my eyes and off my nose.

It tumbled free, landing with a squish and leaving only a chill feeling in its place. Loose from the band's restriction, I tried again, picturing the beloved *aspis* face and reaching with my thoughts toward the only serpent in the Burrow I could still trust.

Viirlahn.

"Viir!" I shouted his name aloud and the walls bounced it back at me. The hollow reverberation made glancing blows against the sides of my head, but the volume was pathetic. No one could hear me down here, not unless...

Viir!

I let my vision fog, blotted out the well and the stink and the despair swirling in the darkness around me. Instead, I filled my head with my *aspis* friend. I pictured Viir swimming through long grass, waiting in our niche, and lounging on his shelf in the gaming room.

Viir, Viir.

I chanted to him. Thinking of the way he laughed, the mischief he seemed to create from thin air, the time we'd celebrated the Awakening and almost...

Viir.

I pressed my need into the song, infused it with my pain and fatigue, my longing and my love for my friend. All the betrayals nagged in the background—Kwirk, Lohmeer, Laarahn. I waged a war with them, pitted Viir against all the others and shivered in my shit hole.

What if? Had I ever had a friend at all?

The skymetal was off. I might be tired, but I was no longer banded. If I meant to survive, I had only myself to rely on. I craned my head back as far as I could manage and stared up into darkness. The top of the shaft would end in a circle, cut into the floor of the closet itself. I saw no light nor hint that any crack existed around the door up there, but I knew where it *should* be. I knew how far I'd have to reach.

Longer than my own body.

If only I had a god's wings. If only the Sage might lend me his, or Viir. My dream Viir might swoop down and snatch me from the pit, but my reality had a bleaker sense of mind. I focused on a random spot in the darkness, a place I prayed the well might end.

My will faltered at the thought. I shook it off, fixed my resolve and my hopes on flying and leaned into it, as I might have leaned into a band of trilling metal. I tried my muscles as well, raising as much of my body physically as I was able.

It was a feeble attempt, and only lifted a quarter of my body from the slimy hole's bottom. I held there, using my will to keep myself steady, upright in the middle of the shaft. I pressed my tail deeper into the slime and levered another four scale rows into the air.

Fly.

"Damn it." I wrapped an invisible hand around my body and heaved with my mind.

Up.

My head rose. My body lifted up and up, until only the tip of my tail touched solid ground. I wavered there for a breath, a single quick inhale, and then forced my will tighter and felt the rush of cool air as I lost all contact and hovered. I could do this. Without my band, I could move anything. I rose higher, fixing my gaze up and reaching for the surface I knew had to be there.

I stretched, flicked my tongue, and fell. Twisting, I brushed the walls, coating my scales in slime and landing with a sick splatter. The impact drove me into a ball, and I tucked my head against my scales and hissed pathetically. The dull aches in my body complained louder, though the fall hadn't been far. I knew, with each twinge, that my last effort had been spent.

I had nothing left, no more chances, and I pressed my nose against my coils and hissed out my misery.

A clattering roused me almost immediately. I froze in place, tilting my head upwards. Had Laarahn returned to finish me off? If so, I had no more fight in me. Nowhere to hide and nothing to fling back at him save a filthy neonate band that I could barely lift in this state.

Light bloomed above. The circle appeared above my head, and I heard a strange voice rumbling.

"Are you serious?"

There was nothing unfamiliar about the reply. "I think I... I just need to check."

Viirlahn!

I'd meant to scream it, but my mind got there first. My tongue dared a quick dance, out and back, and I watched the light with my heart banging against my ribs. "Viir?"

It came out too softly, dry and as quiet as the beetle's clicking. At the top of the shaft, a familiar shaped head appeared, silhouetted and dark but as beautiful as anything I'd ever seen.

"Viir!" I managed a soft croak, but this time it echoed up the shaft and turned the head above. Those huge eyes fixed on the bottom of the hole. "Viir."

"Sookahr?" His voice bounced down, shaky and as weak as I felt. "Sookahr, is that you?"

"Yes."

Yes!

"He's alive!" Viir shouted louder, his words a happier echo of Laarahn's shock. "Alive! By the Dreamer, Soo, what happened?"

"Laarahn tried to kill me," I hollered up, and then bit back any further words. For all I knew my mentor was there, ready and waiting to push Viir into the shaft alongside me. "Viir?"

"Just hold on," he said. "We're getting something." His head twisted, retreating from view.

"Don't." I felt my heart jumping. "Don't leave me, Viir."

For six agonizing breaths I watched that portal. The light remained, glowing through the hole in the floor, but without Viir to make it real, I might have gazed at a pale sun—a distant, unreachable goal. By the time he popped back into view, I squirmed with anxiety.

"We're gonna throw something down. Look out."

Shadows flickered over the circle. A rasping sound descended as something scraped against the walls. I pressed myself to one side of the shaft, but still felt the touch of many soft impacts as whatever they'd thrown landed around me.

"There's a loop at that end," Viir called down. The scraping sounds continued up the wall, and I shifted position and felt rope brushing against my scales. "Can you get through it?"

"Yes." I would get through it, if it killed me I would. "Just a moment."

I fished for my band with the tip of my tail. The rope loop hung around me, and I used my mind to sort it out, to untwist the circle they'd knotted in the end and to hold it open enough that I could glide through. It was too loose, but once around my middle, I found the long end leading up the shaft and wound the front of my body around that as well. The rope brushed against the wall as my tail found the neonate ring and stabbed it up from the muck.

Viirlahn called down to me. "Are you ready?"

"Yes." I held my breath, and when nothing happened, shouted to the light above. "Yes!"

A tug jerked me into the wall. I teetered as the loop dragged me across the shaft. It lifted me, slipping against my scales. I coiled around it, twisting my head and neck around the upright section of the rope and knotting the rest of myself around the loose circle. It jerked again and I left the ground, rising slowly and in stops and starts as Viir worked his magic above me.

I hovered my way up the shaft, not exactly flying, not gracefully, but still working steadily toward freedom. As I neared the circle of light, Viir's nose poked in again. He gazed down at me, and I felt his eagerness vibrating through the rope, broadcasting in his thoughts.

Alive. Sookahr is alive.

"So far." I muttered it to myself. Getting out of this hole had proved too much for me, and now I'd have to summon a miracle, gather enough strength to get to the Circlet's meeting, to get inside, and to stop whatever madness the rats were up to. Not to mention Laarahn himself.

I couldn't believe him guilty of treason. Greed and stupidity, yes. Desperation to get out of his own pit, a life locked into a career he'd never wanted, a caste system that would never raise him from mediocrity, yes. But if he allowed the Circlet to suffer, the Burrow to be invaded, it would be because he'd never believed my threat in the first place.

Maybe he'd been too consumed with his own plans to even hear me.

"Sookahr! Viir's shout warned me just as I reached the hole in the closet floor. I twisted, aiming my head for that opening. The rope lurched again and I spun, keeping my head angled upward and managing to pop through the hole just as Viir poked his head in again.

The rope heaved and I tumbled over the rim and out the door, tangling myself in the line, and in Viir who failed to withdraw in time to avoid the mess. Still, despite my filth and the stench I had to bring with me, he fluttered happily and wound his neck against mine.

"By the Dreamer, Sookahr. It's good to see you."

"Not so much to smell me." I flushed all over, warmth flooding beneath my scales, but I returned the *aspis'* embrace eagerly. We'd fallen out of the closet into the hallway, and I followed the tangle of rope with my eyes. It ended at a familiar pair of constrictors. One of them had the tail of my rescue line tied around his stout body, and the other used his massive girth to block the hallway behind us.

"They told me you were dead." Viir spilled the words in a rush and sighed. "I thought..."

"I nearly was," I said. "More than once, but—"

"You remember the boys from the gaming room?"

"Beetle-tenders. Yes. And thank you. Thank you all, but—"

"Soo, what happened? Where have you been and why would Laarahn—"

"There's no time." I shook myself free of him and began untangling myself from the rope. "Viir, a band of wild rats is going to attack the Circlet. We have to warn them. We have to go now, before it's too late."

"Sookahr?"

I stopped wiggling and looked at them, first at Viir and then at each of his companions. I'd come back from the dead, band-less and raving like a loon. I could see that in their expressions, but I didn't have time to worry about it. I focused my will on shaking free as much filth from my body as possible, then I went to work on the band. I'd need it, if I wanted even a chance at getting near the Circlet.

"I have to go. I know how it sounds. Thank you all for this, but there's no time to explain everything." I looped my tail through the band, unwilling to put it on my face in this condition. It would have to do. *I* would have to do, but there was one more thing I needed help with before I went. "I need to know where they are."

"Is he bonkers?" the saddled constrictor asked Viir.

I held my breath. If Viir couldn't tell me anything, I'd have to find another way. The only thing I could think of was to search through the Burrow at random, to listen for any thoughts that might lead me to the Circlet or the rats. It wasn't the worst plan, but it wouldn't work either. There was too much Burrow and too little time.

"Viir?" The constrictors waited for my friend's answer. How close had they become? I'd been gone, dead, for more than a week, and these three had forged some kind of allegiance in my absence.

"No." Viir shook his head. "If Soo says it, then it's true." He leaned down and stared into my eyes. "He's usually right about everything."

I tilted my head, flooded with relief and trembling from exertion. Viir believed me though, still trusted me, and that was as welcome as a warm shelf.

"Except if he thinks I'm going to let him do this alone," he said, and his eyes never flickered from mine. "You in for some mischief, boys?"

I'd never been able to resist that tone, but I turned toward the constrictors and tried to discern just how far under Viir's spell they'd fallen.

"Yes," the rope-holding one said. "But he can't go anywhere like that."

"I don't have time to bathe," I said.

"I think he meant the band," Viir whispered.

"Oh."

"But you do stink."

"Trust me, I know." I ripple-shrugged and tried not to feel embarrassed, horrified by my predicament. "I have the neonate ring."

"No good." The big constrictor slithered closer, leaving his buddy to shelter our conference from prying eyes. "Can't rig up a fake for him either, not if he's in a hurry. Can we cover him up?"

"Oh," Viir said. His usually perky, dominant pose wilted. "I suppose we have to."

"What is it?" I whispered. I'd never seen him deflate before, and the effect was damn creepy. "What's wrong?"

"Just try not to touch it too much." He stared out toward the hallway, and I heard his band hum to life. While Viir focused, I couldn't help imagining what he might do without his skymetal "helper".

The constrictors ducked their heads low, and a long cylinder drifted into view. It flew over their stout bodies, and settled with one end touching the floor outside the excrement closet. It was soft, rolled tightly and tied with two silken braids. I knew why Viir had doubts about the plan now, and it made my stomach twist for what I had to ask of him.

"Is it the only thing?" I asked. "There's nothing else we could use?"

"It'll be fine." Viir's tone didn't match his optimistic words. "You've gotten most of the filth off."

He stared hard at his weaving and the roll began to unfurl. It lifted into the air, spooling out into a tapestry of fine threads and brilliant colors. I watched, tongue-tied, as the familiar scene spread through the air.

A bright field of long grass and a prickle of black deadwood. Viir had woven the avian attack, complete with five glistening beetles huddling among the needle wood. I knew, now, why he'd befriended the constrictors, why he'd sought out their games and their company. He'd been doing research of his own, weaving his own masterpiece to bring before the Circlet.

"You can't let that touch me," I said, awestruck, unable to look away from his work.

Near the top edge, where he'd left a fine row of fringe, the sun glowed. How he made it seem warm with only thread, I couldn't say, but below it lined out in sparkling strands, the great ave hovered. Its wings spread like waterfalls at its side, and its head... I'd seen it many times already, though

195

I'd never laid eyes on the piece before. Viir had given his avian gods his own face, made them into a snake-bird creature that I'd seen, and spoken to, in my dreams.

"It's you." I breathed the words.

"Artistic vanity," he said. "Something I dreamed of before you left."

"I love it."

I tore my eyes from the tapestry long enough to meet Viir's gaze. His eyes gleamed, and a light shaft in the wall made a halo around his head.

"No time for romance, boys," the constrictor blurted from the hallway. "I thought we were in a hurry."

"Yes." Viir turned away quickly, lowering his nose far more than his norm. "Duck down, Soo."

"No." I couldn't let him soil his masterpiece. There was far too much of him in it, too many hours and too much of his heart and soul. "Drape it over their backs, if you can. I'll travel between them. If I stay low enough the tapestry should be fine."

"Now he wants to cuddle with *us*," the constrictor sniped, but it had more of play than taunting to it. "All right then, let's get it over with."

Viir's band rang out. The tapestry drifted up and over as the two constrictors realigned themselves so that they lay parallel to one another. The weaving flapped into position, settling across their massive backs and making a tunnel between them.

Viir slithered to my side, leaned his elegant head down, and nudged my neck with his nose. "In you go."

They'd dragged me from the lowest place I could imagine, from the bottom of a literal pit. Now, they'd made me a glorious cape, a draping fit for the Circlet. If they didn't reward Viir for that work, then they were stupid as well as corrupt.

"Yes." I slithered beneath the tapestry, pressing my belly against the floor and flattening my body as much as possible. Once I'd hidden away, Viir began to give orders again, directing his new cronies like the master that he was. My bookends moved on, and I was left to travel between them, to keep my head down, my eyes forward, and my brain working.

Alone I'd been desperate, but now there were four of us. We might reach our goal in time, might stop the rats, save the Circlet, preserve the Burrow. But as we traveled through its light-studded hallways, as the familiar scents of musk and dust and rodent filled my head, I couldn't help but wonder if it was worth saving.

I might deliver my warning and stop a foreign enemy, but what would I do then? What would I do about the evil already woven into our lives? By my count, it was tied up in everything the Burrow was, in everything *we* were, as tightly tangled and as intricately designed as Viir's tapestry?

25

The first thing I noticed when we entered the chamber was the scent of rodent. Many snakes had gathered as well, and their musk reached me, but my senses latched upon the aroma of warm fur, sending a shiver of terror through me. So many of them here, always at our sides. How could we have created a danger so fierce and then allowed it to infiltrate our numbers so thoroughly?

It had to be vanity. The blindness of a society unflinchingly certain of their control, of their superiority.

The crowd forced us to press together, and my constrictor escort became a vise at my sides. I peered out from the front of the tapestry and saw Viir's tail as he led us, winding between the gathered serpents in a round room very similar to my old classroom.

If my classroom had expanded to ten times its size.

The tiers were wider too, and the warmth filling the room had more than the press of bodies behind it. We'd traveled deep into the Burrow, deeper than the *aspis* quarters even, and the geothermals flowed all around us, carrying a constant vibration through the floor. The circular walls were draped with fine hangings, though I saw none I felt could stand proudly beside Viir's work. The ceiling mosaic, however, left me staring in stunned admiration.

The room's cap made a concave dome so massive that my eyes had trouble finding all of it, traveling from one side of the lowest circle up and over to the other. Every speck of that surface had been encrusted with tiles, and it glittered like the night sky just before the all-dark.

I would have expected to see the Dreamer there, and though the mosaic included that god, it also bore the image of the others. The Warrior, the Tender, the Mother and the Sage all joined the *aspis* deity in a ring. Five winged serpents with a glowing sun in their middle. I met each heavenly gaze in turn, though the sheer size of the depictions forced me to focus on one eye at a time, and I shivered below their mighty postures.

Viir began his descent over the tiers, squeezing between the gathered serpents who, I noted, were primarily *aspis* or viper. All venomous, all but for a few brave souls who dared to reach above their stations. Like Laarahn, who hid somewhere in the fray no doubt, clutching *my* work to his tattered pride as if it were his own. I swallowed a hiss and waited for my escort to move, but the passage Viir made closed up behind him, and there was no room for the three of us abreast to follow.

I watched my friend's tail vanish into the crowd, felt the constrictors' indecision in the way they tensed and trembled. Though I knew this crowd would not tolerate an un-banded snake in their midst, we would not go any further as we were either. I lowered my head to the tier and rolled my whole length over once, scraping as much of the remaining stench from my scales as I could. Then I lifted my head, raising my body until I could feel Viir's weaving against my scales.

With a small twist and a sideways curl, I relieved my guardians of the tapestry. Keeping as much of my body beneath it as possible, I slithered after Viir, praying to the Sage that I might not damage the art I wore like a cocoon about me.

The crowd also seemed unwilling to risk my cargo, though it might have been the lingering stench that caused each serpent in my path to shift quickly aside. I went easily through the gap they made, and two levels down I caught up with Viir. Two tiers below that, the floor opened into a wide circle and I got my first glimpse of the Burrow's leaders.

Five snakes coiled in an arc around the room's center. Two were *aspis*, and one each of viper, constrictor, and snake. Each dwarfed me in length and girth, and though I hid a full two tiers above them, their noble heads reached much higher than even Viir's. A ring of lesser serpents had formed around them, each with a faithful rodent at their side. Behind the five I saw the glint of beady eyes, and I heard only the shuffling of paws, the slipping of bald tails against the paved floor.

"This is fine work," a pale cobra with scales nearly as white as Sahveen's spoke, and all of the gathered circle cowered before the *aspis*. "But sadly, we cannot accept every design."

I never discerned which hapless candidate he rejected. His final words to the unlucky serpent faded as well, as a sharper sound reached me, a desperate, furious thought.

Devils.

It was not a mind I recognized, but the rage behind it, the fierce sentiment had not left my thoughts since I'd woken with Kwirk's weapon hovering above me. My tongue stretched out, seeking the traitor, but my heart hammered and my body cringed lower.

Freedom.

I swiveled my head as another thought surfaced.

Freedom.

The chant was passed one rodent mind to another, growing in fervor as it shifted around me, an invisible whisper without a definitive source. They were anywhere, everywhere, and only I could hear them.

Freedom, freedom, fight!

The room spun. I turned and twisted until the scaled faces around me blurred. To my right, Viir's voice whispered, but his words drowned in the mental chanting, in the rodent's fury against their masters. I felt their anger like a lash, and their intended target like a clear window directly before me.

Half-stunned, I slithered over the next tier. The cobra's voice managed to reach me, projected for the entire room to hear. His words only dragged me forward, down over the next ridge with my head full of fog and silent hissing.

"Who is the next candidate?"

I lurched ahead, snagging the tapestry in my reckless advance. Whatever it caught on jerked me backwards. I heard Viir then, shouting over the noise in my head. If I'd torn his work, there was no time for chagrin now. My body jerked free of the weaving, and I tumbled the remaining distance to the chamber floor. Gasps chased me as I fell, bodies dodged my flailing coils, and the smooth floor greeted me like a fist.

I hit it belly on, and slid forward as if it were paved in ice.

My head swirled. I lifted my nose slowly, aware the enormous room had fallen silent as a tomb. My tongue stretched out, and hung there limp as a pair of slit-pupil eyes came sharply into focus.

"Who is this?" The cobra's voice hardened into an accusation. "Why is there an un-banded serpent in the heart of the Burrow?"

I lifted my tail, felt the slight weight of the neonate band, miraculously still wedged against my scales. Too small and too low, but a band nonetheless. I trembled as I raised it into the cobra's view, and I shuddered when his tongue fell towards the ring.

"A neonate ring?"

A tide of whispers circled the room, hisses and gasps, but suddenly not

199

a sound from the rodent rebels.

"You're in danger." I forced the words between my lips, but the cobra and his circle remained fixed, coiled and arranged around me as if they hadn't heard.

"Either you're the largest hatchling in history—" The cobra's amusement didn't reach his eyes or his posture. "—or the lowliest of adults. Who are you, snake, and what right do you have to interrupt these proceedings?"

"I'm Sookahr," I said, pausing where I would have added my profession. *The architect* no longer fit me, and I couldn't bring myself to add it. "I'm here to warn you."

"He's a liar!"

The crowd gasped again, taking a sharp, collective breath as Laarahn spilled forth from their midst. He poured himself into the open circle, now devoid of candidates, who all had managed to press themselves back into anonymity the moment I'd seized the Circlet's attention.

My mentor filled their empty space, writhing and stretching nearly as long as the cobra who swayed above me.

"He means to steal my designs." Laarahn lifted himself higher than his station warranted. He puffed out his scales and fixed a vicious expression on me.

I felt his fear behind that look, the risks he'd taken, the desperate lengths he'd gone to. I looked into my own death when I met his eyes, and I knew he'd kill me without hesitation if I stumbled here.

"Screw the design." I spat it and raised my head, slowly and with one eye fixed on the cobra, who might take any sudden movement as a threat. "The Circlet is in danger."

Behind the whispering of the crowd, I felt a ripple, not quite a thought, but a sense of silent panic that didn't originate from any serpent.

"My egg-mother, Sahveen, lent me this band that I might warn you before it's too late." I prayed that mentioning Sahveen might lend my case weight. It had served me at the gates, perhaps, but the *aspis* here did not show any sign I'd impressed them.

"And what is this warning?" The cobra leaned forward, spreading his hood wide.

"Don't listen to him," Laarahn hissed. "He's a criminal. A thief. He left his post, likely killed the constrictor who remained with him."

"He's nothing of the sort!" Viir's voice shouted behind me. I heard him moving, joining us in the circle of death, but I couldn't risk looking, one flinch from the cobra's flat head, and I'd feel the spikes of his venomous teeth. "You tried to kill him! You stole his design, and we can prove it."

Viir's confident tone wavered too much at the end. Even I could hear his doubt ringing. The cobra heard it too, and he spared a second to cast his gaze toward my friend.

"These are serious charges."

Devils.

"And they must all be considered. Theft, desertion, attempted murder."

"Murder," Laarahn said. "Lohmeer has vanished."

Freedom!

"Lohmeer is alive." I hissed, twisted, staying low and praying that the cobra had more patience for my disrespect. "He is, but..."

Attack.

"But you won't be if you don't listen to me." I followed the ghostly thoughts around the room as one after the other of the rodents took up the chant. "The rats are plotting against you. They mean to kill you all."

Now. Quickly, now!

The cobra reared upwards and I fell to my belly, cowering, waiting for the strike that would end me. Maybe I deserved it. Maybe the Circlet deserved whatever the rats had planned. But as I looked up to face my death, I saw the glinting of metal in the shadow of the cobra's coils. I saw his rat, with eyes razor sharp, lifting a blade high over his furry head.

"No!"

Strike!

I launched my body toward the rat, an open-mouthed strike directly at the cobra's coils. As I flew past him, he lashed out. I hit the rat and rolled around him even as I felt the cobra's teeth embedding in my tail. Pain jolted up my spine, but by the time it reached my brain, it was already too late. I coiled tighter around the rat and held him still.

"Devil." His squeak wheezed between razor teeth. "Monsters."

"Folt." The cobra's voice wavered. "What are you doing?"

His rat struggled against my grip. The paw still clinging to the knife flexed, trying to move, still fighting to stab though it was pressed firmly against the rodent's head. I flexed, and his fingers opened. The blade fell to the floor, but the sound of its impact died in the screaming throughout the room.

"Bar the doors!" Another of the Circlet, the huge viper, shouted the order. "Keep them contained."

My attention fixed upon the rat in my grip, but I heard the fray erupting around us. Many of the rodents in the room pleaded their innocence, likely still firmly under the drug's influence. But there were others that fought. Shouts of pain and anger in both rodent and serpent voices all blending together.

The thoughts of our attackers still echoed in my head. Enraged rodents screaming for their liberation, for victory, or for mercy. Outside my head, scaly bodies crashed against one another. Some struck, and others coiled protectively around the faithful attendants who did not join in the rebellion.

I heard Viir shout my name, but when I twisted to find him, the cobra filled my vision. He still loomed over me, and my throbbing tail reminded me that he'd already finished me. Whatever the outcome of this battle, my fate had been decided.

"Why?" He swayed, still focused on the rat I held. "Why would they?"

I knew that feeling, the desperate shock of a most intimate betrayal. At least one member of the Circlet hadn't known about the truth of our attendants' obedience, but I didn't have time to feel sorry for him now. My scarred tail had become a mangled stub, but I had no time to mourn for it. Beyond my misery, a pair of mice charged. They wore the thick garments of the wild rats, and their swords gleamed like the tiles they pointed toward.

"Behind you!" My shout jarred the cobra out of his fugue. He spun, hissing as he went, and the charging rodents faltered. Faced with that hooded fury, I couldn't imagine a creature that wouldn't have.

The tiers thrashed with scales, had fallen into complete chaos. I searched for Viir among the throng, but the squirming rat drew my focus back to my captive. He gnashed his teeth, glaring at me with too-sharp eyes. Only a burbling sound emerged from his throat. If I held him any tighter, he would perish. If I released him, he would kill.

I dragged myself toward the cobra, my front third extended and the rest of me wound like a band around the rebel. My tail bled freely, little comfort knowing the source of the wound, and it pulsed in time to my heartbeat.

Had my warning come in time? It seemed that was still to be determined. A battle raged around me, but I was spent. I'd done what I came to do, and there was nothing left for me but to cling to my prisoner and wait for the cobra's venom to take me.

26

It was Laarahn's voice that told me the battle had resolved in our favor. My rat prisoner had ceased his struggling, choosing to stare his daggers at me now that his real weapon had been lost. I'd watched the Circlet hold their circle, and I'd watched the rats they bit die, convulsing and bleeding from their noses.

Either venom had a far different effect on serpents, or I'd suffered a dry bite only. I couldn't fully nurse that hope until I heard my mentor's crazed voice.

"He was right. He was right about them all along."

That revelation, I planned on living to experience. The cobra had remained at my side throughout the fight, and though a few of the rodents' weapons had pricked his pristine armor, he seemed no worse for the thin trickles of blood marring his perfect scales. The others in the Circlet seemed to have fared better, and I took their condition as a clear sign that we'd been victorious.

I still needed to find Viir, but the final strike to capture the cobra's attendant had done me in physically. It was all I could do to restrain the rodent, and I feared he might discover that at any moment and renew his struggles. I'd wrapped around the portion of my body that held him, lowered my head to the floor, and had no inclination whatsoever to lift it up again.

Until they herded Laarahn from the tiers. He bled from a wound in his neck, but it looked superficial. His head spun constantly from one side to the other, and he continued to babble as Viir's constrictor pals nudged him along. "The mice. He was right."

"This one." The cobra's head appeared beside mine. He whispered, "He tried to kill you?"

"Not just me." I might someday forgive my mentor's assault, but he'd sent us *all* to the outpost to die.

"You saved our lives." He said it quickly, then lifted his head and spread his hood wide. "Seize Laarahn. Take him away. And someone restrain Folt so this one can be tended."

He turned away and I saw the great viper slithering in. Their voices blended into a distant mutter. The room faded in and out, and at some point, someone assisted with unwinding my coils. They took my teacher and my prisoner away, and I was left to sprawl where I was, too tired to lift my head.

I watched them dragging away the bodies from floor height. I scanned for Viir among the wounded, but all I located of my friend was the soft fluttering of a forgotten tapestry. It lay where I'd dropped it, in the center of our battle, and even from here I could see the blood stains on Viir's lovely work.

Dragging my rear quarter, I slithered toward it. When the nearest fringe tickled my chin scales, I heaved my head up enough to assess the damage. The tapestry had played host to more than one mouse death. Blood made dark moons across the woven sky, and an unlucky spatter had wounded the avian version of my friend, as if he rained blood down upon the beetles. There was a tear in one corner, but even so, Viir's threads sparkled like precious metals.

"Is this your work?" The cobra had noted my interest. He reappeared above me and cast a hooded shadow across Viir's work.

"My friend, Viirlahn's," I said. "A masterpiece. Lovely enough to impress the gods themselves."

"I am aware of Viirlan's skill." He surprised me. I twisted and caught the flash of mischief in his expression. It returned to a stoic slate quickly enough, however. "And he has championed you as well. Laarahn's design for the outpost was your work?"

"My final project, yes."

"I see."

What he saw, I couldn't have guessed, nor did I have the energy to press him for answers. I had the attention, it seemed, of at least one of the Circlet, but I had no desire left in me to make use of it. I watched his tongue instead, falling out and then slipping back between his snowy lips. There was only one thing I wanted from him, but I was afraid what the answer might be. "Have you seen Viirlahn?"

"He's fine." Those words removed the last of my worry. I let myself deflate fully. "I've sent him to medical for tending, where you should be."

He stopped talking. The space between us seemed to stretch as his posture tightened. I let the warm floor sooth the throbbing in my tail, and wondered at my own condition. They hadn't sent me to medical yet. Perhaps the bite had been more significant than I'd hoped. Perhaps there was no point.

Finally, the cobra hissed a sigh and nodded. "You need tending as well. I don't know how you discovered this plot, Sookahr, but you've done the Burrow a great service. You've saved the Circlet, and given us time to expel the invaders."

"Are they all gone?"

"There was a secondary attack in the rodent stores. Or perhaps *this* was the secondary attack."

"The food." I spat a pathetic hiss. "The rodent food. Of course."

"Of course?"

I tried to read his expression, to gauge how much he might know, how oblivious my own leaders were. The cobra's eyes were a mystery, however, and if his thoughts gave him away, I was too broken to hear them.

"This one should be with the healers." The viper joined us, dropping his huge head to my level and blotting out the view of anything else. In his eyes I saw more, something urgent and mildly threatening. "I will take him, Mahriil. You must see to the vetting of the remaining rodents."

"Yes." The cobra lowered his head again, smoothed his hood, and faced me. "You have our thanks for now, Sookahr. Expect to hear from me as soon as you're well again."

He moved away from me for the first time since sinking his fangs into my tail. The viper remained, watching me intently. Despite his promise to deliver me to medical, he made no move, did not so much as twitch his tail.

"You know about the mice," I whispered.

His black tongue peeked between his lips. Very slowly, deliberately, he nodded his great head. His voice shook the ground beneath us. "So do you."

It hadn't been a question, but I felt compelled to answer. "Yes."

"Come."

His head raised toward the ceiling and I heard the ringing of skymetal. My body moved without my aid, lifting into the air and floating easily, gingerly, toward the gigantic viper's back. He draped me across his spine, and I did my best to arrange my coils evenly, distributing my weight so as to balance there.

The viper waited until I was secured, and then slithered for the nearest exit. More of his kind guarded the doors, and a queue of *aspis* waited for their turn to be released from the room. Though a crowd still remained beneath the five-god ceiling, not a single rodent was to be seen.

We were allowed through, and despite the viper's grand status, I caught more than one hostile face as we passed those who'd been in line ahead of us. The hallway outside was also crowded, but there it was choked with the piled bodies of fallen rats and mice. If we'd lost many serpents in the battle, they'd stashed those corpses elsewhere. A wise decision if they meant to funnel the *aspis* through these doors.

Not that we hadn't already witnessed the carnage.

Still, I suspected the Circlet would want the day's battle forgotten as soon as possible. They'd claim the victory, have the songs written, the art commissioned, but in my worn down thoughts, I felt a bitter certainty that the truth we'd seen would never make the ballads.

"How is it—" The viper waited until we'd turned into a side passage to speak. "—that an un-banded snake knows what very few inside these walls do?"

"I am not un-banded," I said. "And I was sent to an outpost by my mentor with no suitable food for our mice."

"How many days did it take?"

"Two or three. I'm not sure exactly, but they attacked us soon enough."

He made a noise in his throat, a grunting that told me nothing. We traveled a wide, dim hallway, and I couldn't have said if he delivered me to medical or not. I had no way of knowing how dangerous my knowledge was, or what he meant to do about it. I couldn't fight him, not even with my full strength, and I felt a sudden rush of rage at that. An indignation filled me, erasing the last vestiges of my respect for our caste manners.

"How is it that no one knows our whole society is built upon slavery?"

"Those who need to know are aware. The chemists, many of the higher vipers."

"But not the *aspis*?" That vexed me. I'd assumed our highest caste had orchestrated the system. The fact that he was openly answering my questions did little to assure me that my immediate future was secured just yet.

"The drug made from *aspis* venom induces the dreaming." At the next branch in the hallway, the viper stopped. Voices reached us, but they came from down the next passage, from far enough away to be a slim hope. "*Our* venom, distilled viper venom, produces a very different effect."

"Mind control," I said.

"Complacency." He grunted again. "It's not so bad, is it? To live a life of pampered security in exchange for service?"

"But it's not voluntary."

"Where would our people be without the paws of mice?" His voice lowered even more, and I sensed the words were less his own and more a speech he'd memorized, a propaganda meant to ease his own mind as much as mine. "Would our pyramids still stand, or would we remain scattered and primitive? Still groveling in the dust, freezing in winter, even preying upon the mice? Would they trade *that* for their freedom, do you think?"

I had no answer for him. My head filled with the memory of my first meal, and my stomach clenched. I had to fix my attention on not falling from his back, and yet, he asked the same questions I had. The same circling predicament. What would we be without slavery? How could it ever be justified, and what would we lose if it wasn't?

I imagined the reactions of our people, of Viir and the constrictors, and the line of entitled *aspis* waiting at the doors behind us. The viper took my silent contemplation as understanding.

"You see. We cannot live without them, and if the truth of their situation were known..."

"It would be chaos." That much I could agree with.

"Yes." He twisted sharply, tilting me toward one side and nearly tumbling me from his scales. His flat head came around to face me, and I found the threat in his eyes far less veiled now. "And whoever might let that secret free, even if they were the noblest *aspis*, even if they were a *hero*, would be quickly dealt with."

"I can imagine." I stared back at him, ready for the strike, for him to toss me against the nearest wall and end me. Instead he sighed, hissed a soft note, and shrugged.

"Good."

He turned back around, gave me barely enough time to exhale my fear before starting off again. I'd been warned, and it seemed for the moment that was enough. The next hallway sloped upwards, a gentle rise before it ended in a wide curtain with the green-leaf symbol of the healers' order.

The viper's band circled just behind my position, and it hummed to life as we neared the doors. The curtains parted, and I got my first view of the *aspis'* personal hospital, which looked a great deal more like the leisure baths than its counterparts on my lowly level.

The air inside smelled of herbs and flowers. Long rows of deep basins lined the floor, and a soft mist turned the view of the patient beds hazy. The viper carried me inside the room, lifted his head until his ridged scales brushed the low ceiling, and cleared his throat with a deep vibration of his body.

"I have a hero here in need of tending." His voice boomed. The serpents convalescing in the basins all turned in our direction, and my face flamed beneath my scales.

From the rear of the room, a slender *aspis* appeared. She bore the three-toned shades that signaled a venomous nature, and held her small head nearly as high as the viper's despite her diminutive length. "By the Tender, what is *happening* out there?"

"Rest assured that it would be worse were it not for this one."

The viper's band sang again, and without warning, I lifted from his back and floated down to hover between them. Though I was larger than the doctor, she seemed to dwarf me in my current state, and her dangerous coloring would have cowed me to silence even if I'd been myself. I held my tongue and hoped my silence eased the viper's concerns.

"He's been bit." She leaned over my tail and spoke in a tone that suggested she conversed with herself. "Our mice have been detained, all hell's broken loose, and now serpent is turning on serpent."

"He saved Mahriil's life. You will care for him as if he were one of us."

"I've taken an oath, general. I care for every patient as if they were one of you." Her tone reeked of defiance, and I was inclined to believe her. I wondered if she believed the doctors on our level did the same.

The viper only sighed again, letting me slip a short distance closer to the floor. "Is there a bed I can put him in?"

"Over here!" From the mist, Viirlahn's voice found me.

"That will do," the doctor agreed.

They directed my hovering body between the basins. The mist coated my scales, warm and refreshing. Droplets formed on my lenses, blurring the room even more and urging me to let go, fog over, and sleep.

"Sookahr." Viir called my name and I came back into focus. I'd been settled into the basin beside his, and now my friend's long neck curved between our beds. His eyes, full of concern, stared down at me. "Soo?"

Warmth flooded my body. The basin vibrated from a nearby geothermal, but the heat I felt had more to do with Viir than any external source. My loyal friend. My hero, my champion, and my love.

I moved my head as steadily as I could, reaching for him. Viir met me before I had to exert myself. Our necks twined round and round one another until we rested our chins on the lip of my bed. Wounded and tired...and together.

27

"I can't believe it." Viir had tumbled himself out of his basin when the doctor's attention was elsewhere. He coiled beside mine and we whispered, heads close together. "Not even of Kwirk."

I'd told him my story, even the parts that the viper would not approve of. I needed him to know it all, both to judge his reaction and to hear his opinion. The only opinion left in the Burrow that meant anything to me. We'd spent the whole night talking, and though he'd listened attentively, he seemed to have fixated on the one detail.

"I mean, he was cranky, sure. But murder isn't something I'd think him capable of."

"They're drugged, Viir. All of them."

"Right. Sure. But you don't think all of them would flip, would you?"

I did. In fact, I was certain of it, but the way he said it stopped my tongue. A tremble of fear had entered his voice and I knew he was thinking of his own mouse, of getting out of here and going home to life with a rodent again. I couldn't blame him, but I felt disappointed too.

Viir had shown me one thing. Without witnessing the truth firsthand, it would be very difficult to swallow—maybe impossible for a Burrow citizen to really believe. I doubted I would have, if I hadn't seen the weapon in Kwirk's paw, if I hadn't felt it in my scales.

I shrugged, and Viirlahn nodded his head slowly. He'd think about it, but I saw little of the outrage I felt in his reaction. We fell silent, and I let the warm basin soothe my rumpled mood. The immediate danger was over, our wounds dressed and my strength replenished. I had time to decide what to do next. Both about my future and about Viir, too.

The venomous doctor slithered between our basins, and when she spied Viir on the floor, hissed her disgust. She didn't, however, order him back to his own bed this time.

"You have a visitor." She flicked her tongue and swung her body to one side. In the mist behind her, the enormous white cobra waited. "Here to check on my work."

"I'm sure you've done fine," the cobra said. "They certainly look alive."

He turned to us, fluttering his tongue. The mists swirled around his form, making him even more ghostly, but it was the dark shape huddled beside him that set my heart racing. I pulled into an ess and leaned back.

"No. No, no. It's okay." The cobra threw a coil between the mouse and our beds. "He's new. Yes. Brand new mouse, take some getting used to, but much better. *Much* better. General Gohvaar and his people are systematically interviewing all the Burrow rodents. Won't be long, I'm sure, before they've ferreted out the rebels and we can put this all behind us."

"Behind us." I stared at him, relaxing my strike posture but not my pulse. The general and his vipers were handling the rodents, which meant they were drugging them all for safe keeping.

The cobra took my comment the wrong way. He leaned toward me and flicked the tips of his tongue. "Of course, we still have things in store for you. For both of you, and your two friends if we can find out who they were."

"Why?" Viirlahn might have questioned my story about Kwirk, but he sounded defensive now, must have believed enough to make him nervous.

"Well for one thing, we'd like to reward the four of you." The white hood fanned out, less than when he was angry, but far enough to be intimidating. "There's to be a feast in your honor, a day of holiday, and you'll all be given awards for service to the Burrow."

"I can find the guys," Viir said.

"Wonderful." The cobra nodded and stretched his hood to its full width, then relaxed it and shrugged his upright segment. "And for our hero, there is to be a new job, working for us if you're interested? Comes with lodging that I think you'll appreciate, more leisure, more access. What do you say?"

"I-I'd be working for you?" I felt it then, for a moment, the old stutter of ambition. The desire to make my mark. Well, I'd done that in my own way, and now the Circlet meant to reward me as I'd always dreamed. "Doing?"

"Designing our new outposts, for one thing. After that, perhaps, a few personal renovations, and of course whatever projects you propose."

"I propose?" I stared at him. Was he giving me artistic license? Freedom to suggest the designs I worked on, the changes I made on the Burrow? A chance to leave my mark on my world?

"Of course."

"You're getting promoted, Soo." Viir sounded far more excited than I felt. I wanted to join him, to thrill at seizing the opportunity I'd worked so hard to achieve.

All I managed to say, however, was, "Thank you."

It satisfied the cobra. Perhaps he took it as a sign of humility, but Viir cast me an odd look, and I knew he'd have something to say about it later. I knew I should be happy, really truly grateful. But the last few days could never be erased, and I would never forget the things I knew now. I flicked my tongue and nodded deference to the cobra, but my resolve only solidified when he added his last reward.

"And of course, we'll arrange for a new band."

Despite the heat of my basin, my body went chilly. My tongue froze mid-flutter, and I lost whatever words I'd meant to say next. I stared at the cobra, trembling, and my silence quickly turned awkward.

"Congratulations," Viir interjected, swaying his body and diverting the cobra's attention for me to compose myself. "Where's his new den located?"

"Well, I thought you two might want to see it." The white head turned to me. His slit eyes had shrunk to threads, and I suffered the distinct feeing that he'd seen through me. That I might have saved his life, but I wasn't the hero he claimed I was. Maybe I was imagining it. But maybe he'd been ordered to shower me with gifts, to get me back in line and banded as soon as possible. If so, I suspected the viper's will behind it. And that only made the idea more distasteful.

Maybe I was just paranoid. Either way, I owed him an answer, and I forced as much eagerness into my words as I could feign.

"I would love to see it. How soon can we leave?"

The cobra's head turned toward the doctor. Viir and I mimed his gesture, all three of us staring at her. All three lost in our own secret thoughts, but hanging on her next words as if she alone could relieve our tension.

"They can go now, if they're up to it. But you'll need to take it easy for some time, hero of the rodent rebellion. That puncture will need its dressing changed every other day. You can come back here on your own, or I'll send someone out to find you."

It was less of a threat than the viper had made, but still held the ring of an order to it. I'd only spent one night in the doctor's company, and I most certainly did not want her to come looking for me.

"Well then?" The cobra stared, as if I could release us from the room.

"I'd like to see them now." I managed sincerity there. At least my new den would offer some privacy. "Thank you."

"Very good." The white head nodded, keeping its hood folded. The cobra turned back toward the doorway, and I caught a glimpse of his new mouse. Smaller, darker and huddled in terror beside its enormous new master. Did the *aspis* not see what I did? How could anyone look at a rodent again and not see it?

The cobra paid his attendant no notice, happy in his ignorance. He led us out of the hospital and Viirlahn followed, too quiet for his natural state.

We retraced the path from the previous day, past the hallway where the bodies had lain. Someone had done a fine job cleaning up. If I'd wanted to, in fact, I could pretend nothing bad had happened here. Which had to be the plan, if the vipers were re-drugging our rebels for service. I wondered how they'd explain the event, what words they'd say as they honored Viirlahn and my service.

"It's just up one level," the cobra announced as we reached a spiral ramp. "Not too far from your friend's den."

"That's the *aspis* level," I said, but I didn't miss the excited chirp Viir made behind me.

"And you'll be working for us. Need to have you close, don't we?"

He led us and I followed, stomach churning now. My dreams of rising above my rank had all manifested, suddenly, and in a way I could only conceive of as menacing. I *wanted* these honors, wanted a room beside Viir and a job that allowed me to do my own work. I desperately wanted it. As it was laid out for me, however, piece by piece, it tasted as foul as Ghost's wounds had smelled. Rotten. Full of a slow, creeping death.

"Here we are."

We stopped only a few doors down from the ramp. The cobra faced a curtain easily twice as high and wide as the one that had hung in my den's door my entire life. It was woven from threads as fine as the ones in Viir's tapestry, and bore a faint pattern of rippling lines.

"I will leave you to settle in," the cobra said. "Do take your doctor's advice and get some rest. We can worry about work once you've fully recovered."

"Thank you." I waited for him to leave, waited while he maneuvered his big body easily around in the wide hall, while Viir admired my new curtain, and my stomach danced with both fear and excitement. I watched the curtain, tracing the ripples with my eyes, until Viir's patience ended.

"Aren't you going to go in?"

"Yes." I reached with my mind and stroked the silken fabric. Then, steeling myself, I nudged it aside and slithered through.

The room was not so grand as I'd feared, though it dwarfed my former den and had twice as many light shafts cut into the smooth walls. The bed was larger by half, deeper, and situated in a corner so that it could take advantage of two warm walls. A table sat where my desk would have, and a pile of woven blankets waited beside the bed. A luxury we did not enjoy on the upper levels.

What most impressed me was the water basin. I could easily submerge my entire body inside it, and the flow from the wall spout was far more than the trickle I was accustomed to. Warm water splashed into the pool, and a respectable stream ran out the far end, curving sharply in its trench and vanishing through another curtain.

"What's in there?" I asked. My den had only one closet, and that had been full of Kwirk's cleaning supplies.

"The, uh, waste closet." Viir didn't mock me openly, but I heard his amusement just the same.

"A private one?"

"Yes. With running water instead of beetles."

"And no pit of death?" I poked my nose through the curtain and found a level floor where my river crossed, then vanished beneath another wall.

"Always a bonus." Viir's voice shifted, and I knew he had more to say. We fell silent instead, him holding his tongue and me refusing to look in his direction.

I slithered from wall to wall, tasting the scents of my new home. Would they feed me better as well? Would the Circlet double my leisure time and my meals and then, the second I slithered out of line, slit my throat and be done with me?

"You don't want it, do you?" Viirlahn spoke softly, and so low that I couldn't feel the vibrations at all.

"It's a wonderful den, and close to you."

"I didn't really mean the room."

I'd known what he meant, maybe what he feared, that I would shun the awards and the promotion, that I would reject the entire Burrow and him with it. I wanted to have an answer for him, one that would ease his mind, and so I focused on the only thing I knew for sure I didn't want anything to do with.

"They mean to band me again."

"And that's bad?"

"I'm not sure. How could I be sure? They've never given us a choice."

"You want to do something else? I thought you loved designing buildings."

'I do." I nodded, remembering that he was right, that it gave me so much satisfaction when the lines were just right. Or it *had*, before I thought about doing anything else. "What if I could be more than an architect?"

"It just seems kind of greedy," he said. "What more do you want them to give you?"

"Nothing. No. You don't understand."

Frustration lowered my head toward the floor. Viir didn't get it, and to a Burrow citizen, I must have sounded greedy, ungrateful, insane. To someone who hadn't seen it, but then I could show him, couldn't I? "Viir, without the band I can do more. Look."

I reached for the largest thing in the room, raising the long table from the floor with ease and then sending it into a slow spin for effect. Viir's breath gasped. He curled away from the dancing furniture.

"How?"

"Easily." I kept the table hovering and snatched up the blankets, unfurling them and then sending them flapping in a serpentine between my friend and I. Table, blankets, easy. I could have lifted Viir himself if I'd thought it wouldn't terrify him. "The skymetal doesn't amplify our powers, Viir. I think it might limit them."

I let everything settle to the floor, lined the table back into position and folded the blankets, two at a time, before piling them back in their corner. No sooner than my show ended, Viir raced forward, tongue flicking, to inspect the items. As if it had been a trick. His head continued to shake in disbelief. Even witnessing the demonstration hadn't been enough.

Fearless, adventurous Viir could not swallow what I'd become.

"I won't let them band me again." I hadn't been certain of that decision, but the moment I said it, I knew it was true. The idea of being bolted down again horrified me.

"Who could blame you?" There was resignation in his tone, but also defeat, a deep sadness that didn't fit him.

I wanted so badly to reassure him, to tell him that I'd take the band, take the promotion happily, and remain in the Burrow. But I'd never been able to lie to Viir.

Instead, I reached out with a thought, almost without realizing it. I reached for those glassy scales and I stroked them, comforting, but also asking something else we hadn't gotten around to dealing with.

Viir's tail twitched. His head shot up and he twisted toward me. His huge eyes shone, pleading with me, asking me right back. This time, I had no intention of dodging him.

"I made a god of you," I whispered. "In my dreaming."

Viirlahn shivered once. I held my breath as he moved to me. His nose dipped, tucked under my chin, and then curved around, wrapping my neck with his. A shudder rocked through me, a spasm of longing and affection and somewhere far beneath all of that, sorrow. Viir lined our bodies out, parallel paths, always touching but going in opposite directions. I coiled my neck tighter, clung to him, and slid my tail under and around.

We twisted, twining together until we both shook so hard that it was all we could do to slither across the room. Slither, entwined, to a bed I'd only ever sleep in once.

28

Viir left me in the middle of the night. We said goodbye softly, nuzzling our heads together and pretending that this was the beginning and not the end. As he vanished through my new curtain, I imagined staying. I considered it as I drifted to sleep again, that I still might stay, might take the job, the life... Another band.

My fantasy stopped there.

I pushed the idea of my future aside and let myself settle between the warmth of the walls and the heat of Viir's lingering presence. When I woke, I could hear the soft scrubbing of a broom in motion. It was the sound I'd woken to every day since my hatching, a safe sound, and I almost drifted back to sleep.

"You've too big a day to continue snoozing."

My body froze in place. The warmth that had filled me vanished in a breath, in a single syllable uttered in that voice. Slowly I stretched my tongue out, pulling my neck back into an ess as I turned my head.

"A little too much fuss, if you ask me." Kwirk held only a broom in his paws. His tail slung in a relaxed drape across the floor. Ears forward and eyes down, he tidied up my new den as if he'd always been there.

I hissed deep in my belly, long and low as if the sound began in my tail and drew all the breath I had to its ending. Kwirk's head came up. He turned, still holding the broom, and tightened his whiskers to the side of his furry face.

"Aren't we cranky this morning." Without an ounce of fear, he turned back to his sweeping. "I should think you'd be eager to get moving today."

"Why are you here?" I un-kinked, but lifted my head high and glared down at him. "What do you want?"

"At the moment, I want you to drag your lazy carcass out of that fancy bed and have a bath," he said. "What's gotten into you?"

A prickly sensation traveled down the back of my neck. I shivered again, and Kwirk returned to his sweeping as if nothing horrific had ever happened between us.

Killing the devil.

"Stop." I poured from my basin and coiled into a knot on the floor. "Look at me."

He sighed, but his broom stilled. His nose swiveled in my direction, whiskers wide and ears only slightly drooping in annoyance. His eyes stared into mine, huge and dark and soft as the misty veil inside the hospital.

"They've drugged you again." I spat it, unsure if I was more angry with him or with the serpents in charge of this madness. "They've drugged you and given you back to me."

"What are you talking about?" He flattened his ears and flicked the end of his broom in my direction.

I flinched from it, hit the floor with my belly and hissed again.

"Did you have a bad dream? Perhaps a visit to the dreamers might—"

"No." I buzzed my tail and lunged to one side and then the other. Not striking at him, but managing to fix his attention fully on me. "Stop it."

"Stop what?" Those blurry eyes regarded me levelly, without a trace of guile in them. He didn't remember it, any of it. And I could never forget.

"Why did you return to the Burrow?" I made each word a dart, a weapon like the one he'd turned on me. When he shook his head, I pressed him, not with words, but with the invisible fist of my un-banded will. "Tell. Me. Why. You. Returned."

Kwirk trembled. His fur raised along his spine and he dropped the broom. His paws grasped one another, lodging beneath his chin. He lowered his nose, closed his eyes tight, and shook his head over and over. "No. No, no, no, no."

"Why?" I demanded, feeling my way through the fog of his drug-stupor and digging further. I found the veils they'd draped over his memories, and I did my best to shred them. "Why?"

"Ffff—" He jabbed at his jaw with his fists, but I leaned into my pressure, dragging the truth out of his drug-addled head. "Family."

"Family?"

"My family. Here."

"Who?"

"Wife. Children. Three boys."

"Are you a slave, Kwirk?"

Yes.

He gnashed his teeth together, ground them tight and pushed the word between them. "Yes."

"And your family?"

"Yes."

The truth hissed between us, filled my fancy room, and left us both shaking. I let go my grip on Kwirk's mind, and saw his eyes soften again. This time, I knew the memory I'd opened remained. The drug might've subdued him now, but somewhere behind that, my mouse remembered and hated.

He stared at me, horrified, lost and shaking. "Sookahr..."

I shook my head and his voice trailed away. "Say nothing."

His paws dropped to his sides. His tail curled tightly around his feet and his ears flattened to his skull.

I waited for him to argue, for his head to lift and his eyes to pierce me, dagger sharp again. My rodent didn't even twitch. His complacency would remain until the viper's drug faded. If I continued to feed him here, it might never end again.

They'd given him back to me for a reason, either as a threat or a test. Whatever I meant to do about it, if I meant to do anything about it, I would have to act fast.

"We have a lot to do." I slithered to the table, keeping an eye on him and not quite turning my back. "And we don't have much time."

"I-I..." He stammered and fell silent again. Lost. Oh, how I knew that feeling. Once again our whole world had shattered, but this time I planned on fixing it for good.

"Find me a piece of paper, Kwirk." I stared, watched for the flicker of defiance behind his eyes.

He only nodded, unclenched his paws, and whispered.

"Yes, sir."

The gaming room roared with the usual cacophony. Stone rumbled against table, and constrictors who tended our beetle herds hollered their taunts and pounded their tails against the floor. All but the two I'd come to see.

"Can you get it done?" I asked. Viirlahn was not at the table, nor did he lounge on any of the shelves, at least not yet. I knew exactly where I'd find him at this hour, which is why I'd come here first.

"You bet we can." The big serpent, the one with the scarred nose who'd dragged me from Laarahn's trap, nodded his head. "Of course, but..."

"Are you okay?" his partner in crime finished for him. "Viir was a disaster when they told us you were, you know. He'd flip out if anything happened to you again."

"I'm fine," I said. "And Viir will be fine. I'm going to see him next."

His concern for our mutual companion spiked a surge of jealousy in me that I tamped down quickly. I hoped these two would be there for Viir when I couldn't, but I didn't really want to dwell on that either.

"I really appreciate it. And you can do it in time?"

"Relax," he said. "We'll go straight there."

I nodded, though relaxing wasn't anywhere on my to-do list. I'd passed a dozen rodents in the halls this morning, and each time I had to force myself not to flinch, not to hiss and tremble. "Thank you. For everything. I really appreciate all you've done for me, and for Viirlahn."

"He's gonna be mad about this, isn't he?"

They put their huge heads together and stared at me, waiting for me to tell them the truth. I gave them the closest thing I could find.

"Not for long."

"And if them *aspis* come asking about it?"

I stared across the room, letting the pounding of stones fill me with courage. If I'd tried, I might have lifted them all into the air at once. I considered it, a show of rebellion, but my concentration was fixed on holding the item I'd secreted on my person in place.

"When they do, tell them the truth." By that time, it would be too late to stop me.

When they'd agreed again and wished me luck, I left them, hurrying from the gaming room and half expecting for Viirlahn to catch me in the act. Some things, however, never changed, and I traveled the hallways secure in my belief that he'd be waiting exactly where I hoped.

Despite my lack of a band, the looks I got from the serpents I passed no longer held suspicion. Word of my heroism had swept through the Burrow like a tide, and every gaze I met knew exactly who I was. It made the going faster, but the whispers that followed me set an uncomfortable prickle along my spine.

I stopped making eye contact, hurried my slither, and reached the Spire just as the traffic began to fill it. Leisure hours emptied the ramp of rodents, and I took it without fear, reaching the niche where Viirlahn waited without spying a single mouse.

"I was worried you weren't coming," he said.

Coiling in beside him, I bumped my head under his chin and felt our scales gliding against each other.

"Worried," he repeated.

"I'm sorry."

"For being a little late?" He leaned into me, wrapping his neck around mine and tightening his grip.

"Sorry..." I couldn't say the rest out loud.

"Because you're leaving?" Viir said it for me, and I nodded against him.

"I can't stay."

"Not even for me." I felt him tense then, and though his grip did not relax, I knew he was angry, would be angry for as long as it took.

"If it was just about us, I'd find a way."

"But?" He dragged that word out, waiting for an explanation that he fully deserved and that I couldn't risk giving.

"There's something I have to do."

Viir stiffened more. Our necks slipped apart, and chill air flowed between us. He sniffed, and lifted his head above mine. "What do I tell them?"

"The truth," I said. "You don't know anything. You can't know anything, Viir. Not until they've finished asking their questions. Do you understand that? You have to know nothing."

"You think they'll drug me?"

"They will." I lifted too, matched his height and hoped it didn't piss him off enough to bite me. "But when they've finished, Viir. When it's all over..."

With a thought, I slid the folded paper from beneath a scale near my tail. I let it drift toward him, kept it moving slowly until I was certain his eyes had found it. Then I pried open the compartment on his skymetal ring and let the letter fly to safety inside it.

"When it's over, read that. Read it and remember that I love you."

The hatch snapped shut, not by my will either. Viirlahn had the truth now, all of it, but whether or not it soothed his fury, only time could say. I risked his ire again, just once, with a quick nuzzle, a rubbing of my chin against his neck before I turned away. He didn't respond, didn't twitch a scale in answer, but as I left him, I heard the thought he hadn't meant to voice.

I love you too, Sookahr.

It blazed inside me, that truth, but I still left him. Left my only friend behind, my only love, and went to find my enemy. I had to reach Kwirk, quickly, and I could only hope he'd followed my orders. Or none of this would matter in the least.

DISBANDED

29

The mouse family waited for me in the hallway where Viir's constrictor friends had stashed the cart and beetle I'd requested. Kwirk had brought them all, as I'd instructed, but I couldn't tell if he'd forgotten the part about warm clothing or if they simply had nothing else to wear. The female mouse had a pelt of medium shade, wore a rough vest similar to Kwirk's but longer, and looked absolutely terrified. His children stood in a line beside the cart, looking sullen and fidgeting with their own tails.

"We're going to get in trouble," she whispered to him at a squeaky decibel that made my head hurt.

The boys ranged widely in height. I guessed at their ages by how tall they stood. At least none were still in infancy, though I'd have felt better if they hadn't all looked like exact replicas of their father. Interacting with Kwirk was difficult enough without three echoes standing behind him.

"Tell her it's okay." I'd tried speaking directly to his wife, but she'd cowered and squeaked until I feared we'd be discovered before we could even start out. "Tell her."

Kwirk sulked and repeated my assurance to his wife, who gnashed her teeth and pulled at her whiskers. If she revolted and refused to go, I'd have gone through a great deal of trouble for nothing.

"Load the boys and your wife into the back." I made it an order. "Underneath the tarp."

When he obeyed easily, I made my way forward, sliding near to the beetle's side and reaching for it with a thought. The mind inside the hard exoskeleton was simpler than I'd imagined. I felt nothing that words could make order of, only a dull interest and an underlying question about food and water. I could steer it easily enough, I decided. And when the time came, I'd be able to order it to steer itself at least until the moment it forgot I'd ever existed.

Which might be hours or days, for all I knew.

"They're inside, sir." Kwirk appeared beside me, holding his whiskers and looking nearly as distressed as his wife.

"Are they well hidden?"

"Yes, but—"

"Tell them to remain so, and to be silent until we tell them otherwise." I meant to assist with that as well, to lull our passengers into a gentle sleep before we reached the city gates, but having Kwirk reinforce that would make my job easier. It also gave him something to do while I gathered my courage.

With the mice stowed away in the cart's bed, it would look as though we escorted an ordinary shipment. The constrictors had even stuffed in a crate or two for effect. That, or they'd simply forgotten to remove them. I let Kwirk tuck the tarp around his family, but once he'd finished, I fired off my next command.

"You travel up front where you'll be seen." It would be difficult enough, if we met someone, to explain my lack of band. Having a visible attendant legitimized my possession of the cart and its draft animal. "Can you climb, or should I assist?"

"Of course I can do it." He leapt from the ground to the box, scampering up the tarp to settle at the very front behind the beetle. His muttering went with him, low complaints that had been the backdrop of my life. "Thinks I'm an old man, does he? Thinks I'm on my last leg."

I waited until he fell silent, checked his eyes for any sign of sharpness, and then nudged the beetle's flank with my nose. His mind with mine.

"Stay silent unless I tell you to speak, at least until we're out of the Burrow."

Kwirk pulled on his whiskers and shook his head at me. He wrung his paws together but obeyed, amiably, as if he'd ever had a choice. I steered us out of the side passage after only a few strides. The main hallway here spread wide enough for two wagons. Our little cart rolled easily along, up the gently sloping ground and toward the light ahead which signaled our proximity to the gates.

My neonate band had bought my way into the Burrow, now I hoped my reputation would get us back out. We drove toward the exit, a wounded hero, a traitor now, harboring a family of slaves, and as we went I played out a half-dozen scenarios all of which ended with me fighting my way out and subsequently dying in the process.

More carts joined us as we neared the gates. I forced my head down, leaned into our pace, and did my best not to be noticed. Still, by the time we stood before the guards, whispers circled us. The wagon we followed announced me long before I had to defend myself, and we were waved forward without any more incident than the intrigued expressions on the guard's faces.

My plans might not have worked, but in the end we didn't even have to try them. The bandage around my tail gave me away, that and my status as the only un-banded serpent inside the Burrow's walls.

Kwirk wanted to speak. I could see it in his posture, in the way he stroked his long whiskers. We'd lived together too long, knew each other— at least one version of each other—far too well. I checked his eyes whenever he glanced my way, and when the roadway parted into a fan of branches, I carefully, silently suggested his family fall asleep.

Most of the traffic followed one or the other of the nearer branches, paths that led to the beetle pens, the agricultural fields and the skymetal mines. Only we continued to the road I'd followed home the day before. By the time the sun had reached its zenith, Kwirk, his hidden family, and myself were on our way north.

Back in the Burrow, a great feast was being prepared. The five-god ceiling waited for a party to honor its heroes. Viir waited, to receive his reward and to witness the Circlet's reaction to my disappearance. I'd done everything I could to help him, just by telling him nothing. If he read the letter beforehand, however, my plans would dissolve. The Circlet would find me, and I had no doubt my second final banding would be immediate and permanent.

With that thought chasing me, I pushed the beetle to its limit, slithering beside the cart and earning more confused and disapproving glances from Kwirk. We went swiftly, quietly, and in broad daylight, and by the time the sun kissed the distant horizon, we'd seen only one other vehicle. I'd let them pass, keeping my cart between us to hide the majority of my length.

When the dusk grew deeper and a chill touched the air, Kwirk's restraint failed him.

"Where are we going?"

"You'll see."

"They'll be after us by now; my wife was due back to her serpent hours ago."

"The Burrow is busy this evening." I twisted, staring behind us and gauging how far we'd come, how long it would take for word of my passing through the gate to reach those who meant to do something about it. "But you're right. We'll be followed soon. Come down from there."

He scurried down as easily as he'd climbed. Full of energy after his long ride, and yet I felt fatigue in every scale. The effort of our pace along with the control I'd kept over the beetle and the sleeping mice—it settled on me now like a weight.

"Collect your family, Kwirk, and move them to that side of the roadway, over the berm. Wait for me there."

I leaned against the cart while he woke them. My thoughts relaxed, and the beetle clicked and stamped its feet in relief. The poor thing had a long road ahead of it, and as much as I hated to do it, I could only allow him a breath of rest.

Kwirk's wife and children tumbled from the box, staggering, groggy and confused. Not as much as they would be when the days passed away from their prison. I had to believe they'd have taken this trip willingly if they'd been able to choose.

Once they'd clambered over the berm and vanished behind it, I turned my will back to our draft insect. My mind slipped into its thoughts, full of fatigue now, but to my desperate thinking, not so overloaded that my plot would put it in serious danger. I told myself that, as I whispered to it, filling its mind with the idea of food and shelter, pointing its goal due north and asserting the order to continue, to not stop. *Food and shelter,* I pressed. *Go north. Continue.*

Sharp toes shuffled against the road, and the beetle clicked and started off again. I sent a prayer after him, asking the Sage to guide his path, to keep him moving, and to let him forget me long before his strength gave out. Then I slithered to the berm and, with a deep intake of breath, climbed up and over it.

The mice waited, round eyes gleaming in the dark. Still fuzzy, still under the drug's influence. As it happened, that served my purposes as well.

"Take them and travel west," I said. "Don't stop, and don't go anywhere near a Burrow roadway."

"Sir?" Kwirk's paws twisted together. "I don't understand."

"This is an order. Do you understand that?"

"Yes." He hissed it, and for a breath I caught the flash of sharp light in his pupils.

"You will hide if anyone comes near you, and you will not change direction, no matter what, for at least three days."

"Three days?" His wife stepped closer to his side, clutched at his arm and shook her head. "What will we feed the children?"

"Forage as you go," I said. "You'll find enough to keep going. After three days, well, Kwirk will know what to do then. If you must, there is a great land of grass to the north and west. You may angle in that direction, but steer clear of the road, and give any serpents you see a wide berth."

"I don't understand," Kwirk said again. "This makes no sense."

"It will," I said. "It will, Kwirk, and once it does, you're all going to be fine."

"Yes, sir." He nodded, taking his wife by the paw. "We'll be fine."

I watched them as they trundled off, a family of former slaves walking blindly toward freedom. Kwirk would keep them going, and once he remembered it all, he'd decide what to do for them on his own. Tonight he trusted me, had no choice but to obey me, and that just might've been enough to save them.

My path lay to the east. A bright moon already peeked above the trees, and I still had to climb the berm, cross the road, haul myself over the opposite side. I had to move, to hurry, because despite what I said, I knew they were already at our heels. Too many serpents had seen me leave the Burrow. Too many eyes had followed us as we took the northern road.

I had to be on my way, alone and immediately. And once I'd put a little distance between myself and the road, I'd have to trust the wagon would lead them north. I had to trust my destiny, because as of that moment, I had nothing else.

I slept in a crack beneath a rock. The first half of the night I traveled, found a trickle of water to mask my scent, and followed it northeast for a few hours. Then, in the patchwork forest of shadow and moonlight, I lifted my body with my mind, drifted like a leaf on the wind until my strength waned and I settled again. Hopefully far enough from my track to lose any pursuit by scent.

It was all I could do to slither into the first hole I found and collapse. If I dreamed at all, I didn't remember them. The dawn carried me out of my fog, and I moved again, north this time, keeping my tongue out and tasting, and my journey's goal fixed in my mind.

Behind me lay everything I'd ever valued. Everything, except the freedom I'd never known I wanted. It called me now, carrying me onward between the trees, and I followed it faithfully, unreservedly, until I topped a short rise and spotted a pathway lined with stones.

How far would they chase me before giving up? I weighed my crime against the effort it would take to find me, and decided the Circlet would fold easily. They'd write a different story now, one in which I played no hero. So long as they let me be, I could live with that.

I could live.

Staring at the pathway below, I felt as if that life were just now beginning. Down the slope I slithered, picking my way to the first stones and sliding between them with a lighter heart. To my left, the distant jungle grew to touch the clouds. Ahead of me, a spire of rock pushed upward between the trees. A dark crack split the boulder in two, and from the crevice it made, I heard the sound of laughter.

The wind carried the scent of adequately cooked food.

I paused before that humble home, paused, and thought for the first time that I might not be wanted. Doubt's chill fist gripped my throat, and my greeting died before I gave it voice. Was I welcome here, or should I have gone with the beetle, followed my egg-mother's invitation, and likely been turned back over to the Burrow at first chance?

No. It had to be here, at least for now. And yet I hesitated, staring into that slim doorway with my heart dancing.

When Lohmeer's splotchy head poked out into the sun, I held still, held my breath, and waited for him to pass judgment.

"Sookahr?" The rest of the constrictor spilled from the doorway. His voice echoed through the forest, and I found only happiness inside it. "He's back. Teerahl, Sookahr is back."

"Is that okay?" I eased forward, watching his eyes as if he, too, were drugged into complacency.

"Of course it is." The big head nodded, guileless and sincere. "Teerahl told me you'd be back. She must have said it a hundred times."

"It's only been three days," I said.

Teerahl's lilting voice joined us. She poked her head from behind the stone, and let me know she'd been watching for much longer than I'd guessed. "And yet you've managed to injure yourself again."

"I did." I fluttered my tongue and gave her a laugh in return. "Stopped a war while I was at it. I've been a hero, and now I believe I'm a criminal."

"That sounds like a hell of a story." She slithered around to the doorway and joined Lohmeer. "Come in and tell it. Come in, and see what Meer has found for you."

It was the invitation I'd been waiting for. I hurried to join them, and we all slipped inside the den, crowding into the humble space, but adding to the warmth in a way that was both comfort and pleasure.

"He searched the jungle for it." Teerahl pressed to one side of her living area.

At the back, a stolen pot steamed, filling the air with whatever Lohmeer had tried to cook last. The constrictor lowered his head. His band hummed, and from the bedroom where I'd spent my convalescence, something large and round moved out of the shadows. I stared in horror as Lohmeer fetched my band, and I cringed lower when he settled it on the floor in front of me.

"He spent a whole day searching." Teerahl's tone held a warning.

I forced myself upright and nodded. "Thank you, Lohmeer."

"Just in case you need it," he said.

The skymetal gleamed against the dusty floor, silent and harmless without a bolt to fix it in place. I let out a breath and repeated myself, this time sincerely. "Thank you."

I didn't want the thing, but he had a point. It might be useful in the end. Might come in handy, whatever I decided to do. I was happy he'd found it, and more than that, I felt the gesture for what it was: loyalty, friendship, kindness. These were the things of my future, and they lived here at the moment.

Whatever I decided to do next, I wouldn't be alone. If things went as planned back at the Burrow, Viirlahn would know where I was too. If he ever forgave me, I just might see him again. Maybe. For now I had these friends, this den, and an invitation from my egg-mother to consider.

Coiled inside Teerahl's cozy home, I felt like, perhaps, that was just as it should be. I fluttered my tongue and let my belly rumble. Teerahl laughed, and Lohmeer fetched me a bowl.

Inside my thoughts, Sahveen's voice echoed.

Go forth, beloved. Go forth and change the world.

I'd had a first crack at just that, setting Kwirk free, defying the Circlet. But I had a feeling it was just a first crack. I had a feeling my journey's end was only another beginning. The bowl landed beside my band. Lohmeer settled himself again, and Teerahl's voice broke my reverie.

"What will you do now, Sookahr? Now that you are free to choose?"

"I'm not sure." I lowered my nose to Lohmeer's cooking, not perfect, maybe not even his destiny. My tongue fluttered, tasted delicious freedom in that steam. "I'm not sure, but maybe..."

"Yes?" Lohmeer watched me, eyes sharp and fully his own. They both watched, and at that moment, there was only one answer to give them. One answer that made any sense at all.

"Maybe I'll change the world."

DISBANDED

About the Author

Frances Pauli writes animal stories. From hybrids and shifters to anthros and aliens, she prefers her fiction on the furry side. She's written over twenty-five novels, a dozen novellas, and more short stories than she cares to count. Despite this wordy obsession, her fiction didn't really kick into gear until she focused on animal stories, a place she's happy to curl up in and call home.

Though her worlds are usually speculative in nature, her tales may leak into romance, slice-of-life, and humor. But she almost always circles back around Science Fiction and Fantasy eventually. She has won two Leo Awards, a Coyotl Award, and been nominated for the Dog Writers of America award for short fiction.

She lives in Washington State with her family, a small menagerie—including eight snakes—and far too many houseplants. You can find her contact information, some free short stories, and a reading list of her published work on her website at francespauli.com

About the Cover Artist

Ilya Royz is a digital illustrator and concept artist working primarily within the fantasy and sci-fi genres. While he has little experience of working on large-scale projects, he has illustrated covers for a few books and one table game. He works mostly in Photoshop, but is also growing his knowledge of 3D programs, including Blender and some others.

He hopes to develop his skills enough to work with game or film projects.

About the Publisher

Goal Publications, a subsidiary of Ottercorrect Literature Services, was founded in 2015, and publishes original works of anthropomorphic fiction, striving to publish more QUILTBAG+ work (both authors that fall into that category and/or characters that do), work written by women, work written by people of color, and work by other marginalized groups we have not specifically mentioned here. We want to hear these voices, and our readers want to hear these voices.

For more titles and information, please visit their website and storefront at www.goalpublications.com.

CPSIA information can be obtained
at www.ICGtesting.com
Printed in the USA
JSHW010817050520
5507JS00001B/25